THE F(_ı ı

BROOKE HARRIS

Storm
PUBLISHING

This is a work of fiction. Names, characters, business, events and incidents are the products of the author's imagination. Any resemblance to actual persons, living or dead, or actual events is purely coincidental.

Copyright © Brooke Harris, 2019, 2024

The moral right of the author has been asserted.

All rights reserved. No part of this book may be reproduced or used in any manner without the prior written permission of the copyright owner.

To request permissions, contact the publisher at rights@stormpublishing.co

Ebook ISBN: 978-1-80508-611-6
Paperback ISBN: 978-1-80508-612-3

Previously published in 2019 by Bookouture.

Cover design: Rose Cooper
Cover images: Shutterstock

Published by Storm Publishing.
For further information, visit:
www.stormpublishing.co

ALSO BY BROOKE HARRIS

Memories of You
The Promise of Forever
When You're Gone
The Forever Gift

'We're all just passing through this world like tourists. For some of us, it's a long, winding adventure. For others, it's just a quick visit. But, there's only one question in the end. Did you enjoy the ride? And I did. I really, really did.'

– KAYLA PRENDERGAST DORAN

PROLOGUE

September

There's one minute to the buzzer. My heart is pounding as I race from one end of the school gym to the other, dribbling the ball as I weave in and out through a swarm of sweaty bodies.

'Kayla. Kayla. Kayla,' students, teachers and parents chant from the sideline. The gym is packed to capacity and all eyes are on me.

'If you score this basket we win,' Aiden, my best friend, shouts as he guards me against a really tall player on the other team.

I glance at the scoreboard. Thirty seconds to go. Beads of perspiration trickle from my hairline and into my eyes. I drag a shaky arm across my forehead, stop running and steady myself in front of the basket.

'Kayla. Kayla. Kayla,' the cheering is ringing in my ears.

'Shoot, Kayla. Shoot!' Aiden shouts.

With my feet slightly apart, I focus on the hoop. I bend my knees, throw the ball and a loud scream bursts through my lips.

The gym erupts with cheering and clapping and my team

are running towards me, crowding around me as I sink to the floor, unable to believe what just happened.

'You did it, Kayla. We won,' Aiden says, wriggling his way through the group of our teammates gathered around me. 'What are you doing down there?' he asks, clearly surprised as he finds me sitting, rocking on the floor. 'Can you believe it? We're through to the finals. It's the first time our school has made it in twenty years.'

'Where's my mam?' I ask, choking back tears.

Aiden glances over his shoulder, still smiling. 'She's coming but it could take her a while to get through the crowd. Everyone is going crazy!'

The excitement is electric; stomping feet, clapping hands, laughter and cheering. But all I can think about is the throbbing pain in my knee. Something is wrong! Something is so wrong with my knee. Aiden reaches his hand out to me and pulls me to my feet. I want to scream again, but I press my top teeth down onto my bottom lip and hold the noise inside.

'You okay?' he asks, his smile faltering. 'Blown away by your own greatness? It almost looks as if you're crying.'

'I want my mam,' I say. 'I just want my mam.'

Finally, Mam gets close enough so my eyes can meet hers and as soon as she sees me her expression changes. She knows I'm not crying happy tears. She knows I'm hurt.

I just want my mam.

ONE

HEATHER

One week later

I stand outside my daughter's bedroom door and hold my breath. My feet are slightly apart – my knees wobble less this way and my arms are folded across my chest as if I'm cross. I'm not cross. Kayla never gives me reason to be cross. She's not a stereotypical teenager. But I guess I'm not a stereotypical mother either. Sure, Kayla and I are mother and daughter, but mostly we are best friends. I won't say we never argue. We're human – not perfect. But when we do disagree it's almost always over something silly, like who ate the last slice of pizza or whether Ross really is good for Rachel as we stay up too late watching *Friends* reruns together. And we never, ever keep secrets from each other. Until now. Kayla has been keeping a huge secret from me. My heart hurts when I think about how different everything might be right now if she had just told me she was feeling unwell sooner.

I exhale, making myself light-headed, and raise my hand to knock. But I pause as giggling carries through the gap of the slightly ajar door. I recognise the familiar sounds of Kayla video chatting with her best friend. I smile and shake my head. I often wonder how they can spend all day in school together and come home to spend half the evening chatting more.

'They didn't have Snapchat back in your day, Mam,' Kayla likes to remind me, regularly. 'This is how people talk to each other now. It's just normal.'

Normal, I think. Unsteady again. Suddenly normal feels like a privilege we've taken for granted.

As the carefree, childhood laughter grows louder and giddier I can't bring myself to disturb Kayla. Not right now. I need to keep normal for just a little while longer.

'I can't go to the funfair this year,' I hear Kayla say. 'My mam is in a bad mood. I think she's heard something dodgy from someone else's mam or something.'

'Like what?' Aiden's husky voice says as clear as if he's in the room with my daughter.

'Dunno,' Kayla says. 'Maybe something about kids getting drunk. Half our year were pissed off their heads last year, remember?'

'Ha, yeah,' Aiden laughs. 'The state of some of them; Roisin Kelly threw up in a bush. It was the funniest thing ever, remember?'

I gasp. Mrs Kelly thinks her kids are so perfect. I wonder what she'd say if she found out what Roisin gets up to behind her back.

'Anyway, just tell your mam you don't drink,' Aiden continues. 'She'll believe you, won't she?'

'She knows I don't drink,' Kayla replies, sounding mildly offended, and my heart swells with pride. 'Anyway, I don't think that's even it. She's totally stressed. I think this thing with my wonky knee is really freaking her out.'

'Did you tell her we have a big game next week. You *have* to play. We won't win without you,' Aiden says.

Kayla sighs. 'Yeah. I don't think she'll let me play. She's been obsessed with me taking it easy all week. She's acting all weird since we came back from the hospital. The tests weren't even all that bad. Scans and X-rays. Well, except I had to get blood taken. That was a bit gross, to be honest.'

'I still don't get why you needed to have so many tests for a sprain,' Aiden says.

'Yeah. Me neither.' Kayla sighs. 'It's so boring and there's lots of waiting around.'

Aiden snorts. 'Yeah but it's worth it to get off school. Mr Gibbons gave us three pages of maths homework last night. He's such a dick.'

'Yeah, s'pose,' Kayla says. 'Mam and I get McDonald's or hot chocolate after hospital stuff, so that's cool. I think I'm done with tests now anyway. I'll probably be back in school tomorrow or the next day.'

'What did the tests say?' Aiden asks.

'Dunno,' Kayla says. 'Think it takes ages for results to come back or something. But my knee is grand now, so it was all a big waste of time, really.'

The springs in Kayla's bed begin to squeak and I've no doubt she's jumping on her bed, testing out her *grand now* knee. I'm about to walk in and tell her to stop before she falls. Or cracks the ceiling in the kitchen below her room. The landlord will go ballistic if there's any more damage. He's still bitching about the hair-dye stain on the carpet in my room even though I've told him a million times it was there before we moved in. I bought a rug to cover it. Just so I wouldn't have to think about him every time I saw it.

Aiden's voice suddenly becomes very serious, and I listen, concerned. 'Tell your mam your knee is fine and come to the funfair. Unless you're too chicken to go on the Wall Of Death again and this is just your excuse. Bawk, bawk, bawk,' he teases.

'Seriously,' Kayla snaps. 'Stop that. I told you I can't go.'

'Do something nice to get on her good side,' Aiden says. 'Empty the dishwasher. Or make her breakfast in bed. Mams love breakfast in bed.'

'Aiden come on...' Kayla says.

'What?' Aiden says. 'You just have to know how to butter her up.'

'All these tests are expensive and my mam's had to miss lots of work. She's in a pretty bad mood. So, can we just drop it, okay?'

'Okay. Sorry. I was only joking, Kayla,' Aiden says, sincerely. 'I didn't mean to upset you. Mams are always acting weird. It's no big deal.'

'My mam isn't,' Kayla says, and the tears I've been struggling to hold back begin to fall. 'She's cool.'

'Just not cool enough to let you come out this weekend,' Aiden says.

Silence hangs in the air and for a moment I wonder if Kayla has realised I'm listening. I don't even know what I'm doing. I never eavesdrop on my daughter. I don't need to. We gossip together like a couple of best friends and she fills me in on all her news. I guess I'm just stalling. I know when I knock on Kayla's door that everything will change.

'Look,' Aiden says, 'tell your mam I'll be there. Tell her I'll keep you safe. Cause I will, you know.'

'Don't be creepy, you weirdo,' Kayla laughs loudly. 'Anyway, there's no point even talking about this anymore.'

My heart aches as I hear the disappointment in Kayla's voice. But, she's right. I won't allow her to go to the local funfair with her friends this weekend, despite going the previous two years. But Kayla doesn't know why, and I've no idea how I'm possibly going to bring myself to tell her.

'I gotta go,' Aiden says, suddenly. 'My dinner is ready. Call you later, yeah?'

'Yeah. Sure,' Kayla says. 'Bye.'

There's a sudden silence before Ed Sheeran's latest single blares loud enough to rattle Kayla's bedroom door. I jump back from it somewhat deafened and turn around to face the stairs. Thank God the banister is next to me. I grab it as my knees buckle. I sit down heavily on the top step and drop my head into my hands.

I hate myself for earwigging on Kayla like some sort of creepy spy, checking up on my teenage daughter as if she's done something wrong – especially, when she's such a good kid. I hate myself for being distracted the last few days and seeming distant or *not myself*. I thought I was doing a good job of hiding my worries in front of Kayla – obviously not. Mostly, I hate myself for answering my mobile ten minutes ago and taking a call from a doctor at the hospital. He asked me to come in tomorrow to discuss Kayla's test results.

'What is it?' I asked.

'Would eleven thirty suit?' he said, as if that was an answer.

Eleven thirty definitely does not suit. I've missed so much work already and I have back-to-back meetings from nine until twelve tomorrow. But without hesitation I said, 'Of course.' And then I said, 'Thank you.' I actually thanked the doctor for the opportunity to break bad news to me. *I know it's bad news, because if it was anything else, he would have told me over the phone, wouldn't he?*

I've made my fair share of similar phone calls. I don't talk to people about their health – just their money. Most of my clients think money is the most important thing in the world. I wonder if they saw how much weight my daughter has lost recently, or how she walks with a subtle limp, whether they would change their mind.

'Please come into the office at your earliest convenience,' I say, monotonically and not giving away any clues, but the person on the other end always knows the news is bad. Sometimes they ask for more details. Sometimes they don't. But they always manage to clear their calendars, no matter how busy they protest to be, and make the appointment.

'Mam,' Kayla says appearing behind me and placing her hand on my shoulder.

'Ahh,' I screech, clutching my chest.

I didn't hear her bedroom door open behind me over the music blaring. Kayla giggles. I laugh too and hope Kayla thinks that I'm dragging my sleeve under my eyes to dry the tears of laughter and nothing else.

Kayla squeezes between me and the banister and lowers herself to sit and share my step of the stairs. She drops her head onto my shoulders and doesn't say a word.

'Hey you,' I say, concentrating hard to steady my shaking shoulders. 'What do you fancy for dinner? I'm thinking Chinese? Or pizza?'

Kayla takes a deep breath and nuzzles closer. 'Mam, what's wrong? Tell me, please. I'm worried about you.'

I reach my arms around my daughter and gather her into me. And I plead with the knot in my stomach to back off for just a moment so I can enjoy the smell of Kayla's hair and the warmth of her hug.

'It's a big decision,' I puff out, remaining steady. 'Pizza or Chinese. Could make or break the whole evening.'

Kayla straightens and I release my grip. I look into my teenage daughter's beautiful, sky-blue eyes and I struggle to remember a day before I had her in my world.

'I'm dying for prawn crackers,' Kayla smiles. 'Can we get it delivered?'

'Good idea,' I say. 'That'll give me time to whip up some brownies for after. How does that sound?'

'Yum,' Kayla says, standing up and bouncing down a few steps before she turns a half-circle to look back at me with a cheeky smirk. 'And I'll pick something on Netflix. My choice tonight. No more of that documentary crap that you've been watching. You have to watch *Riverdale,* Mam. Everyone at school loves it. You will too.'

'Okay, sweetheart,' I say, clinging desperately to one more day of normality. 'Okay.'

TWO

CHARLOTTE

The next day

'Molly, honey. Where are your shoes?'

My four-year-old daughter stands by the front door with the evidence of chocolate cereal melted into the creases of her lips.

'Dunno.' Molly shrugs. 'Daddy?' She twists her chin over her shoulder and shouts towards the kitchen.

My husband hurries into the hall sporting the same sugary-breakfast residue around his mouth.

'Shoes?' I say, shaking my head and pointing to our daughter's feet.

'I know. I know. I was just on it,' Gavin says, glancing at Molly, hoping for clues as he drags the back of his hand across his lips to wipe away the chocolate.

I shouldn't sigh, but I can't help it. I appreciate Gavin's efforts to offer me a lie-in this morning, but he doesn't know Molly's routine the way I do. I laid in bed, staring at the ceiling for as long as I could, pretending the confusion about uniform and PE gear hadn't worried me. I came downstairs appearing as unphased as possible with Molly's tie tucked subtly under my arm.

'Your shoes are where you left them last night, Molly,' I say, slipping the tie around her neck and fixing it in place. 'On the bathroom floor.'

'Oh yeah.' Molly smiles, pulling away from me to hurry up the stairs. 'I remember now.'

'God, that kid would forget her head if it wasn't attached,' Gavin says, half-laughing.

'Yup.' I nod, trying not to get frustrated that yesterday I asked Molly three times to put her shoes away in her room.

I walk into the kitchen. Gavin follows me and sits at the table to finish his Coco Pops.

'Coffee?' I ask, filling the kettle.

'Mmm-hmm,' Gavin says, lifting his bowl to his lips to drink the chocolatey milk.

I flick on the kettle and take the cereal bar and packet of crisps out of Molly's lunchbox and swap them for a couple of slices of five-grain bread and an apple. I don't bother mentioning the school's healthy-eating policy. Gavin read the note that we got at registration, just as I did.

'No PE today, Molly. It's Tuesday,' I say as my little girl skips back into the kitchen with her shoes on the wrong feet, carrying her sports kit. 'But you do have piano after school, remember?'

'I hate peenano,' Molly says.

'I know.' I nod. 'But that's because you're just starting out. It's tricky now. But when you're older and you can play all your favourite songs, you'll be so happy.'

'I won't.' Molly stomps her foot. 'I hate songs. I hate all the songs.'

'Okay,' I sigh, trying to ignore my daughter's ridiculous argument.

I'm tempted to point out that for someone who hates all the

music in the world she hums the theme tune from a toothpaste advert every night when we're brushing her teeth. But we're already running late and I know the irony will be wasted on my four-year-old.

'Daddy. Let's go,' Molly says, taking her lunchbox from my hand.

Gavin stands up and doesn't notice Molly jerk her schoolbag from his hand. The zip is open and her pencil case and a plastic folder tumble to the floor.

'Oops.' Molly giggles and bends down to tidy up the mess.

'Molly, really?' I say, coming to help her. 'You need to pay more attention.'

'I didn't mean to,' Molly says, her bottom lip beginning to quiver.

'It's okay, princess,' Gavin says, his eyes narrow on me. 'We all make mistakes sometimes. Even Mammy.'

I groan inwardly and roll my eyes, scolded.

'C'mon, Molly,' I say, aware of precious seconds ticking by – we're going to be late. 'You put these things back in your bag and I'll fix your shoes.'

'My shoes aren't broken.' Molly points to her feet.

'No,' I sigh, losing patience. 'But they are on the wrong feet, aren't they?'

'Are not.' Molly scrunches her nose.

'Molly they are.'

'Are not.' Molly flops onto her bum and tucks her feet under her. She folds her arms across her chest and stares up at me, defiantly.

'Oh for goodness' sake,' I say, bending down to toss Molly's pencil case and folder back into her bag. 'Give me your feet. You'll break your neck on the yard if you don't fix your shoes.'

'No. No. NO!' Molly huffs.

Defeated, I stand up and look at Gavin. My expression is asking him to speak to his daughter about this. But just as my husband points his finger and opens his mouth his phone rings. His fingers quickly retract as he shoves his hand into his pocket to pull out his phone.

'It's Heather,' Gavin says, gesturing at the screen.

I smile, ridiculously brightly out of sheer frustration, because I don't know what else to do at the news that his ex-fiancée is calling.

'Hello,' Gavin says, raising the phone to his ear before I have time to say anything. 'No. Of course it's not a bad time. What's up?'

'*No, it's not a bad time,*' I mimic and roll my eyes as Gavin walks into another room.

Molly laughs. 'You're silly, Mammy,' she says and lunges forward to wrap her arms tightly around my waist. 'I love you.'

'I love you too, baby,' I say.

'I'm not a baby,' Molly says. She lets go of me and lowers herself onto her bum again. She stretches her legs out in front of her and slips off her shoes and switches them onto the opposite feet. 'See. I'm a big girl.'

Result. I smile.

'C'mon,' I say, taking Molly's hand in mine and helping her to her feet. 'Let's see if Daddy is ready. We don't want to be late.'

I toss one strap of Molly's sparkly pink school bag over my shoulder and tuck her even brighter pink lunchbox under my arm. Molly holds my hand and skips alongside me towards the sitting room.

The sitting room door is slightly ajar and I'm just about to push my hand against it when I hear Gavin's voice crackle and break.

'Oh God. Okay. Oh God,' he says. 'Jesus, Heather. This can't really be happening. Tell me this can't be happening.'

I pull my hand away from the door and, I turn, about to direct Molly back towards the kitchen but she wriggles her hand away from mine and pushes the door all the way back until it bangs against the wall.

'Molly, for goodness' sake, Daddy's busy right now,' I say.

'Daddy, look.' Molly skips into the room, ignoring me. 'I fixed my shoes. All by myself. Mammy said I was a baby, but I fixed them.'

Gavin is facing the fireplace and he doesn't turn around. Not even when Molly crosses the room and tugs on the back pocket of his suit pants. His head is low, and his shoulders are round. Gavin is six foot two and broad, he's still carrying some muscle from playing rugby in college, but suddenly my husband seems shorter and almost frail. As if the weight of whatever Heather has said is physically crushing him.

'Molly,' I call. 'Molly, honey, come here.'

Molly lets go of Gavin and spins around to look at me. Gavin is silent and nodding his head as he stands statue-like with the phone still pressed tightly against his ear. I wonder if he's even noticed we are here.

'Molly, will you go upstairs and brush your teeth, please?' I ask.

'I already did.' Molly pulls a funny face as she parts her lips to show me her top and bottom teeth at the same time. 'See.'

'Can you brush them again, please?' I say.

'But...'

'Remember what the tooth fairy said?' I say.

Molly puffs out. 'Shiny teeth are a fairy's favourite.'

'Exactly. So, go on. Good girl.' I move out of the door arch to allow Molly to pass by me on her way to the stairs. 'I can't wait to see how sparkling you can get them.'

'I can get them super sparkly. Sparklier than my school bag,' Molly says, rushing up the stairs. I don't even tell her not to run.

Molly leaves the bathroom door open and I wait until I can hear the tap running before I set her schoolbag and lunchbox down on the couch and hurry over to Gavin. I place my hand on his shoulder and I feel him shaking. This isn't like him. Heather and Gavin have an almost annoyingly good relationship for a pair of exes. They split parenting of Kayla as evenly as they can even though they live on opposite sides of the country. Gavin pays the lion's share of costs: school trips, braces, new shoes. And he never once complains. I think he feels guilty that Heather dropped out of college when Kayla was born, while he continued with his studies.

'I'm the bigger earner,' Gavin tells me when yet another dentist bill comes through the letterbox.

It's true. But Heather is way out of line this week. She must have called Gavin ten times already, all because Kayla fell and sprained her knee. Heather is talking about some specialist that Gavin and I have never heard of, and no doubt Heather thinks the *Bank of Gavin* will cover the cost. It's getting completely out of hand. I'll have to talk to Gavin about it later.

'Gavin,' I say, my fingers curling a little tighter around his shoulder. 'What is it?'

Gavin turns around and his face is pale. His eyes are meeting mine but he's not really seeing me. He's still holding the phone against his ear but I don't think there's anyone on the other end anymore. Suddenly, this doesn't feel as if it's about money.

Light footsteps begin to move around overhead and I know Molly will come bouncing down the stairs any second.

I reach for Gavin's hand and lower it away from his ear. He's clutching his phone so tightly his knuckles are as white as his face. I don't bother attempting to prise his phone out of his hand, or even try to talk to him; instead I slide my hand around his waist and lead him to the couch. He walks, taking baby steps like a small child. A horrible weight settles in my stomach when we reach the couch and I have to reach up and physically press my hands against the tops of my husband's shoulders to guide him to sit down.

'Maaaaammmyyyy, I can't find my school bag,' Molly shouts from the top of the stairs.

I glance at her bag wedged beside and slightly under Gavin on the couch.

'Keep looking,' I say, moving to the door so Molly comes into view at the top of the stairs. 'Try your room. Good girl.'

'Okay.' Molly shrugs, turning and skipping away.

I close my eyes for a second and exhale before I turn around to face Gavin. I know Molly won't stay distracted alone for much longer but I really don't want her listening to whatever Gavin is about to tell me.

I open my eyes to see Gavin sitting with his hands covering his face and he's shaking his head.

'What did she say, Gavin?' I say. 'Is it bad news?'

Gavin doesn't make a sound. When he finally lowers his hands his eyes are bloodshot and I can see he's struggling to hold back tears.

'Mammy, I can't find it,' Molly's shouts. 'I've looked in all the places.'

'Oh, for goodness' sake, Molly.' I roll my eyes and march into the hall.

Molly is standing at the top of the stairs again. Her arms are stretched out wide and she's shaking her head. 'I think Daddy hided it. Maybe he doesn't want me to go to school today.'

I glance over my shoulder at my broken husband. Just minutes ago he was eating children's breakfast cereal with the rigor of a teenager and now he's washed out, shaking and as frail as a man three times his age.

Dammit, why can't we have a normal day for once?

Gavin mentioned something months ago about Heather's job being on the rocks. What if they've finally let her go and she's moving? Gavin would die if Heather moved Kayla even further away. He couldn't cope without Kayla.

'Mammy are you listening?' Molly juts a hip out and points a wagging finger at me.

It's hard to keep a straight face as I stare up at the mini-me scolding me from the top of the stairs.

'Sorry, sweetie,' I say, making my way up the stairs, reluctant to leave Gavin alone. 'Mammy's being silly this morning, isn't she?'

Molly nods. 'And Daddy too. Daddy's very silly. He didn't know today is peenano day.'

'Yes,' I say, taking a deep breath. 'Daddy is silly today, too.'

Molly lowers her pointed finger and she suddenly looks unsure, like she might cry. I hope she hasn't picked up on the tension. Most of the parenting books I've read say children are aware of all sorts of external emotional factors that we don't give them credit for. I would hate if Molly had any idea of how much I struggle with the hold Heather seems to have over Gavin. Or how uncertain it makes me.

'You know what?' I say with a single, enthusiastic clap of my hands. 'We're already a little late for school today. How about we wait until after first break to go in? Would you like that?'

'But I have my shoes on now.' Molly points to her toes. 'And they're on the right feet.'

'I know, sweetie,' I smile. 'But Mammy and Daddy need to talk about something really important right now. I'll walk you to school in a little while. Okay?'

'Are you talking about...' Molly draws in a big breath that makes her stand taller and straighter and then puffs out quickly '... grown-up stuff? I want to talk about grown-up stuff too.'

'Hmm,' I sigh, as I take my little girl's hands in mine and give them a gentle squeeze. 'Not this time, sweetheart.'

Molly lowers her head and she rolls onto her tiptoes and back down. 'Oh,' she says.

'iPad,' I say, panicked. 'Why don't you take my iPad for a little while. Maybe you can watch *Peppa Pig*, yeah?'

'Humph.' Molly jams her hands onto her hips. '*Peppa Pig* is for babies. I like *Teen Titans Go!*'

'Oooh-kay,' I say, making a mental note to check up on what the hell Gavin is letting Molly watch. 'The iPad is beside my bed. If you can't find it I'll...'

Molly's back is immediately to me and she charges towards my bedroom. 'Got it. I got it,' she says, reappearing within seconds with the device tucked under her arm.

If only a school bag was an iPad, I think, rolling my eyes.

Reaching my arms out, I say, 'Let me turn it on for you?'

Molly looks at me as if I've just offered her detox tea and raw kale for breakfast.

'I can do it all by myself,' she says, tugging it out from under her arm to wave it at me like a fan.

'Molly, be careful.' I tut. 'No more than twenty minutes. And only in your room. You're not to bring it downstairs.'

'Twenty minutes,' Molly echoes as if she has a concept of time.

Molly hurries into her bedroom, kicks off her shoes by the door and hops up onto her bed. Sitting cross-legged she turns on the iPad. Upbeat theme-tune music soon fills the air. I use my foot to guide Molly's school shoes to one side then close her door until there's just a crack open and walk down stairs.

The smell of coffee calls to me from the bottom step. Gavin has obviously moved from the sitting room to the kitchen. I'm desperate to ask him what on earth Heather said to rattle him so much, but I don't want it to come out sounding all irritated. As hard as it is, I try to act normal and let him tell me in his own time.

'Oh God, I could murder a cup,' I say, reaching the kitchen and pulling out a chair from the table that there really isn't room for in the cramped space. 'Oh, I said Molly could have your iPad for a little while. She's in her room with it now.'

'Yeah. Okay,' Gavin says, stirring a spoon around one cup, tapping it off the edge and moving it to the other.

'Molly loves that thing, I thought it would be a good distraction. Just for a few minutes so we can talk. I'll drop her into school later,' I say, sitting down.

'Um...' Gavin stirs the second cup.

'By the way, what's *Teen Titans Go!*?' I ask. 'Molly says she loves it. Is it too grown-up? I'm not sure about some of that stuff she watches.'

'*Teen Titans Go!* You're seriously asking me about *Teen Titans Go!*' Gavin raises his hand above his head before he throws the spoon. It misses the sink and clatters against the granite with a sharp, sudden bang before it bounces onto the floor with a less-aggressive clink.

'Gavin,' I inhale, wide-eyed.

'It's just a TV programme for God's sake, and she likes it,' Gavin says as he crouches to pick up the spoon. Standing up again he points it at me, his hand and the spoon shaking. 'But what about piano? And swimming and all the other stuff that we make her do that she hates? And for what, Charlie? Huh? Why do we make her do it?'

'Gavin.' I shake my head, trying to stay calm. 'What's going on?'

'I don't know. I don't know.' Gavin drags his hands around his face and walks, somewhat blindly, towards the table, leaving the two cups of steaming coffee on the countertop behind him.

I hop up and pull out the chair next to me noticing Gavin's lips are losing colour. He flops into it.

'Why do we do it, you know?' Gavin says. 'Why do we push them? Push them to learn. Push them to achieve. They're just kids. Kids! Shouldn't they just enjoy being young?'

I walk around behind my husband and rub his shoulders. 'Talk to me. Eh? Tell me what's wrong.'

'Heather got a call,' Gavin says, tilting his head from side to side as I rub his aching neck. 'From a doctor at the kids' hospital.' Gavin pauses, to gather his thoughts, or catch his breath. 'Not the one Heather has been taking Kayla to. A different one, here in Dublin.'

I dig my thumbs into the stubborn knots below Gavin's shoulder blades, circling. 'Um,' I say, listening. *I just know this is heading towards something I don't want to hear.*

'Heather is meeting him today,' Gavin adds. 'It's important.'

I dig harder into Gavin's shoulders. He doesn't budge.

'He wants to see us both.' Gavin breathes out. 'The doctor wants to see Heather and me.'

'Really? Both of you?' I ask, rolling my eyes again. I can't think of a single time I've taken Molly to the doctor when Gavin would need to be there too. 'Do you think Heather is—' I pause and choose my words carefully. 'Do you think Heather is overreacting? It's a knee injury, after all. Not uncommon for a basketball player, is it?'

'Heather was in an awful state on the phone,' Gavin says, and I can tell from the softness in his tone that he's going to give in to her request.

'I know. I know,' I say. 'But Kayla has already missed the last couple of games and the team are suffering. She'll lose her place as captain if she doesn't start playing again soon. It would break her heart. Couldn't you have a word with Heather?'

'It's not that simple,' Gavin says, running a shaking hand through his hair.

Jesus. I hate this. I hate that one lousy phone call from Heather can have this effect on my husband.

'I know,' I say, 'I get it.' I'm lying. I don't understand. I have no idea what it's like to parent a teenager. I try, of course, to support Gavin, but Kayla is Heather and Gavin's daughter. They have a closeness with her that I can only observe.

'What exactly did Heather say?' I ask, consciously easing

the pressure as I kneed Gavin's tense muscles. 'Is something serious going on?'

Gavin reaches up and catches my hands in his, squeezing a little too tightly. He's pinching. I wince and I'm about to pull away.

'The hospital in Cork sent Kayla's result to the National Children's Hospital here in Dublin,' Gavin says, pausing to draw a deep breath, steading himself.

'Why would they do that?' I ask, confused.

'The hospital say Kayla will need specialist care in Dublin,' Gavin says. 'This is serious, Charlie. I think Kayla is really, really sick. I'm scared.'

I stop massaging and my hands fall limp by my sides. 'Oh God.'

THREE

HEATHER

I drive Kayla to school like any regular morning. Kayla turns up the radio when an Ed Sheeran song comes on and she sings along, out of tune. I catch her glance at me from the corner of my eye and I know she's disappointed I'm not joining in. But I can't remember the words right now. All I can think about is seeing Gavin and meeting the doctor.

'You know, I'm actually kind of glad to go back to school after a weird week. I never want to see a hospital ever again,' Kayla says, turning the radio back down when the song ends. She's surprisingly chirpy for a kid who's most definitely not a morning person. 'It's good to get back to normal, right, Mam?'

I can't bring myself to reply. I search for words that don't feel like a lie or a betrayal but I can't find any. I drive on, numb, as the low hum of morning radio keeps us company.

Usually Kayla hops out while I'm caught in a stream of rush-hour traffic a couple of streets away from her school, but this morning, without overthinking it, I swerve out of heavy traffic and veer down the even more chock-a-block side road leading to the school. Kayla nearly has a heart attack when I drive in the school gates and pull up right outside the front door.

When I stop the car and reach for the door handle to get out, Kayla's eyes widen and she laughs, 'Oh my God, you're not seriously going to walk me to the door are you?'

I make an I'm-worried-about-you face.

'I'm fine. I'm fine, honest,' Kayla assures me. 'Please, Mam. I'll never live it down if my mother walks me in as if I'm a five-year-old.'

'Okay,' I say, when I notice Aiden is waiting for Kayla by the main doors.

I wave and he smiles brightly and waves back.

'Go on,' I say. 'Have a good day. And be careful. No more falling, yeah?'

'Love you,' Kayla says, throwing her arms around my neck and kissing my cheek. 'See you later.'

Kayla opens the door and a blast of cold air charges in shocking us both. I watch as Kayla walks into school with a limp so subtle that if you weren't looking out for it you'd probably miss it.

Kayla knows I'll be late home this evening. She's hanging out at Aiden's after school. There's nothing unusual about that. But there is something unusual about the way she pauses at the door and looks over her shoulder at me. There's a spark of insecurity in her eyes. As if she knows I've been keeping something from her. My heart hurts.

I wait until Kayla and Aiden are out of view before I drag my phone out of my bag and check my messages.

There are some work emails and a missed call from my boss. I skip straight to the text from Gavin.

See you soon.
Try to stay calm.
G x

I take a deep breath, toss my phone onto the passenger seat

and drive towards the train station. Normally I'd drive to
Dublin. I like motorway driving, but not today. Today, I don't
trust myself to concentrate behind the wheel alone on such a
long journey.

The train is packed to capacity and the windows are fogged
before we pull out of the station. The elderly gentleman beside
me makes conversation and I chat back, grateful for the distraction. As much as I don't normally enjoy small talk, the silence
when he gets off halfway is much, much worse.

I find myself checking my phone ridiculously often. I can't
shake the feeling that Kayla's school will call at any moment.
They'll tell me she has fallen. Or fainted. Or fainted and fallen.
And I will feel like an even worse mother than I already do.

I know the doctor asked to speak to me and Gavin alone first
so we can ask all the adult questions that may be too distressing
for Kayla to hear, but I can't help wishing Kayla was beside me
now. I need a big, squishy hug, the kind she used to give me
when she was little. No matter how tough things got over the
years, Kayla's hugs always gave me the strength I needed to
keep going.

The train journey seems to take so much longer than usual.
I count down the minutes until I'm finally outside the large
doors of the children's hospital. I haven't been here since I was a
kid myself and I fell off my bike and chipped the bone in my
elbow. It hasn't changed much in twenty years. It's still the same
intimidating square, red-brick building it always was.

My phone rings as I walk through the doors and I'm greeted
by a large sign expressly forbidding the use of mobile phones. I
answer nonetheless.

'Hey. Where are you?' Gavin's husky voice asks.

'Just here now. Where are you?' I say.

I'm stopped by security at reception and the guard points to
the sign and at my phone.

'Third floor,' Gavin says. 'Doctor Patterson's office is the second door on the right. I'm waiting on the corridor for you.'

'Okay. Okay. Coming,' I say, glancing at the lift right in front of me and the stairs to the side as I try to decide which will be faster.

'Miss, please,' the security guard says, pointing to the sign again.

Oh piss off, I think. But I smile politely and say sorry as I slide my phone into my handbag and decide on the stairs.

I take the steps two at a time, glad I wore flats. I'm surprised Kayla didn't notice. I only ever wear heels to work.

FOUR

HEATHER

I find myself sitting inside the window of a once-familiar coffee shop waiting for Gavin. I left him outside the hospital. He called Charlotte as soon as we stepped outside the main doors. I didn't have anyone to call so I just began to walk. Maybe Gavin thought I was giving him space. Maybe I was. I think I needed some too. I texted him as soon as I sat down and although I didn't expect him to follow, he said he'd be here soon.

The back of my chair is pressed right against the glass and there's a draft blowing in where the latticed window isn't an exact fit in the old stone wall. The chilly autumn air seems determined to work its way between my neck and the collar of my coat to pester me, nagging me to switch seats. But my legs are shaking, and it's not overly dramatic to think I might topple over if I try to stand up right now. Instead, I pull my collar tighter around my neck, fold my arms on the table and stare into a cup of murky coffee.

I haven't been in here in years – not since Gavin and I were teenagers – before Kayla was born. The décor is still exactly the same, although a little tired and worn now. Mismatched chairs dot around oval, mahogany tables. There's a neon-orange couch in the centre of the floor in front of the only rectangular coffee table in the whole shop. A bunch of college kids hog the whole space, sitting laughing and chatting. It reminds me of an early episode of *Friends* and I can't help thinking how much Kayla would love this place.

'Can I get you a refill?' someone asks over my shoulder.

'Ummm....' I say, as if it's a particularly difficult question.

'I'll just take this one away, yeah?' An arm reaches over me and lifts the cup full of cold, white coffee away.

'Hi.' Gavin finally appears next to me. 'Is that dairy?'

'No. It's soya,' I say. 'They do that here now.'

'Cool,' Gavin says, awkwardly unwrapping his chunky, colourful scarf from around his neck – I recognise it straight away. Kayla knitted it a couple of years ago in school and gave it to Gavin as a Christmas present. I didn't think he'd actually wear it.

'Whoever thought this place would be keeping up with the times?' Gavin looks around and then nods to the waitress. 'That's cool. Very cool. Anyway, sorry I took so long. Parking was really hard to find.' Gavin shuffles his arms out of his coat, drapes it over the back of the seat opposite me and sits down.

'I'm sorry,' I sigh, reading Gavin's face as he scans the familiar surroundings. 'I didn't mean to just walk off. But I had to get out of there, you know? I wasn't sure this place would even still be here.'

'It's fine,' Gavin says. 'I get it.'

'And then, I didn't know if you'd remember where to find it,' I ramble on. Neither of us know what to say.

'Here's good. This is good, Heather,' Gavin assures me. 'And of course I remember where to find this place. It's special.'

'Yeah,' I say, remembering. 'It is.'

Gavin and I spent more hours than were healthy in this pokey corner café. Gavin sipping tall black americanos and me guzzling cappuccinos and feeling instantly sick after, because

I'd made it to seventeen and hadn't realised I was lactose intolerant.

'I can't believe it's up for sale,' Gavin says, sounding both nostalgic and disappointed.

'It is?'

'Yeah.' He nods. 'Didn't you notice the huge "For Sale" sign over the door?'

I shake my head. I don't remember the walk from the hospital to here, or coming inside and taking my seat. And I definitely wasn't paying attention to signs above the door.

'So, another?' the waitress asks still hovering, looking at me.

'Yeah,' I nod, realising I'd forgotten she was there.

I really, really don't want to drink another sip of coffee but my hands are desperate for something to hold.

'And, can I get a tall black, please? Double espresso,' Gavin says.

'Anything else?' she asks.

Gavin and I look over at the small glass cabinet next to the till. There's confectionary inside that looks as if it's been there since our college years. It doesn't matter to me, because despite not eating since last night, food is the last thing on my mind.

'That's all,' Gavin says, turning back first. 'Just the coffees. Thanks.'

Gavin and I wait in silence as the waitress walks away. She's back behind the counter before I finally break a silence that's fallen over us.

'Thanks for coming,' I say. 'I don't think I'd have coped alone.'

Tears glisten in Gavin's eyes. 'You don't have to cope alone. We'll get through this together.'

'Yeah,' I nod, not sure I believe him. 'You, me and Kayla. We're a team.'

Gavin swallows hard. 'Where is Kayla today – school like normal?'

Normal. I close my eyes and wish for normal as I tuck a flyaway strand of hair behind my ear. I take a deep breath and open my eyes again, struggling to keep it together. 'She's in school now and she's hanging out with Aiden later. You know Aiden, don't you?'

Gavin nods. 'Vaguely. Nice boy.'

'He is,' I say. 'Aiden's mother is picking them up after school; taking them back to her place. She knows I'll be late home this evening.'

'She knows...' Gavin's eyes widen, horrified.

'That I will be late home,' I reiterate. 'Nothing else. She doesn't know anything else. We have a sort of "Mam's code" arrangement. I pick Aiden up if she's running late and he has no key, she takes Kayla if I get stuck in work. It works out well. And Kayla's happy.'

'Good. Good,' Gavin says, and I can tell he's feeling left out of the loop.

Our coffees arrive, and the waitress sets them down without talking. I'm pretty sure she can sense the vibe at our table and wishes she could be anywhere else.

God, me too. Get me the hell out of here!

'Thanks,' I say, and she offers a mute smile over her shoulder as she carries on to the next table.

'So, what have you said to people?' Gavin asks, picking up his cup.

I don't reach for mine.

'What have I said to people?' I repeat, shaking my head.

Gavin takes a mouthful of coffee with his eyes on me. It's too hot. I can tell by his face as he sets the cup down on the table. 'Kayla's teachers, I mean. They'll need to know, won't they?'

'Yeah,' I say. 'Yeah, I suppose they will.' I hadn't thought about all the people I'll have to tell. I've only thought about Kayla.

'Have you spoken to your parents?' Gavin asks.

I shake my head.

'Mine? You probably talk to them more than I do,' Gavin says.

'*Your* parents?' My eyes round like saucers. 'God no,' I snort, laughing painfully but it's not funny.

'Yeah, okay, sorry,' Gavin says, fidgeting, and I know he wants to reach for his supernova coffee again.

'Christ, don't you remember how your mam and dad reacted when you told them Kayla was going to be born?' I say. 'Imagine how much they'll freak out when we tell them she might die. No doubt they'll find some way to blame us.'

Gavin freezes and makes the same face he does any time I dare to veer towards our teenage years.

'Sorry,' I say.

But Gavin still isn't moving.

'I'm sorry,' I repeat, feeling guilty. 'That was a low blow. But, you brought your parents into this, and I still think they don't approve of me...'

'Dying?' Gavin says.

'No. No. No.' I shake my head. 'Did I say that? I didn't mean to say that. I'm just scared. Scared and talking crap. Don't mind me. You know I ramble on like a tit when I'm nervous.'

I watch as silent tears trickle down Gavin's face.

Gavin. Gavin Doran. The hot boy from my year in school. Liked by everyone. Even parents. My boyfriend for a while. And now happily married. *Not. To. Me.*

This isn't the first time my words have brought tears to Gavin's eyes in this café. The last time was when we were seventeen, a pair of kids about to sit our Leaving Cert and I told him I was pregnant. He crumbled and told me his parents would kill him.

Gavin's parents did make our lives hell. I still blame them for splitting us up. They said we were making a huge mistake and a baby would ruin our lives. I sometimes wonder at what point over the years Mr and Mrs Doran realised they were wrong. Kayla is the best thing to ever happen to Gavin and me, and we all know it. I may never have been good enough for Gavin's parents, but they truly adore Kayla.

'There's hope. The doctors have hope,' I say, my voice cracking. 'They're saying lots of positive stuff, aren't they? There's all sorts of treatments. They said something about...' I pause and suddenly the small coffee shop grows to enormity. 'Something about...'

God, I have no idea what they said. I just became so consumed by fear that anything the doctor said after hearing the words *Kayla* and *cancer* in the same sentence went completely over my head. And as I watch Gavin now I realise it wouldn't matter if I could remember or not, because my words are washing over him in exactly the same way now.

How are we here? *How are we here again?* Gavin and I, in such an unimaginable situation. When I told Gavin I was pregnant I looked into his eyes and I thought I broke him. But I was wrong. So wrong. Because the look on his face then was nothing compared to the way he looks at me now. Telling Gavin that Kayla was going to come into our lives didn't break him. But telling Gavin that Kayla might leave our lives has. It *really* has.

'Surgery,' Gavin says at last. 'That's first.'

He picks up his coffee cup, raises it to his lips but doesn't sip before setting it down.

Surgery, I think. *Maybe? Did someone say that?* I'm not sure. There were so many things said in the hospital. Terms I didn't understand. Lots of big words. And I asked questions. *Didn't I? Surely, I asked something.* Or maybe I just sat there. Useless and barely able to move – a lot like right now.

I rewind my mind to the last time I was thinking straight: on the train this morning. I wrote questions – everything that popped into my head. I got a cramp in my arm because I could barely move the pen fast enough to keep up with my racing mind. But did I write the answers in the meeting? I think I did. *No. No! Maybe I didn't.* I want to check my bag. I want to check my bag now. Maybe there's questions. Maybe there's answers. I don't have any bloody clue what's in there.

I lean over and rummage in my Michael Kors bag. It's a silly, oversized tote but it's real and all. I bought it a couple of years ago on a girls' holiday in New York with my friends from work. I'm not sure which I enjoyed more, shopping for me, or shopping for Kayla. Although Kayla's list was extensive and had to be paired down to a mere fifty million jumpers and thirty billion bath bombs, I loved every minute of the crazy dash around the city in a race against consumer time. Kayla stayed with Gavin that week. And I was the best parent in the whole world when I came home.

'Heather,' Gavin says as I rummage in my bag, half-panicked and half-smiling as I think of Kayla's smile as she tried on all her new designer clothes.

'Heather. Heather. *Heather,*' Gavin says, louder.

'Yeah.' I shoot up, empty-handed.

'Are we going to lose her?' Gavin says, his eyes wide and his jaw slack.

'No.' I shake my head. 'Absolutely not.'

FIVE

CHARLOTTE

I hold Molly's hand as we walk in the school gate.

'Ouch, ouch, ouch,' she protests.

'Sorry, sweetheart,' I say, quickly loosening my grip and slowing my pace, worried I'm walking too fast for her little legs to keep up.

The principal meets us at the door and I smile, trying my best to seem normal. In all the commotion this morning I forgot to call the school to explain we had a family emergency.

'Good morning, Molly,' the principal says. 'It's good to see you.'

'Hello,' Molly says, wriggling her hand away from mine. 'Mammy says we're running late this morning. But I don't think we are 'cos we drived for a quick while in Mammy's car and then we walked from the car park. We haven't run at all.'

'And you like running, don't you?' the principal says. 'But you know there is no running inside school. Even on the mornings we're a little late.'

Molly nods.

The principal reaches her hand out to Molly and says, 'Will

we walk around to your classroom now? All your friends will be happy to see you.'

Molly takes a step back and tucks herself behind my legs. It's not like her at all. She usually skips into school so contently.

'It's okay, Molly,' the principal says, bending to Molly's level. 'Mammy can walk you to your classroom if you prefer.'

Molly doesn't answer but I feel her hand slip around my thigh and I know she needs me to go with her.

'I do hope everything is alright, Mrs Doran,' the principal says, straightening up. 'My door is always open.'

'Thank you,' I say, reaching behind me to find Molly's hand.

Molly and I walk down the long corridor lined with children's colourful artwork.

When we reach Molly's classroom door I hear Ms Martin say, 'C'mon now boys and girls take your seats. Quickly please. Quickly, everyone. Break is over. It's back to work time.'

I knock on the ajar door and wait. Little faces turn to look at Molly and me instead of taking their seats and I feel Molly squeeze my hand a little tighter.

'Boys and girls,' Ms Martin says sternly. 'Seats. Now, please.'

All the children hurry to sit and it's suddenly silent.

'Excuse me, Ms Martin, could I have a quick word, please?' I ask. I try to let go of Molly's hand but she doesn't seem to want to be separated.

Ms Martin comes to the door, smiling.

'Hello, Molly,' she says as she reaches for Molly's other hand, but Molly still clings to me. 'Everyone missed you this morning,' she adds. 'Do you want to go inside?'

A table of Molly's friends wave to her. They've got sticky blocks and they're building a tower. Molly loves building blocks.

'Go on, sweetheart,' I say. 'It's okay.'

Molly shakes her head. 'But Daddy said I need to be a good girl and take care of you today.'

'Ah.' I smile, suddenly understanding Molly's clinginess. She's taken Gavin's considerate words literally. 'You've done a great job of taking care of me. Thank you,' I say. 'But it's school time now.'

'But Daddy said—'

'Why don't you make the biggest, best tower with all the lovely, colourful blocks. You can tell Daddy all about it later.'

Molly finally lets go of me, and without another word she hurries over to the table where all her friends are busy building.

'I'm so sorry Molly is late,' I finally say, watching as Molly picks up a blue block. 'We had some unexpected news and—'

'Blue is stewpid. Brown is the best!' a boy suddenly shouts. 'Ms Martin, Molly is ruing our tower.'

'Excuse me.' Ms Martin turns away from me and points at Molly and the boy.

'Sam,' she says firmly, 'don't you dare shove a block near Molly's eye.'

'Sam you're mean!' Molly shouts. 'You're so mean.'

I like brown,' Sam shouts back, pushing Molly. 'Brown, Brown, Brown.'

I gasp as Molly falls onto her bottom and begins to cry. Ms Martin and I hurry over to the table. Ms Martin speaks to Sam as I help Molly up and give her a cuddle.

'Are you okay, sweetheart?' I ask.

'He pokeded me. Did you see?' Molly points at Sam. 'I tolded him brown was yucky—'

'That wasn't very nice of Sam,' I say, 'but, you have to make more effort to share, Molly. It's everyone's tower and everyone gets to pick their favourite colour.'

'But I like blue and green,' Molly says.

'And Sam, quite obviously, likes brown,' I say.

'But, brown is yucky!'

'Molly. That's enough,' Ms Martin cuts in.

The children at the table stare at the commotion and my face reddens and I very much feel I'm intruding in Ms Martin's classroom.

'You like blue, Sam likes brown. Okay? And we're all going to be friends now,' Ms Martin says.

Molly looks at me; I nod and smile trying to reassure her.

Ms Martin claps her hands suddenly and all the children instantly give her their attention.

'Okay, boys and girls, play nice and quietly. I'll be back in a minute,' she says. 'I'm just at the door so I'll see if there's any funny business.' She points her finger at Sam. And then at Molly.

Ms Martin guides me to the door and I walk beside her feeling like one of the school children.

'Appointments with parents are usually scheduled for after school,' she says when we step onto the corridor. Her kind eyes sweep over me and I can sense her concern. 'Is everything okay?'

'Erm, I'm not sure.' I shake my head, suddenly realising how confused and scared I really am.

SIX

CHARLOTTE

Toilet water splashes over the top of my bright-green rubber glove and trickles down my arm on the inside of the sleeve as I sweep the toilet brush around the loo in the main bathroom. I put the brush back in the wobbly chrome holder and peel off the gloves as quickly as I can. I toss them angrily into the sink, rinse my hands and sit, exhausted.

I've been cleaning the bathroom for at least an hour. The smell of bleach is making me light-headed but I'm not sure what else to do. I keep replaying Molly's teacher's comments from this morning over and over in my mind.

'Kids are emotionally stronger than we give them credit for,' Ms Martin said. 'Molly is a clever little girl. She will understand. In time, she will.'

Ms Martin meant well. I've no doubt. But her words cut through me like a blade. I left quickly after that. I knew I couldn't keep it together much longer and I didn't want Molly to see me fall apart. She was so content among her school friends after the initial squabble with Sam. She was giggling as I walked away.

But now I'm alone all I can think about is Molly. And those

damn words, *Molly will understand.* Because, Molly won't understand. She absolutely will not. Christ almighty, she threw a tantrum two weeks ago because I told her that even Santa can't bring a real, live unicorn. How can she possibly understand that her big sister has cancer?

I can't believe I hadn't thought about how this would affect Molly sooner. My first thought was about how Gavin was coping, or not coping, with the news. Immediately after, I thought of Kayla. Poor Kayla. Beautiful, lovely Kayla. Then my thoughts seemed to drift organically towards Heather. One mother to another. I seemed to automatically slip myself into her shoes. They were uncomfortable and terrifying, and I quickly shook them off, distraught. But, I forgot Molly. How could I possibly forget my own daughter? She might be just four years old, but she has a big heart and this news is going to crush it. For the first time, ever, I have no idea how to protect my child.

I've been checking my phone all afternoon. I've an endless string of WhatsApp messages from a group I was added to this morning inviting Molly to a birthday party. One of the boys in her class is turning five this weekend. Molly's been telling me about his party plans for the last week. Molly said they're going to Bouncy Land and then for ice cream. Today's invite confirms Molly's story. The class mothers have been replying all morning with lots of emojis: smiley faces, birthday cakes and balloons. I haven't replied.

I don't have any other messages. I was hoping for an update from Gavin. He called earlier, but he was a mess and I didn't want to start firing questions at him over the phone. I suggested he grab a coffee and call back, but I've heard nothing for hours and I'm slowly cracking up.

I have a headache. The bleach is getting to me and I desperately need fresh air. Despite it only being a couple of degrees above freezing outside, I fling open the window. Chilly, angry wind nips at my face like sandpaper but I laugh at its efforts because it's surprisingly refreshing.

I glance around at the several other houses, identical to mine, that sweep around the horseshoe of our cul-de-sac. The morning dew hasn't lifted from the grass on the large green all day and I doubt any of the children will be out playing this afternoon because it looks like rain. But despite the grizzly weather the street looks as warm and inviting as always. Gavin and I lied through our teeth to the bank to get the mortgage that we could barely afford to buy this place. Gavin had niggling doubts at first, but I was so in love with the house I convinced him it would all be worth it because someday we would raise a wonderful family here.

Kayla had just turned seven when we moved in. She loved coming over every weekend. And we loved having her. We spent a small fortune in IKEA, money we didn't really have at the time, turning her bedroom into a pink palace. That changed to purple when she was nine, and then a very sophisticated ivory and mint when she was eleven. I'd chosen the calm, pastel colours for the baby's room when I was pregnant with Molly because we didn't know if she was a boy or a girl and I wanted something neutral. Kayla was so excited about become a big sister that she wanted her room to be exactly the same as the baby's. I remembering secretly hoping I was carrying a girl so the three of us could enjoy days out shopping, and I looked forward to lazy afternoons going for coffee together when the girls grew up.

We've painted Molly's room since. And I've offered to paint Kayla's too but she shrugs, smiles and doesn't seem bothered. But I guess that's because she's not here very often anymore. At first, Kayla missed the odd weekend here and there when she made the transition from primary into secondary school. Heather would text Gavin to apologise, sometimes at a moment's notice, and explain Kayla was sleeping over at a

friend's house. Gradually every weekend turned into every
second weekend, then once a month and lately we haven't seen
much of Kayla at all. I understand, she's busy being a teenager
and her friends and social life are all in Cork. She FaceTimes
Gavin and Molly often though. But it's not the same as actually
having her around and I know they miss her. I do too. A lot.

When my headache has eased and my face is completely
numb I duck my head back inside, close the window and make
my way downstairs to the kitchen deciding that I'll flick on the
kettle and have another coffee before it's time to pick up Molly
from school. The doorbell rings before I reach the bottom step
and I groan inwardly. I'm in no mood to make small talk with an
unexpected visitor today. I drag my hand around my face trying
to shake some life into myself before I answer. The smell of
bleach, that despite wearing rubber gloves seems to have found
its way onto my fingers, jolts me upright and I open the door
semi-startled.

SEVEN

CHARLOTTE

'Gavin,' I say, confused when I find my husband standing on the other side of the door.

Gavin doesn't speak. The top button on his shirt is open. His tie is still around his neck but it's so loose it's almost slipped out of view below the top button of his jacket. And his hair is messy, almost greasy as if he hasn't washed it in days. He looks completely different to the suave man who left our house earlier this morning.

'Hey,' I say. 'No keys?'

I look at Gavin's car parked in the driveway and then at the keys he holds in his hands.

'It's okay,' I say. 'Come on. I was just about to put the kettle on. You look like you could use a cup.'

I reach out and drape my arm around my husband's waist, ushering him inside, but I pause when the passenger door of Gavin's car creaks open slowly.

Kayla, I think, hopeful, but my breath hitches in the back of my throat when Heather steps out of the car. My eyes dart back to Gavin looking for an explanation. But he's watching Heather, protectively. Heather looks awful. Her eyes are red and puffy, it's noticeable even from a distance. Her usually bright skin is dull and grey and she's shaky on her feet. Gavin doesn't look much better and I can understand why he didn't text to let me know he was on his way with Heather – neither of them seem capable of thinking straight right now. *Oh God.*

Gavin wriggles away from me and hurries back to the car and around to Heather's side. He drapes his arm over her shoulder as if she can't walk unaided.

'C'mon,' he says. 'Let's get you inside where it's warm.'

Heather snuggles into him. She's as slim and petite as ever and Gavin's six foot three seems positively gigantic beside her. He holds her as if he could sweep her into his arms at any moment and promise to keep her safe for ever. I can't take my eyes off them.

'Stick the kettle on, Charlie,' Gavin says, as they reach the front door, still huddled together, and I step back to let them brush past me.

'You forgot to say please,' I mumble under my breath as I close the door and turn around and watch Gavin settle Heather on the sitting-room couch.

I turn away, shake my head and make my way into the kitchen.

'Sorry. I'm sorry,' Gavin says, appearing behind me with his hand on my shoulder. 'She's a mess. She was in no state to head back on the train alone. And I couldn't sit in a coffee shop any longer with a nosey waitress listening over our shoulder. I thought bringing her here for a while was a good idea. Help her calm down a bit, you know.'

'Yeah. Good idea,' I say. 'A text would have been nice though. A heads-up, you know,' I add still walking towards the kitchen with Gavin trailing behind me.

Gavin shakes his head. 'Did I not text? Oh God, sorry. I meant to. It's just—'

'It's okay,' I say quickly, feeling like a bit of a bitch because a text seems like the least important thing in the world right now. 'Will she even be okay to get the train alone at all today? She really doesn't look good.'

'Actually,' Gavin says, 'that's something I want to talk to you about—'

'Sorry,' Heather's voice calls behind us and we both turn around. 'Mind if I use the loo?' Heather points upstairs as if to ask, *Is it up there?*

I smile. 'There's one under the stairs, but we don't really use that one. The main one is upstairs. Second door on the right.'

'Thanks,' Heather says.

I continue into the kitchen and pour the lukewarm water out of the kettle, pop open the lid and shove it under the tap. The cold water hits the bottom of the kettle with force and splashes onto my blouse, freezing me. I look at Gavin, hoping he'll pass me a towel. But he hasn't noticed. He's standing with his back against the countertop and his arms are folded across his chest as he stares into space.

I flick on the kettle and fetch the hand towel hanging over the handle of the cooker. I listen for the sound of Heather's footsteps coming down the stairs but there's no sign of her reappearing yet. *Good.* I'm grateful of the opportunity to speak to Gavin alone.

'How did it go?' I say, at last.

Gavin shakes his head. I'm not sure what that means.

'What are they saying?' I try being more specific.

He shakes his head again and I hear the toilet flush overhead.

'Gavin, please,' I say, racing my words now. 'What did the doctors say? I've been waiting all day for news. Will Kayla be okay?'

The water begins to bubble noisily in the kettle but I still hear Gavin exhale loudly. He's a bloody mess. I don't under-

stand how he can be a tall, composed pillar of strength for
Heather but he can't even string a sentence together for me.

'Gavin. Please, answer me,' I say. 'Are things really that
bad? You're scaring me.'

'It's cancer,' Heather says, walking into the kitchen.

I jump. I didn't hear her coming back downstairs over the
noise of the kettle boiling. A lump forms in my throat and tears
blur my vision. I shake my head, feeling I can't cry – not in front
of Gavin and Heather. Kayla is their child, I know that. But my
heart is breaking nonetheless.

'It's a sarcoma,' Heather explains.

'A sarcoma,' I find myself repeating the strange word I've
never heard before. 'But I thought she hurt her knee. She's a
basketball player. She's the school captain for God's sake—'

'I don't think cancer cares what team she plays for,' Gavin
cuts across me.

'Gavin. I'm sorry. I didn't mean...' I pause and shake my
head. 'I just don't understand.'

'It's cancer in the soft tissue around the bone, Charlie,'
Gavin continues. 'It's called Ewing's sarcoma. That's what's
been hurting her. Kayla has a tumour in her knee.'

'Oh,' I say, trying to take it in. I feel crushed.

'I'd never heard of it either,' Heather says, as if she reads my
mind. 'Not until this morning.'

'Leg cancer,' I say. 'I mean, that's treatable, right? It's not
like blood cancer or something in her organs?' I wait for Gavin
or Heather to tell me I'm right. I wait for someone to say it will
be okay, but silence falls over us as the kettle bubbles dramatically in the background.

'Sarcomas aren't common in kids and they can spread,'
Gavin finally says, his voice cracking.

'But we don't know much for certain,' Heather adds.
'There'll be more tests and stuff before they decide a treatment
plan.'

'Okay,' I say, as a tear that I've fought to hold in trickles down the side of my nose and I catch it quickly with my fingertip. 'And when will they know all that?'

'They want to start tests immediately,' Heather says.

'And they want to get family in for bloods,' Gavin says. 'Hopefully one of us is a donor.'

I nod as if I understand.

'They've suggested tomorrow,' Gavin says.

'Tomorrow?' my eyes widen, and I say it much too loudly just as the kettle flicks off.

I swallow, struggling to keep up. 'But, tomorrow. It's so soon. No one has had time to get their head around this.'

'They don't want to waste any time,' Heather says.

'Depending on the results they'll call Molly in after that,' Gavin adds.

'Molly?' I say, shaking my head, confused.

'For bloods,' Gavin says.

'Molly,' I say again. 'Why would they need Molly to have a blood test? She's only four.'

'They're sisters,' Heather says.

My brain seems stuck and I'm so confused. I have so many questions for Gavin, but I know now is not the time. I imagine in Gavin and Heather's emotional state they've picked up something wrong. Molly is just a baby. They won't need her.

I open the press above the sink on auto pilot and fetch some cups. I pop open the lid on the jar of instant coffee that I left on the shelf earlier and spoon some into each cup. I add boiling water and stir. And then, I come to a sudden standstill, and my arms flop uselessly by my side.

'Does Kayla know yet?' I ask, my back to Gavin and Heather as my heart aches waiting for their answer.

'Not yet,' Gavin says. 'Actually, we wanted to talk to you about that.'

'Me?' I tap my chest, turning around.

'I think it would be best if Heather and I tell Kayla together,' Gavin says.

'Of course. Yes,' I nod, walking to the fridge to fetch milk. 'That's a good idea. A great idea.'

'Tonight,' Gavin says.

'Well, yeah, sure. If she has to have all these tests tomorrow, then of course you need to talk to her tonight.'

'I spoke to work earlier,' Gavin says. 'I told them I won't be coming in for a while. They understand.'

I'm nodding. Listening.

'No milk for Heather,' Gavin says as I hover the carton of milk over the first cup.

'I can't have dairy,' Heather says. 'Sorry.'

'Me neither,' I say, surprised to discover Heather and I have something in common. Gavin never told me.

'So what do you think, then?' Gavin says, knocking against my shoulder as he takes one cup with milk and one without over to the table.

Heather and Gavin sit down and Gavin looks over his shoulder at me, waiting for me to join them. I pick up my coffee and take it to the table.

'What do I think?' I repeat, pulling out a chair. I don't know what I think. I'm not sure I'm even thinking at all.

'About me going to Cork tonight?'

I stare at Gavin blankly. There's so much to take in. He's losing me.

'Kayla is going to her friend Aiden's house after school today,' Gavin says.

'Okay,' I say. I've never meet Aiden but his name is familiar to me. Kayla and Aiden have been friends for a long time and she talks about him often. At one stage I thought they were more than just friends, but Kayla quickly set me straight.

'I thought I could drive down this evening with Heather,' Gavin says.

'Oh,' I say, concentrating hard to understand what he's saying. 'I thought you meant tell her over the phone. What was I thinking? You're right. God you're so right. This is something you should do in person. Of course it is.'

I look at Heather. She's sipping her coffee that I know is still too hot and keeping very quiet. I imagine she's completely overwhelmed, but I wish she'd say something. Let me know what she thinks of this plan. I wonder if she wants Gavin there. Or if she needs the space to cope with this on her own terms. I wish there was some way of knowing what the right thing to do is.

'Heather and I will pick Kayla up at Aiden's and head straight to Heather's place. We'll tell Kayla together there,' Gavin says his voice cracking.

'I want her to be at home when she finds out,' Heather says. 'Maybe we'll get a takeaway. She loves takeaway. I think it's important to keep everything as normal as possible.'

I wonder how telling a fifteen-year-old she has cancer could ever be normal but I understand what Heather means.

'Then she can pack her stuff and I'll drive all three of us back up,' Gavin says.

'Back up?' I ask.

Gavin nods. 'To here.'

'But you said Kayla needed tests tomorrow?' I say, so confused.

'The tests are in the National Children's Hospital here in Dublin,' Heather says, putting down her cup and when her eyes meet mine my heart aches. 'Cork just doesn't have the same facilities. And since Kayla is only fifteen...'

'She's still a child,' I say quietly.

Heather nods and lifts her cup back to her lips with shaking hands.

'So, we'll be back tonight,' Gavin says. 'But I'm not sure when. Kayla is going to need some time to adjust to the idea of staying in Dublin for a while. She'll be away from school and her friends in Cork. It'll be hard.'

I nod. I can imagine. 'Take your time,' I say.

'Obviously Kayla can stay in her own room here, but would you mind making up the bed in the spare room for Heather?' Gavin asks.

My eyes widen. The idea of Gavin's ex sleeping in our guest room is so weird. It makes me uncomfortable or maybe even jealous. And I hate myself, considering the circumstances.

I pull myself together and nod. 'Yeah. Sure.'

'Thank you,' Heather says. 'I know this is all very sudden, but I'm really grateful to have somewhere to stay that's so near the hospital.'

'It's no problem, really,' I say.

Heather's phone rings and startles me, and I jump again. *God, I'm all over the place today.*

'Sorry, excuse me,' she says, fishing in her bag and pulling out her phone. She places it to her ear as she walks out into the hall. 'Hello. Heather Prendergast speaking...'

Gavin stands up and clears the cups from the table. 'Don't wait up tonight, eh?' he says, kissing the top of my head.

I'm about to ask him about the blood tests and Molly but I can hear the cups rattle against each other as he walks over to place them in the sink and I know he's trembling. I bite my tongue.

'Jesus, you're white as a ghost,' I say when Heather reappears in the kitchen. I hop up and pull out the chair she was sitting on and hold out my arm to steady her.

'That was the hospital on the phone,' Heather says. 'They'll have a bed ready for Kayla first thing in the morning.'

'Already?' Gavin asks, turning away from the sink, and I notice his face is suddenly as white as Heather's.

Heather nods. 'Yeah, they want her ready as soon as a slot

becomes available in theatre. They're hoping for something in a day or two.'

'Surgery?' I say.

Heather nods.

Gavin clasps his hands and presses them down on the top of his head as he takes a deep breath and puffs it back out. 'Jesus. Is this really happening? How can this really be happening?'

'Hey. Hey,' I say, hurrying over to him and wrapping my arms around him.

He grabs me tight and nuzzles his head into the crook of my neck. His breath is laboured and warm and I feel I can't hold him close enough or tight enough.

'Can we leave now? Can we go now?' Heather asks. 'I just want to get home to her. Please?'

Gavin pulls away from me and straightens up.

'Yeah,' he says. 'Let's go. If we leave now, we might make it in time before school closes.'

'School closing. Oh Jesus,' I say, twisting on my chair to look at the clock. 'It's ten past two. Molly. I forgot Molly. I should have picked her up ten minutes ago.'

EIGHT

KAYLA

I can't believe I'm crying in front of my whole class. And not even just a few tears, I'm bawling my eyes out. I'm never going to live this down.

'My leg. It hurts,' I sob, my eyes slammed shut as if it will help with the pain if I block out everyone. 'It really, really hurts.'

Half my class are gathered around me in a circle. I open my eyes and look up from lying sprawled on my back at their heads bowed and staring down on me. I'm still crying. I can't stop even though I want to. Everyone's faces are so serious. No one is laughing or pointing, the way people usually do when someone falls and makes a show of themselves at PE.

'Excuse me. Excuse me,' Miss Hanlon our PE teacher says, trying to shuffle her way into the circle. 'Guys, move. Now.'

The circle parts and Miss Hanlon hurries over, her runners squeaking as she crouches down on the gym floor next to me.

'What happened, Kayla?' she asks.

I shake my head and try to catch my breath. My heart is racing and my whole body is shaking.

'She fell,' Aiden says, suddenly crouching at the other side of me after fighting his way through the circle too.

'Yes. Thank you, Aiden. I think we can see that. But did anyone see how it happened?' Miss Hanlon asks.

Blank faces stare back at her and the usually noisy PE hall is quiet except for the echo of my crying.

'Well, something must have happened,' Miss Hanlon says, sternly. 'I turn my back for two minutes to fetch some bibs...'

Miss Hanlon is tiny. Everyone in my year is at least a head taller than her and she's not even up to most of the boys' shoulders. She only wears tracksuits. Nice ones though, and she's super skinny and toned. From running around all the time, I guess. She's young too. Well, not too young, like thirty maybe. But that's super young compared to some of our other dinosaur teachers. And if I ever had a problem or someone was being an asshole or bullying me or whatever, Miss Hanlon is the teacher I'd talk to. I think Miss Hanlon is the teacher our whole year would talk to. She has a way of making everything seem calm and okay, even when it's not. Like now.

'She was just running with the ball, about to score a basket when she went down,' Aiden says.

'Guys, it's just a game,' Miss Hanlon says. 'There really is no need for all this pushing and shoving. Look at poor Kayla.'

Everyone looks at me again. I pull myself to sit up and pray that my face isn't as red as if feels. I bet I'm an actual tomato. *Oh. My. God. Shoot me. Shoot me now.*

'No one pushed her, Miss,' Aiden says.

'Is that true, Kayla? Did you just slip?' Miss Hanlon asks, unconvinced.

'She didn't even slip,' Aiden says. 'She literally just fell over. I mean, like, just splat for no reason.'

There's some giggling and snorting from the other kids. *Ugh.* As if this wasn't bad enough already, Aiden is making me sound like an old granny. I'm going to kill him later.

Miss Hanlon breathes out slowly. I can smell the garlic something-or-other she had for lunch.

'Okay, Aiden, thank you,' she says, 'But Kayla really can speak for herself.'

'I- I-,' I begin. The pain in my leg has changed from sharp to throbbing and I dry my eyes. The hall starts to become noisy as my classmates lose interest, thank God, and begin talking among themselves.

Aiden is staring at me with wide eyes and I know he wants me to tell Miss Hanlon about the tests Mam's been taking me for. I shake my head and scrunch my nose, pleading with him to keep his mouth shut. If Miss Hanlon thinks I've a recurring injury she might make me sit out the rest of the season.

'I don't know what happened,' I say, attempting to stand up. 'I had the ball and then I was on the ground.'

'Hang on,' Miss Hanlon says, placing her hand gently on my shoulder and encouraging me to stay sitting. 'Let's take a little look, eh?'

I nod.

'Knee or ankle or both?' Miss Hanlon asks.

'I... I... I dunno. All of it.'

The hall gets noisier. Someone's bouncing the basketball. I can feel the vibration in the floor under me. I wish they'd stop.

'Okay, Kayla,' Miss Hanlon says. 'Tell me to stop if this hurts. I'm going to take off your shoe and sock to see if your ankle is swollen.'

I nod again. 'Ouch, ouch, ouch,' I say as Miss Hanlon unties my laces and slips off my runner.

There's some laughing and pointing and I remember the huge hole in my sock that I noticed this morning. I wasn't bothered about changing it because I never thought my whole class would be staring at my foot before we even had eleven o'clock break.

'Ew, what's that smell? It's like cheese,' one of the idiots in my class says. 'Ugh. It's gross. I think I'm going to be sick.'

Of course, laughter erupts as if the stupid comment is even funny. And I wish I could be anywhere else. Or at least be wearing any other pair of socks that I own. Like all the millions of pairs without stupid holes. *Could today possibly get any worse?*

The sharp, high-pitched screech of Miss Hanlon's whistle brings all the messing and laughing to a sudden stop.

'Right. That's enough,' Miss Hanlon says lowering her whistle from her lips. 'Everyone into the changing room and get changed for your next class. And with no messing. I'm in no mood, guys. No mood at all.' She points a warning finger and wags it. 'Go. Go on. Now.'

Everyone shuffles out the doors of the hall and into the corridor, the noise and mumbling and, no doubt, slagging me off about my holey socks fades with them.

'You too, Aiden,' Miss Hanlon says. 'Go on now. You'll be late for your next class.'

'But Kayla,' Aiden says, looking at me with pitiful eyes that I know are more about his desperation to get out of our next class than sympathy for me.

I know where he's coming from. It's almost worth mangling my leg to miss Irish verbs and poems.

'Kayla will be just fine with me,' Miss Hanlon smiles. 'Won't you, Kayla?'

I pull a face. Irish class is bad. But Irish class without your best friend to keep you sane for an hour is torture.

'Miss please, can Aiden stay?' I ask.

'Ha, nice try,' Miss Hanlon says. 'But this is not an excuse to get out of class and you two know better, don't you?'

'Yeah. Okay,' Aiden sighs. 'It was worth a try though, wasn't it?'

'Yes. I s'pose it was,' Miss Hanlon says. 'Now, c'mon. Hurry.

You're already running late and I don't want you getting into trouble with your next teacher.'

Aiden stands up and drags his feet so slowly towards the door anyone would think he's the one with a sore leg.

'I'll be sure to get the homework for you, Kayla,' Aiden teases, turning back as he reaches the hall doors. 'Check your Snapchat later.'

'Oh great! Thanks,' I groan.

Aiden pokes his tongue out at me while pulling a funny face, then hurries off to class.

'Will he really text you the homework later?' Miss Hanlon asks.

'Nah,' I smile. 'He's just having a laugh.'

'It's good to have a friend like that,' Miss Hanlon says in a soft almost-whisper voice.

I wait for her to ask me if we're going out – most of the other teachers think we are. It's fair enough, we spend lots of time together, but I've known Aiden since playschool. It would be super weird.

'You'd talk to Aiden if you had a problem, wouldn't you?' Miss Hanlon says.

'Yeah.' I scrunch my nose, so confused about where this conversation is going and really wishing we weren't having it while I sit on the ground with one runner on, one off and a giant hole in my sock.

'It's just I've noticed you're not quite yourself lately,' Miss Hanlon says, gently twisting my ankle. 'Does this hurt?'

I shake my head.

'Good. Good,' she says, moving her attention from my ankle to my knee as she begins to bend my leg. 'Is everything okay? Is anyone being mean to you?'

'Ouch. Ouch,' I say. 'That hurts.'

'Sorry.' Miss Hanlon lets go.

I reach for my runner without talking. I'm weirded out by

Miss Hanlon's strange questions and my knee is killing me again after moving it. Suddenly Irish class doesn't seem so bad.

'Kayla you would talk to someone if something was bothering you, wouldn't you? A friend? Your mam. Me maybe?' Miss Hanlon says, standing up and giving me a little space to put my runner back on.

'There's nothing wrong, Miss, I swear,' I say.

'Okay. Okay,' Miss Hanlon says, helping me up and shuffling towards one of the side benches with me. 'You're just not yourself at the moment, that's all.'

Miss Hanlon and I sit on the bench next to each other in awkward silence. I wish she'd say something. She obviously has more questions and it's not as if I can get up and walk away. God, I never thought I'd see the day where I was wishing I was in Irish class, but nothing could be as bad as this weirdness.

'Kayla have you been eating properly?' Miss Hanlon asks, turning towards me making the bench squeak like a loud fart under us.

I totally want to laugh but Miss Hanlon's face is scarily serious and I wonder how she could hear that and not even smile a little. It's not like her, she's usually our fun teacher.

'It's just, you've lost a lot of weight recently. You're pretty pale too, if I'm honest. And you clearly fainted before you fell. I would be lying if I said alarm bells aren't ringing, Kayla. I'm really quite worried about you.'

'Miss, there's nothing wrong. I swear. I love takeaways and popcorn and chocolate. Seriously. Chocolate! I could never give that up.'

'Cadbury's Fruit and Nut,' Miss Hanlon says.

'What? No. Chocolate and fruit is just wrong. And gross.' I pull a face. 'Dairy Milk, though. Now you're talkin'.'

'Ah, Dairy Milk. Keep it plain and simple. That's the spirit.'

I smile.

'Well, it just so happens I have a bar of Diary Milk in my

handbag. It's in the staff room. Let's call your mother and let her know what's happened and then I'll get you some tea and chocolate. How does that sound?'

I shake my head. 'My mam's in work meetings all day today. I'm supposed to be going to Aiden's after school.'

'Oh,' Miss Hanlon says, sounding disappointed, and I bet she wants to talk to my mam about more than just my knee. 'Well, I'm sure I'll catch her on her mobile and we can figure it out from there.'

It's hard not to start crying. I've no idea why, I just feel weird. Aiden is such a laugh and his mam is so nice, but, suddenly, I don't want to go to his house after school. I just want to go home. I really, really want to go home.

'Try not to look so worried, Kayla. I'd say it's just a sprain. Nothing too serious, but best to get an X-ray anyway. Let's see what your mam thinks.'

'Okay.' I nod.

Miss Hanlon smiles. 'And if you change your mind and ever want to talk about anything you know where I am, okay?'

'Yeah,' I say, knowing she's never going to drop this now. 'Thanks.'

NINE

KAYLA

'Does it still hurt?' Aiden asks as I sit on the couch in his parents' sitting room with a bag of frozen peas wrapped in a tea towel on my knee.

'Nah. Not really,' I say as Aiden flicks through channels on the TV.

'Ha. Knew you were faking,' he laughs.

I wish. The pain is darting the whole way down my leg in these weird waves that start at my knee and kind of trace the bone all the way to the ankle and then work their way back up. I don't want to say anything to Aiden because he'd probably tell his mam and she's been fussing over me all afternoon as it is. She's so lovely, but it's mortifying. I already had Aiden's older sister who's home from college moan, 'Jesus, Mam never took care of me like that when I broke my arm, did ya, Mam?'

'Ah, go away, you,' Aiden's mam said, laughing as she swatted her daughter out of the room as if she was a manky fly. 'Don't mind her, Kayla. You rest up and I'll see if we have any ice cream in the fridge.'

Aiden says his sister was only joking but I definitely think she was at least half pissed off.

'Right, what do you want to watch?' Aiden asks, flicking through the channels on the telly.

'I don't mind,' I shrug.

'Do you want to go up to my room to watch Netflix? I think the new episode of *Riverdale* is ready.'

I glance at my knee.

'Can you walk?' Aiden asks, and I know he's more concerned than he's pretending.

'Course I can,' I lie. 'But can we just stay down here? Your mam will be all weird if we go upstairs together. She'll start thinking we're going out again.'

Aiden scrunches his nose. 'Good point,' he says, and his eyes drop briefly to my knee and I know he knows I'm firing out excuses because my knee is killing me.

'Anyway, my mam just texted.' My eyes sweep over my phone screen as I'm talking. 'She says she'll be here in fifteen minutes. She's leaving work early.'

'What? Noooo,' Aiden says, pointing to the TV. 'Look, *Friends* is just starting. It's the one where Joey doesn't share food.'

'Joey never shares food,' I correct, laughing. 'Anyway, sorry. She seems in a hurry to go. She said, "be ready, please," and she added a tonne of exclamation marks and no kisses.'

'Oooohhh,' Aiden jokes. 'Someone's in trouble. What have you done now, Kayla Prendergast Doran? Huh, huh? Speak up, young lady. Speak up.'

Aiden's impersonation of our principal complete with her silly pout and hands on hips is hilarious and I'm laughing like a donkey when his mam comes back into the sitting room.

'Well you two certainly seem to be enjoying yourselves.' She smiles, and I cringe waiting for her to make some joke about me being her future daughter-in-law like she usually does. But Aiden shoots her a warning look and she nods back knowingly.

Oh. My. God. Wait? Did Aiden seriously tell his mam to

stop making jokes about us being a couple? What the hell! That's even more cringe than her actually making jokes about us being a couple. I'm going to kill him for a second time.

'I've thrown a pizza in the oven. It'll be ready in ten minutes. And I've no ice cream but I'll nip to the shop and get some in a bit. How's the knee now, Kayla? Any better?' Aiden's mam says.

I nod. 'Yeah. Loads. Oh, Mary, my mam just texted. She said she'll be here soon. I'm not sure I'll have time for pizza.'

'Don't be daft,' Mary says. 'Your mam will probably be starving after a hectic day. I'll throw another pizza on and she can stay for dinner too.'

'Thanks, Mary, but I think she's in a bit of a hurry, I'm sorry,' I say, cringing a little because it's really hard to be polite while basically saying *my mam sounds pissed off about something in her text and I doubt she wants to come in for frozen pizza*.

'Not at all,' Mary shakes her head. 'If she wants to take you for an X-ray you'll be in the hospital half the night. She'll be glad of a bite to eat, don't worry. Anyway, I haven't seen your mam in ages. I'm looking forward to a catch-up.'

'Okay,' I say, knowing it would be rude to protest. Mam can explain herself when she gets here. And maybe Mary is right. Mam will probably be starving. The pizza won't be a patch on the one from the takeaway that I was hoping we could get tonight but at least it means I can stay and watch *Friends*.

Canned laughter fills the sitting room as Aiden and I watch Joey and Phoebe sit on the couch in Central Perk and Joey tries to explain that food is not for sharing.

'That's me,' Aiden says wrinkling his lip and nodding his head, confidently. 'Aiden doesn't share food.'

I snort and can't hold in a laugh. It makes my whole body shake. Including my knee, but the pain is worth it because Aiden's face is both insulted and hilarious.

'You don't even eat the crusts of your pizza!' I say.

'Shut up,' Aiden folds his arms, losing. 'Crusts hurt my gums. There's sneaky crispy bits that get stuck there. Sometimes they even bleed.'

I can barely breathe I'm laughing so hard as Aiden throws a cushion and it hits me in the face.

'Ouch,' I say, still laughing. He throws another but misses. 'Stop,' I say holding my hand up to surrender. 'Do you smell that?'

'Pizzzzzaaaaa,' Aiden jumps up.

The smell of melted cheese and pepperoni wafts from the kitchen just as the doorbell rings.

'Ugh, my mam,' I say. 'Seriously, her timing.'

'I'll get it,' Aiden says, picking up the cushions and placing them back on the couch exactly as they were before so his mam doesn't kill him later. 'I'd tell you to wait here, but I know I don't have to, you cripple ya.'

Aiden leaves the sitting-room door open and walks into the hall.

'Hi, Heather,' he says and I feel the draft of cold air from the open door almost straight away. 'Kayla's on the couch. She's been a terrible patient. Moaning all day.'

'Is your mother here?' Mam says, and she sounds weird, cranky like a teacher or something.

'Um yeah,' Aiden says, and I can tell he's picked up on her mood. 'She's cooking pizza. She's put some on for you too.'

There's a moment of silence and I wonder if they're not talking or just talking really quietly.

'I can't stay,' Mam says.

'Oh. Yeah, sure okay.' Now Aiden sounds weird, like he doesn't know what to say or do.

'Can I have a word with your mam?' Mam asks. 'I just want to thank her for today.'

'Yeah. Okay. Come on in. Mam's in the kitchen if you want to go in to her.'

I hear the front door close and the noise of my mam's heels clip-clopping across the hall floor. She doesn't stick her head in the sitting-room door to say hi as I was expecting. Instead, it's Aiden's head in the gap. And his eyes are wide and round and he looks full-on traumatised.

'Okay. Your mam is in the worst mood ever,' Aiden whispers. 'That was so weird.'

'Really?' I say, confused. Mam loves Aiden. She's usually so cool around him. I slag them both for getting on so well and joke that they are actually the ones who are best friends.

'Did the school say something to her today when they called?' Aiden asks. 'Miss Hanlon was super weird around you, wasn't she? What did she say?'

'Nothing.' I shake my head, Miss Hanlon's conversation instantly replaying in my mind.

I bet Aiden is right. Miss Hanlon must have said something to my mam about food and now Mam is all freaked out. That would explain her snappy text too. *Oh great.* Now I'm going to have to listen to a lecture on body image all night. *Thanks a bunch, Miss Hanlon.*

Aiden hits mute on the telly so we can listen as my mam and his mam come into the hall, talking.

'I really am sorry, Mary,' my mam says. 'You've gone to all this trouble. And Kayla loves pizza. It's just I want to get to the hospital and get this knee business seen to.'

'No need to apologise, Heather,' Mary says. 'We'll catch up another time. And, between Aiden and his sister, I doubt very much the pizza will go to waste. Sure, I can't keep that boy fed. He'd eat the legs off the table, given half the chance.'

'I'm so grateful for today,' Mam says. 'And you had to pick the kids up early and everything. You're so good, Mary. Coffee on me soon, yeah?'

Mam sounds weird. It's freaking me out.

'Ah, would you stop. You'd do the same for me,' Mary says. 'And coffee would be great.'

The sitting-room door finally swings back all the way and Mam appears, smiling, but she looks awful.

'Hey you,' Mam says and I think she's going to cry.

I bet Mam's boss was horrible when she had to leave early. Mam says he's an asshole. *I feel so bad.* All this fuss. And my knee feels kind of okay now. I really wish Miss Hanlon hadn't called home.

Aiden stands up as Mam walks in. Mary comes in behind Mam. Everyone is standing except me. It's insanely uncomfortable.

'Bad fall?' Mam asks.

'Nah,' I shake my head. 'More annoyed that I fell just before I scored the winning basket.'

'Ha, cocky much,' Aiden tries to joke, reminding me he was on the opposing team but no one laughs and he blushes.

'Right, missy,' Mam smiles again and her eyes glass over more. It's as if every time she tries to pretend to be cool and happy she really wants to cry. 'Let's get going.'

'Okay,' I say, slowly swinging my legs from using the couch like a bed to sitting upright like usual.

'Your dad will carry you to the car, okay?' Mam says.

'Dad!' I screech, realising by everyone's faces that my reaction was way too dramatic, but seriously... 'What is Dad doing here?'

'Hey, love,' Dad says.

'Heeeeyyy.' I blush, turning much quieter as he comes into view.

'C'mon.' His voice is so deep and calm and normal. Not like Mam's at all. 'Let's get you into the car.'

Dad nods as he brushes past Mary and I realise this must be

mega awkward for them 'cos they've never actually met before. Dad stands in front of me and bends.

'Okay, wrap your arms around my neck and I'm going to lift you,' he says.

'Seriously?' I pull a face.

'Seriously,' Dad replies.

'Okay. Fine. Whatever.'

I slide my arms around Dad's shoulders and he slides his arms under me and there's no count to three or anything; he just lifts me into the air and I kinda slide down his arms until I'm pressed against his chest and I can smell the familiar aftershave I really like, the one that's all herbal and spicy, and I start crying. I've no idea why. It's so bloody embarrassing and I try to keep it under control so it's just tears running down my face and stuff, no actual sobbing, but I really want Dad to hurry and carry me out to the car before Aiden or Mary notice.

'You're okay, Kay,' Dad says, noticing. 'I have you.'

What the hell, Dad? Are you trying to make it worse? I think, his comforting words making it so much harder to keep it together.

'We'll call you,' Mam says as Dad carries me out the door. 'And, thanks again, Mary. Thanks, Aiden.'

'Bottom button,' Dad says as Mam holds the car keys in her hands, pointing them at the driver's door without anything happening. 'Double click,' Dad explains.

Dad's Audi plays a celebratory melody when Mam finally presses the right button and I wonder what it must be like for Molly to sit in a car this posh every day to go to school. And then I wonder what it must be like for Dad to love two kids leading such different lives.

TEN

KAYLA

'Will we get a takeaway?' Mam asks, as Dad drives out of Aiden's estate and turn towards town. 'There's a fab pizza place on the main street, isn't there, Kayla?'

'Yeah, it's fine,' I say, wondering when one of them is going to tell me what on earth is going on.

'Or Chinese,' Mam says. 'Do you still like Chinese, Gavin?'

Mam doesn't give Dad time to answer before she rambles on. 'I have their number.' She roots in her handbag and pulls out her mobile. 'I can call our order ahead and it'll be ready to pick up in ten minutes.'

'Anything is fine,' Dad says. 'I'm not really that hungry.'

Mam slides her phone back into her bag. 'Oh, well, maybe I could just make us some sandwiches back at the house—'

'Okay,' I say, folding my arms and sitting a little straighter. 'What is going on? This is way too weird. Why is Dad here? Why are you two together? And if we're getting pizza now, why didn't we just stay and have pizza at Aiden's?'

'You're right,' Mam says, slackening her seat belt so she can turn to look at me. 'Pizza is the best plan. I'll call now and get them to deliver. It'll probably arrive just as we get home.'

I drop my head back and stare at the ceiling. I'm obviously in trouble or Mam and Dad wouldn't be here together. It looks like it's pizza with a side of lecture for dinner. *Great!*

Back at the house, Dad is super careful as he carries me to the couch and Mam runs upstairs. She comes back with the teal fleece blanket from my bed even though it's not cold.

'There now,' Mam says, tucking me in, and it's surprisingly comfortable.

There's a knock on the front door and Dad pulls out his wallet before he even leaves the sitting room. 'I'll get this,' he says, hurrying as if something might happen if he's out of the room for too long.

Mam doesn't talk while he's gone. She's staring at me with teary eyes and the only sounds are the mumbles from Dad talking to the pizza guy at the door.

'Okay what?' I say, pressing my hands onto my hips.

'Let's just wait for Dad,' Mam says.

I'm momentarily distracted by the delicious smell as Dad comes back carrying two large pizza boxes. I can tell they're pepperoni before he even opens a box, and as much as my tummy is rumbling pizza will have to wait because I can't take this weirdness anymore.

'Will one of you please, please, please tell me what's going on? If I've done something wrong—'

'Kayla, no. God no,' Dad says, quickly. 'You haven't done anything wrong, kiddo. None of this is your fault.'

'None of what?' I ask, more confused than ever.

'I- I-' Mam stutters, looking at Dad. 'Gavin.'

'Your test results are back, Kay,' Dad says, and I watch as he looks like he might drop the pizza boxes.

'And?' I say, my tummy somersaulting.

'It's not great news,' Dad says. His face has gone weird, as if he's frozen.

I exhale and shake my head. 'But I can still play basketball, right? I mean, whatever the problem is they can fix it.'

'Kayla,' Mam says, sitting on the couch beside me and taking my hand the way people do with old people in movies when they're about to break bad news. 'Your father and I met a doctor in Dublin today and—'

'And,' I cut across her, 'can I still play basketball? We have the county finals in six weeks. I have to play, Mam. Please? I'll take it easy after that. I'll rest up until Christmas or whatever. But I have to play the final. Please, you know how important this is.'

'Kayla you're very sick,' Dad says, finally putting the pizza boxes down on the coffee table.

I exhale really sharply and make myself light-headed. *This isn't fair. They're ganging up on me!*

'Kayla, sweetheart,' Mam says, stroking her thumb over and back across my hand. 'The doctor says you have cancer.'

What? I take a deep breath and close my eyes. *Cancer. What the fuck? No. Just. No.*

'Kayla?' Mam calls me.

I don't answer. Dad comes to sit beside me on the couch and kisses my head like he used to when I was little.

'Kayla, I'm sorry,' Mam says, 'but we're going to see the best doctors in the best hospital and—'

'So I really can't play anymore,' I finally say. 'I mean, that's it. Everything I've worked so hard for, that's it. It was all just a big waste.'

'Kayla, I really am so sorry sweetheart. I'm sorry,' Mam says.

Mam and Dad continue to talk but I'm not really listening. Mam is apologising over and over as if any of this is her fault and Dad is being *Mr Overly Positive*, so I know how freaked out he actually is. I open my eyes and stare at Mam's favourite photo of me above the fireplace. My face is all red and sweaty and I'm smiling like crazy after shooting hoops with Dad and

Charlotte for hours. I'm missing my two front teeth so I think I was about six-ish. I remember how I couldn't wait to grow up and play for a real team. I never realised I was wishing my life away. But I guess I was. *This isn't fair.*

I close my eyes and try so hard not to cry. Suddenly basketball isn't the most important thing in the world. Staying alive is.

ELEVEN

CHARLOTTE

The house is eerily silent apart from the low hum of the old pipes in the attic. God only knows how long I've been lying in bed, staring at the ceiling in the dark. Cold and unable to sleep I feel around on the bedside table for my phone, smiling when my wedding ring clinks against the chrome cover. I drag it into bed with me and the insanely bright screen lights up half the room in a foggy blue hue.

'Ten past three,' I say aloud, as if anyone was listening. 'And still no word from Gavin.'

I texted him a few times. And I tried calling him once when I was waiting in the car while Molly was at her piano lesson. I tried him on WhatsApp and Facebook Messenger too but I can see that he hasn't even opened the messages.

I shove my phone under my pillow and toss and turn trying to get comfortable. I'm desperate to sleep but my mind is racing. I can't stop thinking about Kayla and all our chats about her future – studying physiotherapy and playing basketball for the university team.

I close my eyes and try counting backwards from one hundred. I make it to zero and I'm more awake than ever. I try again. Endless rounds of counting ensue until, finally, I hear a key turning in the front door.

The sound of hushed voices talking carries up the stairs like a tap on the shoulder, suggesting I get up and join them. I reach for my dressing gown on the end of the bed. But I decide against it – Kayla had a horrible day and the last thing she needs is another adult struggling to keep it together in front of her. Besides, I need to talk to Gavin and it would be better if we're alone. I have some questions about Molly and blood tests. I'm sure he has more information now after talking to Heather on the way to Cork.

There are footsteps on the stairs and the door to Kayla's bedroom opens and a few moments later closes. I I have to fight the urge to run into her room, wrap my arms around her and tell her that I love her. 'I'll get you something to sleep in,' I strain my ears to hear Gavin say as his footsteps circle the landing and the linen cupboard opens and closes.

Heather mumbles something but I can't make it out. Then I hear Gavin's voice again, followed by more walking around and I assume Gavin is coming to bed. I wait for the slightly ajar bedroom door to swing open fully.

Seconds tick by in slow motion until I hear Gavin on the stairs again, walking back down. His deep voice is whispering downstairs and I can hear Heather replying but I'm not sure what they're saying. Cupboards gently open and close in the kitchen and the kettle flicks on. It's becoming increasingly noisy and I hope that Molly doesn't wake up.

I slide my legs over the edge of the bed and the cold of the floorboards nibbles my toes as soon as I stand. I'm throwing on my dressing gown when Gavin comes into the room.

'Hey,' he says, as if he's shocked to find me in our bedroom. 'What are you doing up? It's so late. Did we wake you? I'm sorry.'

I shake my head and sit back onto the edge of the bed. 'I couldn't sleep.'

'Yeah,' Gavin nods. 'Molly?'

'She's asleep. She went to bed as usual,' I say. 'She was wrecked after her piano lesson.'

'Is she okay?'

'Yeah. She asked where you were, of course. And she was disappointed that I was reading her bedtime story instead of you. But she hasn't picked up on anything.'

Gavin swallows and nods. 'She just likes my funny voices.'

'Yeah,' I say, 'she does.'

I want to ask about Kayla. But I can't seem to find the right words and Gavin looks so exhausted I'm not sure he'd be able to find the right answers. So I just say, 'Is Kayla okay?'

'I dunno,' Gavin sighs. 'She fell asleep in the car and she can't walk very well so I carried her into bed—'

There's a loud bang downstairs and I jump. 'What was that?'

'Heather,' Gavin says, getting undressed for bed.

'She's still downstairs?' I say.

'She's baking cookies, or brownies or something.' Gavin flops onto the bed on his side and slides under the duvet pulling it right up to his chin.

'Baking?' My eyes widen as I reach for my phone and check the time. 'At half three in the morning, she's baking?'

'She bakes when she's stressed.'

'Sure,' I say, sliding under the duvet.

I turn my back on Gavin, close my eyes and find my spot. He drapes his arm around my waist and pulls me close to him. The heat of his body wraps around me and I snuggle into him, trying to ignore that his ex is downstairs in my kitchen.

My eyes fly open again as the sound of Molly crying in her room makes its way across the landing to shake me fully awake again.

'Daaadddyyy,' Molly cries.

'Gavin,' I whisper. 'Can you check on her?'

'Daaadddyyy,' Molly's crying grows louder and more upset.

'Hmm?' Gavin says, clearly already half asleep.

'Molly,' I say, turning around to face him. His eyes are closed. 'She missed you at bedtime. Maybe you could give her a goodnight hug now?'

'So tired, Charlie,' Gavin mumbles. 'Can you do it? Sorry.'

'Sure,' I huff out, blowing warm breath in my husband's face.

I stand up, throw on my dressing gown and march across the landing and into my daughter's bedroom.

'Hush, hush, sweetheart,' I whisper. 'I'm here. Mammy's here.'

TWELVE

KAYLA

The next day

I'm sitting in a leather armchair in the doctor's office. I'm trying really hard to concentrate, but I'm so tired after last night. It's nothing like I expected in here. It doesn't really feel like a hospital at all. It's more like the principal's office, only much posher. The walls are cream and there's a really soft, but kind of gross, browny-pink carpet. There's a filing cabinet in the corner and a water cooler beside it. The doctor has a pretty impressive flat-screen computer monitor on his desk and there are certificates framed on the wall behind him. He's kind of good looking for someone in his thirties or forties. Mam keeps staring at him, so I think she fancies him. Dad hasn't really noticed.

'So, Kayla. Have you any questions for me?' Doctor Patterson asks after a big long explanation about what Ewing's sarcoma is and how none of this is my fault – it just happens sometimes.

'Am I going to die?' I ask.

Mam and Dad gasp, as if they're shocked by my question, but I know by Mam's face she wants an answer too. Mam is sitting in the chair beside me. Her legs are crossed. She keeps crossing them and uncrossing them and switching which one is on top. There isn't another chair for Dad so he stands behind me with his hands gripping the back of my chair. I sort of wish he'd let go because he's shaking and it's making my chair wobble and that's making me nervous.

No one says anything for a moment.

'Well. Am I?' I ask again.

'Kayla, I know this is scary,' Doctor Patterson says. 'But we'd like to start your treatment as soon as possible, okay?'

I nod, realising I'd stopped listening at some point while he was explaining all about treatment. I look at Mam and her eyes are all glassed over and she's not doing a great job at pretending to be okay. And I just keep thinking about why he won't answer my question.

'So, I *am* going to die,' I say.

'Kayla. No. No you're not,' Dad says.

'Kayla, there are so many treatment options,' Doctor Patterson says. 'I don't want you to be worried or scared. You're in the best possible place. And everyone here, all the nurses and doctors and me, of course, we just want to help you to get better.'

'I'm only fifteen,' I say. 'It's not fair. I'm really fit and kinda healthy. I mean, I eat a lot of chocolate but I'm captain of the school basketball team. I just thought I was running it all off.'

'Your fitness will help you,' Doctor Patterson says, standing up and walking to the water cooler. He pours two glasses of water. He gives one to Mam and the other to Dad. I wonder if he'll go back and pour me one. I'm actually pretty thirsty but he walks past the water cooler and back to his desk. And I can't help but be disappointed that for a kids' doctor he's one of those people who thinks grown-ups are more important than kids. He doesn't sit down but he opens his drawer and he pulls out a can of Coke and a KitKat. He walks back around his desk and passes them both to me.

'I like chocolate too,' he says, winking.

I smile and wonder if it's okay to open the can in his office.

'Look, Kayla. I'm not going to patronise you,' he says, staying standing beside me. 'This is not going to be a picnic. You're in for one heck of a battle here, okay?'

I nod, listening.

'But as a team captain you know that when the going gets tough you just have to be a little tougher.'

I nod again. He sounds like Miss Hanlon. She's always giving us pep talks about how if you stay strong you can achieve anything.

'So, can I count on you to fight hard?' he asks.

'Yeah,' I say.

'Good,' he smiles, walking back to his desk and sitting down. 'Now are you going to open that KitKat, or what? And can I have a bit, please?'

THIRTEEN

KAYLA

'So that was super weird, wasn't it?' Aiden says as I hold the phone to my ear.

'What was?' I ask, switching ears. I never talk on the phone like this. It feels strange, but I don't want to video call. Not right now. I don't want Aiden to see the huge, bright-green Peter Pan painted on the hospital wall behind me as I sit cross-legged on a lumpy hospital bed. I think Wendy used to be painted too but she's flaked off and all that's left is half her dress and part of her shoe. It's actually a bit creepy.

'Your dad turning up at my house randomly?' Aiden says.

I sigh. 'Yeah. A bit unexpected.'

'So, c'mon then. What's going on?' Aiden says.

'Nothing really,' I lie.

'Kayla Prendergast Doran you can't lie to save your life, you know that?'

I smile. Aiden is right. I go all squeaky and sound like Molly when I lie. It's as if I pre-empt getting caught and panic.

'Just some family stuff, that's all,' I sigh, and console myself that I am technically telling the truth.

'Where are you?' Aiden asks. 'There's an echo or something.'

'Dublin.'

'Haha, smartarse.' Aiden laughs. 'Where in Dublin? You're not at your dad's.'

'How do you know that?'

'Because you said the WiFi is crap and that's why we have to talk on the phone like old people. And I know the signal at your dad's is great 'cos you're always boasting about how fast you can stream Netflix at his house.'

'Oh yeah,' I say, realising that this is another reason I don't lie. I can never remember what I said just seconds ago and I trip myself up.

'Okay, Kayla,' Aiden's voice takes a sudden serious turn and he sounds as grown-up as my dad, 'What's really going on? Don't make me call your mam. I will you know.'

He actually will, I think.

'Okay, okay,' I say, 'But you're not to freak out...'

'Kayla what do you mean I'm not to freak out. Now I'm freaking out.'

'Aiden. I'm serious,' I warn. 'Everyone else is already acting so weird and I can't handle it if you do too, okay.'

There's silence for a moment and I know he's thinking.

'Yeah. Okay. I promise I won't freak out,' Aiden says, calmly. 'Just tell me.'

I take a deep breath as I stare at Mowgli from *The Jungle Book* painted on the wall opposite me and shake my head. I look around for Tinker Bell. She's not on any of the walls. *Seriously where are they going with this theme?*

'Kayla,' Aiden grumbles. 'Say something. Please?'

I close my eyes and shake Mowgli out of my brain. 'I have cancer,' I blurt, running all the words together to get them out in case they burst in my mouth and taste gross.

'What?' Aiden says and I swear I can hear his eyes widen.

'You said you wouldn't freak out,' I warn.

'No, I actually mean *what*. What did you say? You said it so fast I couldn't hear you.'

'Oh.' I smile. 'I said...' I take another breath, not as deep this time. 'I said, I have cancer.'

'No, seriously,' Aiden says, seeming to lose patience. 'What did you really say?'

'I have cancer,' I repeat, no deep breath, no rushed sentence, just three simple words said with certainty.

'Kayla that's not funny.' Aiden is the one taking a deep breath now.

'It's not meant to be.'

'You have cancer,' he says slowly.

'Yes.'

There's silence and I'm going to remind him that he promised not to freak out, but I stop myself, and just let the silence hang in the air for a moment while the reality of what I said seems to sink in for us both.

Finally, I feel ready to explain. 'That's why my dad was at your house last night. My mam wasn't at work yesterday. She was at the kids' hospital, meeting my doctors. Dad drove down to Cork with her after so they could tell me together.'

'Fuck,' Aiden finally says.

'I know.'

'You're fifteen, like. Are fifteen-year-olds even supposed to get cancer?' Aiden says. And now it's his voice that goes squeaky.

I sigh. He's doing a terrible job at this not-freaking-out thing.

'You know they can,' I say.

'Yeah. Yeah.' He puffs. 'But not fifteen-year-olds like us. Or people we actually know.'

'Ha.' I smile, his argument is very sweet. Stupid. But sweet. 'I don't think cancer really works that way.'

There's more silence between us. I listen to footsteps on the corridor. And there's a rattle of teacups in the distance and there's the smell of toast – slightly burnt, wafting from somewhere. I wonder if these are sounds and smells I'll have to get used to. *I don't want to have to get used to them*, I think, cursing bloody Mowgli as he stares back at me with big blue eyes and a cheery smile.

'What the hell are you smiling at?' I snap.

'What?' Aiden says. 'I'm not smiling.'

'Not you.' I blush, glad he can't see me. 'Mowgli.'

'Who?'

'Mowgli,' I repeat. 'You know, from *The Jungle Book*.'

'Okay, have they put you on drugs already or something?' Aiden says.

I laugh. 'He's painted on the wall here in the hospital. There's a whole kids' cartoon-character theme thing going on.'

'I'm sure you love that,' Aiden says.

'It's fine,' I shrug, my shoulder crashing against my phone and bashing it against my ear. I wince. 'I mean, some of them are headless though so I'm not sure who they're supposed to be.'

'Headless cartoon characters?' Aiden laughs. 'Jesus, Kayla, what kind of kids' hospital is it?'

I laugh too. 'Not decapitated, you eejit. Just here years and the paint is flaking off. It's kind of gross.'

'All hospitals are gross,' Aiden reassures me. 'Do you have your own room, at least?'

'Yeah,' I nod, looking up at the closed door. It's kind of lonely. 'But, I think that's 'cos I'm contagious or something.'

'Cancer isn't contagious,' Aiden says. 'It's probably so you don't pick up the vomiting bug or something rotten like scabies.'

'Right, I gotta go,' I say, suddenly.

'Ah, Kayla. I was only joking about scabies. I don't even know what scabies are,' Aiden says.

I giggle. 'My mam is outside the door. I can hear her in the corridor taking to the doctor. I'm not hanging up because you tried to give me scabies.'

'Oh okay.' Aiden sighs, relieved. 'It's just—'

'Seriously,' I begin to whisper, 'I really gotta go. I want to pretend to be asleep when they come in so they don't start talking treatment crap to me again. Bye. Bye. Bye.'

I hang up, stuff my phone under my pillow and lie down with my eyes closed.

'Hey, you,' Mam's voice washes over me as the door creaks open.

I breathe deeply for effect.

'Kayla,' Mam says gently.

I breathe some more. A little louder.

'I know you're not asleep,' Mam says. 'I just heard you on the phone to Aiden.'

Damn you Aiden. I smirk and open my eyes reluctantly, trying not to laugh.

FOURTEEN

HEATHER

'I brought you some fluffy socks,' I say, rummaging in my large paper bag to show Kayla the fleecy, blue-and-pink stripy socks.

Kayla smiles.

'And I got jammies and chocolate too, but they're in the car. I'll bring them in later,' I say.

'You went shopping?' Kayla says, her eyes glassy.

I nod. 'Just to grab a few essentials. I just nipped around the corner. I didn't go to Penneys or anything without you. I know better.' I throw in an awkward laugh and I hate how forced it sounds.

'Who doesn't love Penneys?' the nurse says, coming into the room behind me. 'Did you see the Winnie the Pooh jammies they got in last week?'

I nod. I did see them. They're cute. Kayla isn't smiling even though she loves Winnie the Pooh. She has a Pooh teddy at home that she's had since she was a baby. He only has one eye and patches of his fur have been hugged off but she will never throw him away. I wonder if I could find him. It would be nice for Kayla to have something special with her now.

Kayla is staring at the characters painted on the wall and I wish I knew what she was thinking. I wonder if all the rooms are like this, or if Kayla will be moved to something more suited to her age when she comes out of surgery later. I make a mental note to ask. But not in front of Kayla, stuff like that embarrasses her and she's dealing with enough already without feeling like her mother is nit-picking at the décor.

'I'm going to buy some of the chequered ones with the honey pots on the legs for my nieces,' the nurse says, catching my attention again. 'I'll put them away for Christmas.'

'Good idea,' I say, looking away from Kayla reluctantly to make eye contact with the nurse. *Did she really just mention Christmas?*

'Might get the slippers too,' the nurse continues. 'You know the ones with the bobble Eeyore head. Eeyore is my favourite.'

'Um,' I nod. 'I like Tigger, myself.'

Why do I sound so weird? I think. My voice is gruff as if I've been out partying all night and I'm hungover. This small talk is torture. Out of the corner of my eye I notice Kayla looking at me with her head tilted a little to one side and her forehead wrinkled as if to ask, 'What the hell are you saying, Mam?'

'Is it okay if I take a little blood, Kayla?' the nurse asks, as she walks towards some drawers at the side of the room that I hadn't noticed before.

Kayla's neck elongates and her expression changes drastically. I try to reassure her with a wide smile, but I feel like such a fraud. I'm as caught off guard as she is. It's not my veins getting a needle, but I wish it was.

'Mam?' Kayla whispers.

'She had bloods taken in Cork last week,' I say.

'I'm sorry, Kayla,' the nurse says, looking genuinely regretful. 'I really do need to take some before your operation.'

'It's just a quick prick,' I add, meeting Kayla's beautiful blue, unsure eyes with mine. 'Kind of a sting, but over before you know it.'

'Do you want your mam to sit beside you, Kayla?' the nurse asks as she rummages in the drawer.

'Yeah,' Kayla nods.

Tears prick the corners of my eyes. *Why didn't I think of that?* Of course, I should be beside her. Of course I should.

I walk over to the hospital bed, which is much higher than a normal bed. Kayla uncrosses her legs and slides over until she's pressed right up against the wall and I know the uncomfortable position is more about getting away from the nurse than making room for me.

The nurse looks at Kayla and then me. I shoot her a look that says, 'Just give us a moment?' and she smiles at me knowingly and pretends to be distracted with something in the drawer. I realise she must see this every day; parents having to coax scared children away from the wall, but I wonder if the nurse knows that the parents are probably just as scared. I never realised how goddamn terrifying something as simple as a blood test is until this very moment. It's not the needle, of course, and I know that's not what's bothering Kayla either. It's what the needle represents. It's that start of a journey none of us want to be on. Poking and prodding and operations and nights in hospital.

'C'mere, Kayla,' I say stretching my arm out to her and waiting for her to take my hand. 'It'll be easier if you're sitting up.'

Kayla shakes her head and I can feel pressure in my chest as if something horribly heavy is sitting on my heart, crushing it.

'Trust me,' I say.

Kayla doesn't budge. I can hear the nurse close the drawer and I hope she doesn't say anything. Not yet. I really want Kayla to take this step for herself and not because she feels pressured into it. God knows, I feel enough pressure for the both of us.

'You know what?' the nurse asks. 'This is all a bit sudden,

Kayla, isn't it? I think I should give you and your mam some time alone. Maybe some time to try on those lovely fluffy socks would be good, wouldn't it? I'll come back later.'

'Thanks,' I say, looking down at the comfy socks I didn't realise I was squeezing so tightly my knuckles are white.

'No,' Kayla says, sitting up and shuffling over to the edge of the bed while rolling up her sleeve. 'Let's just get this over with.'

I nod and smile at Kayla, proud. And, maybe a little confused. Then, I nod at the nurse. She nods back. I had no idea there would be this much nodding involved in Kayla coming into hospital. I wonder if gestures are easier than words when your whole life is turned upside down. But, as my legs wobble and my tummy is a single rumble away from throwing up in the bright-yellow bin behind the door, I realise: nothing is easy when your child is *this* sick. Gestures. Words. Eating. Functioning. They all go out the window.

'Ready, Mam?' Kayla says, her wide eyes searching mine for answers I don't have.

'Yeah,' I say, pulling myself straight as if I have the confidence of Goliath. 'Let's do this.'

I drape my arm over Kayla's shoulder as I lower myself to sit on the bed beside her. It's bouncier than I was expecting and Kayla giggles when I almost fall off. Getting my balance, I smile and kiss the top of her head. The smell of coconut shampoo from her golden hair smacks against my nose.

'You smell great, kiddo,' I say, choking back tears.

'Like holidays,' Kay replies and I instantly think of the coconut sun cream I'm obsessed with slathering us in every time we go abroad. Factor 50 million, because our Irish skin burns easily, and those cancer warnings are all over the news and radio ads. 'Tanned skin is damaged skin,' they warn. But no one warned us about this.

To hell with sun cream, I think, staring at a mural of Baloo on the wall opposite Kayla. My God that thing is scary. It's teeth are huge; painted oddly out of proportion with the rest of its body. I doubt it bothers Kayla much but I can only imagine that a small child would be terrified by a big grey bear ready to pounce off the wall to eat them while they sleep. Maybe I should say something?

'That's a girl, Kayla,' the nurse says before poking her tongue between her teeth as her eyes squint with concentration. 'You're doing great.'

I hold my breath, wishing the nurse was stabbing the needle into me instead. And, when Kayla gasps and snuggles her head into the crook of my neck the way she did when she was a baby, my heart feels as if it drops from my chest and sinks into the pit of my stomach to weigh heavy there.

I compose myself quickly, afraid that Kayla will pick up on my fears. I watch as the nurse draws crimson blood into a vial. Kayla doesn't budge.

'So, did Aiden have any news?' I ask, my fingertips stroking her hair.

Kayla lifts her head off my shoulder and turns to stare at me. She shakes her head. 'No. I'm pretty sure I'm the one with all the news.' She narrows her eyes and adds a sarcastic air quote with her free hand. I know her snappiness isn't directed at me, but it still stings.

'Did you tell Aiden?' I ask.

'Yeah.'

'And?'

'And what?' Kayla snaps again.

'And, what did he say?'

Kayla shrugs.

'Okay all done,' the nurse says, securing a ball of cotton wool against Kayla's arm with some white surgical tape.

'Really?' Kayla smiles.

'See that wasn't so bad, was it?' she says.

The nurse makes her way over to the drawer again and my

attention drops to the vials of dark blood resting on a metal tray with a mint surgical cloth draped across it.

'This is for you,' the nurse says, pulling a bright-purple lollipop out of the drawer that seems to have everything. 'I know you're probably too grown-up for lollies, but these blackcurrant ones are delicious and a little sugar after giving blood will make sure you don't go all dizzy on me.'

Kayla looks at the lollipop, uncertain, and I think she might cry.

'Would you prefer lemon?' the nurse asks. 'The strawberry ones are all gone, I'm afraid.'

'Blackcurrant is good,' Kayla says, composing herself and taking the lollipop. 'Thank you.'

'You're very brave, Kayla,' I say. 'Well done.'

Kayla slides the wrapper off the lollipop. 'Sorry for biting your head off,' she says, before popping the lollipop in her mouth.

I don't reply, I just kiss the top of her head reassuringly.

'I'm going to get these off to the lab,' the nurse explains, lifting the tray. 'And the doctor will be in to see you soon.'

The nurse isn't wrong because as she walks out the door Doctor Patterson walks in. They stop for a chat in the middle and the nurse walks all the way out the door and the doctor walks all the way in. It all seems to play out in slow motion.

'Kayla. Heather.' The doctor nods, looking at each of us in turn. 'How are you?'

Kayla looks away and I groan inwardly, and I wonder if that answers his question.

'Did I tell you I used to play basketball myself when I was younger?' the doctor says sitting into the uncomfortable-looking plastic chair next to Kayla's bed.

'Nothing as cool as on my school team, mind you. In fact, I wasn't very good at all,' he says. 'But, I tried. That's all that matters, right?'

I'm not sure what the doctor is expecting Kayla to say but I see her smile while crossing her legs to get comfortable. I breathe a sigh of relief.

'Yeah, trying is really important,' Kayla says. 'I wasn't great when I was little. But I kept practising and last year I got made captain.'

Kayla and the doctor chat effortlessly about shooting hoops and dribbling and who their favourite player is and I sit back down on the bed and listen, joining in only very occasionally because it's just so lovely to listen to Kayla talk about something without the wobble of fear that crept into her voice last night when Gavin and I told her how sick she was.

Time flies by as the three of us chat. And, after half an hour, maybe more, I wonder when Doctor Patterson is going take on a sudden seriousness and start talking about surgery and medication. I find myself fidgeting and staring at the cartoon characters on the wall wondering if somebody, someday, is going to paint a new head for Wendy. The sound of Kayla's girly giggles grabs my attention. The doctor laughs too. I wonder what's so funny and I wish I'd been listening.

'Right,' the doctor says, standing up as he looks at his watch. 'I'd best be off. My lunch break was over ten minutes ago.'

'You're on your break?' I ask.

'I was,' he smiles. 'I should be back downstairs by now, but I was enjoying talking about my glory days so much.'

'Will you be back later?' Kayla asks.

He nods. 'I will. I'm going to check up on those bloods of yours, see what they tell us. I already know you're an amazing basketball player, let's see what else I can find out.'

'Thank you,' I say.

I can't quite believe he sat with us when he should have been enjoying lunch with his colleagues in the canteen. And I realise that it isn't what Doctor Patterson does with a stethoscope or blood pressure monitor that makes him a great doctor;

it's how at ease he puts his patients. *He's such a lovely person*, I swoon, blushing when I realise I'm staring at him and his gorgeous hazel eyes.

'Bye, Kayla,' he says, winking. 'Take care of your mam and I'll see you both later.'

'Byeeee.' Kayla grins. 'See you later.'

'Goodbye, Heather,' he says, placing his hand gently on my shoulder.

FIFTEEN

HEATHER

'Oh my God.' Kayla laughs as soon as the doctor walks out. 'Could you have made that any more obvious?'

'Made what obvious?' I ask, knowing exactly where Kayla is going with this. I will my embarrassed cheeks to cool down. My face is actually stinging.

'Can't say I blame you.' Kayla smirks. 'I mean he is actually gorgeous, isn't he?'

'Kayla,' I say, pretending to be shocked.

'Oh c'mon. I saw the way you looked at him.'

'I looked at him like he's your doctor and I appreciate his time,' I nod. 'That's all.'

'Oh. My. God. You're so full of it.' Kayla is laughing so hard she snorts, which makes her laugh even harder. It's quite hard to keep a straight face. 'You looked at him like you fancy the pants off him. You do, don't you?'

'Kayla,' I say.

'Ah, c'mon, Mam. Admit it. You've a thing for my doctor.'

'He's a good-looking guy, yes, but—'

'But nothing. He's hot and you fancy him. Wow. I've never really seen you fancy someone before,' Kayla says, and I pull a face realising she's right and I wonder if that's a good thing or if it's a little depressing. 'You know your face went super red when you were talking to him, right?' Kayla tells me.

'It's hot in here,' I say.

'Yeah. Hot like Doctor Hot.' Kayla crosses her hands across her heart and pouts her lips dramatically.

'Okay. That's enough now,' I say, my face stinging more than ever.

'Ah, Mam,' Kayla says, sounding disappointed. 'I'm only having a laugh.'

'I know, sweetheart.' I smile. 'I know.

I walk towards the window, wishing it opened so I could get some fresh air. But I take a deep breath anyway and the unnatural smell of hospital fills my lungs.

I turn around and look at Kayla. She's sitting cross-legged on the bed with a monster grin on her face and her eyes are sparkling with giddiness. She doesn't look sick at all. She just looks like Kayla. My beautiful Kayla full of fun and life and silliness. It's hard to believe there's a disease inside her trying to cause so much damage.

'Where did you put that lollipop?' I ask. 'We don't want it to get stuck in your hair.'

I flinch, as Kayla runs her hand over her hair and I wonder if she's thinking about when she might lose it. Because it's what I'm thinking about. I really need to learn to watch what I say. *God, this is hard.*

'It was gross and all sticky so I wrapped it in some paper and Doctor Patterson put it in the bin for me.'

'He did?'

'Yeah.' Kayla narrows her eyes. 'Didn't you notice? The bin was right behind you.'

I shake my head, feeling so overwhelmed.

'So, are you going to ask him out?' Kayla asks.

'What?' My eyes shoot wide open. 'No. God. No.'

'Why not?' Kayla says. 'Don't be nervous.'

'I'm not nervous. He's your doctor.'

'Yeah, and—'

'And it would be highly inappropriate,' I say. 'Okay, seriously, can we please talk about something else?'

Kayla folds her arms. 'Fine. But I think you're being a big chicken.'

'You're entitled to your opinion, but—'

There's a gentle knock on the door and it creaks open slowly. 'Sorry,' Doctor Patterson says, appearing in the gap. 'I forgot my phone.'

I glance at the chair he'd been sitting in and his phone is resting in the middle, face down. An awkward silence falls over us as I stare at Kayla and hope to God he didn't over hear us.

He takes the phone, stuffs it into an inside pocket on his pristine white coat and smiles. 'You've gone very quiet suddenly, Kayla,' he says. 'Is everything alright?'

Oh God. Oh God. Oh God. I hold my breath, praying Kayla doesn't think it's funny to say something.

'Yeah. I'm okay,' Kayla says. 'Are we allowed phones in here? There's a sign in the corridor that says no phones, so I wasn't sure.'

'A sign that everybody ignores,' he says. 'Of course you can talk to your friends, Kayla. You'd crack up in this place otherwise, wouldn't you?'

Kayla nods.

'Do you want to call Aiden back?' I say.

Kayla nods again.

'Okay,' I say. 'I'll give you some space. I'll go call your father and get the jammies and chocolate out of the car while you're busy.'

'Actually, Heather,' Doctor Patterson says. 'Would you mind if I grabbed a quick word before you jump on the phone.'

'Sure,' I say.

'In the corridor,' he adds, tilting his head towards the door.

I take a deep breath, terrified that whatever Doctor Patterson has to say, he doesn't want to say in front of Kayla. I don't think I can cope with much more bad news.

'I'll be right outside,' I reassure Kayla, as Doctor Patterson takes a step back to allow me to pass out the door and into the corridor first.

'Um-hmm,' Kayla nods, her attention already passed over to her phone screen.

Doctor Patterson closes Kayla's door behind us and points towards some waiting chairs lined up against the far wall.

'Let's take a seat,' he says.

I nod, grateful for his suggestion as my knees begin to tremble.

SIXTEEN

HEATHER

The metal seats are cold and the chill works its way through to my legs, as I sit leaning to one side so I'm more hovering on my hip than resting on my bum. I wonder why most hospital waiting chairs are made with countless tiny holes in the base that press against the cheeks of your backside like a cheese grater digging into a block of Cheddar. I've no doubt when I stand up I'll have an imprint on my backside that will last for hours.

Doctor Patterson sits similarly. He's turned towards me and I can tell from his pensive expression he's waiting for the right moment to speak.

'So,' he finally says, 'how you doin'?'

'Excuse me?' I allow my full weight to flop onto the cold metal chair. 'How you doin'?' I repeat, shaking my head.

Doctor Patterson looks at me blanky.

Friends plays in my mind so vividly I can literally hear the characters talking. 'How you doin'?' I hear Joey say. I can't wait to tell Kayla that Doctor Patterson has used the worst chat-up line in the book. I doubt she'll think he's so cool then, but it should give her a laugh, at least.

'I'm fine thank you. How are you?' I say.

My God this is awkward.

Doctor Patterson shakes his head. 'No. I mean how are you *really* doing? How are you coping?'

'Oh,' I say, my smile slipping away. 'I- I- I-'

Doctor Patterson places his hand on my knee and my eyes fall to his fingers, but I don't move.

'This is all happening so quickly. Your head must be spinning,' he says.

'Yeah. It is,' I admit. 'It's just Kayla, you know.' I feel tears swell in my eyes and I beg myself not to cry. 'She doesn't get sick. Not really.'

'It was a pleasure chatting to her earlier,' Doctor Patterson says, taking his hand off my knee. I instantly miss the warmth. 'I enjoyed learning about her love of basketball. It was good to hear in her own words and in her own time how the pain started to affect her game.'

'Oh,' I say, enlightened. 'You asked her all about her life to find out about her cancer. That's clever.'

'I wasn't trying to trick Kayla,' Doctor Patterson explains. 'Kids...' he pauses and shift his weight a little so he's sitting a little straighter '...teenagers especially, are more astute than we often give them credit for. If we bombard them with medical questions upfront, they build fortresses and associate us with pain and misery and shut us out.'

I nod, understanding.

'And I can't say I blame them. I wouldn't talk to some guy with a clipboard and a fancy degree, just because he wears a white coat.'

'So, you want her to think you're her friend,' I say.

'No,' he shakes his head. 'I want to be her friend. I want to help her to the absolute best of my ability.'

'That's lovely,' I say, the lump in my throat so huge I can barely breathe.

'I like friends,' Doctor Patterson says.

Friends? I smile ridiculously brightly, and he looks at me as if I've lost my mind.

'Friends or *Friends?*' I ask.

'Chandler, Monica, Ross, Rachel, Phoebe and Joey. Who doesn't like *Friends?*' he says.

My mouth opens but no sounds comes out.

'Your T-shirt says, *We Were On A Break.*' He points at it.

'Oh. Right. Yeah.' I blush, remembering the old T-shirt Gavin gave me last night when I confessed I'd been so busy packing for Kayla I'd forgotten to pack for myself.

'Kayla and I argue about this all the time.' I smile, reminiscing.

'What do you think?' he asks.

'About *Friends?*'

'Yeah.'

'They really were on a break.' I shrug. 'Rachel said so herself. I'm team Ross.'

'Team Ross.' He shakes his head.

'Yes, Ross,' I say, my eyes narrowing. 'Why? Whose side are you on?'

'Rachel's,' he says as confident as if the characters are real people we know personally.

'Ha,' I snort. 'Kayla will love you for taking her side.'

'It's not sides.' He smiles. 'Just my honest opinion. I'm with Kayla on this. You're wrong.'

I try not to giggle as I fold my arms, but I fail miserably and begin to laugh. And for a moment, just a fleeting moment, I feel lighter; floating above the nightmare the last twenty-four hours have been.

'You still haven't answered my question. Not honestly,' he says, the moment over as I plummet back to reality with a painful bang. 'How are you doing?'

Shit! I'm doing shit, I want to confess. But instead I smile and act brave and he shakes his head knowingly. I wonder if he's this good at reading all his patients' parents, or if I have any right to feel special because he's damn well reading me like a book.

I meet his eyes and I shake my head. He's giving me time.

Exhausted and broken and thinking, *In another life and another set of circumstances we might actually be friends,* I let my guard down.

'I'm not really doing great,' I hear myself say, somewhat subconsciously.

'Kayla worries about you, you know?' he says, placing his hand back on my knee.

'Me? No. Kayla is the one who's sick. Not me.'

'She knows this is hard for you too,' he says. 'Like I said, they know stuff we don't give them credit for. It's always better to be honest with them. And yourself.'

'Kayla is my whole world,' I say.

He smiles. 'She's a great kid.'

'I have a job I hate, a house I can barely afford, and I'm single at thirty-three, but it's all okay because I have Kayla,' I say. The words are spilling off my tongue and I can't seem to stop them.

We sit opposite each other in silence and it's not as awkward as it should be and I think he's really good at this friends thing. And not just knowing the names of the characters from the show.

'Work said I could have as much time off as I need while Kayla is sick,' I say.

'That's great,' he says.

'Unpaid,' I add.

'Oh.'

'I know. That's kinda lousy, right? I mean, I work myself to the bone for those bastards. Sorry, pardon my French. But really.'

'You'd be surprised the stories I hear from parents in your shoes.' He shakes his head. 'Makes me glad I work for the state. Well, not really. Don't quote me on that.'

'It's just hard, you know,' I rant. 'Kayla's dad is minted. He has his own company. His parents are very proud.' I pull my head back until I have three chins and then put on a voice like Gavin's dad as if my head is so far up my own arse I've reached my small intestine. '*Oh, Gavin had a baby and still made something of himself.* They remind me all the bloody time. Well, maybe I had a baby and raised her, loved her and spent lots of time with her, you absolute judgemental arse.'

An older nurse walks by and throws me a disgusted look.

'Ooops,' I say.

'Don't worry,' he says. 'She's, erm, she's like your in-laws, who aren't exactly in-laws, really. Right?'

'Outlaws.' I snort.

'Kayla tells me you bake,' he says, unexpectedly.

'I can't believe Kayla told you about my baking. She doesn't really tell people. She's usually embarrassed.'

'Well, she was full of pride when she told me all about your skills.'

I blush.

'Look,' he says, running an awkward hand through his hair. 'Please don't take this the wrong way, but, the canteen are looking for someone part-time to bake confectionary. It's nothing very exciting I'm afraid, just scones and muffins—'

'I'm not really qualified,' I interrupt him, 'I mean, I never went to college so...'

'If your muffins are as great as Kayla says they are then let me see if I can pull a few strings.'

I smile.

'Nothing is guaranteed of course, but I know they've been looking for a while because the hours are so unsociable, but if you're interested?'

'Yes. Yes. That would be great.'

'And, I think if Kayla were to bring a basket of brownies down to the kids' games room one day, she would be pretty popular, really quickly.'

'You think it would help her makes friends?' I ask.

'I know it would. Kids love brownies, and if your brownies really are the best in Ireland...'

'Kayla said that?' I ask, blushing. 'I didn't hear her.'

'That's because you couldn't take your eyes off that drawer near Kayla's bed.'

'Sorry?' I say.

'You know, I can get you a lollipop if you really want one that badly,' he jokes.

I shake my head and I'm smiling again.

'Lollipops are usually only for patients, but I can pull a few strings. I know people.'

I relax. As embarrassing as his teasing is, it helps. I'm so glad he's Kayla's doctor. His ability to find fun in even the most horrible moments will be just what Kayla needs.

'I think I'll pass on the lollipop, thank you,' I say. 'Now, if it was a glass of wine on the other hand...'

He smiles. 'Unfortunately, my connections don't stretch quite that far. But if you want my medical recommendation? There's an off-licence on the corner, just after the car park; they do a fantastic French Chablis and it's on special offer at the moment. Try two glasses before bed, see if that helps.'

The metal chairs creak under me as I stand up. I drag my hand around my face trying to compose myself before I walk back in to Kayla. I turn my back on him as I reach for the handle of Kayla's room and slowly creak it open.

'Thank you,' I mouth without sounds.

He scrunches his nose. 'You're welcome,' he replies, equally as silently.

SEVENTEEN

CHARLOTTE

Heather's car is parked in the drive behind Gavin's, so I pull up against the curb and hope my cantankerous neighbour in number ten doesn't start ranting and raving about people blocking the path in the event of a fire again.

'Okay, sweetie,' I say, twisting around too sharply so that the seatbelt digs into my neck. 'Shit. Ouch.'

Molly gasps. I groan inwardly as I slacken the belt and rub my neck. I know at some point over the next day or two I'm going to hear my daughter repeat that word and when I try to correct her she'll proudly tell me, 'But you said it, Mammy.'

'We're home,' I say, looking at Molly who has started giggling now as she no doubt commits the word to memory.

I exhale, undo my seatbelt and open the car door. I swing my legs out and stand up, realising how tired I am. I duck my head back inside, press the button on Molly's car seat and say, 'Okay, sweetheart, grab your bag out of the boot and let's get inside. I'm starving, are you?'

'So hungry,' Molly says.

Molly is always starving when we come home from swimming. The instructor pushed hard this week and I think Molly's little arms must have swum an extra length or two. I left lasagne defrosting on the shelf and I hope Gavin got my note to stick it in the oven. If not, I'll chop Molly some carrot sticks and turn on CBeebies to tide her over until dinner is ready.

Heather's car is parked crooked and there's no room to pass by without stepping on the grass. I swing Molly and her absurdly large swim bag into my arms and hop across the grass so at least I'm only dealing with one pair of mucky shoes.

Opening the hall door the heat hits me first, followed by a delicious smell.

'Oh yummy. What's that smell?' Molly says, kicking off her shoes as I put her down.

'Not lasagne anyway,' I say, confused.

Molly drops her bag in the corner and races into the kitchen.

'Daddy,' I hear her squeal and I know she's excited he's home. He's rarely home from work when we get in from swimming. It's really lovely having him home early, but I wish it was under different circumstances and not because Kayla is sick.

I pick up Molly's swim bag so no one trips over it going up the stairs and breaks their neck and make my way into the kitchen. *God that smell is fabulous*, I think as my tummy rumbles.

'Oh, hello,' I say, sounding as surprised as I am to find Heather and Gavin sitting at our small kitchen table eating.

Gavin is tucking Molly's chair into the table in the space they've made between themselves for her.

'Heather cooked,' Gavin says.

'Mmmm,' I say, the swimming bag starting to dig into my shoulder as I stare at the scene of domestic bliss in front of me.

There's a white lacy tablecloth on the table. It was my grandmother's and I rarely use it because it stains easily and has to be hand-washed. The last time I used it was Christmas and Gavin's birthday was the time before that. A bottle of red wine sits open in the centre of the table. The label is fancy, cream with a swirly font, and I've no doubt it was expensive and highly unlikely to be organic. Gavin will no doubt complain of a headache later like he always does because he's allergic to sulphites. The thick-cut steak on their plates, that they've already started eating, looks mouth-watering and there's a selection of veg and a tray of some sort of fancy potato thing.

'What's this?' Molly says, sticking out her tongue, clearly unimpressed by the potato. I try not to laugh.

'That's potato gratin.' Heather smiles. 'But don't worry, Molly, that's only for the grown-ups.'

I'm about to explain that in this house we all eat the same food. There's no definition between grown-up food and children's food but Heather keeps talking.

'Your daddy told me you love chicken nuggets,' Heather says.

Molly's face lights up. My hand tightens around the strap of Molly's swim bag and I swear if Heather produces a McDonald's Happy Meal from somewhere I'll scream. I've told Gavin countless times I don't want Molly eating that stuff.

Heather stands up and slips on an oven glove.

'Heather made them herself. Especially for you,' Gavin says.

Heather pulls a tray of, no doubt, hand-battered chicken breast chunks and home-made chunky chips out of the oven. I hate myself for thinking they smell even more delicious than the steak.

'Yummy,' Molly squeals with excitement. 'Heather. You're the best.'

Finally, my shoulder on fire, I drop the swim bag. The gentle thud gets Gavin's attention.

'Aren't you going to join us?' Gavin asks.

Heather places a colourful plastic plate of nuggets and

chips in front of Molly and warns Molly that they're hot before she sits back down.

I stare at the already overcrowded table that only has three chairs and I don't even bother asking the redundant question of 'Where will I sit?'

'I'm not hungry, thanks,' I say.

'Yes you are,' Molly corrects me. 'You said so. In the car. You said you were starving.'

'Well I'm not hungry any more,' I say, firmly.

Heather's eyes shoot up to find mine. I glare back. 'There really is plenty here, Charlotte. I can toss your steak on the pan now. It'll only take five minutes. Three if you like it rare.'

I glance at the worktop where a single piece of fillet steak is waiting on some brown paper.

'Charlotte doesn't eat meat,' Gavin says, his eyes widening. 'I should have said something earlier, but with everything going on I forgot.'

Heather winces. And I think she's embarrassed. 'I'm sorry,' she says. 'I had no idea.'

'The veggies are fab, Charlie,' Gavin says. 'And the potatoes are dairy-free so you can have those.'

'You're vegan?' Heather asks.

I nod.

'Charlie hasn't eaten meat in twenty years but she's been vegan about five,' Gavin says.

'Six,' I correct, bending down to fetch the swim bag again. 'I'm going to get this stuff in the wash. You enjoy dinner.'

'Charlotte I really am sorry. But I've a recipe for a fab vegan stew. I'll make that next time, yeah?'

Next time?

'Sure,' I say opening the door into the utility room and walking away.

'Why didn't you tell me she's vegan?' I hear Heather say in a similar tone I use with Gavin when he's screwed up.

Her tone is way too familiar and way too comfortable. I fling open the door of the washing machine and tumble in everything out of Molly's swim bag, possibly including her goggles but I'm too exhausted to check. I slam the door shut, dump the empty bag on top and march back into the kitchen.

'You know what?' I say. 'I'm not that hungry, but I could murder a glass of wine. I think I will join you after all.'

'Great,' Gavin says, hopping up.

He fetches a glass, sets it on the table and fills it almost to the brim.

'You take my seat,' he points, pushing his plate over to slide the glass into its place. 'I'll grab one of the foldaway stools. Are they still under the stairs?'

'Yeah,' I say. 'I think so.'

Gavin hurries into the hall and I sit. Heather and I are face to face. She's stopped eating despite there being three quarters of her food still on her plate and I've no doubt she feels as awkward as I do.

I glance at Molly hoping to catch her eye so she'll begin chatting but she's too busy enjoying her delicious nuggets.

'Found it. Found it,' Gavin says, returning.

He's almost out of breath from rushing, so I know he's aware of how uncomfortable this whole situation is. He opens the stool out and sits next to me. He's much lower than the rest of us on chairs and Molly begins to laugh. Heather laughs too and finally, I giggle, so grateful for something, anything, to lighten the atmosphere.

I pass Gavin his plate and he tucks back in. I watch everyone eat for a moment and hope that my tummy doesn't rumble loud enough to be heard.

'Did Heather tell you the good news?' Gavin asks, reaching for the wine and topping up Heather's glass first and then his own.

'No.' I arch an eyebrow, relieved it's good news for a change but unsure if we should discuss Kayla in front of Molly.

'It's not that big a deal.' Heather blushes. 'And nothing is definite yet.'

'Don't be so modest,' Gavin says, chewing on some steak.

Heather shakes her head and my stomach aches, and not just with hunger, as I watch the banter between my husband and his ex. I slug a large mouthful of wine and wait for them to share the secret. I was expecting Gavin and Heather to share conversations I'm not privy to. They need to talk about Kayla's treatment and make decisions. I understand that. I just wasn't prepared for how weird watching them develop this relationship would make me feel.

'Heather's only gone and got herself a new job,' Gavin says.

'A new job.' I press the wine glass to my lips again and drink. 'What about Kayla?'

'It's at the hospital,' Gavin says. 'Couldn't be more convenient.'

'I'm sorry, what?' I say, lowering the glass before I spill some. 'What's going on?'

'Work have given me as much time off as I need to be with Kayla,' Heather explains. 'But, unpaid.'

'Oh,' I say, feeling awful that I hadn't realised.

'Doctor Patterson said the canteen are looking for someone to bake. Scones, croissants, muffins. That sort of thing.'

I shake my head. 'But won't that take up lots of time you need to spend with Kayla?'

'I suggested Heather could bake some stuff here. Like a practice. And she's going to bring some muffins in for the kids on the ward too,' Gavin says.

'Bake here?' I say, looking around the kitchen.

'If that's okay,' Heather says.

I don't reply. I reach for the wine again.

'I'll buy all my own ingredients and I won't get in the way. I can wait until everyone has gone to bed so I don't take over the kitchen or anything.'

'Well it sounds like this is all planned out then,' I say, guzzling the remainder of my glass.

'I could leave some brownies for Molly for school,' Heather says.

'I love brownies,' Molly says, her mouth full of mushy chips.

'They're not allowed treats in school,' I say, my head feeling light already from the wine.

'Can I have a brownie now. Please? Please?' Molly says, stuffing the last nugget into her mouth without biting.

'There are no brownies, Molly,' I say.

'Actually,' Heather says, 'there might be a little surprise in the fridge.'

'Brownies,' Molly squeaks, and jumps off her chair to run over to the fridge.

'Only if your mammy says it's okay,' Heather says, as Molly flings open the fridge door and it bangs off the wall behind it.

Molly spins around to look at me with huge, pleading eyes.

'What can I say?' I shrug.

'I eated up all my dinner.' Molly points to her empty plate.

'Okay, Molly.' I smile. 'But, just one, yeah?'

'There's some there for us too,' Heather says, 'if you fancy some dessert.'

'Nice one,' Gavin says, his eyes as wide as Molly's at the mere mention of something sugary and chocolatey.

Gavin stands up and lifts the plate of brownies out of the fridge for Molly to choose one. He takes one too and leaves the tray down on the countertop next to the cooker.

'C'mon, Molly,' he says, taking a bite of his. 'Let's watch a little telly together before bedtime.'

'*Teen Titans Go!?*' Molly says, biting her brownie.

'Definitely.' Gavin bends and scoops Molly into his arms

and she squeals excitedly. 'Let's leave Mammy and Heather on their own for a little while.'

'Grown-up talk,' Molly says as they walk out of the kitchen.

Gavin glances over his shoulder and nods at Heather and I see her smile back. *What the hell?*

'More?' Heather asks, reaching for the wine bottle.

'No,' I say. 'Thank you.'

Heather pulls her hand away from the bottle and doesn't top up her glass either. I crane my neck towards the utility room door and the thump, thump, clatter that's coming from the washing machine. I've no doubt Molly's goggles went in the machine and are now being spun around furiously. I'll probably need to buy her a new pair. *Great!*

Heather clears her throat and pushes some food around her plate with her fork. I'm getting ready to stand up and excuse myself when her eyes seek out mine. I notice the dark half-moons under her eyes and her usually dewy skin is pale, except for her flushed cheeks.

'Thank you,' she says, and there's an unmissable quiver in her voice.

I eye up the bottle of wine and wish I'd let Heather pour me another glass.

'I know this can't be easy for you,' Heather says.

I stiffen, unsure where this conversation is going. I grab the wine and pour the remainder of the bottle into my glass.

'It's not easy for any of us,' I say, before taking a mouthful.

'I know. But I feel like I've come in here, taken over your home...'

'You haven't taken over my home,' I say, and I realise that's more of a warning than a polite reassurance.

Heather nods and I can tell she realises that too.

'It's just this baking,' she says. 'I know it's your kitchen and I would normally never—'

'Heather,' I cut across her, suspecting she's about to cry and knowing I'm not far from the same. 'It's just an oven and some shelf space. The main thing is Kayla. And if this helps, then that's great.'

'Thank you,' Heather mouths, and there's no sound, but the tears she had been doing so well to hold back trickle down her cheeks.

EIGHTEEN

CHARLOTTE

I'm exhausted when I finally flop into bed. Molly was hard work tonight. She was overtired after swimming, but she wouldn't settle down and close her eyes. I read two stories. Gavin read another and finally we both had to get cross and threaten her with no screen time tomorrow if she didn't stop getting in and out of bed and running around on the landing.

'What the hell was in those brownies?' I say, wrapping myself up in the duvet.

Gavin sticks his head out the door of our ensuite bathroom and pulls the toothbrush out of his mouth. 'I dunno,' he says, 'but they were delicious.'

'They were loaded with sugar,' I say. 'That's why Molly was so hyper. I thought we were never going to get her to sleep.'

I hear Gavin spit into the sink and the tap runs. He swings the door open wide and the sudden burst of light from the bathroom shines in my face and makes me squint.

'She's just excited about seeing Kayla soon,' Gavin says, closing the bathroom door and turning off the light, plunging us into darkness.

'Huh. Sorry, what?' I say, sitting up dramatically despite the darkness.

'At the hospital,' Gavin says, and I feel him roll into bed beside me. 'You know Kayla's surgery is coming up.'

'Yeah of course,' I say, trying not to let Gavin hear the worry in my voice.

'Well, Heather thinks it would really cheer Kayla up to see Molly. With Kayla starting chemo straight away, there's no way of knowing what that will do to her immune system. This really is the best time.'

'When were you going to talk to me about this?' I ask.

'Charlie, we have talked about this.' Gavin sighs, and I can hear the exhaustion in his tone. 'It's surgery first, then chemo.'

'I mean about Molly visiting the hospital.' I inhale. It's so hard not to let my emotion spill.

'Oh,' Gavin says. 'Well, we're talking about this now, aren't we?'

'No.' I exhale, and it hangs in the air heavier than I mean it to. 'This is you making a plan with Heather and filling me in after all the decisions are made. You've talked to Heather about this. Not me. Heather.'

'Charlie, I'm sorry,' Gavin says, and I can't tell from his voice if he's frustrated or upset. The darkness isn't helping. The bed bounces and I know Gavin has turned his back on me. 'I've so much on my mind, I guess I just forgot to mention it before now. But you knew we'd be bringing Molly to see Kayla at some point, obviously.'

'Gavin,' I say, throwing my legs over the side of the bed to stand up.

'Mmm,' he says, sleepily.

I walk across the room with my arms held out in front of me like a zombie as I feel around for the light switch. I flick it on.

'Gavin,' I repeat, louder this time. 'Seriously. This isn't okay. I get that you're in hell right now. But Molly is our child. Ours.

You don't get to make these decisions without me. Can we talk about this please?'

'Charlie, we just did.' Gavin turns around, squinting as the light blinds him.

'And?'

'And what?' Gavin rubs his eyes.

I glare at my husband, so hurt and infuriated.

'Kayla's surgery is soon, and Heather and I thought it would be good to get the girls together once Kayla is feeling up to it. Maybe over the weekend,' Gavin says. 'Is that okay with you?'

'Heather and you thought.' I slam my hands onto my hips. 'Heather. And. You. Thought. Oh, well, that's just bloody fine then, isn't it? Because if Heather thinks, then, what the hell does it matter what Charlotte thinks?'

'Charlie, what's wrong?' Gavin says, sitting up. 'You know Molly has been asking questions about Kayla.'

'What's wrong?' I say. 'What's wrong?'

Gavin shakes his head and looks at me confused. It only upsets me more, a hard lump rising in my throat.

'I want you to talk to me, Gavin. That's what's wrong. Talk to me. Please. Me!' I tap my chest. 'I'm your wife. Not Heather.'

'Charlie...' Gavin begins but he trails off without saying anything.

'I understand this is awful. I do,' I say, half-crying, half-apoplectic. 'Awful for Kayla. Awful for you and Heather as her parents. But it's awful for me too.'

'I know you care about Kayla,' Gavin begins. 'I know you love her, too.'

I know he's going to steer this in the wrong direction and make this about medicine and operations and fears, so I cut across him.

'It's awful because you're cutting me out. And I don't mean from Kayla's treatment. I know those decisions are up to you and Heather. I mean you're cutting me out as your wife.'

Gavin shakes his head. 'I'm sorry. That was never my intention.'

'I've barely seen you since you got the news. Tonight you even forgot that I don't eat meat,' I say. 'And when I do see you, Heather is with you. I can't talk with her there. For God's sake, I can't even ask you if you're okay.'

'Yes you can.' Gavin shakes his head. 'You can always ask me that, Charlie. Always.'

'No. No, I can't,' I say. 'I'm not comfortable. And now she's staying here. I mean, I get it, I do. I'm happy that Heather staying in Dublin helps. Honestly, I want to help. I want her to be close to Kayla – to see her all the time. I just...' I pause to catch my breath and Gavin looks at me so intensely it feels like I might snap in half. 'I just... I'm overwhelmed. I walked in tonight to find the two of you sharing a romantic dinner for two, for God's sake.'

'No. C'mon, Charlie.' Gavin grows very serious. 'I can't believe you just said that. That's not what dinner was at all. You must know that Heather was thrilled about the baking news. She was so stressed out about money before. This was a Godsend. I was happy for her. Jesus.'

I take some deep breaths and try to calm down. My heart is beating out of my chest and I remember I forgot to eat any dinner. I'm regretting the couple of glasses of wine now as the reeling sensation in my head threatens to topple me over.

'I don't want Molly to go to the hospital,' I say, folding my arms across my chest. 'I'm sorry. But I don't.'

'What? Why?' Gavin's eyes cloud over with disappointment.

'I don't think it's good for her. She's too young to understand.'

'But I told Heather I'd bring Molly in,' Gavin says.

'Well, you shouldn't have. Not without checking with me first.'

'I'm checking with you now,' Gavin grunts, growing angry.

'And I say no.'

'Charlotte, they're sisters.'

'Half-sisters,' I correct, immediately hating that I went there. I've never gone there.

Gavin throws the duvet back and stands facing me in just his boxers. 'They. Are. Sisters.'

I don't speak.

'Kayla is sick, Charlie, and all she wants is to see her little sister.' Gavin sways, a broken man. 'I don't care about halves or whose feelings might get hurt. I am bringing my little girl to visit her big sister. They are both my daughters.'

'Gavin... I...' I trail off. There's nothing more to say. This isn't how I wanted this conversation to go. I'm too upset with Gavin and Heather, too worried about Molly, and too terrified for Kayla to even try to make sense of it all.

'Where are you going?' I ask, as I watch Gavin pull on a tracksuit.

'For a drive,' Gavin says.

'Heather's car is parked behind yours. You're blocked in.'

'Then I'll take your car.' Gavin looks at me, his eyes are bloodshot with fury and puffy with hurt. 'Unless, of course, I need to ask permission for that too?'

'Gavin, c'mon,' I say. 'That's not fair.'

Gavin shakes his head, walks past me without looking at me and reaches for the door handle. I know he won't ask Heather to move her car so he can take his. As hurt as he is, I know he wouldn't let me down that far, but I don't doubt he'd go out walking instead. He's wearing all black and the roads into town aren't the safest at this hour. And he's too angry and upset to suggest he goes back to bed, and, being honest, I'm too angry and upset to be around him either.

'The keys are on the hall table. Drive safely,' I say. 'It's late.'

NINETEEN

HEATHER

A few days later

The morning of Kayla's surgery seems to sneak up on me and now that it's here it has wrapped itself around my neck and tries to choke me. I'm standing in Gavin's kitchen in his fancy, expensive house at four o'clock in the morning baking muffins. I could only ever dream of a kitchen like this. A house like this. A life like this. The smell of the muffins is good but the feeling in my stomach is horrendous. This time last week my biggest concern, as I lay in bed, awake at stupid o'clock, was finding the best way to ask my boss for a day off to go to an Ariana Grande concert. I'd bought tickets for myself and Kayla months ago and forgotten about them. If it wasn't for the reminder on my phone, I'd probably have missed the concert altogether. Now I can't help but think about how we're missing it anyway, and I really, really wish it was only because I have bad time management.

The smell of coconut wafts towards me from the batch of coconut-and-raspberry muffins cooling on the wire rack next to the sink. There's another tray of cinnamon-and-apple and some orange-chocolate ones too. They're Kayla's favourite.

She loves chocolate. I stare through the glass on the oven door as I watch a fourth batch rise inside. I doubt the hospital canteen is going to sell this many tomorrow. But, the couple of dozen yesterday weren't enough and the manager said I'd need more. She didn't specify exactly how many *more* was. I've taken the liberty of making triple. If the canteen can't sell them I'll bring them up to Kayla's ward. The kids loved them the other day and the staff did too. The manager also didn't give me permission to bake from home but with Kayla's surgery happening first thing I need this head start on the day.

The oven timer buzzes and I shut it off almost instantly, hyper aware of waking anyone upstairs. I slip on Charlotte's novelty oven glove, which I'm pretty sure she never uses because it's impossible to grip anything with it, and slide a tray of golden muffins out of the oven. I set them down on the countertop next to all the others and turn off the oven. Exhausted, I slide onto the floor. The cold from the porcelain tiles works its way through my jeans but I don't budge. I tuck my legs into my chest, and I don't bother to take off Charlotte's oven glove as I wrap my arms around my knees and rest my chin on top. If I'm going to get any sleep at all tonight, I'm confident this is the spot.

My eyes are closed and I'm drifting somewhere between cinnamon, apple and chocolate when I hear footsteps approaching. I pull myself to my feet and pretend to clean as someone opens the kitchen door behind me.

'Heather,' a little voice whispers.

I turn around to find Molly bare foot and bleary-eyed in My Little Pony jammies behind me.

'Something smells yummy,' she says.

I swallow hard as I look at the pretty little girl looking up at me with huge, oval blue eyes. Kayla used to look at me with the same eyes when she was little. Kayla and Molly also share cheekbones and a nose. But Molly's smile is all her mother's and so is her curious nature.

'What are you doing?' Molly asks.

'I'm baking,' I say. 'I'm going to sell these muffins at the hospital tomorrow.'

'The hostable where Kayla is asleep?' Molly asks, rubbing her sleepy eyes.

'Yes,' I nod.

'Why does Kayla sleep at the hostable?' Molly asks.

I take a deep breath and look at the little girl who reminds me so much of a time gone by. I wonder what Gavin has told her about Kayla getting sick. Or what Charlotte has mentioned. I don't know what to say.

I puff out and smile. 'Kayla isn't feeling very well.'

'Does she have a pain in her tummy?'

I take a deep breath. I'd forgotten how simplistic life at four can be. It's lovely to remember. Hard. But lovely. 'It's not her tummy, Molly,' I say. 'Kayla has a problem with her knee.'

'Did she fall?' Molly asks, rubbing her eyes.

I can see her little legs grow tired. I bend and pause, smiling. Molly reaches her arms up, ready for me to lift her. I scoop her into my arms and swing her onto the worktop.

'Yes, Molly,' I say, tears pricking the corners of my eyes. 'Kayla did fall. In school.'

'Oh no,' Molly says, her eyes wide with concern. 'Did she cry? I cry when I fall.'

I take a deep breath as I struggle to keep it together.

'I know you think Kayla is all grown-up,' I say. 'But she's really just a kid, like you.'

Molly shakes her head and laughs.

'She is,' I nod, enthusiastically. Anxious to explain. 'She's just a kid. And sometimes kids fall or get sick and the grown-ups get very worried about them.'

'Are you worried about Kayla?' Molly asks, and I wonder if she truly understands the question.

'I don't like that she's sick, Molly,' I try to explain as best I can.

'Does she need some Calpol?' Molly points to the cupboard above the fridge. 'Mammy gives me Calpol when I get sick. And it's yummy.'

'That is a good idea, Molly,' I smile. 'But I don't think Calpol will help this time. I think the doctors have special medicine for Kayla.'

Molly nods.

'Do you understand, Molly?' I ask.

'Yes,' Molly nods again, smiling and satisfied with my answer. 'Can I have a muffin now?'

'At this hour of the morning, you most certainly cannot,' Charlotte says.

I cringe. I didn't hear Charlotte come into the kitchen behind us. I wonder how long she's been there. How long she's been listening to Molly's questions and my efforts to answer.

'Molly Doran do you think there is somewhere you should be?' Charlotte asks.

'In bed,' Molly whispers.

'Yes! In bed,' Charlotte says with her hands on her hips. 'C'mon now. Lickety split please?'

Molly's eyes glass over and I'm sure she's about to cry. I place my hands on her hips, give a little nod so she's ready, and swing her down from the shelf.

'Your mam's right, Molly,' I say. 'It's a little too late for a muffin right now, but how about taking one to school tomorrow instead?'

'Really?' Molly's eyes brighten.

'If that's okay with your mam.' I look at Charlotte, conscious that I'm treading on very thin ice.

'Unfortunately, the school has a strict healthy-eating policy,'

Charlotte says sternly and the explanation is clearly for me and not Molly. 'No treats allowed, except on Fridays.'

'Oh.' I swallow, remembering.

Molly sighs and drags herself sluggishly towards the door.

'But...' Charlotte exhales loudly. 'Maybe we won't be going to school tomorrow.'

Molly spins around, suddenly animated and giddy.

'Okay, missy,' Charlotte says. 'That's enough excitement for one night. We'll talk about this more in the morning.'

'But I don't have to go to school?' Molly bounces on the spot.

'No.' Charlotte shakes her head.

'And I can have a muffin?' Molly grins.

'Yes.' Charlotte smiles.

'And I can see Kayla?' Molly adds.

My heart races.

'Molly,' Charlotte says, serious and stern. 'It really is bedtime now. I said we can talk in the morning. Not tonight. In the morning.'

'So, I *can* see Kayla?' Molly's head nods to complement her bouncing.

'Molly. Bed.' Charlotte sighs.

'But it's scary all by my own,' Molly says, suddenly still.

'Okay,' Charlotte says. 'Go upstairs and climb into bed with Daddy. He's asleep, so can you please be careful not to wake him? I'll be up soon.'

'Okay,' Molly says, instantly chirpy again as if someone flicked a switch on her mood.

I take a deep breath as Charlotte and I watch Molly leave the kitchen, neglecting to close the door behind her.

'Daddy,' Molly calls at the top of her voice ascending the stairs. 'Daddy. I'm coming. Daddy.'

I muffle a laugh at Molly's ability to royally misconstrue

Charlotte's idea of silence and wait for Charlotte to turn around and tell me off over the whole muffin thing.

Charlotte waits until we hear voices upstairs before she closes the door and turns around. She looks me up and down without words and makes her way to the table.

'I'm sorry,' I say. 'I forgot the school's eating policy was so strict. I never would have...' I trail off, doubting Charlotte is listening.

Charlotte pulls a chair out from under the table and somehow manages not to make a sound. She sits.

A stagnant silence hangs between us for way too long and I wonder if I should start boxing up muffins so I can clean her kitchen, or join her at the table, or just piss off out of the kitchen entirely.

'So, can I have one or what?' Charlotte eventually says.

'A muffin,' I gasp, hating how startled I sound.

'Is there a cinnamon one? I smell cinnamon, right?' Charlotte elongates her neck and sniffs.

'Yeah. Yes there is. Apple and cinnamon, actually.'

'Will you have one, too?' Charlotte asks. 'I don't want to sit here like a plonker scoffing a muffin on my own.'

'Eh, yeah. I don't usually eat when I'm baking. Always afraid if I start I won't be able to stop. But sure. Why not? Will I stick the kettle on too? For coffee.'

'Yeah.' Charlotte nods. 'But tea for me. I won't sleep a wink after coffee.'

'Okay,' I smile. 'Tea and muffins at 4 a.m. it is.'

Another silence descends. It's still awkward but it's bearable. The kettle rattles and hums as the water begins to boil and I slide a still-hot cinnamon-and-apple muffin onto one plate and place a coconut-and-raspberry one onto another. I open the drawer next to the cooker and take out a couple of knives. I make a tea and a coffee and shake my head, wondering what the hell I am doing. Charlotte doesn't look over, despite me taking over her kitchen. I place everything on a tray I spotted resting behind the knife block and carry it over to the table.

'Muffins.' I swallow, setting the tray down in the centre of the table.

Charlotte finally looks at me as I reach for her cup of tea.

'Sit down, Heather,' she says, and I wonder if she means for it to sound like an order.

I sit.

Charlotte does the dishing out. Coffee and muffin for me. Tea and muffin for her. She gets the muffins right, which is impressive. And then she sits back, watches me and folds her arms. *Jesus this is horrendous.* I find myself glad that Molly has woken Gavin and I hope he'll come downstairs to rescue me.

'So, how's the baking business going?' Charlotte says.

'Good, yeah.' I nod overly enthusiastically. 'They didn't have enough muffins the other day so I've made more.'

'I see that,' Charlotte says, glancing over her shoulder at her kitchen countertops strewn with trays of cooling muffins.

'I might have got a little carried away,' I say.

'Hmm.' Charlotte smiles sympathetically and if it wasn't for the look in her eyes that says, *I wish you'd get out of my house,* I might actually relax.

Another silence descends, thankfully broken by Gavin's deep voice and Molly's happy giggles, muffled as they rain down on us through the floorboards overhead.

'So, Molly's not going to school tomorrow?' I say, slicing through my muffin.

'No,' Charlotte says stiffly.

I stuff some muffin into my mouth and wonder why I'm the only one eating, since this whole middle-of-the-night muffin binge was Charlotte's idea.

'The school called today,' Charlotte says, lifting her cup to her lips.

'Molly's school?' I say, realising these muffins are a little too dry as they stick to my teeth.

'Um-hmm.' Charlotte takes a mouthful of tea. 'Apparently some boy in her class has been teasing her about Kayla.'

'About Kayla,' I say.

'Yeah,' Charlotte says. 'This kid is a little brat at the best of times, he's hit Molly with Lego bricks and pushed her before, but this is a new low.'

'What did he say?' I ask.

Charlotte lowers her cup, and I don't miss the tears that smear across her eyes. 'Nothing. Nothing in particular. Just, he's a nasty little boy. And if he thinks Molly is upset he'll use it against her.'

I know Charlotte is lying. It's the same kind of lie I told Kayla the other day when she asked if everything would be okay and I answered with an unequivocal *yes*.

'You're worried that if Molly visits Kayla she will believe whatever nonsense this little boy is saying?' I say, realising.

Charlotte nods.

I nod too. I look at the muffin on my plate. The thought of another bite makes me feel sick.

'Does Molly know?' I ask. 'About how sick Kayla really is.'

'She's four,' Charlotte says.

'But she knows Kayla is in hospital,' I say. 'She told me. Just now.'

'She doesn't even know what a hospital is.' Charlotte slices into her muffin and her knife scratches against the plate with a frustrated squeak.

A shiver runs down my spine.

'Kayla has been asking to see her,' I say.

Charlotte nods. 'I know.'

'Gavin told you,' I say.

'Yes. He did.'

'And?'

Charlotte shrugs. 'What would you do?' she says. 'If you were me. If the shoe was on the other foot. What would you do?'

I pick up my coffee and the warm, familiar smell comforts me. 'Honestly?' I say, before taking a long, dramatic sip. 'I have no idea.'

Charlotte sighs.

'But,' I continue, lowering the cup and stuffing another huge chunk of muffin into my mouth realising it's the first time I've eating since morning. 'We're thinking about this like adults. Like mothers. And we're both just trying to protect our child as best we can.'

'Yes. Exactly.' Charlotte's eyes soften. 'We are.'

'Kayla and Molly are just kids,' I say. 'Kids who want to see each other. I think we'd probably feel differently if we thought about it from their side.'

'Yeah,' Charlotte says, taking a bite of her muffin for the first time. 'That's what Gavin said. They're sisters.'

'They are,' I say.

'Oh. My. God,' Charlotte says with wide eyes and a mouth full of muffin. 'This is delicious. I mean, actually amazing.'

'Thank you.' I smile.

Charlotte takes another bite. And another.

'Molly isn't going to school tomorrow.' Charlotte shrugs, chewing. 'She is going to see her sister after her operation.'

'Thank you. I know this isn't easy for you, Charlotte, but I just...' I begin, but Charlotte shakes her head and I close my mouth.

'This is about Kayla and Molly,' Charlotte says, polishing off the muffin. 'Sisters. That's all. I'm not doing this for Gavin. Or for you. Or even for me. It's for the girls.'

'As it should be,' I say, looking at Charlotte's empty plate. 'And, do you want another muffin?'

'Yes.' Charlotte nods. 'Yes. I do.'

TWENTY

CHARLOTTE

I open the door and press the button on Molly's car seat.

'She can do that herself now,' Gavin says. 'Can't you Molly?'

'Um-hmm.' Molly grins, proudly.

'Really?' I say, wondering how Gavin can think it's a good idea to teach Molly to unbuckle herself. What if she does it while I'm driving?

'I don't think Mammy knows how grown-up you are getting, Molly,' Gavin says.

My tummy somersaults. I know Gavin is trying to keep the atmosphere light but Molly is little more than a baby. *My baby*. Gavin's phone rings as I lift Molly out of the car.

'We've had to park in the overflow car park. Where is Kayla?' Gavin asks. 'Okay. We'll be up in a minute.'

'Where are they?' I ask, my palms staring to sweat. 'Molly, don't run off. There are cars reversing. You need to be careful.'

Molly pulls a face. 'I was just checking where the hostable is,' she tells me with her hands on her hips.

'Kayla is back on the ward, and doing well,' Gavin says.

'Oh thank God for that.' I exhale, realising I've been holding my breath. 'Let's get going.'

I reach for Molly's hand and she skips along happily beside me.

'Clip-clop. Clip-clop,' she says, copying the noise of my wedges hitting the ground.

'Molly, stop that, please,' I say. 'I can't hear myself think.'

'Clip-clop. Clip-clop,' Molly whispers. 'Clip-clop. Clip-clop.'

'Molly, for goodness' sake,' I snap, my head pounding. 'I said stop it.'

Molly's eyes cloud over and her bottom lip quivers. I feel awful.

'I'm sorry, sweetheart,' I say, coming to a standstill so I can bend down and hug her. 'I didn't mean to upset you. I just need you to be a very good girl today. Okay?'

'I am a good girl,' Molly says.

'Yes. You are,' Gavin says, placing his hand on my back and I can feel him shaking. 'You're a very good girl, Molly.'

I straighten and look away for a moment, taking some deep breaths. I don't want Gavin to see how rattled I am. He has enough on his plate. I need to stay strong.

'C'mon, Charlie. It's okay,' he says, rubbing my back. 'Molly just doesn't understand. That's all.'

'I know. I know.' I nod, hating this feeling. I have no right to take my worries out on Molly, especially when it's her I'm so worried about. 'I'm sorry, Molly.'

The overflow car park is ridiculously far from the main building and I've no doubt Molly's legs are growing tired. Gavin must be thinking the same because just as I'm about to bend down to pick her up, he scoops her into his arms and kisses her cheek.

'Nearly there,' he says.

'I'm hungry,' Molly says.

'I know.' Gavin sighs. 'Me too. We'll get lunch after we see the doctor, okay?'

'I still don't know why she had to fast since midnight,' I say, struggling to hide my frustration in front of Molly. 'It's crazy expecting a small child to understand. They really should have given us a morning appointment.'

'Well, we're here now,' Gavin says. 'And you're all ready, Molly, aren't you?'

'Yes.' Molly nods, certain, and my heart pinches knowing she has no understanding of what is going on.

'You're going to be a big brave girl today, aren't you?' Gavin chokes and I can tell he's struggling. I can only imagine how hard this is for him.

Molly reaches her chubby arms around Gavin and rubs his shoulders the way she's seen me do countless times. 'There. Is that any better?' she says, copying the words I use.

'Oh, Molly,' Gavin whispers, barely able to form words. 'What would I do without you?'

'Daddy, don't squeezy me so tight. Your scratchy bits are yucky,' Molly protests as she points at Gavin's woollen jumper. And for the first time in a while I hear Gavin laugh.

'C'mon, Charlie. We can do this,' Gavin says, draping an arm over my shoulder as he holds Molly in the other. 'We just have to keep it together.'

'Yes, Daddy,' Molly says. 'Keep it together.'

Gavin laughs again. Louder this time. I laugh too. But Molly shakes her head and makes a face, clearly unimpressed.

Gavin puts Molly down as we reach the main door and our little girl seems full of renewed energy as her curious eyes sweep over the large old building.

'It's huger than my school,' she announces. 'And there's magic doors too. Like the ones at the shops.'

'Magic doors?' Gavin asks.

'Automatic doors,' I say, quickly. 'Remember when Molly was afraid of the doors at the supermarket?'

''Cos they might eat me,' Molly adds, reaching for my hand, suddenly much less enthusiastic about a big building.

'They won't eat you,' I say. 'Magic doors aren't scary. They just open wide so you can go inside.'

''Cos they're magic,' Molly says, and I'm not sure if she's telling Gavin or reminding herself.

'Ah. I see.' Gavin nods. 'Magic doors. Well, should I go first?'

Molly nods squeezing my hand as we follow Gavin.

'It's stinky,' she says, scrunching her nose at the intense smell of antiseptic as soon as we step inside. 'Hostable smells like the toilet.'

'Molly, shh,' I say, as Gavin leads us towards reception. 'Don't be rude.'

We pass a packed waiting area of children and their parents waiting outside A&E. There aren't many teenagers. I only notice one boy about Kayla's age slouched in his chair. He's scrolling through his phone while pressing a blooded cloth against his elbow. I assume it's deep. The poor kid will probably need stitches. But then he will be fine. I can't take my eyes off him, wishing that Kayla was in his shoes. Wishing that Kayla's problem was a messy sports injury and one day soon she'll be as good as new.

'Mammy, look, look,' Molly calls, pointing at the teenager. 'He's all bleedy.'

'Molly, stop that. Pointing is rude,' I say, hoping the boy won't notice.

'But look.' Molly tugs on the sleeve of my top. 'His arm is all bleedy. He's going to die.'

'Molly, he's not going to die,' I whisper, taking her hand and leading her to the side. 'Lots of people come to the hospital to get better.' I force a smile trying to be reassuring.

'Like Kayla,' Molly says.

My breath catches and I can feel my face fall before I answer. 'Yes,' I say, lifting Molly into my arms so I can feel the warmth of her little body close to me. 'Like Kayla. There are lots and lots of doctors and nurses working here. It's their job to help Kayla. Look, there's a doctor right now, doesn't he look helpful?'

I point at a doctor in scrubs.

'It's rude to point, Mammy,' Molly reminds me.

'Oh, Molly.'

'Why is he wearing his jammies?' Molly asks, scrunching her eyes trying to get a better look. 'I like his blue jammies but I like my unicorn jammies better.'

Molly's innocence lifts me. 'C'mon,' I say, leading Molly back towards the reception desk. 'Let's see if Daddy is ready.'

'Tell her Kayla is my sister,' Molly says, jumping up and down trying to see the receptionist behind the high counter.

'Molly, shh.' I place my finger over my lip. 'Daddy is talking.'

'Do we just go through these doors, then?' Gavin points.

'Pointing is rude, Daddy,' Molly says, still jumping.

'Molly please,' I say, placing my hand on her shoulder to steady her. 'This is important.'

'Yes. And then take a left. The lifts are right there,' the receptionist says, but her directions wash over me making little sense. 'There will be someone there to meet you and talk you through the test.'

'Thank you,' Gavin says.

'Bye-bye, sweetheart,' the lady says, waving at Molly. 'You're a very brave girl.'

'I can't wait to see Kayla,' Molly says. 'I'm going to tell her all about how I learned to play "Twinkle Twinkle" on the peenano with no 'istakes at all at all.'

'That's great, Molly,' Gavin says, looking up to read overhead signs as we navigate our way. 'I'm sure Kayla will be delighted to hear all your news, but we have to see the doctor first, remember?'

'The doctor in his jammies,' Molly giggles.

'Here we are,' Gavin says, pressing the buzzer on large double doors. 'I think it's through here.'

'That's very silly.' Molly shakes her head. 'Doorbells go on the outside. Not the inside.'

'Hello,' a voice carries through the intercom.

'Hello. I'm Gavin Doran. I'm here with my daughter Molly.'

There's a loud buzz and Molly laughs as the doors release. 'Magic doors,' she squeals excitedly, and my heart aches as I wish there really was such a thing as magic.

TWENTY-ONE

There's a paper cup of coffee in my hands as I sit on the uncomfortable metal chairs outside Kayla's room. I have no idea how I got the coffee I'm holding, or if I've drunk any of it. It's cold now and I really should throw it in the bin, but I just don't trust my legs to hold me up if I try to stand.

'Hey,' a male voice hovers above me.

I look up and smile. 'Doctor Patterson.'

'Mind if I sit?' he asks, pointing to the empty chair next to me.

I nod. 'Yeah. Sure.'

The metal bench creaks and groans as he sits down and he looks almost as exhausted as I feel.

'I wouldn't drink that stuff if I were you,' he says. 'I've seen them clean those machines. It's not pretty.'

I lift my coffee cup and tilt it towards him. 'This?' I say. 'I don't think I've tasted it. I mean, I don't remember getting coffee. Maybe someone got it for me.'

Doctor Patterson takes the cup from my shaking hands and tosses it into the bin beside him. 'Right. Let's get you something to eat and some proper coffee before I have two patients on my hands.'

'I... I...'

He looks at me with such kind, understanding eyes, I really wish I could go for coffee with him.

'I can't leave Kayla,' I say.

Doctor Patterson looks up at the door of Kayla's room. It's closed but Molly's excited giggles filter through every so often.

'Was that Kayla's dad and little sister I saw go in earlier?' he asks.

'Yes. Molly. She's a little dote.'

'Ah, I thought so. I couldn't see Gavin's face, but an excited little girl with Kayla's eyes was dragging a man by the hand insisting he hurry up, so I put two and two together.'

'Yeah.' I smile. 'That sounds like Molly alright.'

'I'm sure Kayla is delighted to see them,' he says.

I nod. 'She is.'

'And you're just out here giving them a little space?' he asks, but I know there's no need for an answer.

'Molly's mother is here too,' I explain. 'Charlotte.'

'Oh,' he says, and I instantly wonder if Charlotte should be on the ward at all or if it's just immediate family. I never thought to ask.

'Do Kayla and Charlotte erm...' He shuffles, and I can't tell if it's the metal seat underneath him making him uncomfortable or if it's what he's about to say.

'They get on great,' I say, hoping I'm pre-empting his question correctly and the look on his face quickly tells me I am and that I've put him out of his awkward misery. 'Charlotte has been in Kayla's life since she was three. I doubt Kayla even remembers a time before Charlotte. They're very close.'

'That's good,' he says.

'It is.' Despite my jealously over the years I am glad Kayla and Charlotte have a good relationship. Kayla is lucky to have a stepmother who is disappointed when Kayla doesn't turn up for the weekend rather than some bitch who resents a teenage step-daughter.

'I was going to pop in and check on Kayla, but I think it's best to leave her enjoy this family time,' he says. 'I'll come back in half an hour or so.'

'Okay.'

'In the meantime, can I please get you a coffee? You're frighteningly pale.'

'Oh,' I say.

'Sorry. Sorry,' he says. 'Occupational hazard. I tend to refer to people's level of wellbeing by their skin tone. Washed-out, flushed, jaundiced, and the list goes on. I have many more unflattering and unhelpful ways of putting my foot in it when what I really mean to say is, *I'm a little worried about you.*'

'You're worried about me?' I say, glancing at the door of Kayla's bedroom.

'It's not every day your child undergoes major surgery, Heather,' he says. 'Kayla is going to need time to recover. But so are you.'

'It was scary.' I swallow. 'All those hours she was in surgery. And I was just sitting around. Waiting.'

'Sitting around waiting, being right here ready to hold Kayla's hand the minute she woke up was so important,' he says. 'When she woke up you were the first person she asked for.'

'Well, then, why do I feel so useless?'

'Being the person Kayla wants to see most in the world is more help than you can possibly imagine. When the fight gets too hard for Kayla, you're going to fight for her and keep her fighting. You have the most important job in the world, Heather. Your job is being her mother.'

I shake my head and concentrate to keep the wobble out of my voice. 'I didn't think it would be this hard.'

'No one ever does,' he says. 'It doesn't mean you're not doing great.'

'I stayed up all night last night baking,' I say, though not really sure why.

He looks back at me but he doesn't talk.

'I made, like, eighty cupcakes or something.' I shake my head.

'Oh, Heather, I'm sorry. I had no idea the canteen was going to put pressure on you for crazy orders that big. Did you tell them Kayla's surgery was today? I'll have a word with them.'

'No, no.' I shake my head. 'It wasn't them. I just went crazy. I was emptying bags of flour and sieving and whisking and... and...'

'Heather, you do know if it wasn't muffins it would be something else, right? I see parents take up knitting. These uber-cool mams with pointy heels and designer handbags with a big ball of colourful wool sticking out the top of them.'

'Knitting?' I smile.

'Yup. Or sewing, if you don't like wool. Painting, pottery, basket-making.'

'Basket-making. Seriously?'

'Don't knock it till you've tried it.' He smiles.

'Ha, no.' I relax a fraction. 'Thank you. I think I'll stick to muffins.'

'My point is, don't be so hard on yourself. It's just a distraction. And a delicious one at that. I had one of your raspberry-and-white-flaky-things muffins this morning.'

'Coconut,' I say.

He looks at me with unsure eyes.

'The white flaky things. They're coconut flakes.'

'Ah. Yes. So they are. Well, they're good. You're quite the legend among the staff. We've never been able to eat the pastries at work before and now we're keeping the diabetes department busy.'

I laugh. It's just for a moment until I remember where I am, why I'm here, even why we're having this conversation. But the moment was wonderful, the split second it lasted, and I feel lighter after.

'I hear you even dropped some extras up to the wards for the kids,' he says.

'Yeah. I took your suggestion on board,' I say. 'I've dropped a couple of baskets up. They probably had two or more each—' I cut myself off mid-sentence, suddenly remembering Molly's school's healthy-eating policy. 'Sorry, that was probably too much.'

'What? Why?' he asks.

'Is there some rule about sugar or something?' I wince.

'No. Not at all.' He scrunches his nose. 'I was just joking about the diabetes thing. Kids love muffins. So do doctors and nurses. It was a nice thing to do, Heather. I appreciate it.'

I take a deep breath but it's hard to let it back out because I feel as if there are giant hands around my chest compressing me. 'Thank God,' I say. 'I don't know if I could handle almost poisoning a child with too much sugar.'

His eyes narrow and I realise I better explain my throwaway comment, especially since half the doctors in the hospital ate some of my muffins this morning.

'Sorry,' I begin. 'That was dramatic. It's just I'm struggling a bit with Charlotte.'

'Kayla's stepmother,' he confirms.

'Gavin's wife. Yeah,' I say.

'But you said Kayla and Charlotte get along.'

'They do.'

'Oh,' he says, knowingly. 'But you don't.'

'It's not actually that. Charlotte is nice. Or at least as nice as anyone can be when their husband's ex-girlfriend moves in with them.'

I wait for him to gasp or at least raise an eyebrow but he doesn't flinch.

'Ah,' I say, 'Kayla told you, didn't she?'

'She mentioned you moving to Dublin and living with her dad. I guessed the rest.'

'It's just so damn messy,' I say. 'I think she was okay with me staying there. Well, okay-ish. Less okay with me taking over her kitchen. But she doesn't really seem okay with the Molly stuff.'

'The Molly stuff?'

'She was barely okay with Molly coming to the hospital to visit Kayla. But we talked and I thought she was better. But now, Molly's blood test seems to have freaked her out again.'

'Ah,' he finally gasps.

I wait for him to explain, the way the nurses have and the phlebotomist has, that it was just a simple test nothing invasive blah, blah. But he doesn't. He sits silently as if he's waiting for me to say more. Despite not really wanting to say more, the words seem to tumble from my mouth uncontrollably.

'She says she's just protecting Molly. But why can't she see I'm just doing the same. I'm just protecting Kayla. If Molly is a match she can help.'

'I see,' he says.

'Gavin had to put his foot down,' I say.

'Wait,' Doctor Patterson says. 'Was Charlotte in agreement? She must have signed the consent forms, surely.'

'She did,' I say. 'But she really didn't want to. I don't understand. I know she loves Kayla to bits. Why is she so afraid of these blood tests?'

'And if it was the other way around?' he says. 'If Molly was sick—'

I cut him off before he has a chance to say another word. 'In a heartbeat,' I say. 'And it wouldn't even be my decision. Kayla would want to help her sister no matter what.'

'Yes.' He nods. 'But Kayla is fifteen. She's old enough to

understand. Molly is only three. She has no idea what's going on.'

'Molly is four,' I correct, as if one year makes such a huge difference.

'Charlotte has to be Molly's decision-maker while battling her own conscience,' he says.

'I can't believe you're taking her side,' I say.

'There are no sides,' he replies.

'It was just a simple test,' I say. 'It took two minutes.'

'Unless she's a match,' he says. 'And if she's a match...'

'If she's a match then, thank the Lord.' I choke back tears. I stand up and the stupid metal bench creaks loudly again. 'Excuse me,' I say, 'I have to get back to my child.'

'Heather, wait, I didn't mean...' he starts.

I keep my back to him as I open the door and step inside.

TWENTY-TWO

KAYLA

Mam is pale like a ghost when she comes back in but at least she's not holding that paper coffee cup that's she been clinging to for the last couple of hours. One of the nurses gave it to her earlier. I think they were worried she was going to faint or something. To be honest, I can't say I blame them. She looked awful. I don't think she drank it though because she looks even worse now.

'And then they 'jected me,' Molly says, and I drag my eyes away from Mam and drop them onto Molly's arm. She's pointing to the colourful plaster on the squishy bit inside her elbow. 'It was so hurty.'

'They injected me too,' I say, showing Molly the cannula in the back of my hand.

'Ew. Yuck,' she says. 'I don't want one like that.'

I laugh. Dad laughs too. Mam doesn't laugh. Mam is pressed up against the door, with her back leaning against it. *She's smiling, but she's not really here at all*, I think, as I watch her stare into space. I really wish she'd drink some coffee.

There are two chairs beside my bed. They're both black plastic with wobbly metal legs. They're exactly like the ones we have in school. Dad sits in one and Molly sits in the other. Well, when I say sits, I mean climbs on, climbs under, runs around, but she's taken a liking to it and calls it *her* chair.

'Molly calm down,' Dad says, and has said several times. 'They gave her a lollipop downstairs,' he explains. 'She's a bit hyper.'

'Yeah.' I shrug. 'They love to give lollipops here.'

'It's was brown,' Molly says, flopping into the chair and sending it sliding back against the floor tiles with a brain-numbing screech.

Dad catches the back of the chair, and Molly, before they both tumble over. Molly hops up again, oblivious. It's hard not to laugh especially because Dad's about to blow his top.

'I don't like brown,' Molly says. 'But it was a yummy lollipop, so I like brown now.'

'That simple, eh?' I say.

Molly talks and talks. She tells a story about a Lego tower, and her teacher's cross voice and something about a meany-head boy in her class. She asks me some questions too, about school and my friends. Everything is just like normal with Molly. She doesn't look at me any differently. Not like Dad, who's useless at keeping it together. I think he's nearly started crying at least twice since he came in. And Charlotte couldn't even be in here. She gave me a hug and said she needed to use the loo. That was ages ago. So unless it's a number two, which she'd never do in a public loo, she's just avoiding me.

And Mam. The state of Mam. I mean, I'm the one who had half my knee chiselled out, but Mam actually looks as if they chiselled out half her soul or something at the same time. I hate what this is doing to her. She's standing like Gran. All slouched and droopy. This stupid cancer is turning my mother into an old lady. I hate it.

I try to move over in my bed. I press my hands onto the mattress at either side of me and the bed bounces as I slide my bum to one side. I move my good leg first. The bad one is a little tricky to move. It's mega heavy after the operation and there's a monster cast on there. It's hard at the back and soft at the front with a tonne of padding all around my knee making it impossible to bend, so I kind of have to move my hip and foot all at once and hope my leg moves in the process. It does, and surprisingly, it doesn't hurt.

'You okay, chicken?' Dad says, noticing me shuffle. 'Are you uncomfortable? Can I help?'

Mam looks over and I can see the worry in her eyes immediately.

'I'm fine,' I say. 'I'm just making some room for Mam to sit beside me.'

I pat the mattress and smile at Mam. She smiles back and peels herself off the door.

'Are you sure?' Mam says, looking at the space I've made for her. 'I don't want to bounce the bed and hurt you.'

'Please,' I say, 'I'd really like a hug.'

'Okay,' Mam says.

She's so careful lowering herself onto the bed that Molly offers to help.

'Is it too high up for you, Heather?' Molly says.

'It is a little high,' Mam says.

'Daddy can lift you,' Molly says. 'Can't you, Daddy?'

'I... I...' Dad blushes.

'Daddy lifts me into bed all the time,' Molly adds. 'And sometimes he lifts Mammy too when he gives her a grown-up kiss.'

'Oh,' Mam says, finally sitting onto the bed next to me. The bed bounces a little and Mam gasps, but nothing hurts and I hold Mam's hand to reassure her that I'm okay.

'Molly, I don't go around picking Mammy up all the time,' Daddy says.

The bed bounces more and I know Mam is trying to hold in

a laugh.

'What?' Dad says, staring at me and Mam now. 'I don't. Honestly.'

I can't keep it in. A huge, gurgling laugh bursts out of me and Mam laughs, too.

'Ah, here,' Dad says, throwing his hands in the air and I can see he's struggling not to giggle. 'There's no talking to the two of you when you get a silly idea in your head.'

'Speaking of Charlotte,' Mam says as she drapes one arm over my shoulder and I snuggle into her the way I used to when I was little, 'Where is she?'

Mam is all warm and cosy and she smells nice. I think she's wearing the Victoria Secret body spray I bought her for Christmas. It's lovely. I must borrow it.

'She went to find the bathroom,' Gavin says.

'Yeah, like, a million years ago,' I add.

'I think she might have escaped to the canteen for a coffee too,' Dad says, sliding his phone out of his pocket and checking the screen. 'Yup. Text. She did. She says the queue is mad and does anyone want anything?'

I'm about to request a hot chocolate when dad continues. 'Oh wait. That was sent ten minutes ago. She's probably on her way back up now.'

'She didn't have to leave on my account,' Mam says.

'She didn't,' Dad replies, kind of snappy.

'Okay,' Mam says gently.

'She just needed some air,' Dad explains. 'Molly was quite distressed giving blood. I don't think Charlotte was prepared.'

Mam snorts and her breath dances across the top of my head.

'What does "stressed" mean?' Molly asks.

'Upset,' Dad explains.

'I wasn't upset,' Molly frowns.

'It's okay, Molly,' I say, sitting up straight and leaning

forward so I can see my little sister clearly. 'Needles are scary. I get that. I'm scared of them too.'

'They're not scary.' Molly folds her arms and shakes her head. 'They're hurty.' Molly points to the plaster on her arm again and her bottom lip begins to quiver.

'Yes, Molly,' I say, and my bottom lip starts to go too. 'I know they hurt. But you don't ever have to do that again, okay?'

'Kayla,' Mam squeaks, looking at Dad. And Dad stares back, equally put out by my revelation.

'Kayla don't tell her that,' Dad says. 'Don't make promises you can't keep.'

I shake my head and pull myself to sit up even straighter. I move too quickly and sharp pain darts from my knee right down to my toes and it feels as if my whole leg has burst into flames. Mam notices immediately and hops off the bed.

'Oh God, Kayla,' she says. 'What is it? What hurts? Is it your knee?'

I catch my breath and choke back some tears. 'I'm okay,' I lie. 'I'm fine.'

'Maybe we should go,' Dad says, his voice even wobblier than he is as he stands up. 'You should probably get some rest. It's been quite a day.'

'I agree with your dad.' Mam starts ruffling the pillows behind me, actually making me super uncomfortable. 'You really should get some rest.'

'But I don't want to go,' Molly says. 'I like it here with Kayla.'

'C'mon, Molly,' I say, patting the space Mam has left on the bed beside me. 'You wanna sit up with me? I got a new game on my phone. I think you'll like it.'

'Sneaky sneak?' Molly squeaks.

'Sure.' I nod, having no clue what that is; it'll probably take me two hundred years to download on the crappy hospital broadband.

Molly hurries over to the bed and it's hilarious to see her try her best to climb up. She grabs the sheets for grip but has as much luck as she would climbing Everest.

'Dad,' I say. 'A little help, please?'

'Oh, Kayla. I'm not sure...'

'Dad. Please. Put those lifting skills to good use.'

'Gavin,' Mam says, looking at him unsure.

'Guys,' I say, firmly catching both my parents' attention at once. 'I'm fine. Molly is fine. We just want to sit together and play a game on my phone like normal. Can we please do that?'

Mam and Dad look at each other, both shaking their head and I actually want to scream. Molly continues to tug on the sheets and she's either going to tumble back and burst her head open or drag me right off the bed while they hum and haw.

'Okay, Molly,' Dad says, sliding his hands underneath her arms and scooping her off the ground. 'But you have to be very, very careful. Kayla has a very sore leg and you can't hurt her,' he warns.

'Like my hurty bit.' Molly points to her plaster again, and I smile.

'Yes,' Dad says as he sets her down on the bed next to me. Molly snuggles into me, and straight away tears burn in my eyes and if I blink, they're going to come spilling down my cheeks and Mam and Dad are actually going to flip out with worry.

I pass Molly my phone and bury my face in her delicious, apple-smelling hair. Mam and Dad huddle in the corner whispering, as if when they keep their voices low and calm I won't notice they're talking about me.

'You don't have Sneaky Snake,' Molly says.

'Oh, sorry.' I lift my head, ready to take my phone back and offer her a different game.

'S'okay,' she says. 'It's downloading now.'

'Molly you're my hero. Do you know that?' I giggle.

'Don't be silly, Kayla,' Molly says. 'I can't fly.'

TWENTY-THREE
KAYLA

The door creaks open and Charlotte comes into view.

'Mammy!' Molly yells, too loud for the small room and much too loud for right next to my ear. 'I'm playing Sneaky Snake on Kayla's phone. Do you want to see how long my snake is? He's super big, isn't he, Kayla?'

'He is,' I say.

'In a minute,' Charlotte says as she opens the door wider but doesn't come in.

A smell of mashed potato and Dettol wafts through. It's rank. Molly and I look at each other and scrunch our noses and stick out our tongues. But Charlotte doesn't close the door behind her, she remains standing in the doorway awkwardly with her hands behind her back. It's as if she's waiting for someone to tell her it's okay to come in.

I look at Mam and Dad, they're still deep in whispery conversation. Dad is looking at Mam, nodding and agreeing with whatever she says, but Mam is looking at Charlotte the same way I looked at Roisin Kelly for a month after she put chewing gum in my hair in science last year.

'Mammy close the door, quick, quick,' Molly says, as if the

corridor is some dark portal and my room is another dimension where it's safe. 'It's stinky out there.'

'Yeah.' Dad looks up and makes a face. 'It really does smell awful out there, what is that?'

'Lunch,' I say.

'Oh Jesus, really?' Dad says.

'Well, hospitals aren't exactly known for their delicious food, now, are they, Dad,' I say.

'God, I don't know which is worse. Your poor leg or having to eat that crap,' Dad jokes, and I laugh.

'Gavin,' Mam says, crossly.

'What?' Dad shrugs. 'Oh c'mon, Heather, something has to lighten the mood. I thought it was funny.'

'It was,' I say.

'I do know your knee is very painful, Kay,' Dad says. 'I was just trying to cheer you up, that's all.'

'I know,' I say.

'I also know I'm bringing you something decent to eat tomorrow,' Dad adds. 'How does McDonald's sound?'

'I love McDonald's,' Molly shrieks and bounces on the bed.

'Molly, Molly, calm down,' Charlotte warns, hurrying towards us.

The door shuts with a loud bang behind her and startles us all. I laugh. So does Molly. But my parents and Charlotte are all mega serious.

'I don't think you can bring food from elsewhere into the hospital,' Mam says.

'What?' Dad folds his arms. 'Why not?'

'I don't know,' Mam says. 'Health and safety, I s'pose.'

'Rubbish,' Dad says. 'If you can bring in home-made muffins, then I can bring a burger and chips. And if I can't, I'll sneak it in under my coat. They'll never know.'

'Dad.' I smile. 'You absolute rebel, you.'

'Speaking of sneaking things in,' Charlotte says, finally revealing her hands from behind her back.

'What's that?' Molly asks, pointing to the takeaway cup Charlotte is holding.

'Oh my God. Is that a hot chocolate?' I ask, hopeful.

The large cream-and-gold cup isn't from the canteen downstairs. I recognise the logo from the place around the corner that Mam was telling me about.

'With extra marshmallows,' Charlotte says.

'Yesssss.' I smile.

'I like hot chocolate,' Molly says, sad that there is only one cup.

'We can share,' I suggest, quickly.

'You, young lady, need lunch,' Charlotte tells Molly. 'They have a nice tomato soup downstairs. We should go get some.'

Molly shakes her head. 'I hate soup.'

Dad lifts Molly into his arms and she wraps her legs around his waist and her arms around his neck.

'I like McDonald's and hot chocolate,' Molly says. 'It's not fair.'

'C'mon, munchkin.' Dad smiles, patiently. 'You know Mammy doesn't like you eating that junk.'

Charlotte passes me the hot chocolate without words and winks. She turns her back and walks towards the door.

'Right,' she says, opening the door. 'Let's get you some soup, Molly.'

'Charlotte,' I call. 'Can you stay? Just for a little while.'

Charlotte turns around and looks at me with wide, unsure eyes.

'It's just, I haven't really seen you in ages. It would be nice to catch up.'

Charlotte smiles and I can see she's searching for the right thing to say.

'I'm sure Dad can get Molly her soup, can't you, Dad?'

Dad nods.

'So,' I say. 'Can you stay?'

Charlotte looks at Mam and neither of them even blink. Jesus, this is worse than any beef I have with Roisin Kelly.

'Actually, Mam. Maybe you could go downstairs with Dad,' I say. 'I know you haven't had a chance to eat anything today. And no, offence, but you look awful.'

Mam snorts and forces a laugh. 'Ha, thank you, Kayla.'

'You know what I mean,' I smile. 'Seriously, though, go get a coffee at least. I'll still be alive when you come back.'

'Kayla.' Mam shakes her head, and I wish I'd phrased that differently.

I point to the door jokingly. 'Go. Go on.'

Mam looks at Charlotte. 'Well, if you don't mind?'

'Of course not,' Charlotte says. 'I'll stay with her.'

'Okay. Thank you. I won't be long.'

'Can we go to McDonald's, Heather?' Molly says, leaning out of Dad's arms to reach for Mam.

Dad puts Molly down and Mam takes her hand.

'You know what, Molly?' Mam says. 'That's a great idea.'

TWENTY-FOUR

CHARLOTTE

I sit in the plastic seat next to Kayla's bed as she sips on her hot chocolate. There's a slurping sound every few seconds and Kayla giggles with her big blue eyes peering out over the top of her cup.

Kayla isn't as pale as I was expecting, or as frail. In fact, if it wasn't for the cannula in her hand I could easily believe she's just tucked up in bed enjoying a lazy Friday afternoon.

'How are you feeling?' I finally build up the courage to ask.

Kayla lowers the cup and looks at me very seriously. My tummy somersaults.

'Full,' she says. 'This thing was huge.'

I take the empty cup from her, twist in my chair and toss it into the small chrome bin behind me. It rattles more than I thought it would as the cup lands in the centre.

'Score!' Kayla cheers, raising her hands about her head.

'Ugh, not exactly,' I say, standing up when I notice the cup wasn't completely empty and milky chocolate has dribbled down the side of the bin and onto the floor. I pull some baby wipes out of my bag and clean up. 'You can never have enough of these with a four-year-old on your hands.'

I know it was a lame joke but I thought it might have roused at least a sympathy giggle from Kayla but she's miles away. There's obviously something she wants to talk to me about. And in private, if she tried so hard to get rid of her mother. But I've no idea what it would be and waiting is making me nervous. I don't want to bulldoze my way in and drag it out of her, but if it's important I'm sure we'll need time to talk about it and I doubt Heather will stay gone long. Even if they do take a trip to bloody McDonald's.

'Does it hurt?' I finally ask, throwing the grungy wipes in the bin and using some fresh ones to wipe my hands. I toss those in too and make my way back to the seat.

'Not really,' Kayla says when I sit down. 'It's more annoying than sore. It's boring just sitting here, not even being able to walk down to the games room. Even though it's crap down there. Broken jigsaws, half-coloured-in colouring books. But there's a TV and a pool table.'

I study Kayla's bright eyes and fed-up expression. I remember after my C-section I couldn't move for days and it took me weeks to feel semi-normal again. Kayla is so full of energy. It's hard to believe she's recovering from a general anaesthetic. I guess that's the difference between surgery at fifteen and at thirty.

'This hurts, though.' Kayla raises her arm and my eyes fall to the cannula that's half the size of her hand. 'It keeps stabbing me. Last night, I forgot it was there and I rolled over and Oh. My. God. It was torture.'

'Yeah,' I say. 'I'm not great with needles either.'

'Or Molly,' Kayla says. 'She really doesn't like them, does she?'

'No,' I admit. 'She doesn't. And I don't blame her.'

'Dad said she freaked out when they tried to take blood earlier.'

I take a deep breath and wonder what the hell Heather has been saying.

'She doesn't understand, Kayla,' I say, gently. 'She's only four. And, to be honest, even if I tried to explain, I doubt it would make any sense.'

'It doesn't make any sense to me either,' Kayla says, suddenly looking tired.

'What doesn't, sweetheart?' I say.

'Why would you let them do that to her?' Kayla shakes her head. 'She's not sick. I am. She shouldn't have to be poked and prodded like that.'

'It was just a blood test, Kayla,' I say, calmly. I sound exactly like Gavin when he tried to reason with me. 'It hurt for a little minute, but she's fine now. She will be fine.'

Compared to everything Kayla is going through, a simple blood test seems inconsequential. But then that's no consolation to a confused four-year-old. Kayla is so sweet to be concerned for her little sister. I smile, proud of her.

'What's the test for?' Kayla says. 'Mam and Dad had blood tests too. But no one has told me why exactly. Are we all at risk of this cancer?' Kayla takes a deep breath, and horror splashes across her face. 'Oh. My. God. Could Molly get this? Could she get sick too?'

'No, no, no.' I swallow, and I stand up and turn my back on Kayla for a moment feeling like such a damn hypocrite. Of course, one of my first concerns was that Molly could get sick too. It could be a gene. Something Gavin has passed to his kids. I'd be a liar if I said I don't still worry. But I can't let Kayla see that. 'These tests see who's a match for you, Kayla. No one else is sick. Okay?'

'A match for what?'

'I don't know, Kayla,' I say, pacing. 'Options, I suppose. They want to keep all options open.'

'Is that why you and Mam are fighting?' Kayla asks.

I shake my head. 'We're not fighting.'

'Oh come off it, Charlotte. You and Mam barely said two words to each other earlier.'

'It's complicated.'

'Not really.' Kayla shrugs. 'You're Molly's mother, Mam is mine and then Dad is in the middle with both of us being his kids. I can kind of see why you're all killing each other.'

'We're not,' I say, and it comes out sharper than I mean it to.

'Mam is living in your house,' Kayla says. 'That has to be awkward for a start.'

'Well...'

'And then there's Dad trying to keep the peace.'

Not exactly, I think, realising I'm growing bitter, feeling that he's growing close to Heather while pushing me aside.

'And Molly. Poor Molly. She hasn't a clue what's going on,' Kayla says. I'm about to reiterate Molly's age and innocence but Kayla keeps talking. 'And me. Then there's me. And it's all my fault.'

'Kayla, no,' I insist, devastated that she feels this way. I push the chair out of the way and climb up on the bed beside her. 'None of this is your fault. None of it. You can't control getting sick.'

'My knee has been sore for ages. Like really bad. And getting worse and worse.'

'Oh, sweetheart.' I wrap my arms around her as she cuddles close to me.

'I didn't tell Mam,' Kayla sniffles. 'The last time I told her she said I was overdoing it. Training too hard, playing too many matches. I thought if I told her how bad it was she'd make me stop playing basketball altogether.'

'And you love it so much, don't you?'

Kayla nods and I feel her shoulders rise and fall as gentle crying shakes her body.

'It's my whole life. It's the only thing I'm good at.'

'That's not true, Kayla. There are lots of things you're good at.'

'No there's not. Mam is all arty and bakes these amazing cakes that everyone loves, and I can't even get a C in Home Ec. Dad is mad clever with his big maths brain. I hate maths. Molly is so good on the piano already even with her tiny fingers. I just have basketball. I'm crap at everything else. And now I don't even have that anymore.'

'Oh, Kayla, sweetheart. Time. Give it time.'

'No.' Kayla shoots upright and twists to look me in the eyes. 'It hurts, Charlotte, it really, really hurts.'

'Your knee?' I ask.

'I should have told Mam,' Kayla cries. 'I should have just told her. If I told her last year, then none of this would have happened. See, do you believe me now? It really is all my fault.'

I don't bother with words. There's nothing I can say that will make her feel any better right now. I just sit and hold her as large angry cries shake her whole body. I take slow, deep breaths and I know the pain in my chest is the feeling of my heart breaking.

TWENTY-FIVE

KAYLA

October

I lie in bed with the blanket pulled right up to my neck. Someone must have tucked me in at some point. *Mam, obviously.* I'm roastin'. The hospital is always mad warm. But, even though I'm cooking away under the covers, I don't move. It's way too much effort. I'm awake but my eyes are closed. It's early. Before seven. I know without checking my phone. At seven the breakfast commotion starts. Bowls of cereal and glasses of juice rattle on trollies pushed along the corridor. And no matter how badly I've slept, or how exhausted, or how sick I am, there's no sleeping past seven in this place. I don't mind so much this morning. I've been awake for ages already. Hours maybe and I'm glad everyone else is finally awake, too. And I'm hungry for the first time in days. I think I'll try some toast. The nice catering lady will be so happy. She's spent all week trying to get me to eat and when I kept refusing, mostly because I was too busy throwing up from the chemo, she seemed so disappointed.

There's a soft knock on the door and I open my eyes. My

mouth goes fizzy thinking about hot toast with melted butter and a glass of orange juice. I giggle – I never thought I'd see the day I got so excited about toast.

There's another knock, but the door doesn't open like usual.

'Erm, come in,' I say, and it comes out like I've a really sore throat or something.

The door doesn't open. *Oh for God's sake.* I pull myself to sit up. My arms are wobbly, and the effort knackers me. I clear my throat and it's a bit phlegmy and gross. *Don't be sick. Don't be sick. Please don't be sick.* I check that there's a puke tray on the locker next to my bed, just in case. I take deep breaths and it helps. My tummy calms down. I'm not going to start today by throwing up. *Progress.*

There's another knock.

'Okay, seriously, just come in,' I say, surprised by how loud I can be even when I'm this tired.

The door finally creaks open.

'Hey,' Aiden says, looking like he wasn't sure he had the right room until he opened the door and he saw me stuck to the bed.

'Oh my God,' I say, not really sure I'm seeing him either.

'Can I come in?' he asks.

'What?' I'm flagging already, seeing Aiden is so great, but I think I got so excited I used up all my morning energy. Also, I really want some toast. 'Do you have to ask? Of course, you can come in.'

Aiden pushes the door open until it knocks against the wall. He leaves it there when he walks in. I think about asking him to close it. I don't like when the door is open and I can hear everything going on out on the ward; like some of the little kids crying because they want to go home, or someone puking their guts up. But Aiden seems so nervous I think he'll be freaked out if I ask him to close it.

'Right, don't take this the wrong way,' Aiden says, 'but, you look absolutely awful. Like, seriously bad.'

'Thanks.' I smile.

Aiden smiles too and shuffles a little further into my room. 'Be honest, Kay,' he says. 'How you doin'?'

Aiden's Joey impersonation is terrible and I shake my head.

'That good, yeah?' he says.

'What are you doing here?' I rub my eyes and wake up more. 'Visiting hours aren't for ages.'

Aiden scrunches his nose. 'Kay it's five past one.'

'In the afternoon?' My eyes open wide.

'No. In the morning,' Aiden laughs and tilts his head to one side. 'Of course in the afternoon, you eejit. I was here earlier but your mam said you were sleeping and wouldn't let me in.'

'You were here earlier?'

'Yeah. I got the train up. My mam went off on a mental one about travelling alone to the big smoke, blah, blah and at rush hour, blah, blah. But I got here. And Dublin is awesome. Kinda smelly though. Does the Liffey always stink this much?'

I nod.

'Well, anyway. I'm here and it's great to see you,' he says.

'I can't believe you convinced your mam to let you get the train by yourself. You're usually so... so...'

'Chicken,' Aiden finishes for me.

'Careful,' I say, my eyes closing without me telling them to. 'You're in danger of growing up.'

It's so hard to stay awake. I'm really happy to see Aiden, but a part of me wishes he wasn't here so I could go back to sleep.

'Is it really 1 p.m.?' I ask.

'Yup. And my God can you snore. I actually thought there was a donkey in here. *He-haw, he-haw,*' Aiden teases.

'I do not snore.' I jam my hands onto my hips, pretending to be deeply offended. 'Ouch.' I wince when the stupid cannula in my hand pinches.

'You okay?' Aiden says, his eyes widening, and I know I've
scared him.

'Yeah. Just this stupid thing.' I point to the needle in my
hand. The tape around it is peeling off and grubby and there's
some gross dried blood on it and under it.

'Wow, Kay. That looks sore,' Aiden says.

'It's a killer,' I inhale. 'Seriously. I think this thing is the
worst part of the whole stupid nightmare. It really, really stings.
I thought I'd get used to it, but I just hate it and wish they'd take
it out.'

'Have you asked them?'

'Yeah, a bunch of times. I'd just have to get a different one in
my other hand and that's no fun.'

'I'd say.' Aiden goes pale just looking at it.

'Dude. You should sit down.'

Aiden nods and hurries over to the set of chairs next to my
bed. He flops into the one furthest away from me and I don't
know why but it really hurts my feelings. Like he doesn't want
to get too close. He knows I'm not contagious, so I don't get it.

'Everyone is asking after you,' he says, sitting a bit straighter.

'In school?'

'Yeah. Miss Hanlon got everyone to make a card in PE.
Here...' Aiden swings his schoolbag, that I didn't notice him
wearing, off his back and onto his lap and rummages around
inside. He unfolds a giant card and passes it to me.

'Thanks,' I say, stuck for better words.

There's a big tatty grey teddy on the front. He has sad eyes
and a bandage around his head and the swirly, lilac font at the
top says, *Get Well Soon, Champ*.

'Champ?' I say, running my finger across the letters.

'Miss Hanlon thought it was appropriate, cause you're
basketball captain and all.'

I look down at my padded and bandaged knee and struggle

to hide how emotional I am. 'Yeah,' I say. 'That was thoughtful of her.'

'So, what's the story, anyway?' Aidan says, pulling himself fully upright, recovered from his dizzy spell. 'When will you be better? The team sucks balls without you. We've lost the last two games, Kay.'

'I... I...'

'We actually had an assembly for you, too,' Aiden cuts across my spluttering.

'You what?' I say, my eyes raised and my neck poking forward.

'Yup.' Aiden smiles and I know he's loving this. 'The principal. Vice. Year head. They were all there. There was a prayer and poems and it was super weird. You'd have bloody loved it. Been pissin' yourself laughing too.'

I shake my head. 'What the hell, Aiden. That's not funny.'

Aiden's stupid grin disappears and he becomes serious all of a sudden. The same way he does when a teacher gives out to him.

'Does everyone in school think I'm dying or something?'

'What?' Aiden says. 'No.'

'Well, what's with all the prayers and stuff then?'

Aiden doesn't answer and the silence that falls over us is weird and awkward and I'm not sure I want him to be here. I'm not sure I want anyone to be here.

'I miss you,' he finally says. 'School is so boring without you.'

'School is always boring,' I correct.

'Yeah, but it's extra boring without you.'

I take a deep breath and look around at the four walls I'm growing to hate, the window that tries to be all bright and reassuring but overlooks the car park and the door that creaks open and closed during the night when nurses come in to poke me, check my blood pressure or dose me up with drugs.

'I never thought I'd say this,' I admit, 'but I actually miss school.'

Aiden looks away and I can hear him puffing out deep breaths.

'Jesus, dude. You're failing miserably at this reassuring me thing,' I say, teasing. I'm trying hard to make this easier – for both of us.

'Wanna go to the games room?' Aiden says, without turning back.

I don't. I have no energy. 'Sure,' I say. 'It's just down the corridor.'

Aiden turns slowly back at last and I can see the tears in the big eejit's eyes. 'Do you need help... you know... getting out of bed or anything?'

'Noooo,' I lie. 'I'm fine.'

Aiden stands up and opens the door way before I'm ready. He stares at me as my good leg shakes when I throw it over the edge of the bed. I wriggle my hip, certain I'm pulling a weird concentration face as I guide my bad leg to follow. I shuffle into giant Winnie-the-Pooh-head slippers and I'm so light-headed standing up, I'm pretty sure I'm going to topple over. I can hear Doctor Patterson's voice play over in my head, 'Listen to your body, Kayla. It will tell you when you're ready to be up and moving.'

'Ready? Aiden asks, his relief to leave my room written all over his face.

'Ready, ready, ready,' I say, using up so much energy getting from the bed to the door.

TWENTY-SIX

KAYLA

It takes us two hundred years to reach the games room. I had to keep stopping every couple of steps to draw deep breaths like I've been smoking like a trooper since the day I was born. Aiden rubbed my back sometimes. It was a bit weird and it didn't help, but I didn't want to offend him and ask him to stop when he was trying so hard.

Aiden's reaction when we reached the games room was also weird.

'Oh my God,' he said. 'This place is great.'

It's not great. I mean, really, really not great. But, to be fair, compared to my boring-as-hell room, it's a lot better.

There's a pool table in the centre of the room, a couple of cues hung up on the wall behind it, and blue chalk that's worn down to a stub on the side. There's also a play kitchen and book shelf overflowing with fairy tales for little kids. Also, there's a not-too-shabby huge TV on the wall. It's mostly taken over by *Peppa Pig* or *Paw Patrol*, but in the evenings when the little kids are asleep, a few of us get together to watch *Friends*.

'Game of pool?' Aiden says, bouncing into the room with a nervous energy.

I groan inwardly. My hand is fanning the wall just outside the door, weirdly over Aladdin's crotch and I know if Aiden looks over I'll never hear the end of it, but it's way too much effort to move.

'Kay, c'mon. You love pool, don'tcha.'

I don't know where he's got that from. Because sick or not, I hate pool.

'Yeah, yeah,' I say, wondering why the hell I didn't think to bring my crutch. It was right beside my bed. And it's just one, so it's not really obvious that I'd be leaning on it so much.

Aiden grabs a cue off the wall and chalks it up like he's some sort of pool champion who knows what he's doing.

'Kay, c'mon. You have to chalk it.'

'Do you?' I pull a face, wondering why you would.

'Of course,' Aiden says, as if that's a reasonable answer and I try not to smirk knowing he has no clue either.

I peel myself off the wall and shuffle into the room as if I'm one hundred on my next birthday.

'Game of eight,' someone says, like a whisper scratching against your window when you can't sleep.

'Who's there?' I say, craning my neck to search the seemingly empty room.

The beanbag in front of the telly rustles and the boy who seems to always be morphed into it finally stands up. I've seen him before. He's stuck to the beanbag in the evenings before I come down for *Friends* and he's always still there when I leave. I'm shook to see him standing up. I kind of assumed he had something wrong with his legs, but he stands up no bother and it irrationally irritates me. *Why is he even here?*

'Who's first?' he says, looking at me.

'Aiden,' I say pointing at him, since he's holding the cue, and I've yet to make it over to the wall to reach mine.

'Right,' Beanbag Boy says to Aiden. 'You pot first. Hit a

stripe. That's what you're aiming for. Hit a plain, you're aiming for that. Get me?'

Aiden nods, but his eyes aren't on Beanbag Boy, they're on me.

'Need help, Kay?' Aiden asks.

'I've got it,' I say, closing my eyes for a moment before I hobble forward. I take down the remaining cue and hold it across my chest like a warrior ready for battle.

'Your shot,' Beanbag Boy says.

'You look like you wanna play more than me,' I say, offering my cue to him.

'Nah, Healthy Boy here thinks he can take you on. I say let him have it.'

'Healthy Boy,' Aiden snorts under his breath as he searches under the table for something.

'What's your name?' I ask.

'Sean,' beanbag boy says with a lisp, and I see that his jaw doesn't open and close properly when he's trying to speak.

I hate myself for gasping. I'm missing half a leg, for God's sake – I'm not one to be shocked. It's just, Sean seemed so normal, so unaffected; his struggle catches me off guard.

'Got it,' Aiden says, straightening and holding a plastic triangle above his head.

'It's mouth cancer,' Sean says, ignoring Aiden's announcement. 'And before you say anything, I don't drink or smoke, I'm fourteen, gimme a break. But yeah, it sucks. And yeah, I'm screwed.'

'Knee,' I point to my padding and plaster. 'Well sort of, more the bits around it, but my knee is still mangled.'

'Ouch,' Sean says.

'What's your excuse, Healthy Boy?' Sean smirks, his eyes shifting to Aiden. 'Why are you here?'

'I'm visiting. Just visiting,' Aiden says.

'Ha,' Sean snorts. 'Alright for some.'

'Aiden is my mate from school,' I say.

'Just a friend?' Sean asks.

I laugh, probably a little harder than is necessary. 'God, yeah. We're not going out. That would never happen. Not in a million years.'

'Okay, Kay,' Aiden grunts, as he gathers all the balls into the plastic triangle that he's placed in the centre of the table. 'I think he gets it. We're just mates.'

'So, do you have a boyfriend, then?' Sean asks.

I glance at my plaster and wonder if he's flirting. *And if he is, why? Look at the state of me. Who would want to flirt with me like this?*

I hear the crack of balls knocking against each other and I look up, relieved to find Aiden has started the game. Maybe we can get back to talking about pool and Sean will stop making this awkward.

'Nice break, Healthy Boy,' Sean says. 'You're stripes.'

'Please stop calling me that,' Aiden says.

'Healthy Boy, Healthy Boy, Healthy Boy,' Sean chants.

'Seriously, dude. What are you? Like six? Cop on,' Aiden says, slamming the cue down onto the table. Some of the balls rattle and move from position. The blue one rolls into the middle pocket.

'C'mon,' I say, placing my hand on Aiden's shoulder. 'Let's just play on.'

'You can't play on now,' Sean snorts. 'Healthy Boy here is cheating.' Sean points at Aiden and pulls a face. 'Cheater, cheater, cheater.'

'Okay.' Aiden's eyes widen with frustration and he shrugs my hand off him. 'You're just a wanker, do you know that? If you weren't sick I'd punch your bleedin' lights out.'

'Aiden,' I squeak, horrified.

'What?' Aiden snaps. 'You heard what he said.'

I shake my head.

'Oh, is Healthy Boy sulking now cause his missus gave out to him?' Sean says.

'Okay,' I say. 'That's enough. You're being rude. We're leaving now. C'mon, Aiden. Let's go. I don't even really like pool anyway.'

'Ah, what?' Sean says, sounding disappointed. 'Don't go. I was only having a laugh.'

'It wasn't funny,' I say.

Sean raises his hands above his head and frowns. 'Look, I'm sorry. I was just messing. I didn't mean to piss you off. You guys stay and play. My gran is coming in to visit soon anyway. I gotta go.'

I hear Aiden puff out and gather up balls, I guess he's reset-ting the table to start over. But my eyes are on Sean as he walks towards the door with his shoulders flopped forward and his head down. He seems genuinely sorry that he offended us. I think his tough-guy thing is all an act. And I get it. Maybe it's easier to pretend to be something you're not, than face up to never being the way you were before, ever again.

'Hey,' I call just as he's about to walk out the door. 'I'll see you later for *Friends*, yeah?'

He stops and twists his head over his shoulder. '*Friends*.'

I think Sean could really use a friend in this place. So could I.

TWENTY-SEVEN

HEATHER

I'm downstairs in the canteen trying to talk some sense into the manager when my phone begins to ring. I ignore it. Someone has complained about too many blueberries in their muffin, and the manager has pulled me aside for a quick word. That was over five minutes ago and I'm anxious to get back upstairs to Kayla. I left her alone on the ward over an hour ago and I told her I wouldn't be long.

'This is the third complaint,' the manager says with her hands on her hips.

'It's the same patient complaining each time,' I say. 'If they don't like blueberries they should order a plain muffin.'

'We take complaints very seriously, Heather.'

'And so you should,' I say, my phone buzzing furiously in my pocket. 'But this is just stupid.'

'Heather!' The manager's eyebrows shoot up. 'I'm disappointed to hear you say that. We pride ourselves on good customer experiences and we would never consider any of our customers stupid.'

My phone stops ringing.

'Someone found a hair in their tomato soup, yesterday,' I

say, becoming increasingly impatient with this ridiculous conversation. 'And I never said the customers are stupid. I said complaining about too much fruit in a fruit muffin is stupid. And it is.'

'Just don't be so heavy with blueberries in future, okay?'

I'm about to retort with a question about where we stand on raspberries and chocolate chips but the respite from my ringing phone is short-lived and it starts buzzing again.

'Less blueberries moving forward. I got it,' I say through gritted teeth, as I reach into my pocket and pull out my vibrating phone. 'Now, if you'll excuse me, I need to take this.'

'Hello,' I say, holding the phone to one ear and pressing my finger against the other, trying to block out some of the noise bellowing from the clusters of people eating and drinking all around me.

'Heather?' a man's voice says.

'Yes.' I hurry through the double doors of the canteen, instantly relieved by the sudden silence on the corridor as I make my way towards the lifts.

'Heather, it's Jack. Jack Patterson.'

'Doctor Patterson,' I say, taken aback that *he's* my incessant caller. The lift doors open and the woman who gets in ahead of me holds the door, but my feet are frozen to the spot. I wave my hand and she lets the doors close. 'What's wrong? Are there more results back? Is it bad?'

'Where are you?' Jack asks.

'Erm,' I swallow, glancing over my shoulder at the door to the canteen. 'I'm on my way up to the ward.'

'Okay. Good. I'll see you there in a few minutes.'

'What's wrong? You're freaking me out, Jack.'

'Nothing's wrong,' he says, in that soothing voice that I've come to learn precedes a *but* of some sort.

I bang the button on the wall, frantically calling back the

lift. *Bing!* The doors part and I can barely contain myself to wait for the man inside to get out before I jump in.

'Jack, just tell me,' I say, pounding on the button for the third floor. The lift creaks and groans and obediently begins rising. 'Jack?' I say, but the line is dead.

I lower my phone and stare at the screen. I should have known I'd lose service in the lift. I count along with the digital display above the door. One... two... stop! Dammit. We're stopping on the second floor.

'Going down?' a young women says as the doors part.

'Up.' I point, ready to push the button to close the doors again.

'I wanna goooooo. I wanna goooooo,' the toddler in her arms screeches.

She grabs another, older, child by the hand and I move over as they step into the lift. The doors creak and groan and seem to take forever to close and the toddler and older kid poke their tongues out at one another and scream and shout, obviously in the middle of a sibling war. Their mother tosses them a look that warns them they're in big trouble as soon as I get out.

Bing!

'How dare you, both,' I hear her growl before the doors fully close behind me. 'I'm sure that lady is shocked. I'm mortified by your behaviour.'

I take a deep breath and shake my head. I can remember scolding Kayla in the same way for similar silly behaviour when she was little. I remember when she was about two she had a meltdown in the sweets aisle in Tesco because I wouldn't, and couldn't afford to, buy a giant bar of Toblerone. I was embarrassed as strangers watched her kick her arms and legs and scream at the top of her voice. I remember how my face burned and my temper flared, and I thought being a mother was too hard, too intense. What I don't remember is who the people staring at me were. I don't remember if they were young or old.

If it was a man or a woman or both. I just remember the sinking feeling of *I can't do this.*

The feeling grabs me again now as I stand in front of the security doors outside Kayla's ward. My legs are shaking, and my palms are sweating. I want to hurry inside and hug Kayla tight. I want to apologise for not buying the Toblerone back then and buy her as much chocolate as she can possibly eat. But, I can't seem to get my legs to move forward. Jack is waiting behind those doors and I know I don't want to hear whatever he's about to tell me.

'You goin' in, love?' I jump as one of the nurses from the ward appears behind me.

I nod, a bit lost for words.

She places her hand on my shoulder. 'You're not the first parent to be overwhelmed by these doors.'

'I just...'

'Is it your son or daughter we're looking after?' she says as she swipes her security card through a box near the door and there's a buzz and a click and the doors release.

'My daughter. Kayla.'

'Ah, Kayla,' she says, as we step inside. 'She's a great kid. Although I think I might be in her bad books. I suggested changing her cannula this morning and she didn't say anything but...'

'If looks could kill,' I say, thinking of Kayla's angry stare. 'Oh God, I didn't mean,' I add quickly, trying to back pedal, wishing I hadn't said that.

'Oh don't worry,' the nurse says. 'I've heard worse.'

'I'm sorry,' I add.

'Listen,' she says, taking both my hands in hers and giving them a gentle squeeze. 'You don't have to watch every word out of your mouth. If you start doing that then you won't be yourself and Kayla will pick up on it. Kids with cancer are just kids and they need their parents to be just parents. Try not to be so hard on yourself. You're going through enough already.'

'Thank you,' I say. 'I'll try to remember that.'

'Well, best get back to work,' she says squeezing my hands once more, which I wish she hadn't as my palms are too sweaty, and it's a little disgusting. 'It was lovely meeting you.'

'Yeah. You too,' I say.

I reluctantly put one foot in front of the other as I walk towards Kayla's room further down the corridor. I can hear familiar voices and laughter as I get closer. The sinking feeling eases and I allow myself to consider that I overreacted to Jack's call. Maybe he just wanted to go over Kayla's notes or give me an update or something. I've really got to stop thinking the worst all the time or, as the nurse said, Kayla will pick up on it.

'Hey, Mam,' Kayla says, sitting up in bed when I walk into her room.

'Hey, you,' I say.

'You were ages. Everything okay?'

'Yes. Yes. Just a silly muffin crisis. Hello, Jack,' I say, assuming the white coat sitting on the edge of Kayla's bed is Doctor Patterson.

'Hi, Heather,' he replies, too busy checking Kayla's leg to turn around.

'Hello, Aiden,' I add.

Aiden steps aside so I can pass by and get closer to Kayla. I drop my bag onto the chair next to her bed and lean over her to kiss her forehead, as seems to have become habit every time I enter or leave her room.

'Did you get some time to chat?' I ask, looking at Kayla and then Aiden.

'Yeah. Yes we did,' Kayla says. 'It's been good.'

I smile. My eyes are on Aiden. He's unusually quiet and he's pale. As pale as some of the kids on the ward.

'That's good. I'm glad you had a chance to catch up—' my

breath catches in the back of my throat as I catch a glimpse of patches of bright red on Kayla's bandages that weren't there earlier. I point. 'Jesus Christ, what's happened?'

'Mam, don't freak out,' Kayla says.

More bloodied bandages are thrown in a kidney dish on Kayla's bed and Jack is sitting next to them wrapping fresh, white bandages around Kayla's knee.

'Kayla had a dizzy spell in the games room. She took a little tumble,' Jack says.

'Is she okay?' I search Jack's face for an answer but he's not looking at me. My gaze moves to Kayla. 'Are you okay?'

'She's absolutely fine,' Jack says. 'These things happen. They're not ideal, and we're going to be more careful to make sure it doesn't happen again. Aren't we, Kayla?'

Kayla nods.

'But it's really nothing to get upset or worried about, Heather,' Jack continues. 'There's no damage and we'd be changing the bandages soon anyway.'

'Is this why you were calling me?' I ask.

'Yes.' Jack smiles. 'I thought Kayla could use a cuddle. She's been very brave.'

'Or very stupid,' I snap. 'Kayla what on earth were you thinking? If you're dizzy you know you shouldn't get out of bed. How many times can we go over this?'

'I was bored.' Kayla folds her arms and narrows her eyes. 'It's boring in here. It's not a crime to want a change of scene.'

'Aiden, what were you thinking dragging her around the hospital like that? She's not well. How can you not understand that?'

'I- I- I'm sorry,' Aiden splutters.

'It's not Aiden's fault,' Kayla says. 'The games room was my idea.'

I look over at the wall. Kayla's crutch is in exactly the same place as it was when I went downstairs earlier. 'Did you even think to bring it with you?'

'I forgot,' Kayla shrugs.

'You forgot,' I say. I shake my head with my lips pursed together.

'I don't think there's any real harm done,' Jack says.

I exhale sharply until I'm light-headed. 'Maybe not this time, thank God. But Kayla, I think we need to talk.'

'Oh great,' Kayla groans.

'Aiden would you mind?'

'Sure,' Aiden says. 'I'll wait outside'

'I think it's time to go home now, Aiden,' I say, shaking my head. 'It's been a long day.'

'Maaammm,' Kayla grumbles. 'That's not fair. Aiden's come all the way up just to visit.'

'It's okay, Kay,' Aiden says.

'Aiden I *am* sorry,' I say. 'But Kayla needs some rest.'

'S'okay, Heather. I get it. Anyway, my mam says I have to be home before six. She doesn't want me on the train when it's dark.'

'Are you sure your mother is okay with you getting the train alone, Aiden?' I say, trying to hide my suspicion that Aiden has skipped off school and come to Dublin without his parents knowing. I wonder if I should text Mary, but I don't want to get him into trouble.

Aiden nods, wide-eyed and emphatic. 'Yeah, she's cool with it.'

'Okay, then. Well, text us when you get home, won't you?' I say, reaching a compromise with my conscience. 'You know, just so we know you made it back okay.'

'Will do,' Aiden says. 'Oh, I nearly forgot.' He bends down and reaches into his school bag and pulls out a large Toblerone. 'Your favourite, Kay.'

'Oh my God, is that a white chocolate one?' Kayla asks, sitting a little straighter.

'Yup.'

'You absolute legend.'

Aiden passes her the giant bar of chocolate and she pulls him in for a hug. She catches him off guard and he wobbles. I hold my breath, panicked for a moment that he'll lose his balance and come crashing down on her.

'Maybe you could come visit again soon,' Kay says.

'Yeah,' Aiden says, zipping up his school bag and sliding one strap over his shoulder. 'But, it'll have to be the weekend. If I skip another day of school my mam will kill me.'

I glare at Aiden, waiting for him to realise what he's confessed.

It takes a bit longer than it should but eventually he says, 'Ah, Heather. You're not going to tell my mam are you?'

'Not this time,' I say. 'But you really can't do this again, Aiden. It puts me in an awful position. And now I'm worried about you making it back home safely. I'm already worried enough about Kayla, I don't need this on top. Do you even know what bus you need to catch to get back to the train station?'

'Erm...' Aiden mumbles, unsure.

'Oh Aiden,' I say.

'You know, my shift finished forty minutes ago,' Jack says, standing up and lifting the tray of Kayla's murky bandages with him. 'I'm heading home once Kayla is okay. I drive through town on my way. I can give Aiden a lift to the station, if it helps.'

'Oh.' I wince, unsure. *Gosh, I could choke Aiden for going behind his mother's back and making this all so awkward.*

'That'd be cool. Thanks,' Aiden says, sliding his arm into the other strap of his bag.

'That would be really helpful, Jack. Thank you,' I say.

'Ah, look,' Jack says. 'We were all teenagers once and did

silly things. But next time I see you on the ward, young man, I want to be certain your parents know you're here.'

'Yeah. Definitely,' Aiden's says. His cheeks are flushed and I'm sure he's learned his lesson.

'Thank you,' I mouth to Jack and he smiles back at me with big, beautiful hazel eyes.

'Bye, Kay,' Aiden says.

'Go home, you eejit,' Kay says, opening the Toblerone and taking a bite. 'But I'll see you soon, yeah.'

'Yeah. Soon.'

'Come on, young man,' Jack says, draping his arm over Aiden's shoulder. 'Let's get you on that train.'

TWENTY-EIGHT

CHARLOTTE

Molly skips up the steps between the ground and third floor. I'd happily have taken the lift but Molly wanted to see all the characters painted on the wall as we make our way up the stairs.

'That's Jas-bin,' Molly says, pointing excitedly.

'Jasmine,' I correct.

'And A-lad-bin,' Molly adds.

'A-lad-din, Molly.' I exhale. 'Aladdin. We've watched the film twenty times.'

'I can't wait to see Kayla,' Molly says, her hand in mine swinging back and forth.

'Me too.'

'Oh, oh, look,' Molly says as we round the first half flight of stairs. 'That's Mooblee.'

'Oh God Lord, Molly.' I smile. 'That's *Mowgli*. Mowgli from *The Jungle Book*.'

'I love *The Jungle Book*,' Molly bounces. 'I really like when the ele-fant goes flying high and high.'

'Molly,' I say as we round the next turn, 'that's *Dumbo*.'

'No.' Molly pulls a face and throws her head dramatically

over her shoulder to look back at the mural on the wall we've passed. 'That's Mooblee.'

'No, I mean the flying elephant is *Dumbo*.' I shake my head, exhausted already. 'You know what? Never mind.'

Molly's hand pulls in mine and I know without looking she's trying to get closer to the paintings on the wall as we ascend the staircase.

'I'm tired,' Molly announces as we round the next flight.

'Well taking the stairs was your idea, missy. C'mon. Not much further. Kayla is waiting for us.'

'And lollipops. Kayla will have lollipops.'

I come to a sudden stop and Molly's hand jerks in mine as she tries to skip ahead.

'Molly, there won't be lollipops every time we come to see Kayla. Do you know that?'

Molly's bottom lip drops and she shakes her head.

'Didn't Daddy explain this to you, sweetheart,' I say.

Molly stares at me blankly. For a kid who almost never stops talking, Molly is a mute statue now. I turn away and roll my eyes. I asked Gavin to speak to Molly last night; ease her gently into what we're facing.

'What *did* Daddy tell you Molly?'

'That we could see Kayla after school...'

'And...?'

'And that we'd see Aladbin and Mooblee.'

'And?'

'And that's all,' Molly says sweetly, smiling as she tugs on my hand, ready to get moving again.

I tug back, gently. 'Did Daddy tell you Kayla might not be feeling very well?'

Molly shakes her head. 'Does Kayla have a pain in her tummy again?'

'Great! Thanks, Gavin,' I groan inwardly.

'What's great, Mammy?' Molly asks.

'Nothing. Nothing,' I say, wishing my kid didn't have the ears of a bat. 'Come on now, let's go see Kayla. Yeah?'

'Yay,' Molly says, beginning to skip again and clearly forgetting that less than two minutes ago she was complaining about tired legs.

Molly complains about tired legs, a pain in her finger, and needs to stop off on the second floor for a wee, before we finally reach Kayla's ward. Bleach and disinfectant seem to seep from the walls up here. The smell is so much stronger in this part of the hospital than anywhere else. I wonder if it's my imagination or if everything has to be more sterile because the kids are so sick. A lump swells in my throat and I try not to think about it.

Molly's fingers wriggle away from mine and she charges into Kayla's room with renewed energy. I hurry after her, wishing I'd reminded her not to jump on Kayla's bed. I told her in the car but, in her excitement, she might forget.

'Shh.' Heather is in the chair by Kayla's bed and places her finger over her lip. 'Kayla is asleep, Molly.'

'But it's daytime.' Molly points to the window where autumn sun shines through the panes of latticed glass and creates squares on the floor tiles like a patchwork quilt of light.

'She's very tired,' Heather explains.

I try not to act visibly shocked by how pale and thin Kayla looks tucked up in bed. The chemo has stripped the colour from her cheeks and the shine from her hair. *Oh, Kayla.* Heather looks positively awful too. Her hair is messy, looking as if she hasn't brushed it today. There are deep, dark circles under her eyes and her skin is almost as grey as her jumper.

'How is she?' I ask, tilting my head towards the bed.

'She fell earlier,' Heather says, her voice crackling.

'Fell. Oh Jesus.'

'I fell in school,' Molly says and pulls up the leg of her school tracksuit pants to show off a scab on her knee that's at least a week old.

'Is she okay?' I ask. 'I mean, she didn't hurt herself, did she?'

'Oh, it hurt.' Heather nods. 'They gave her morphine, I think that's why she's so sleepy. Thankfully there's no damage done. Just a bit of bleeding.'

'Oh thank God. But how did it happen?'

'She was playing pool in the games room.' Heather rolls her eyes. 'She doesn't even like pool.'

'There's a games room?' Molly bounces. 'I want to go to the games room. Please, Mammy. Pleeeaaassseee.'

'Molly we came to see Kayla,' I say.

Heather shakes her head. 'I don't think Kayla is up to visitors today, Molly. I'm sorry. She's just very sleepy.'

'So we can't play?' Molly's face falls.

'Not today, Molly,' Heather says.

'But I want to play,' Molly shouts, and Kayla stirs.

'Shh. Shh,' Heather says, leaning forward to stroke Kayla's hair.

I bend to come down to Molly's level. 'Molly, we have to whisper when someone is sleeping. You know that.'

Heather looks at me crossly as I straighten. Then she glares at Molly. I'm not sure what more she wants me to say.

'I'm really sorry.' Heather exhales, standing up and ushering us towards the door. 'You've had a wasted trip. But Kayla is just too sick today. Maybe come back another time.'

'But I don't want to go home,' Molly begins to cry.

I scoop Molly into my arms and she nestles her face into my neck. 'I want to play with Kayla,' she sobs.

'We'll be back again another day, Heather,' I say. I don't mean it to sound as threatening as it does, I was just really looking forward to seeing Kayla.

'Okay. Thanks.' Heather smiles and closes the door behind us.

I'm reeling as I put Molly down and her small, chubby fingers wrap around my hand.

'I'm really sorry, sweetheart. I know you wanted to spend some time with Kayla.'

Molly doesn't reply. She sniffles and drags the sleeve of her coat under her nose.

'I know,' I say, trying hard to sound chirpy. 'There's a shop downstairs. Did you see it when we came in?'

Molly nods.

'I bet they sell lollipops.' I pull a silly face and hope I can extract a smile from my daughter.

It works. Molly grins and says, 'Strawbee?'

'Let's go find out.' I swing Molly's hand back and forth as we skip away together.

TWENTY-NINE

CHARLOTTE

It takes forever to get home in evening traffic. Molly is asleep in the back of the car when I finally pull into the driveway.

I turn off the engine and flop my head back against the headrest. I've only closed my eyes for a second when there's the tap of a nail against my window.

I open my eyes and sit up straighter. *My nosey neighbour!* I groan inwardly as I reluctantly lower the window.

'Hello, Trish.'

'Hey, Charlotte. I hope this is a good time.'

'A good time for what?'

'A quick chat,' Trish says, with an irritating grin that tells me she knows full well there's never a good time for one of her interfering chats.

I twist my head over my shoulder to check the back seat. 'Actually, Trish. Molly's asleep so—'

'Ah, good, we can talk while she snoozes,' Trish says.

'Well, I should probably get her inside and settled,' I say, turning back and almost crashing face to face with Trish because she has her head shoved in my window trying to glance back at Molly.

'I won't keep you long,' Trish says. 'I just thought you should know that I've been keeping an eye on the house and—'

'My house?' My eyes widen.

'For neighbourhood watch,' Trish says. 'And, well, gosh I'm just not sure how to put this.' Trish places her hand across her chest as if she's protecting her heart. 'I've seen Gavin with another woman.'

I hate that my face registers an *oh-my-God* expression before my head catches up and I say, 'Heather. She's he's ex.'

'Oh. Oh,' Trish stutters.

Oh God, I groan inwardly. *Why did I say that? That must sound worse than whatever Trish was thinking.*

'Their daughter, my stepdaughter, isn't well,' I explain. 'Heather is staying with us for a while.'

Oh my God, Charlotte stop talking, I think as I watch Trish's lips twitch as she savours that little nugget of juicy gossip.

'Little Kayla?' Trish says.

'Not so little anymore,' I say. 'Kayla is fifteen now.'

'Gosh, time flies.'

I nod, wondering when Trish will peel her nose out of my business and go back to her house.

'Will Kayla's mother be staying long? Here, I mean.' Trish points to my house as if I need clarification about where I live.

'I really have no idea,' I say, realising that I really *do* have no idea how long I will be sharing my house with the woman my husband used to sleep with.

'It's just it's an extra car to park and the cul-del-sac is already crowded enough. Neighbours are beginning to complain,' Trish says.

'Really?' I reach for the door handle and push the door open, not caring if Trish has time to jerk her head back through the window or not. I stand up and tower over my short neighbour. 'If anyone has a problem, they can talk to me.'

'You know what people round here are like.' Trish pushes

her shoulders back trying to stand a fraction taller. 'They expect me to do all the talking. Sometimes I wish people wouldn't expect so much.'

I ignore Trish as I open the door behind mine and bend inside to unbuckle Molly. Molly hums and groans as I gather her into my arms. I duck back out, wrestling with my daughter's floppy body. Balancing on one leg, I push the door closed with my foot.

'So, if your guest could park her car around the corner where there's more space, I know everyone would be very grateful,' Trish drones on.

'Shh, shh, sweetheart,' I say, running my hand through Molly's hair as she stirs; Trish's talking is waking her.

'I miss Kayla,' Molly mumbles in her sleep.

'Me too,' I whisper. 'Me too.'

I think Trish is still talking as I turn my key in the front door. I turn on the step and face my neighbour whose lips are moving but I'm so tired I don't even hear the words coming out of her mouth.

'Goodbye, Trish,' I say, turning back, stepping inside and slamming the door so roughly behind me the whole frame rattles.

I'm shaking as I place Molly on the couch in the sitting room. I pull off her shoes and take the throw from the back of the couch and drape it over her.

'I love you, Mammy,' Molly says, snuggling into the soft throw.

'I love you too, my little princess.'

I flick on CBeebies and think about the bottle of red wine beside the fridge. The doorbell rings and I ignore it. I'm certain it's Trish wanting to rant at me more.

I pull my phone out of my pocket and hit call on Gavin's number as I make my way into the kitchen.

'Hey you,' my husband's voice says after a single ring.

'That was quick,' I say.

'I had my phone in my hand reading a text as your call came in.'

I'm comforted and calmer just hearing Gavin's voice. 'I'm just about to open some red and get a start on dinner. How do fajitas sound?'

'Eh. Maybe just make something for yourself and Molly,' Gavin says. 'I'll get take away later.'

'What? Where are you?' I ask. 'I thought you'd be on the way home by now.'

'I was. But Heather called. Kayla had a fall today.'

'I know. Poor thing.'

'Heather asked me to come in,' Gavin says.

'Oh. Is Kayla awake?'

Gavin pauses, and I guess he's picked up on the surprise in my voice.

'Molly and I were at the hospital earlier but Kayla was asleep.'

'Ah, that's a pity,' Gavin sighs. 'Kayla will be disappointed she missed Molly.'

'Molly was disappointed too,' I say. 'I had to bribe her with a lollipop.'

Gavin chuckles. 'Molly's answer to most things is sugar.'

'If Kayla is still asleep why are you going in? Would it not be better to wait until the morning when she actually knows you're there?'

'I think Heather could do with the support, to be honest,' Gavin says. 'She sounds completely worn out.'

I stop talking. *I could do with the support. I'm completely worn out.* I've barely seen Gavin in weeks. Molly hasn't seen him at all because he's gone in the morning before she wakes up and she's in bed again before he makes it home.

'Charlie, you there?' Gavin says.

'Yeah,' I say.

'So, I'll see you later, okay?'

'Okay.'

'Love you,' Gavin whispers.

I hang up and slam my phone down on the kitchen counter. I grab a glass out of the cupboard and unscrew the lid on the wine and pour until it's nearly flowing over the top of the glass. I guzzle a huge mouthful, followed by another and another. The glass drained, I set it on the counter and decide I better get on with making dinner before I pour any more or I'll be pissed. I'm already light-headed.

I open the fridge and I'm just pulling out the vegetable crisper when there's a thud in the sitting room followed by a high-pitched squeal and crying, and I hurry in to find that Molly has rolled off the couch.

THIRTY

HEATHER

I turn my key in the lock, but the door doesn't budge. Wiggling it doesn't help much, and I'm afraid if I twist too hard the key will snap. I step down from the doorstep and sweep my eyes over the house. Everything is still and there are no lights on downstairs. There's light on the landing but the bedrooms are all in darkness.

I really don't want to ring the doorbell and wake Charlotte or Molly. I pull my key out of the door and I'm considering sleeping in my car when the door rattles from the inside and slowly creaks open.

'You're home,' Charlotte says, as she swings the door back. 'Oh.' Her face falls and she pulls her already closed dressing gown a little tighter across her chest. 'It's you.'

My cheeks sting. I was already embarrassed, assuming I've woken her, but she makes her disappointment that I'm not Gavin so obvious, I'm not really sure what to say.

'Sorry. I hope I didn't wake you. I couldn't get my key to work.'

Charlotte shakes her head, but her eyes are sleepy and even

if she wasn't upstairs in bed, I've clearly disturbed her from napping on the couch or something.

'You have a key?' she says.

'Gavin gave it to me a couple of days ago. Didn't he tell you?' I say, wishing I hadn't brought it up because clearly he's forgotten to mention it and Charlotte is pissed off. I wonder if I should offer to give it back to her. I don't really need a key; I'm never here unless either Gavin or Charlotte are home.

We both look up at the sky when a loud clatter of thunder rumbles overhead.

'How's Kayla?' Charlotte asks, moving aside to let me in as an angry sky warns us it's about to rain.

'Not great,' I say, shivering as the night wind clings to my bones. I wish I had a heavier coat than the leather biker jacket I grabbed when I left Cork in a panic.

'Oh.' Charlotte seems surprised; I thought she understood earlier that Kayla wasn't well today.

'She was awake and talking to Gavin when I left, but she didn't touch her dinner and I know by her face she's in pain even if she's too stubborn to admit it.'

Charlotte shakes her head and her eyes round. 'You know, Molly and I had fajitas tonight. There're leftovers in the fridge.'

My tummy growls at the mere mention of food.

'They're vegan, of course,' Charlotte warns, nodding firmly. 'It's a new recipe I got online, but you're welcome to them.' She twitches, unsure. 'If you're hungry, that is.'

'Really?' I say. 'That would be great. I'm starving.'

'Didn't you get something to eat at the hospital?' she asks.

I shake my head. 'Didn't really get the chance. I was in the canteen earlier, but I was so busy with muffins and the manager from hell – I just, sort of forgot... and then Kayla fell and...'

'What's the manager's problem?' Charlotte asks, switching places with me as I step inside.

'Ugh, long story,' I say, not wanting to get into it.

Charlotte stands on the doorstep for a couple of seconds, turning her head left and right and left again. A second clap of thunder, louder and angrier than the first, shakes the sky and Charlotte jumps.

'Um, is everything okay?' I ask.

'Where are you parked?' Charlotte asks, oddly.

'Erm...' I point, towards the opening of the cul-de-sac. 'Around the corner. Is that a problem? I can move.'

'No, no, no. Everything is fine.'

'Ooo-kay,' I say.

Charlotte is so odd, I think. *Gavin's mother must love her.*

After a weird amount of time when I'm not sure if I should head into the kitchen and pop fajitas in the microwave or wait for Charlotte to lead the way, she finally closes the door with a ferocious bang. I cock my ear and listen for Molly upstairs. She doesn't stir, and I don't realise I'm holding my breath until Charlotte is right beside me in the hall.

'Fajitas.' She clicks her fingers, and even though this is her house she's somehow inadvertently let me know she feels as weird as I do.

'Thank you,' I say, following her into the kitchen.

I pull out a chair from the table but stop it halfway between the table and me. I wonder if I should offer to help; although there's not much to reheating fajitas. Or maybe I should just sit and let her plate up. I wonder what would make her comfortable. I know neither will help me.

'Erm, don't suppose you'd like a coffee?' I ask.

'No.' Charlotte doesn't elaborate, and if I felt awkward before, now is positively painful.

Charlotte places a plate of shrivelled fajitas in the microwave. A flash of lightning strikes and illuminates the whole garden for a split second and the kitchen lights flicker as if shivering with fear.

'Oh God, I hope the power doesn't go out,' Charlotte says,

turning on the microwave as if she's racing time. 'Molly is terrified of the dark.'

'Do you usually lose power in a storm?' I ask, trying to sound casual while panicking inside about how on earth I'm going to bake a couple of dozen brownies and muffins without an oven.

'Depends how bad the storm is.' Charlotte shrugs, looking out the window for clues about how the weather might behave.

The microwave beeps, demanding attention, but both Charlotte and I are staring out the window at the torrential rain that's erupted and is pounding the patio with large, angry drops.

'Drink?' Charlotte says suddenly, breaking into my worried thoughts.

I nod. 'That'd be great Thanks.'

'Red or white?'

'Wine?' I ask, exhaustion and hunger catching up with me. 'I don't really mind.'

'Okay.'

Charlotte pours the remainder of one bottle of red into a glass before opening the microwave and lifting out the plate that I know by her expression is much too hot to hold. She drops it onto the countertop and fetches another bottle of wine from the rack above the fridge.

'I only have red,' Charlotte announces as if that's some sort of failing.

'I like red,' I say, wondering why I said that. I do like red wine, but I really don't feel like alcohol right now. I really need food, water and sleep.

Charlotte fills a second glass and sets one down on each side of the table. She walks away again to retrieve the plate of shrivelled fajitas and reluctantly places them next to me.

'They looked better earlier,' she says.

'They look great,' I say. I'm lying and we both know it. But they do smell good and I wonder if I should wait for Charlotte to sit down before I tuck in.

Charlotte ignores the wine she's poured for herself and walks back to the sink. She pulls on a pair of bright-yellow rubber gloves as if the washing up is suddenly important.

'Gavin loves fajitas,' she says, turning on the taps.

'I know,' I say, biting into a fajita. They may not look like much but they taste great.

'I was keeping those for him.'

I stop chewing and look down at the plate that Charlotte has suddenly made clear is her husband's dinner.

'I've been keeping dinners for Gavin and then throwing them out when he doesn't get home.' She sighs.

I begin chewing again, too hungry to be polite.

'I'm not sure why I bother, really,' she says, staring into the sink. 'It's usually so late when he gets home that he's too tired to eat.'

I swallow. I'm not sure if Charlotte is blaming me or if she just wants to vent and I'm the only person here to listen.

'It's exhausting,' I say as Charlotte drags steel wool vigorously over and back against a baking tray. 'For all of us.'

'Molly misses him,' Charlotte says.

I don't reply. Instead, I take another bite and keep my eyes focused on the plate in front of me as Charlotte continues to wash up. I munch my way through the remaining fajitas in silence. When my plate is empty I stand up.

'They were amazing,' I say, placing my used plate on the countertop next to the sink. 'Thank you.'

Charlotte snatches the plate out from under my fingertips and ducks it under the water. 'I'm glad someone got to enjoy them. Do you have any idea when Gavin will be home?'

I look at her blankly and wonder why she's asking *me* that question and not him. I shrug. 'I think he'll wait till Kayla's asleep. I hope so, anyway.'

'Yeah,' Charlotte says. 'I'm sure he'll text.'

'Yeah,' I say, my eyes weighing heavy with tiredness. I walk back to the table and reach for the wine. I surprise myself with how easily the first mouthful slides down. 'This is really nice.'

'It's French,' Charlotte says. 'And organic. I only drink organic. Anything else gives me a headache and an even worse hangover. I think it's the sulphites.'

'I'm not sure what a sulphite is, but it doesn't sound good,' I say.

'It's just a chemical. And I think there's enough chemicals in our life without adding more. If I can eat and drink healthily, I do.'

'But isn't alcohol technically a poison?' I say.

Charlotte turns away, but I don't miss her roll her eyes as she does. 'Do you need to charge your phone or anything?' she asks, pointing towards a socket with a charger plugged in. 'You know, in case the power goes.'

'Yeah. Good idea,' I say. 'I bought a power bank in the hospital shop the other day but suppose I should keep that for emergencies.'

Charlotte nods and I know she's stopped listening. She peels off her rubber gloves, hangs them over the edge of the sink and walks over to the table to fetch her glass of wine. 'Right. I'm knackered. I'm going to go watch some telly. You're welcome to join me. Help yourself to s'more wine too, if you like. I don't plan to get up again once I sit down.'

My glass is still full to almost overflowing and something from the fajitas is repeating on me. I tell myself that half an hour of telly could be good. It might help me unwind rather than lying in bed tossing and turning for hours the way I've done the last few nights. I take another mouthful of wine, and another, and I can feel myself slowly relax. I wonder if Charlotte is onto something with this sulphur business because this is genuinely nice. I tilt the glass slightly and give it a little swirl the way they do on those posh cookery shows. The wine swirls more vigorously than I mean it to and a smidge splashes out over the edge and onto the cream porcelain floor tiles.

'Don't stain, don't stain, don't stain,' I mumble as I stare down at the small, burgundy circle of wine sinking into the grooves of the porous tile. 'No, no, no!'

I pop the glass down on the table and snatch some paper towel off the shelf. My legs creak, exhausted, as I bend down to dry up the wet patch. I close my eyes as I stand up. I'm afraid to look in case a stubborn red patch stares back it me. Opening my eyes I breath out, relieved to find the tile in mint condition. I pop the paper towel in the bin under the sink. I reach for my glass again and, drinking quite a bit so the glass is empty enough to carry in confidence of no more spills, I make my way into the sitting room to join Charlotte.

THIRTY-ONE

CHARLOTTE

I check my phone on the arm of the couch. There's still no word from Gavin. *Surprise! Surprise!* And I can't help but wonder if he can't be bothered to text. Or, if reception is terrible, or if he's chatting to Kayla. But it would be great to hear from him at some point; it's killing me not knowing what's happening half the time.

I'm regretting drinking two glasses of wine so quickly now as a small, frustrated vein in my temple pulsates. I'm surrounded by noise; rain pelts against the glass as the storm grows angrier, there's still the odd crash of thunder. At least there is no more lightning and we still have power. But it's just as noisy inside as out. I'm surrounded by snoring. A faint wheeze puffs in and out upstairs as Molly sleeps soundly, and there's the odd noise overhead every so often, which I recognise as the sound of one of Molly's giant teddies being shoved out of bed.

The snoring next to me is more violent and intense. Like the sound of air passing through a narrow tube when there's a blockage halfway. I'm squashed into one corner of the couch. Heather and I started out on opposite ends but she fell asleep after less than half her glass of wine, and she gradually stretched out and is taking up more than three quarters of the space now.

It was Heather's suggestion to watch *Friends*.

'They're repeats,' she said. 'We spent hours watching them when we were younger and now Kayla and I watch them all the time too.'

Heather got a bit upset at the mention of her telly time with Kayla so I didn't bother to ask if the *we* she was talking about was her and Gavin. Anyway, I don't have to ask. I already know. I don't know why I'm so worried about Gavin and Heather, I know it's ridiculous.

My fingers hover over the screen on my phone. I want to text Gavin. I want to ask how Kayla is. I want to ask if he's had dinner. Mostly I want to ask when he's coming home. I exhale until I'm light-headed and think about the bottle of wine on the shelf in the kitchen. Heather's glass is sitting on the coffee table. I turn off the TV and pull the throw over Heather, deciding against more wine. I'll regret it in the morning.

I'm just about to head up to bed when the doorbell rings. I smile, glad I'll actually get to see Gavin tonight before I fall asleep.

I'm taken aback when I find my neighbour and not my husband on the doorstep.

The man in running gear standing on my step introduces himself as my new neighbour. He moved in a couple of houses down last month with his pregnant wife or girlfriend, but we've never actually spoken. I was at a piano lesson with Molly when he came around to introduce himself.

'He said his name was Ben or Sam or Tom. Something with three letters anyway, I can't quite remember,' Gavin said. 'Seems like a nice guy. About our age. And athletic too, big rugby fan.'

I remember thinking how nice it would be to finally have a neighbour we have something in common with. The rest of the cul-de-sac are older than us; mostly retired couples with grown-up children. But seeing Mr three-letter-name standing on my doorstep at stupid o'clock with wet hair and a weather-beaten red face I'm wondering if Trish has intercepted him and he's here as her messenger to scold me about the parking situation. He's clearly walked from somewhere in the storm and I wonder if it's because Heather's car is sitting in his spot.

'I'm so sorry,' he says, shivering. 'It know it's very late, but I saw the light on in your sitting room and I guessed you might still be up.'

'I'm just on my way to bed,' I say, closing the door over a little to keep the freezing wind from zipping past me and into the house.

'It's just I noticed your car window is open and' – I crane my neck past him to look at my car – 'I thought you'd want to know.'

'Oh God. I do. I do. Thank you.'

I grab my keys off the hall table behind me and I'm about to dash outside when my neighbour looks at my bare feet and shakes his head. 'It's cats and dogs out here. If you give me the keys, I'll close it for you.'

I must look uncertain or scared because he backs off the step and says, 'Only if it helps. I won't drive off in it. You know where I live, after all.'

'That would be great. Thank you,' I say, reaching my arm out into the rain to pass the keys to him.

He opens the driver's door, starts the engine and rolls up the window.

'Thank you so much. I'm not normally this distracted.' I shake my head, mortified.

'One of those days,' he says, locking the car and passing me back the keys.

'One of those weeks, actually,' I say.

'No real harm done. But that rain is heavy stuff,' he says,

pointing towards the sky as he returns to the shelter of the doorstep. 'And it's been coming down for a while. You might want to put some plastic on that seat before you sit into it next. You'll get pneumonia otherwise. Should dry out in a day or two though.'

I glance across the green at Trish's house. The curtains in an upstairs bedroom twitch and I've no doubt my busybody neighbour is peeking out. We'll be the talk of the estate tomorrow. Of course, Trish will put her spin on it. I can hear her now.

'Poor neighbour had to come to Charlotte's rescue in the storm when her terrible husband abandoned her. And do you know they have another woman living with them?'

'Oh really,' some other busybody will reply. *'I'm not surprised.'*

The twitching curtain steadies and I know Trish has spotted me glaring in her direction.

His phone rings and I've never seen someone drag a phone out of their pocket and press it to their ear so quickly. I look on as he uses a hand gesture to excuse himself and he steps aside on the porch. I wonder if it's his fiancée checking where he is or maybe it's a business call. It's definitely something very serious if the expression on his face is anything to go by. He's very serious and concerned as he speaks. I wonder if I should mouth a silent goodnight and close the door or wait until he's finished on the phone to say goodnight properly. It's all rather awkward. All I want to do is go back inside and go to bed.

THIRTY-TWO

HEATHER

A sharp, icy draft shakes me awake. I rub my eyes and sit up. I've no idea how long I've been asleep, but my head is pounding and I've a horrible crick in my neck. Charlotte isn't here and at first I assume it's late and she's gone to bed. But as I wake a little more I hear voices outside and I realise the draft is blowing in from the open front door. I peel the warm throw off me and stand up. I shake it out and drape it over the back of the couch. Charlotte must have put it over me. I'm exhausted and all I want to do is flop into bed but I decide I better clean up first. I pick up the two glasses from the coffee table and drag myself towards the kitchen. I don't think Charlotte notices me as I pass behind her. I'm barely able to keep my eyes open as I wash and dry the glasses and put them away, hoping I chose the right cupboard.

Charlotte and the man at the door move to the shelter of the porch as they continue talking. I'm about to make my way upstairs and go to bed when my phone rings. I hurry back into the kitchen and dig around in my handbag, that I've left hanging on the back of the chair.

'Hello.'

'Heather it's Gavin.'

'Oh. Gavin. Hi,' I say, the hairs on the back of my neck standing to attention as I notice the wobble in his voice.

'It's Kay,' he says. I can tell he's holding his breath.

'What's wrong?'

'Her temperature is through the roof. The nurses have been in and out like a yo-yo since you left and now they've called the doctor. They can't seem to get it to come down. Even with paracetamol or whatever those little white tablets they give her are.'

'Oh Jesus.' My chest tightens. 'Is she awake?'

'Sort of. Yeah,' Gavin says. 'She opens her eyes every now and then, but she's floppy and can't really talk. I know she's trying to tell me something. But I don't know what.'

'I'm on my way. On my way right now. I'll be there in less than twenty minutes.'

'Okay. Yeah. Okay,' Gavin's voice is cracking like a needle scratching a record.

'Gavin calm down,' I say. 'Don't let Kayla know you're freaking out. Okay?'

Gavin doesn't reply.

I raise my voice. 'Listen to me. Keep it together. I'm leaving now.'

There's still no reply.

'Gavin. Please. Please keep it together. Don't scare her. I'm begging you.'

'Heather, hurry. Please,' Gavin finally says.

THIRTY-THREE

CHARLOTTE

My new neighbour finishes on the phone almost as abruptly as he answered. 'Sorry. I have to go,' he says, sliding his phone into his pocket as he turns to face me.

'No worries,' I say. 'It's late. Thanks again for your help. And I'll be sure to put some plastic down in the car before I sit in.'

'Good. Good.' He nods.

'Is everything alright?' I ask, sensing his sudden distress.

He shakes his head.

'Do you want to come in?' I ask, hoping he'll say no, but feeling like I should ask, at least.

'Thank you, but I really must get going. It was lovely to meet you, erm...'

'Charlotte,' I say, shaking his extended hand. 'And you too. Great to meet you.'

'Jack,' he says.

'That's four letters.'

'Sorry?' he says, squinting and tilting his head.

'Oh. Erm, Gavin. My husband. He's terrible with names.

He couldn't remember yours. He insisted you had a three-letter name.'

'Oh right. No worries.' He straightens up. 'Well, as I said, I'm Jack. Jack—'

'Jack in-a-hurry,' I say, as if guessing his surname wins me some sort of prize.

Jack snorts. 'Well, Patterson, actually. But everyone who knows me would agree that I'm Jack In-A-Hurry when it comes to work.'

I nod, familiar with the excuse. Gavin uses it all the time.

Jack says something more but I'm distracted by rustling behind me and my attention shifts towards the kitchen and I suspect Heather is awake. The rummaging grows louder and closer. I freeze, knowing Heather will burst through the house at any moment and I'll be forced to explain to yet another neighbour why a woman is living with us.

I'm relieved when Jack steps out from under the porch light. 'Good night, Charlotte, it was lovely to meet you. And, I'm sorry to dash—'

'No worries, Jack,' I say.

Heather comes skidding into the hall as Jack walks away. Her bag is flung over her shoulder and she's trying to get her coat on at the same time as stuffing her phone into her bag. Her hands are shaking so much she can't seem to coordinate them.

'What's going on?' I ask. 'Where are you going?'

'I- I- I have to go to the hospital.' Heather finally manages to get her phone into her bag and when she looks up and her eyes meet mine, my heart skips a beat. There's terror in Heather's eyes and it reaches out to grab me.

'Now?' I ask.

'Gavin called,' Heather says.

'And?' I say, inhaling sharply.

'It's Kayla,' Heather says. 'Her temperature is through the roof.'

'Oh. Oh God,' I say, processing, trying desperately to catch up.

'They've given her medication,' Heather continues.

'Well that's good,' I say, feeling relief wash over me. 'She's probably picked up some sort of bug. You know yourself there's all sorts going at this time of year. Half of Molly's class was out sick last week with the vomiting bug. Try not to worry.'

'Try not to worry.' Heather snorts. 'Would you worry if it was Molly?'

'Heather I didn't mean—'

'I have to go,' Heather cuts across me. 'I shouldn't have left.'

'Gavin is with her,' I say reassuringly. 'She's not on her own.'

Heather's eyes narrow as she stares at me as if I'm something horrible and sticky on the bottom of her shoe. 'I should always be with her,' she says.

'You're right.' I nod. 'You're her mother. I understand, Heather. I do. If it was Molly—'

The anger in Heather's eyes turns to sadness and desperation and my heart breaks for her.

'I- I- I- I have to go,' Heather stutters, charging past me and out the door.

'Heather, you can't drive,' I say, stepping out after her. The icy wind nips at every inch of my skin. 'You've had wine.'

Heather drags her keys out of her bag. 'I need to get to the hospital.'

'I'll call you a cab,' I say.

'A cab?' Heather says. 'How the hell long will that take? I don't have time. I don't have any time.'

'Heather, please,' I say, grabbing her arms, terrified she'll do something stupid.

'Let go!' Heather shouts.

I don't.

'Heather. Heather is that you?' Jack says, turning back from halfway out the gate. 'I thought that was your voice I could hear.'

'Jack, it's Kayla.' Heather begins to cry. 'Something's wrong. The medicine's not working.'

Jack hurries forward placing his hands on Heather's shoulders, steadying her as I let go. 'Okay,' he says calmly. 'Deep breaths. Big deep breaths.'

Heather does as Jack suggests.

'That's it,' he says. 'Nice and calm. That's it.'

I step back into the doorway and watch with trepidation. Heather and Jack clearly know each other but I've no idea how. And now really doesn't seem like the appropriate time to ask. Heather must clearly trust this guy because she's calmed down a lot since he's taken hold of her.

'It's okay,' Jack says, pulling his phone out of his pocket. 'I've just got off the phone with them.'

What? How would he know? I think.

I'm about to intervene when he continues talking. 'I'm on call tonight. I'm going in to check on her, but this kind of thing happens all the time, Heather.'

'It does?' Heather asks.

'Yes. Unfortunately it does. C'mon, I'll give you a lift.'

Realisation sweeps over me like a gentle breeze. Gavin never told me our new neighbour was a doctor. And he certainly never mentioned that Jack is Kayla's doctor. But I guess that's just another thing to add to a long list of stuff Gavin hasn't had a chance to discuss with me since Kayla got sick and Heather moved in.

Heather looks completely lost. 'Um, Charlotte, this is Kayla's doctor.'

'Ah,' I say. 'Heather, take care, okay? Ring me if you need something.'

'Thanks, Charlotte,' she says, turning to leave.

I watch as Heather and Jack walk away and I close the door. Another thunder clap erupts and upstairs I hear Molly.

'Maaammmyyy... Maaammmyyy...'

'I'm coming, Molly. I'm coming,' I call, as I make my way up the stairs.

Loud thunder erupts and the whole staircase illuminates as lightning streaks across the sky and shines through the Velux window. Complete darkness follows as the power to the whole street goes out.

'Oh, you have got to be kidding me.'

I stretch my arms out in front of me, feeling the air all around as I make my way up the remaining steps. I stub my toes on the final one, and by the time I reach Molly's room she's stopped crying but I'm ready to start.

THIRTY-FOUR

CHARLOTTE

I really don't want to light the cinnamon-and-spice candle that I've been saving since last Christmas, but the torch on my phone is draining the battery super fast and Molly and I will be in complete darkness soon.

'I won't be a minute,' I say, peeling myself away from Molly as the two of us lie, arms around each other in her bed.

'I don't like the dark,' Molly says as I stand up.

'I know. I know. Me neither,' I say, wondering where I last hid the matches; I always keep them out of Molly's reach. 'But I'm going to light some candles and then it won't be dark anymore.'

'I want Daddy,' Molly says.

'I know sweetheart, so do I. Here, let's try this,' I say, pressing the light-up love-heart tummy on Molly's Glow Bear. It doesn't have much impact on the dark room, but Molly seems pleased as she gathers the teddy into her arms and cuddles him. 'I'll be back in a minute. I just have to find some matches.'

I hurry down stairs before Molly has time to object.

'Maaammmyyy...'

'Yes. Yes!' I shout back, making my way into the kitchen, the light growing weaker on my phone. 'I'm still here, sweetheart. I'm still here.'

Dammit where are the bloody matches? I think as I rummage in the drawers and swing open cupboards.

'Mammy, I'm scared,' Molly cries loudly. 'Maaammmyyy...'

'Coming. I'm coming,' I call, remembering that Heather smokes. There must be a lighter in her room.

I hurry back up the stairs and pop my head around the door of Molly's room. 'See, darling. I told you I was here. Isn't this a fun game?'

'It's not fun.' Molly sulks.

'Sure it is,' I lie. 'Just like hide and seek.'

'It's. Not. Fun,' Molly repeats as I duck my head out of her room again and hurry across the landing to the guest room.

Curling my fingers around the handle of the closed door feels weird, as if I'm intruding in my own house, and I pause. I know what's on the far side of this door off by heart. I traipsed all over the city when I was seven months pregnant with Molly to find the perfect duvet cover to match the curtains I'd fallen in love with weeks prior. I stripped back the antique chest of drawers and painstakingly re-varnished it. Yet I can't help feeling I shouldn't open this door. Not right now. Suddenly the space on the far side of it feels as if it belongs to Heather and not to me. I shouldn't impose.

'Mr Glow Bear isn't working!' Molly's cry carries across the hall.

Knowing Molly has been plunged into complete darkness, I turn the handle and charge inside the guest bedroom. I make a beeline for the bedside table hoping that's where Heather would keep any spare lighters. I'm right and I'm delighted when I find a black lighter with the Guinness logo printed across the side. I grab the lighter and am turning to leave when I'm distracted by a letter underneath it with Molly's name in italic font on the first line. I shine my phone over the paper for closer inspection. There's a book resting in the centre of the letter, hiding most of the words, but I can clearly see the hospital logo in the top left-hand corner.

I'm lifting the book out of the way when Molly's crying becomes more distressed.

'Mammy, where are you?' Molly cries. 'It's too scary.'

'I'm here, sweetheart,' I shout back.

'Where? I can't see you?'

My eyes sweep the paper. Kayla's treatment. Molly. Donor. Stem cell. *Match!*

'Maaammmyyy.' Molly's crying shifts to a distressed shriek. 'There's a monster. Help. Help.'

I slam the book back down on the letter and march out of the room, not bothering to close the door behind me.

'I'm here, sweetheart,' I say, hurrying into Molly's room. 'I'm here.'

'Quick. Quick, Mammy,' Molly says. 'He's under my bed.'

'There's no monster, Molly,' I say, the battery on my phone finally giving up.

Molly gulps. 'He's here. See, I told you.' She can barely draw breath between her sobs. 'I want Daddy.'

'Okay. C'mon,' I say, feeling my way to Molly's bed in the darkness.

I feel the mattress against my leg and I pat my way along the edge, shuffling forward. I smile instinctively when Molly's chubby arms reach out to me and I guide them around my neck as I lift her out of bed.

'I'm here, Molly,' I whisper. 'I'm always here.'

I pull my little girl close to me and I can feel her rushed breath and rapid heartbeat.

'I don't like it,' Molly says, tucking her head into the crook of my neck, guided by instinct.

I clutch the Guinness lighter tight in my fist and I can't stop thinking about why Heather has a letter with my daughter's name on it hidden in her room. I march towards the bathroom with blind determination, with Molly still cradled in my arms, and seek out the three-wick candle on the windowsill and light it.

'Look, Molly,' I say, drawing her attention to the burning light. 'There are definitely no monsters here.'

'When is Daddy coming back?' Molly whimpers, not lifting her head off my shoulder and holding me extra tightly.

Molly's words cut me like a knife. *Coming back?* Gavin hasn't left us. He comes home every night. He kisses and hugs her in her sleep. But Molly has no idea. To Molly, Daddy's been gone a long time. My heart aches.

'Do you want to sleep in my bed tonight?' I ask.

'Are you scared of monsters, too?' Molly asks, finally lifting her head.

'Yeah,' I nod. 'I guess I am.'

'Okay.' Molly pats the top of my head with both her hands in turn. 'I'll sleep in your bed. You don't need to be scared, Mammy. You have me.'

'I do, Molly, don't I?' I say, suddenly overwhelmed by the thought of not having her. The thought Heather must face every day.

THIRTY-FIVE

CHARLOTTE

It's only November but the smell of Christmas hangs in the air as the rustle of a key turning in the front door rouses me. I haven't fallen fully asleep since Molly climbed into my bed. The front door creaks open and I listen without opening my eyes. The sound of the door closing followed by Gavin's familiar footfall downstairs helps me to relax. I hadn't realised being alone with Molly in the darkness was bothering me so much until just now. I open my eyes and untangle myself from Molly's sleeping grip and roll out of bed. The cold of the timber floor drives into the soles of my feet instantly and I skip my way across the room. I fetch my dressing gown, which is hanging on the back of the door, and quickly slide in my shivering arms and tie the belt around my waist. With a deep breath I leave my room.

'Hey,' I say, meeting Gavin as I step off the bottom step of the stairs. 'Is Kayla okay? What happened?'

'Hey,' Gavin says, holding a pint glass full of water in his hand. 'She has a kidney infection. They've started her on antibiotics. She was really distressed and scared but she calmed down when Heather came back.'

I sigh, relieved, and a weight I didn't realise I was carrying lifts.

'We've no power,' Gavin says.

'Eh, yeah,' I say. 'It's been out for ages. And Molly is afraid of the dark.'

'What are Electric Ireland saying?' Gavin asks. 'When will it be back?'

'I dunno. I didn't call them.'

'Why didn't you call?'

I close my eyes and inhale. I want to explain that I had too much on my mind. I want to tell Gavin I was worried about Kayla. And tell him about Heather falling asleep on the couch. I need to tell him I miss him and can't sleep without him. Most of all, I want to ask Gavin if he knows anything about the letter in Heather's room. But I find myself frustrated instead and I turn on the bottom step and make my way back up the stairs without another word to my husband.

Upstairs I wrestle with Molly's floppy, sleeping body as I lift her up and cautiously cross the landing to tuck her into her own bed. I'm exhausted by the time I feel my way back to my room and flop into the sheets.

Cold and exhausted, I lie awake for ages listening to Gavin walk about downstairs wondering what he's doing in the darkness. Finally, I hear him creep up the stairs, making an effort to be quiet, obviously assuming both Molly and I are sleeping.

'Can you blow out the candle in the bathroom?' I say, when I think he's close enough to be in earshot of our room. The darkness doesn't seem so bad now, with Gavin here to share it.

'Did I wake you?' he says, ignoring my request to quench the candle as he walks into our room, the torch on his phone blinding me as he shines it towards the bed.

'Nope,' I say. 'I haven't been asleep yet.'

'But it's late...'

I roll out of bed as Gavin begins to undress. I scurry across the dark landing, into the bathroom, and puff out the glorious-smelling candle. I'm plunged into complete darkness as Gavin's and my bedroom door swings closed. *For goodness' sake.* I slow down, stretch my arms out in front of me and feel my way back to the bedroom.

Moments later, when Gavin and I are both in bed, back to back, I allow my thoughts to wander to the letter in Heather's room and what the hell it means.

It doesn't take long for Gavin's familiar gentle snores to rustle through the air. I pull the duvet up close to my neck and drift off to sleep. But seconds later Molly is crying and afraid again.

'Gavin,' I say, placing my hand on his shoulder. 'I think Molly is awake.'

'Hmm?'

'Can you go check on her?'

'Can you?' Gavin sighs, barely awake. 'I'm so sleepy.'

'Gavin she misses you. She hasn't seen you in days. I know she'd love a hug.'

'Tomorrow,' Gavin whispers. 'I'll see her tomorrow.'

I exhale, exhausted, and throw the duvet back on my side. I'm just about to stand up when the lights all come back on and the house is painfully bright for this time of night. Molly appears at our bedroom door, dangling a teddy by her side.

'Daddy,' she squeals, noticing Gavin asleep beside me.

'Hey, princess,' Gavin says, sounding drunk his words are laced with so much sleep. 'C'mere.'

Gavin lifts the duvet on his side and Molly hurries into our room, around the end of the bed and climbs in beside her father. Gavin's arms wrap around her and he shuffles into the middle until he's touching me too. Tucked between us both he sighs and says, 'Goodnight.'

Finally, all three of us together in bed I close my eyes. I think all the lights are on downstairs, but I'm too content to move and I fall asleep within seconds.

THIRTY-SIX

CHARLOTTE

The next day

'Daddy, daddy,' Molly says, shaking Gavin awake. 'It's morning time.'

'No, Molly.' Gavin grunts, reaching for the duvet to tuck it closer to his neck. 'It's not morning.'

'Yes it is!' Molly insists, struggling to get out of our bed, which is much higher than hers. I watch sleepily as she reaches for the curtains and tugs, sliding them back a fraction. 'See' – she points – 'It's all morning outside.'

I cover my eyes with my hands, the sudden burst of sunlight blinding me. 'Oh God. What time is it?'

'Oh for God's sake, Molly, it's only half six...' Gavin says, no doubt checking his phone.

'And it's Saturday,' I say, waking a little more. 'Molly let go of the curtain. You'll tear the hook and eyelets.'

Molly giggles. 'Curtains don't have eyes. You're so silly, Mammy.'

'C'mon, Molly,' I croak, getting up, exhausted. 'I'll put some cartoons on downstairs for you.'

'And make a dippy egg?' Molly suggests, rubbing her tummy so I know she's hungry.

'Later, Molly,' I say, barely able to function. 'Let's just watch cartoons first. We can have an egg later.'

Gavin sits up and rubs his eyes. 'You know what? Eggs would actually be great. I didn't get any dinner last night.'

'Mammy and me eated fajitas last night,' Molly says, rubbing her tummy some more. 'They were yummy.'

'I'll come down with you,' Gavin says, throwing back the duvet. 'I can make us omelettes.'

'Yay! Yay! Yay!' Molly jumps up and down and I wish I had a fraction of her energy at this time of day.

'No. Wait here. We need to talk,' I say to Gavin.

'Is everything okay?' he asks.

'No. Not really,' I say, trying to hide how pissed off I am in front of Molly.

'Do you not like omelettes?' Molly asks. 'We can have dippy eggs. And then you can be happy.'

'Later, Molly,' I say, taking her hand. 'It's just cartoons now. Eggs later.'

'Do curtains really have eyes, Mammy?' Molly asks as we're walking down the stairs.

'What?' I laugh. 'No, Molly. Of course they don't.'

'But you said...'

'I suppose curtains do have eyes, Molly. But they are called "eyelets" and it's what the rail goes through.'

'Eye-lights,' says Molly slowly, and I ruffle her hair.

I open the sitting-room door to find the lights and TV on.

'It's magic,' Molly says, and I don't tell her otherwise.

'Oh, look,' I say. '*Peppa Pig* is on.'

'Yuck.' Molly scrunches her nose. 'Sam says *Peppa Pig* is for babies.'

'You are a baby, Molly,' I sigh.

'I. Am. Four!'

'Okay, Molly. Okay. You're four. And not a baby,' I try not to laugh. 'So, what do you want to watch?'

Molly doesn't answer for a moment. Peppa is jumping in muddy puddles and Molly can't seem to pull her eyes away from the screen.

'Sam said *Peppa Pig* is for babies,' Molly says again, obviously sad as she shakes her head.

'This Sam little shit again?' I say.

Molly gasps and pulls her eyes away from the screen to stare at me with her mouth open.

'Sorry,' I say quickly, trying not to wince as I study Molly's horrified expression. 'I just don't think Sam is a very good little boy. He doesn't get to tell you what you can and can't watch, Molly. Or what colour blocks you can play with. Or anything like that.' I can feel myself grow crosser just thinking about this kid.

'Do you want to watch *Peppa Pig*?' I ask.

Molly nods.

'Right, good,' I say. 'Hop up on the couch and stay here for a while. I need to go back upstairs and talk to Daddy.'

'And then is it dippy egg time?' Molly asks.

'Yes,' I nod. 'After I talk to Daddy we'll all have yummy dippy eggs, all of us together.'

It doesn't take long before Molly is engrossed in TV and I go back upstairs.

I find Gavin asleep again but this conversation can't wait until later. I slam the bedroom door behind me and stare at the bed, waiting.

'Jesus,' Gavin grumbles, his eyes opening slowly.

'We need to talk.'

'Later, Charlie, please? I'm so tired.'

'I'm tired too.' I fold my arms.

'I know.' He closes his eyes again. 'Come back to bed.' Gavin pulls the duvet around him and turns his back.

'Are you kidding me?' I shout.

'Charlie. What?' Gavin throws back the duvet, clearly pissed off as he sits up. 'It's barely morning. Will you calm down.'

'Don't you bloody tell me to calm down, Gavin. Just don't.'

'Charlie, come on.'

'When were you going to tell me, Gavin, huh? Huh?' I shout louder. 'Were you ever going to tell me? Or did you think I wouldn't notice when you and Heather started using our daughter for spare parts?'

'That's a horrible thing to say.' Gavin's eyes darken and I can't tell if he's angry or upset.

'That's not an answer.' I shake my head as I turn my back. I can't even look at him right now.

'Charlie,' Gavin calls after me as I open the door. 'Charlie, c'mon,' he shouts, reaching our bedroom door as I walk down the stairs. 'You're the one who said you wanted to talk and now you're walking away.'

'Don't you dare try to turn this on me,' I shout back. 'Just go back to bed, Gavin. I don't want to be anywhere near you.'

Fighting back tears I return to the sitting room. 'It's dippy-egg time, Molly.' I'm surprised to find an empty couch. 'Molly,' I call, walking towards the kitchen. 'Molly!'

She's not in the kitchen either. I'm about to check her bedroom when I hear gentle whimpering coming from the larder cupboard. I open the door to find her sitting between the sweeping brush and the ironing board. Her knees are tucked into her chest and her little hands are covering her eyes.

'Oh, Molly.'

THIRTY-SEVEN

KAYLA

It's hard to wake up. I blink a lot. I'm not sure if it's morning or night. Napping during the day and then being awake for hours at night staring at the ceiling is messing with my sense of time. Finally, I manage to keep my eyes open and I realise it's bright outside. There's a tray of breakfast on the end of my bed. Someone has come and left cornflakes, orange juice and a bowl of shrivelled-looking fruit. I'm surprised I didn't hear them come in. Usually the noise in this place around breakfast time would deafen you, but I've been sleeping right through the last few mornings. And I still wake up tired. I'm constantly tired the last few days.

'Morning,' Mam says.

'Jesus.' I jump, suddenly noticing her slouched in the chair next to my bed.

'Sorry, sorry, didn't mean to scare you.'

'Were you here all night?' I ask.

Mam nods. 'Yup.'

'Did you sleep?' I add.

'Of course.'

Mam is the worst liar. Her eyes go all squinty, as if she's

afraid you'll look into them and call her bluff. To be fair, all of
her looks squinty today. As if her whole body is closing in on
itself. It's bloody creepy. She's so skinny. Like, weirdly thin. I
can't remember the last time she wore make-up and her hair is
in bits. The roots are shocking, and I don't think I ever noticed
she has such dark hair before. She's been blonde all my life but
there's a big chunk of black-brown sitting on the top of her
head now.

'How are you feeling?' Mam says, standing up and pouring
some milk onto my cornflakes.

'Okay,' I say.

'You gave us a bit of a fright last night.'

'I did?'

'Don't you remember?'

I shake my head.

'Your temperature was sky high and you were passing out
and shaking and...'

'Oh,' I say, slowly remembering some madness last night,
but it feels like a dream. I remember dad freaking out and
calling the nurses. And then the nurses getting panicked and
calling the doctors. They gave me some medicine and I thought
I fell asleep after that. I don't remember Mam getting here, or
Dad leaving. What a weird night.

'Orange juice?' Mam says, dragging the trolley-table thing
from the end of my bed closer to me.

I shake my head.

'Okay, okay.' Mam sounds weirdly disappointed that I don't
fancy juice two seconds after waking up.

I try to sit up but it's so hard. My arms are insanely heavy;
as if they belong to someone else and I can't really control them.
My breathing feels a bit funny too, like someone really big is
sitting on me. Squashing me.

'Okay, let's take it easy,' Mam says, sliding her hands under
my arms. She puffs out as she hoists me up.

'I'm sorry,' I say.

'What? What on earth are you sorry for, kiddo?' Mam says, letting go of me to adjust the pillows behind me.

I'm wobbly, trying to sit by myself for a few seconds. Mam places her hand on my shoulder and eases me back. When I'm supported by a mound of soft, fluffy pillows I realise how uncomfortable I've been all night.

'Just for everything,' I say.

'Listen to me, Kayla.' Mam suddenly becomes very serious and I think she's about to cry. I wait for her to excuse herself for a second. She thinks I don't notice when she goes outside the door to take some deep breaths or dry her eyes.

'None of this is your fault. None of it.'

I want to believe Mam but I know it *is* my fault. If I'd just told Mam when my leg first started hurting last year my cancer wouldn't have spread and I'd probably be better by now like some of the other kids here. But I was so obsessed with basketball. I didn't want to miss a single game. *Look at me now. I'll never play a game again.* And I'm starting to worry I might never even leave this room.

'Some water?' Mam asks.

'I'm not really thirsty,' I say, my eyelids starting to droop. I think I'm ready to go back to sleep.

'Kayla, you really need to drink something.'

I pull a face.

'You heard what the doctors said last night.'

I stare at Mam blankly. I don't remember the doctors coming in and I definitely don't remember them saying, '*If she doesn't drink orange juice, she has to drink water.*'

Mam stops fidgeting and sits down again, taking my hand. She squeezes it gently.

'What did the doctors say last night?' I ask, not sure I really want to know.

'Ah, you know, this and that.'

'Mam. Please?'

'It's the chemo,' Mam's voice crackles. 'The doctors aren't happy with how it's working. It's making you really sick...'

'Chemo makes everyone sick,' I say, pausing to take some breaths as if I'm puffed out after scoring five baskets. 'Sean threw his guts up in the games room a few days ago. It's was so gross. All bile and carrots—'

'Kayla...'

'Why are there always carrots in puke? Like, always. Even if you haven't eaten carrots in ages, I just don't get it—'

'Kayla,' Mam repeats, gently.

I finally look up at Mam and her eyes are so serious and teary.

'Kayla your kidneys are struggling,' she finally says.

'And...?' I ask, not really that surprised. The other kids in the games room talk about stuff like this all the time. Everyone is affected in different ways. Everyone loses their hair like me, obviously, but one of the girls on the ward had blonde hair all her life but when it started to grow back after chemo it was black and curly. I thought it was nice but she was completely freaking out. And one of the younger kids is so skinny I'm afraid to touch her but she's always so smiley and running around with lots of energy. I guess wonky kidneys is going to be my thing. I wonder if that means I'll have to pee more, or maybe my pee will change colour – that would be weirdly cool. Maybe I should bring Mam down to meet some of the other kids. I'm sure they wouldn't mind talking to her about how their treatment is going. It might help her to understand and freak out a bit less.

'Kayla,' Mam says again and I realise I've zoned out trying to think of everyone's chemo schedule today and wondering who'll be in the games room later for a game of Fortnite. I still haven't got a win and it's bloody mortifying. There're six-year-olds kicking my arse for God's sake.

'Kayla, sweetheart, the doctor's want to stop the chemo,' Mam whispers.

'Oh my God, really?' I say, suddenly more energetic than I have been in days. 'Really? Really?'

Mam shakes her head.

'What?' I ask. 'This is good news. I mean chemo is over. I think we can deal with all the kidney stuff as an outpatient. The girl with the blonde-now-black hair only comes in once a week or something like that now.'

Mam's face is blank.

'It means we can go home soon, right?' I ask, scared that the doctors are talking to Mam about serious stuff and leaving me out of the conversation. *It's always bad when they leave me out of the conversation.*

Mam is as still as a statue. The only thing moving are her eyes as she blinks.

'Home to Cork, Mam. I know it's been weird for you staying with Dad...'

Tears start streaming down Mam's cheeks. 'There're trials, Kayla. We can try trials.'

'Trials?'

'Yes. It's complicated.' Mam sweeps the tips of her fingers under her eyes. 'It's new stuff; cutting edge. Not every patient is even eligible, Kayla.'

I didn't realise I was crying but tears are running down my cheeks now too. 'Mam, I don't understand. I thought you meant I was done with chemo because it had worked. I want to go home.'

'Sweetheart, we have to keep trying. These clinical trials—'

'I don't want to be part of some experiment,' I say, frustrated.

'They're not experiments, they're scientific advances. I'm meeting Doctor Patterson today.' Mam looks at her watch. 'In an hour. And I'm going to ask him all about it. I'll know more then and we can talk about it, okay?'

'Whatever.' I flop my head back, way too exhausted to think about any of this anymore.

'Kayla. You will get better. Okay?' Mam says.

'I know,' I say, and I wonder if I suck at lying as much as Mam does. If I was going to get better, we'd be packing our cases now that chemo is over. Not talking about other options that mean more needles, more blood transfusions, more operations, more hell. And it might not even work. Suddenly, I realise that Fortnite isn't the only battle I'm not winning.

THIRTY-EIGHT

HEATHER

'Shh, she's asleep,' I say, as Gavin comes into Kayla's room.

Gavin looks as bad as I feel. 'How is she?' he asks.

'Better than last night but still not great.'

Gavin shakes his head as he watches our sleeping daughter.

'Did you talk to Charlotte?' I ask.

Gavin doesn't answer as he continues to watch Kayla. He's jumpy and agitated and I know the answer, but I ask again anyway.

'Gavin? Please tell me you at least tried to bring it up with her?'

'She brought it up with me, actually.' Gavin sounds annoyed and I'm not sure if his frustrations are directed towards me or at Charlotte.

'Really?'

'Yeah.' Gavin shoves his hands into his pockets and shuffles on the spot. 'She found a letter. One explaining all the donor stuff.'

'Oh.' I'm almost certain I put that letter away in my room. Maybe it fell out of my bag in the kitchen or something. I need to be more careful. It must be the tiredness.

'She's not happy,' Gavin says.

'About the letter?'

Gavin shuffles, awkwardly. 'About us not telling her. Not telling her sooner that stem-cell donation might be an option.'

I shake my head. 'Yeah, okay. Fair enough. But we didn't even know until last night whether any of this was going to be necessary.'

'I thought I was doing the right thing,' Gavin says, dragging his hands around his face. 'I didn't want to stress her out unnecessarily over something that might never even happen.'

'Well, now that it is happening what has she said?'

'We didn't actually talk about it,' Gavin says. 'Not properly.'

'What?' My hands slam onto my hips. 'Why not?'

'Because, Heather, it's not that simple. This is a messed-up situation. And Charlotte is scared. And now that she thinks I've been hiding stuff from her she's completely freaked out and doesn't trust me. And she definitely doesn't trust you.'

'So, you had a fight?' I say, worried that Gavin is putting a silly row with his wife over something as important as Kayla's treatment. It's almost as if he doesn't know how serious this is. Or as if he doesn't *want* to know.

'Eh, it's a bit more than a fight, Heather,' Gavin snaps. 'It's not as if she's annoyed with me for leaving the toilet seat up, you know.'

'You're acting like a child,' I say, pretty annoyed by Gavin's snarky attitude.

'Heather, I will talk to my wife. But you need to calm down and stop pushing so hard. The time has to be right.'

'Jesus. Gavin, how can you be so calm? Will Charlotte sign the consent form or not? I can bring the forms home with me. She doesn't even have to come into the hospital if she doesn't want to. But we need her consent.'

Gavin looks at me with teary eyes and it's the first time I

notice how bloodshot they are. I wonder if he got any sleep at all last night.

'Call her,' I say, softening. 'Ask her now. Or, I can ask her if you want to avoid another row.'

'No. Jesus no. Are you mad?' Gavin says, and I immediately shift my glance towards Kayla, worried that he'll wake her. 'Charlotte would lose her mind all together if you jump in.'

'But I can explain.'

'Heather, no.' Gavin's eyes widen and round like saucers. 'It's not your place. Molly is Charlotte's daughter. Mine and Charlotte's. This really is nothing to do with you.'

'Nothing to do with me? Are you for real?' I hiss. 'Look at her, Gavin. Just look at her.'

Gavin's eyes swell with tears as they sweep over our sleeping daughter tucked into her hospital bed.

'Tell me again how this has nothing to do with me.'

'This is so hard.' Gavin sighs. 'It's too hard.'

'Gavin, sit down,' I say, pointing to the chair beside me, noticing how pale he's suddenly become. I'm worried that he's going to keel over.

'I know it's hard,' I say, but I'm lying. I can't understand why Gavin is so reluctant to talk to Charlotte about this. I can't understand how he's not ecstatic that Kayla and Molly are a match. Molly's stem cells could save Kayla's life. It's fantastic news.

'I have to go into work for a few hours today,' Gavin says, dragging shaking hands through his hair.

'What? Now? But you only just got here.' My eyes narrow, suspecting this is an excuse to put off going home and talking to Charlotte.

'The place is falling to pieces without me. We've lost two big clients already this month. I need to be more present.' Gavin pauses and drops his head into his hands. 'But I need to be here too.'

'I know,' I say, and this time I really do understand. My life before Kayla's diagnosis seems like a lifetime ago already. I exist now only as a mother of a sick child. I'm not a person in my own right anymore, I don't have the time or inclination to be.

It's taken me quite a while to realise that I'm lonely. Kayla is spending more and more time sleeping and I miss our chats and *Friends* binges. When I'm at Gavin's place I usually hang out in my room, trying to give Charlotte her space and not invade her privacy. My friends at work who were so supportive when Kayla was first diagnosed only call or text now when they realise they haven't in quite a while and their moral compass compels them to check in. One of the girls told me last week that someone new has been hired to fill my role and our boss loves her, so goodness knows if my job is even there to go back to when the time comes.

It's a similar story with Kayla's school. The teachers called and offered support initially. They even held a fundraiser and donated the funds to the National Cancer Organisation in Kayla's name. But as days and weeks drag on, life continues for everyone else as normal while we're stuck in this never-ending loop of treatment and surgeries and ups and downs. And despite my best intentions, I can feel myself growing bitter and jealous.

I'm jealous for Kayla. Jealous of her teammates continuing to play basketball without her. Jealous when Kayla shows me photos on Instagram of her friends out shopping or going to the cinema or simply being normal, healthy teenagers.

I'm jealous for me. Jealous of the girls in work chatting and gossiping over morning coffee. I'm jealous of their friendship with my replacement. I'm jealous of their financial stability, bonuses and day-to-day routine.

But mostly I'm jealous of Gavin. I'm jealous that although he's here as much as he can be, he goes home to a healthy, happy child. A child he can hug without worrying he will hurt her delicate bones. A child he can watch eat a meal without fear that everything is going to come back up. A child he can play with, run with, skip with. And mostly, a child he can watch grow, become a woman, maybe get married and have children of her own. In recent days, as I watch Kayla lose even more weight, I worry that all of those things will be snatched from her. From me.

'Will you tell here I was here?' Gavin asks, cutting into my burning thoughts.

'Yeah,' I say. 'I'm not expecting her to wake for a while. They've given her some pretty strong meds.'

'Okay, well, I'll only be a couple of hours and—'

'And then you'll talk to Charlotte,' I cut across him, seizing the opportunity to try again.

'You know I want Kayla to get better more than anything in the world,' Gavin says.

'Prove it,' I say, resenting him for feeling the need to tell me that. Of course, I know how much he wants our daughter to be well again.

'Molly is four, Heather. She is four years old,' Gavin says.

'I do know how old your little girl is, Gavin.'

Gavin takes a deep breath and stands up. He lifts his hand out of his pocket to place it on my shoulder. 'You're an amazing mother, Heather. You always have been. I know you would do anything for Kayla. Anything at all to help her.'

I nod, a little thrown by his sudden change of direction and calmness.

'Well, Charlotte is an amazing mother, too. She adores our little girl and she will stop at nothing to protect her. Do you understand?'

I nod again, and I can't find words. Fear settles into the pit of my stomach as I begin to worry that Gavin is trying to tell me that he won't talk to Charlotte about this, or worse still that if he does she'll say no.

'This is hard for her, Heather. Charlotte loves Kayla. She loves her as if she were her own. But the honest truth is that she's not and Molly is.'

'So, what are you saying?'

'I'm saying, give me some time. Let me talk to her when she's calmer. Less upset. Less afraid for Molly and how traumatic all this could be for her.'

'But we don't have time,' I say, tears gathering in the corners of my eyes. 'They want to stop the chemo, Gavin.'

'They what?' Gavin's voice is suddenly too loud for the confined space. 'Why didn't you tell me?'

'Shh,' I say, pressing my finger against my lip, worried Gavin will wake Kayla. 'I'm telling you now.'

Gavin looks at our sleeping daughter and shakes his head. 'You know what? It doesn't matter. They can't stop chemo. We'll tell them they can't do that. It's madness.'

'Gavin, her kidneys are failing.' The look of disbelief on Gavin's face cuts through me. 'And... And...' I pause and try to catch my breath, as if just trying to say the next words out loud is choking me. 'And they've found another growth.'

Gavin sniffles and drags his arm across his teary eyes. 'Where?'

'Her pelvis. It's only small, but it's new and...'

Gavin makes a sound like an animal caught in a trap. I know this sound. I make it too. Sometimes just inside my own head when I can't bear to watch Kayla go through any more. But I push the noise deep down and don't let it out because Kayla is leaning on me and I have to be strong.

'Is it... is it spreading? Gavin asks.

I don't reply. I can't form words.

'Does Kayla know?' he asks.

I shake my head.

'Good. Good. We don't want to scare her.' Gavin picks up his coat off the chair and slides in his shaking arms.

'You're going?' I say.

'I have to.'

'Right. Yeah. Work,' I say, unable to believe work is even coming into his head right now.

'I'm going home,' Gavin says. 'To talk to Charlotte.'

THIRTY-NINE

HEATHER

The door to Jack's office is slightly ajar and I can see him through the gap, sitting at his desk writing. He looks stressed out. I can only imagine how difficult his job must be. I don't think I could ever work here. I take a deep breath, raise my hand and knock three times.

'C'mon in,' he says, casually.

I push the door back and step inside, unsure whether to close it or not behind me. Maybe he likes it left a fraction open for some fresh air. I think I'd like it to be. I decide to leave it open.

'Hi, Heather,' he says, dropping his pen on his desk and standing up.

He's not wearing his usual white coat over scrubs and he has a tie around his neck today instead of a stethoscope. His tailored navy suit is a stark contrast to the running gear he wore last night. He's dapper.

'Have a seat,' he suggests, pointing to two large leather chairs waiting at the far side of his desk.

I nod and sit into the nearest one as he walks out from behind his desk to close the door.

'Thank you again for the lift last night,' I say, the brief silence making me anxious.

'No problem,' he says, coming back to take his seat at the opposite side of the desk. 'Drink?' he asks. 'Tea, coffee, glass of water?'

'Um, no,' I say, looking around his office. There's no coffee machine or even a kettle. There's a bottle of unopened Lucozade on top of the cabinet behind his desk but I doubt he wants to split it. 'Thank you, but I'm fine.'

'You sure? I'm having a coffee.'

'I'm sure.'

'Okay,' he says and reaches forward to press a button on his desk phone. 'Hi, Matilda. Could you grab me an americano and a muffin when you get a moment please? Actually on second thought...' He pauses, and his eyes shift from his desk to find mine. 'You didn't get a chance to bake yesterday, did you?'

I shake my head and he smiles, understandingly.

'Matilda, make that just a coffee today, please.'

'What?' A women's voice carries over his loudspeaker. 'But you love the muffins in the canteen.'

'I do,' he says. 'But just a coffee today. Can you get two, actually? Thank you.' He smiles at me. 'Just in case you change your mind.'

'I'm sorry,' I say, not really sure why. 'Hopefully I'll have time to bake a double batch later. Kayla is so much better today.'

Jack's jaw twitches but he doesn't contradict me. I look around his office some more. His running gear is folded neatly on a suede armchair that sits under the window. There's another energy drink next to his clothes, only that bottle is empty.

'You didn't go home last night,' I say, and I hate that it comes out accusatory.

'I wanted to be nearby,' he says.

'In case she took another turn?' I ask.

'That armchair is surprisingly comfortable,' he says, avoiding my question. 'I think I spend more time asleep there than I do in bed.'

'Really?' I say. 'It looks kind of stiff and firm.'

'Yeah okay. You're right,' he agrees. 'It's awful and uncomfortable. But I do catch a few Zs there. Quite a lot. It keeps my colleagues in osteopathy in business. My back is in bits.'

I know how he feels. My lower back has never been so sore. Every time I wake up in that horrible plastic chair next to Kayla my butt cheeks are numb and my back is knotted like a pretzel.

'I'm sorry,' I say, feeling somehow responsible. 'But thank you, I know you stayed to keep an eye on her. I really appreciate it.'

'She's a great kid,' he says.

'Yeah.' I nod. 'She is. She's also full of questions.'

'Oh,' Jack says, clearly concerned as his eyebrows crinkle. 'Is there something she's worried about? Or something confusing her? I do my best to make sure I explain everything that's happening to all the kids. I don't want Kayla to ever be scared. And kids get scared when they don't understand or feel we're keeping things from them. Is there something I can help explain?'

'About her treatment,' I say. 'Or, more, why it's stopping.'

'Oh.' Jack sighs. 'Her treatment isn't stopping. Where did she get that idea from?'

'No. I mean her chemo is stopping.'

There's a knock on the door, interrupting us, and a middle-aged woman comes in with a grey paper tray cradling two take-away cups of coffee with steam swirling out the small holes in the lids.

'Ah, lovely. Thank you, Matilda,' Jack says as she sets the coffee down on his desk.

'And no muffin.' Matilda sounds disappointed.

'No,' Jack says. 'Not today. Thank you, Matilda. Would you mind closing the door on your way out, please?'

'Of course,' Matilda says, leaving.

The door closes with a gentle click and I feel overwhelmed again now Jack and I are alone. It's such a strange feeling, I can't quite put my finger on it.

'My first cup today,' Jack says, taking both coffees out of the paper tray. He places one in the centre of his desk, right between us, and he sits back in his chair cradling the other between both hands. 'You're really not going to make me drink this alone, are you?'

The delicious smell of thick, black coffee wafts towards me and my mouth waters. 'Okay,' I say, reaching for the cup. 'It does smell great.'

'I drink way too much of this stuff,' he admits, taking a sip. 'But if there's one thing working here has taught me, it's to enjoy the little things.'

I try not to let his words make me cry. I attempt to slip the lid off my cup to look inside, but it's finicky. And the flimsy paper cup is so hot it's hard to hold without burning my fingertips.

'It's just black,' Jack says. 'I don't take milk.'

'Oh, great' I say, giving up on the lid.

'Kayla told me you're lactose intolerant.'

'She did?' I wonder why. And when.

'She talks about you all the time,' Jack says, a warm smile lighting up his face as he enjoys the rich taste of coffee.

'She does?' I say, not entirely surprised. I talk about her all the time too.

'You're really close,' Jack says.

'Yeah.' I raise the cup to my lips and take a mouthful, only realising how exhausted I am as the warmth works its way towards my belly. 'It's just the two of us usually, so you know, it's nice.'

'Heather, you know that I am going to do everything I can for as long as I can to help Kayla, don't you?'

'I know,' I say, sipping more coffee.

'Would it help if I talked to Kayla? The three of us could have a chat this afternoon, maybe. I don't want to get ahead of ourselves scaring her with big intimidating medical terms. But maybe I could answer some of her questions, and yours, and put her mind at ease.'

'That would be great,' I say, but don't you need to get home? 'You've been here all night. You must be exhausted.'

'Don't worry about me. Let's just make sure Kayla is okay, yeah?'

'Thank you,' I say, feeling lighter than I have in days.

'Actually, there was something else I was hoping to talk to you about today.'

'There was?'

'Yeah.' He nods, suddenly seeming unsure and I can feel my new-found confidence fading fast. 'There's a ball on next week. It's a fancy dinner and speeches. It can be horrendously boring, I'm not going to lie, but there's dancing after and the wine is great. I was hoping you might be my guest.'

'Me?' I almost spit coffee across his desk.

'And Kayla too of course,' he adds, quickly.

'Oh.' I blush, realising I misread him.

'Every year a couple of patients give a speech. About their treatment, their experience in the hospital. I thought Kayla might like to do it. I've heard her chatting with some of the other kids in the games room. She's so kind and compassionate. And the nurses adore her. I can't think of anyone better to speak.'

'Wow that's... that's huge.'

'I wanted to ask you, of course, before I made any suggestion to Kayla.'

'Thank you. Wow. Yes. That would be fantastic. I mean, if

she's up for it. I'll have to talk to her about it and see if she's comfortable.'

'Of course,' he says. 'I thought maybe I could come up to the ward in an hour or so and we could ask her together.'

'Yes. Great,' I take another mouthful of coffee, it suddenly tastes better than ever. 'That would be great.'

Jack places his coffee cup on the table and stands up. I do the same, except I keep my coffee with me. It's just about the only thing keeping me awake right now. We walk to the door together.

'Okay, well I'll speak to you again soon,' Jack says and I'm probably reading too much into it but I think he sounds nervous. I wonder if he thinks Kayla might say no.

He stretches his arm out to me and I switch my coffee from my right into my left hand so we can shake. Jack leans forward as our hands connect and I do the same. I think it's odd that he's going to kiss my cheek goodbye as if we're French or terribly posh. But I don't want to be rude and just walk away, and we're still shaking hands. However, we're misaligned as we lean in, and instead of catching my cheek, Jack's lips press onto mine. It's mortifying, and he's not really kissing me. We're just standing still with our lips together and I realise that his hand is on the door handle behind me. Jack wasn't leaning in to kiss my cheek, he was leaning in to open the door. *Oh my God.*

'Gosh, I'm so sorry.' Jack rubs the back of his neck, cracking his head from side to side with an audible pop. 'That was awkward. I hope I haven't embarrassed you.'

'No. No, it's fine,' I say, mortified.

'I can only apologise,' Jack says, as if it's not equally our fault.

'Perhaps the ball isn't such a good idea after all,' I say, not sure what the bubbles popping in my tummy right now mean. I think I haven't been kissed in so long that feeling Jack's lips on mine, accident or not, felt like something special.

'Okay,' Jack says. Disappointment is written all over his face. 'I understand. I'm sorry you feel that way. But I respect your decision.'

'And don't say anything to Kayla,' I add. 'Please? She'll read way too much into this. You know what kids are like.'

'Of course.' Jack frowns and I know I've insulted him by even suggesting that he might talk to Kayla about this. Part of me is desperate to leave. But another part wishes everything could be different and I could stay, maybe even kiss him for real. 'I don't think we need to discuss anything further today, okay?'

'But, Kayla's questions,' Jack says.

'Not today. I've got to get back to Kayla now,' I say and I pull back the door dramatically and throw my half-full cup of coffee into the bin that's waiting on the far side.

'Bye. Goodbye,' Matilda chirps as I pass.

'Bye,' I say.

I can feel Matilda's eyes on me as I walk away and Jack is possibly watching too. I'm walking so fast my hips waddle uncomfortably as I round the corner and come to a sudden stop. Out of view I press my hand against the wall and bend in the middle to catch my breath, unable to believe exactly what just happened.

FORTY

KAYLA

November

'Oh my God, you stink,' Aiden says, holding his nose as he tries not to laugh.

'Do I?' I ask genuinely.

Aiden nods.

'Sorry. I forgot you were coming,' I say, lifting my shaky arm over my head to try to sneak a cheeky sniff. *It's not that bad,* I decide.

'Today is Tuesday,' Aiden says, much more horrified that I wasn't expecting him than by the fact that I just measured my body hygiene by inhaling a whiff of my underarm.

Aiden comes to visit every Tuesday without fail. And not just because he has double Irish on a Tuesday morning and I know he'd trade his signed Messi jersey to get out of class, but because it's become our routine. Mam doesn't even ask if he has his mother's permission to be here anymore. I think both our mothers came to a realisation a few weeks into my treatment that there wasn't any punishment they could threaten, or inflict, that would stop him from cutting class and catching the 9.15 a.m. train to Dublin to come visit me every single week.

'Where is everyone?' Aiden asks.

'Mam has a meeting with the doctor. And the nurses are floating about. They come in and out all day. I'm never on my own for very long.'

'Is your mam still baking for the hospital?' Aiden asks, and I think he's hoping for a brownie or muffin later.

'She hasn't had time to bake anything for a few days,' I say, hoping he won't ask why. 'I think she's getting worried they'll let her go.'

'Oh God.' Aiden becomes serious. 'They won't will they?'

'I hope not.' I shrug, and a sharp pain instantly shoots out my shoulder. 'It's not about the money, you know. I don't think they even pay her that well.'

'They should,' Aiden says. 'Your mam's muffins are the best.'

'Thanks.' I smile, realising that I can't remember the last time I ate one. Mam brings them in to me all the time, but it's an effort just to nibble the corner and I wait until she goes to the loo or something, wrap the giant muffin in a tissue and throw it in the bin so I don't hurt her feelings.

'You okay?' Aiden asks. 'You don't seem yourself today. Do you need a break from your mam? Must be pretty intense just the two of you here all the time.'

'Nooo,' I say, trying not to take offence. I know Aiden doesn't understand how close Mam and I are. Most teenagers my age hate their mothers, or at least they pretend to, but it's always just been Mam and me. I could spend all the time in the world with her.

'What then?' Aiden asks. 'Is it really worries about your mam's job or is there more going on? Do you want to talk?'

'I am a little worried about her losing the job. It's been so good for her. Mam needs the head space. Baking is a perfect distraction. She's getting mad stressed over all this medical stuff.'

'Understandable.' Aiden nods, making his trying-to-look-wise face, which I know doubles up as his I-don't-know-what-to-say face. 'Your mam worries when you go out in the rain without a coat, I can't even imagine how much all this must be stressing her out.'

'She's extra stressed since...' I take a deep breath, not sure if I'm ready for the next words, but I really, really need someone to talk to. The kids in the games room are great and they really *get* cancer. I'm just not sure they *get* me. We've become cancer friends, but right now I need an old friend. I need Aiden.

'Since...?' Aiden asks, his eyes narrow with concern.

I shake my head. If I can't find the right words to tell my best friend that I'm getting sicker and I don't want any more treatment, how the hell am I supposed to tell my mother? Mam's face lit up yesterday when she was taking about experiments or whatever it is, but I can't try it. I really, really can't. When Mam said, 'No more chemo' a few weeks back, I nearly burst with excitement. I was ecstatic even though deep down I knew it wasn't that simple. I knew chemo couldn't just stop and everything would go back to normal. Normal is long gone. But I was still so happy just to hear the word 'stop'. I want it *all* to stop!

'Kayla since what?' I hear Aiden say and I realise my eyes are closed and I've drifted into that relaxing state somewhere between awake and asleep that has become my favourite place. The pain never feels quite so intense when I'm in that place.

I open my eyes and the words tumble from my lips. 'Since I'm dying.'

Aiden doesn't back away or shake his head the way my mam and dad do when the doctors break more bad news to them that basically spells out the inevitable. Instead Aiden nods and says, 'What can I do?'

'Aren't you going to freak out?' I ask.

'Would it help if I did?'

'No,' I say, 'not really.'

'Right then, tell me what you need me to do. Because let's face it, Kayla, there's no way that head of yours isn't formulating some sort of a plan, is there?'

I smile. I'm so glad this isn't going to be a battle of acceptance for him the way I know it will be with Mam. 'Help me with something very, very awesome,' I say. 'Please?'

Tears gather in the corner of Aiden's eyes. 'Have you told your mother you want to stop treatment?'

'You know me too well, Aiden,' I say. 'You really, really do.'

'So you haven't told her,' Aiden says.

'Not yet.'

'Oh, Kayla,' Aiden says, becoming a little unsteady on his feet. He's acting a bit more like my parents now and I wait for him to make a U-turn and tell me this is all crazy. He'd be right.

'Is this going to get us in trouble?' Aiden asks.

'Maybe.' I shrug. *Ouch, ouch, ouch, my spine hurts.*

'Oh God, it isn't illegal, is it?' Aiden adds.

'Ha! Eh no, but there might be time for that yet.'

'Kay—'

'Jokes. Jokes,' I say. 'This is all perfectly legal'. A bit out there. And really, really cool. Are you in?'

Aiden takes a deep breath and says, 'I'm in.'

FORTY-ONE

KAYLA

'Hey, hey, hey,' I say as Molly bounces into my room. I laugh as I watch Charlotte desperately try to wrangle her hyper daughter but Molly charges towards me, as happy and cheerful as always.

'I missed you soooooo much,' she says. 'I learned a song in school. Do you want to hear it?'

I don't have time to answer before Molly breaks into song.

'Zoo, zoo, who's in the zoo?'

'How are you, kiddo?' Dad says, talking over Molly as she stomps around the room as if she's a single troop lost from a marching band.

'I'm okay,' I lie.

'Shh, Molly. Not so loud,' Charlotte says. 'Sorry, Kayla. She's just so excited to see you.'

'I'm excited to see her too,' I say, struggling to speak loud enough to be heard over the noise Molly is creating.

'Hello, Aiden,' Dad says, acting awkward, as if he knows he's interrupted an important conversation between Aiden and me.

'Hey, Mr Doran. Kay and I were just watching some videos

on YouTube,' Aiden says.

Ugh, I groan inwardly, painfully aware that my phone is on the locker beside my bed and Aiden's phone is peeking out of his backpack on the seat next to him.

'Really?' Dad asks, raising a curious eyebrow.

'No, not really,' I say, attempting to cover up. 'We were talking about school actually.'

'Yeah,' Aiden jumps in, way too enthusiastic.

'Zoo. Zoo. Zoo,' Molly continues to sing and dance.

Aiden twists in his chair and unzips his rucksack to pull out something. 'Look,' he says, holding a colourful flyer over his head.

'Is that my name?' I ask, pointing at the large neon-pink font on the top of the page.

'Yup,' Aiden says. 'It's Sports Day soon and the school is getting everyone to bring in two euros so we can wear our own clothes instead of the mouldy PE gear.'

'And why is my name on there?' I ask.

'Well, 'cos it's for you,' Aiden says, lowering the flyer.

'For me?' I tap my chest and try not to wince when the side of my nail clips the cap on the central line leaning into my heart. 'How is everyone in school getting a non-uniform day anything to do with me?'

'Kay, I'm sorry.' Aiden shoves the flyer back into his bag. 'I didn't mean to upset you. I thought you'd be happy. It was Miss Hanlon's idea. She's always talking about you. Asking me how you're doing. Coming up with fun stuff for us to do to raise money.'

'You can come tooooooooooo,' Molly sings at the top of her lungs. Her squeaky little voice is going through my head.

'Fun stuff for *you all* to do,' I say.

'Yeah, okay,' Aiden says, looking around my small hospital room that tries depressingly hard not to be depressing. 'I see the irony. I'm sorry. Forget I said anything, yeah?'

'Is there a basketball game?' I ask.

Aiden nods.

'Are you playing?'

'Yeah. But we won't win. Not without you.'

'So why play?' I say, hating myself for being so bitter. I don't want Aiden to miss the game. I just desperately want to play alongside him.

'All the proceeds go to Cancer Research,' Aiden says. 'I thought you'd be happy. It was my idea. I'm sorry, Kay. I can ask them to cancel. It's not for another week so...'

'No. No, don't do that. It's good. It's a nice idea. Thank you.'

'You're not mad?' Aiden asks.

'No. Course not, you big eejit. I'm excited,' I say.

'You are?' Aiden is so confused, it's sweet.

'Yup. I can't wait to go.'

'Whoa, whoa, whoa, young lady,' Dad cuts in. 'You're kidding, right?'

'No,' I say.

'Kayla. No. No way.' Dad inhales and stands up very straight.

'Dad, I'm going,' I say, trying to hide how exhausted this conversation is making me.

'Kayla, this is not up for discussion.' Dad points his finger as if he means business. 'Aiden, I'm sorry. You're a good lad organising a fundraiser in Kayla's name but this is just crazy. She's much, much too sick.'

'Don't blame Aiden,' I say, annoyed. 'I'm a big girl. I can make my own decisions.'

'You are fifteen, Kayla,' Dad reminds me, as if cancer has somehow stripped the knowledge of my age from me. 'You most certainly cannot make your own decisions.'

Aiden looks at me and fear and worry are scribbled all over his face. I know exactly what he's thinking. If my dad is flipping

out this much over Sports Day, imagine what he'll say when I
tell him that I plan to refuse all further treatment.

'Zoo, zooooooo....' Molly sings.

'Jesus Christ, Molly. Will. You. Stop. It?' Dad snaps.

Molly begins to cry.

Charlotte bends and gathers a whimpering Molly into her
arms. 'Shh, shh, shh,' Charlotte says as Molly tucks her head
into the crook of her mother's neck.

'Hey, Molly,' Aiden says. 'Do you want to come to the
games room with me? I hear they have My Little Pony there.'

Molly lifts her head but she's clearly unimpressed. 'Do they
have Peppa Pig? I like her now.'

'I think they do,' Aiden whispers as if Peppa Pig is the best
kept secret the hospital holds.

'You sure you don't mind, Aiden?' Charlotte asks. 'Especially when you've come all this way to see Kayla.'

'Actually, I came all this way to see Molly,' Aiden says,
reaching his hand up to my sister. Molly grabs on tight and
when Charlotte bends and puts Molly down her feet barely
touch the ground as she skips her way towards the door hand-in-
hand with my best friend. Aiden looks over his shoulder and
smiles.

I smile back, telling him without words that I'm ready to
share my secret with Charlotte. I just have to hope she'll understand the way Aiden did.

'You coming, Mr Doran?' Aiden asks. *God love poor Aiden.*
I know he'd rather boil his head than be the decoy for my dad
but I only need a few minutes to talk to Charlotte, and Aiden
did ask if there was anything he could do to help.

'Me. What?' Dad says.

'Come on, Daddy,' Molly says. 'I can show you the big telly.'

'T-h-a-n-k y-o-u,' I mouth, as Aiden winks at me and walks
away with my dad's hand firmly on his shoulder and my little
sister skipping happily beside him.

FORTY-TWO

CHARLOTTE

'So how are you feeling?' I ask, cringing as I hear the stupid question pass my lips.

Kayla smiles, as if she knows how uncomfortable I am and she's trying to hold in a laugh. I wonder if she's equally as uncomfortable. I find myself trying to sneak a sideways glance at my watch. I know Heather never leaves Kayla alone for long, so I'm hoping she'll be back soon. I hate feeling this way. I've known Kayla since she was a little girl. I've wiped her bottom after the potty for goodness' sake, but we've grown apart in recent years. I'm not sure what her interests are or who her friends are. That Aiden boy seems nice. I wish I could think of something to talk about but my mind is blank and racing at the same time.

'Charlotte I need your help,' Kayla says, suddenly.

'My help?' Of all the things I was hoping Kayla might say, this wasn't it.

'Please,' Kayla adds.

My breath catches nervously and I wonder if Heather has stooped as low as putting Kayla up to asking for Molly's stem cells. 'What is it, sweetheart?' I ask, nervously.

'It's big, Charlie,' Kayla says. 'Like, kinda huge.'

'Oh, Kayla.' I exhale. 'Are you sure I'm the person you want to talk to about this? Maybe your mam would understand more.'

'No. Not Mam.' Kayla shakes her head and I can see the simple movement leaves her exhausted. 'Charlie, please?'

'Okay, okay,' I say, trying to keep her calm. 'Okay.'

'You can't tell my mam. You have to promise.'

'Oh, Kayla.'

'Promise, Charlie. Please promise.'

'Okay,' I say, worried. 'I promise.'

'I've stopped getting better,' Kayla blurts without warning. She's not teary or upset. Her body language, although exhausted and worn out, is still confident and certain. She seems to have come to a grown-up acceptance that the rest of us just can't seem to manage.

'Kayla, I really think this is a conversation for you and your parents.' I find myself looking over my shoulder at the door, hoping that someone, anyone, will walk in.

'Charlie, you promised,' Kayla reminds me, sinking a little lower in the bed. I hurry over to her and help her back up and re-fluff the pillows that are almost as weary as her.

'You're right. I did promise.' I exhale again, making myself light-headed. I ease myself into the chair waiting beside Kayla's bed and I take her hand. Her fingers curl around mine and I fight back tears as I remember her chubby little hand that used to hold mine when her dad and I first started going out. We'd take her on day trips and for walks in the park. I never, in my wildest dreams, thought I'd ever sit beside her hospital bed, facing the horrifying thought that she might leave this world before I do. 'You know you can ask me anything.'

A painful silence hangs between us, as if Kayla knows I'm bluffing. Just this morning I told Gavin again that asking for Molly to be put through more was too much. Too far. Too great an ask.

'I overheard Mam and Dad and Jack talking about my options,' Kayla says, as if she's a forty-five-year-old woman discussing the best way to approach mortgage-interest relief. No fifteen-year-old should ever sound this solemn. 'They never check if I'm properly asleep; they never include me.'

'Kay, look, it's grown-up stuff and—'

'And, you're all still fighting.' Kayla shakes her head, disappointed in us.

I think about lying. Or at least trying to make out that we're all simply having heated discussions, but I feel I owe Kayla more than a bullshit generic response. 'Yes. We are all killing each other. But that's stress, Kay. It happens. We're all so stressed out.'

'I know. And I'm sorry. I know it's because of me.'

'It's not, Kay,' I say, only just realising. 'It's because we're afraid of losing you. We can't bear it. None of us can.'

'Does Molly know about any of this?' Kayla asks.

'No.' I shake my head, guilt swirling in the pit of my stomach. I can't bear to tell Kayla I have reservations about these damn trials.

'Good. Don't tell her.'

'What?'

'Don't tell her,' Kayla repeats.

'Kayla, I know she's only four, but I have to talk to her about this. In some way. I have to try to explain. Help her understand how she can help. She'll be scared, but you're her sister. She adores you.'

'No,' Kayla says, again. 'She can't help. I don't want her to.'

'Kayla.'

'Charlie, I said no.'

'Kayla, what exactly is it you want my help with?' I ask, suddenly realising that whatever it is Kayla wants to discuss there is a reason she has chosen me and not her parents. This has unorthodox written all over it and I'm not sure I'm in a posi-

tion to disagree. And I'm even more certain I'm neither qualified genetically or medically to agree. 'Oh, Kayla what are you
up to?'

FORTY-THREE
CHARLOTTE

There's a knock on the door and I hold my breath, hoping Gavin is on the far side.

'Come in,' Kayla says in a sing-song voice that seems very grown-up for her. I can only imagine she's adopted the tone to usher in the constant flow of medics who weave their way in out of her room daily.

'Hey,' Aiden says.

'Where's my dad and sister?' Kayla asks, seeming surprised or perhaps disappointed to see her friend.

'Molly was hungry so your dad said he'd take her to the canteen. I told him there's a McDonald's around the corner – so I think they've gone there.'

I groan inwardly at the thought of Molly eating more junk food.

'I best be going,' I say, glancing towards the door. 'I'll call Gavin when I'm on the corridor and let him know that I have fresh soup waiting at home for Molly.'

'What? No.' Kayla shuffles to sit up straighter and she looks as if she's in pain. Her floral bandana slips back a little and reveals that although she hasn't lost her hair completely, there isn't much more than a few stray strands left. Suddenly avoiding chicken nuggets and a sugary drink seems inconsequential. 'You can't go,' she says. 'We haven't finished talking.'

'We can chat more next time,' I say, my breathing feeling laboured and uncomfortable. 'I'm sure you and your friend want some alone time to catch up.'

'Alone time.' Kayla laughs. 'Me and Aiden, God no.'

Aiden. That's his name, how could I forget?

'Jeez, thanks,' Aiden says, folding his arm and tilting his head to one side.

'Ah, you know I didn't mean it like that,' Kayla says, blushing.

'Have you asked her yet?' Aiden says.

'I was trying to but then you barged in.'

'Oh, right. Sorry.' Aiden blushes. 'Do you want me to go again?'

'Nah, you're grand.' Kayla smiles. 'Charlie doesn't mind if you're here, do you Charlie?'

I shrug. If Kayla is going to ask me something huge, or personal, I would rather we were alone. But of course I don't say that.

'Well go on then,' Aiden encourages and I'm not sure how I feel about this boy. I must ask Gavin about him. I hope he's not a bad influence on Kayla.

Kayla takes a deep breath and says, 'I want to buy a bakery.'

A strange throaty gargle seems to escape my lips, but no actual words follow.

'She's serious,' Aiden says, as if he suspects I need that clarification. And, to be honest, I do.

I try not to look so blatantly flabbergasted. Of all the things I thought she might say this was definitely not one of them. 'You what?'

Kayla nods. Certain. 'For my mam.'

'Oh,' I say, understanding, but no less shocked. 'Kayla that's very sweet, but businesses like that cost thousands to set up. And even more to run. Especially in the early days.'

Kayla nods. 'I know.'

'We learnt all about setting up small enterprises in school,' Aiden says. 'We did a whole project on it.'

'Oh, did you now?' I laugh, wondering how long these two have been concocting this master plan.

'I know that the premises is only the start of it. I know it will take a lot of money to buy equipment and ingredients and stuff,' Kayla says.

'And insurance and marketing and accounts,' I say, hating that I'm bursting their bubble.

'I know. I know,' Kayla says. 'That's why I need your help.'

'Oh, Kayla.' I shake my head. 'Your dad and I don't have that kind of money.'

Kayla giggles. 'I know that, silly.'

Aiden laughs too. I'm glad they see the funny side.

'But it was a very nice idea. I'm sure your mam will appreciate the sentiment,' I say.

'What? No. You can't tell her.' Kayla straightens suddenly and I know for sure she's in agony.

I hurry over to the bed, gently nudging Aiden out of the way. I ease Kayla back against the mound of pillows waiting behind her and hope that the tears gathering in my eyes won't start to trickle down my face. Not in front of her.

'There now,' I say, when she's resting. 'Is that better?'

Kayla takes some deep breaths, exhausted, and her eyes seek out Aiden's. She's obviously requesting he be her spokesperson for the rest of this conversation. I glance over my shoulder. Aiden looks nervous but determined and I decide that maybe I do like this boy after all.

'Kayla needs an adult's help to raise the funds,' Aiden says.

I don't answer. Kayla is looking worryingly pale and I

wonder if I should press the buzzer above her bed and call a nurse.

'She can't ask her parents.'

'Mam can't know,' Kayla says, her voice crackling like static on the radio.

'Kayla wants it to be a surprise for her mam,' Aiden explains. 'And Gavin is too stressed out to be any help.'

'Kayla, you don't look well,' I say. 'I think I should call a nurse, or your dad.'

Aiden stops talking.

'No,' Kayla whispers. 'Water.'

I reach for the jug of water next to Kayla's bed and pour some into the waiting glass. My hands are shaking as I lift the glass towards Kayla's lips and she manages several sips.

'It's warm,' she complains.

'You look better already,' I say, placing the glass back on the bedside table.

'We want to try crowdfunding online,' Kayla says, her eyes closed but her colour improving.

I study her. She seems to have aged years in a matter of weeks. Dark circles hang under her beautiful blue eyes and her cheekbones protrude. Her neck seems longer than ever with no hair to cascade down around her shoulders and she's painfully thin. My heart hurts.

'Crowdfunding is where you put your story online. You know, like what's happening and why you need the money. And then people donate whatever they want. It's really very cool,' Aiden says, excitedly.

'I'm familiar with the idea. Thank you,' I say. 'I just don't think it would work.'

'Why not?' Kayla asks.

'Well, it's pretty unorthodox. I'm not sure how people would feel about something like this.'

'People love a sick-kid pity case,' Kayla says, her eyes open again and colour returning into her cheeks. I wonder how often she wilts like that. So suddenly. It's terrifying.

'You're not a pity case, Kay,' Aiden says. *I do like this boy.*

'You're the same girl you have always been,' I add.

'It's okay,' Kayla says. 'I know the point we're at. The nurses are extra cheery when they come in to check my blood pressure. And the doctors make silly small talk to hide the fact they're surprised I'm actually still alive. I know I'm screwed. They know it too. But Mam and Dad don't know it.'

My heart pinches as I realise Kayla is right. Gavin is so convinced Kayla is going to get better. We all are. I don't think he's thought for a moment what might happen if she doesn't. *Oh God...*

'Baking is the only thing Mam loves as much as she loves me. I don't want her to lose both.'

Aiden suddenly becomes very quiet.

'You should sit down,' I say, realising he has gone white.

'Yeah.' He flops into the bedside chair and I realise that if what Kayla says is true and she doesn't have feelings for this boy, it doesn't stop him being head-over-heels crazy about her.

'There was a fund a few years ago for a girl about my age to go to the States to try some mental expensive treatment that we don't have here. She was honest with people and said it mightn't even work but people still donated so she could at least try,' Kayla says.

'People are generous,' I agree.

'And then there was another one where a family of this ten-year-old boy in a wheelchair wanted to take him to Disney because he loves Buzz Lightyear. They raised a fortune and gave the extra money to some charity,' Aiden says, brightening up again.

'Well who doesn't want to meet Buzz Lightyear?' Kayla smiles.

'Kayla be serious,' Aiden scolds like a teacher trying to

demand a pupil's attention in class. 'Seriously though, Mrs Doran,' Aiden says, making me feel as old as my mother-in-law. 'If people donate so a family can go down Splash Mountain then I don't see why they wouldn't donate to this.'

I take a deep breath and think about Gavin being so distant and stressed out. I think about him not telling me about Molly's stem cells. About how every time I even mention Kayla's name he has to leave the room. I know Kayla getting sick has pushed him and Heather closer together. And not just as the parents of a sick child; I've seen them become each other's rock. And I'd be a complete liar if I pretended it didn't hurt or fill me with jealousy. I'm an outsider looking in. I'm watching Heather and Gavin be there for Kayla, and be there for each other, and I stand by helpless and useless. Maybe this is how I can help. I can't make medical decisions for Kayla. And I don't want to. I realised that the moment Molly got dragged into this. But I can help be there for Kayla as a confidant. As a friend. As someone who loves her as if she was my own child. And I make two decisions. I will help Kayla raise as much money as possible and I will give my blessing for Molly to help her sister, even if all we get is a little more time. *We all need more time.*

I choke back tears. 'So, you want to buy a bakery?'

FORTY-FOUR

KAYLA

'Hey, you,' Mam says, coming into my room carrying a bottle of Coke Zero in one hand, a huge box of chocolates in the other, and her laptop tucked under her arm. 'I watched *Riverdale* at last. Oh my God, you're right. It's so good. We have to watch the next episode together.'

'Oh, sure. Yeah. Okay,' I say, pulling myself to sit up.

Mam drops all the stuff onto the bedside chair and hurries around behind me to fluff my pillow or whatever, but she puffs it up too much and I suddenly feel as if I'm sitting on an aeroplane all stiff and awkward. I don't say anything. I'll wait until she sits and then I'll slouch down and get comfortable.

'Where's your dad? He hasn't gone home already, has he?' Mam sounds disappointed. Or maybe annoyed. 'He knows I want to talk to him.'

'He's in the games room, I think,' I say. 'Molly wanted to go play after they got something to eat.'

'Right,' Mam says. 'And Aiden?'

'Gone with them.'

'And I suppose Charlotte is down there too. Don't they know that area is for patients only?'

'I'm sure it's okay,' I say, my eyes heavy with sleep. 'Lots of the others bring their brothers and sisters down. I don't think anyone will mind.'

'I mind,' Mam mumbles under her breath.

I ignore her bad mood and ask, 'How did the meeting with Doctor Patterson go?'

'Yeah. Good. Yeah. Fine.'

'What?' I say. 'Well that was a weird answer.'

'It was fine, Kayla,' Mam says. 'We couldn't really talk for long. He's a very busy man.'

'Okay,' I sigh, not believing a word out of her mouth. He's obviously told her something terrible and she's too freaked out to talk about it. I'll ask him myself tomorrow when he comes around to check on me.

Mam sits into the chair next to my bed and stares out the window.

'Okay, seriously,' I say, unable to hold it in. 'What did he say?'

Mam doesn't look at me as she shakes her head.

'Um, you're kind of freaking me out,' I say, sounding as if I have much more energy than I actually do.

Mam takes a deep breath and sighs. I don't mind that her warm coffee breath hits me. *Coffee.* At least she's had something warm to drink, I think, realising that I can't remember the last time I saw her eat or drink anything.

'So, *Riverdale*,' I say, changing the subject as I eye up the chocolates. *Cadbury Milk Tray. Awesome!* Except Mam can eat that gross new apple flavour one. I don't even know what Cadbury were thinking. Yuck.

'Yup, it's so good. It's great, I'm really glad you told me to watch it,' Mam says, trying to sound excited even though her mind is obviously on Dad and I've no doubt she's desperate to talk to him about all the Molly stuff. 'Did Dad say when he'll be back?' Mam adds.

I shake my head and a sharp, sudden pain darts down my spine. It happens all the time when I move too suddenly. I'm getting used to it.

'Great,' Mam groans. 'That's just great. What's the point of him coming in to visit if he's not going to spend any time with you? Sure, he might as well be in work.'

'Are you okay?' I ask. 'You're in a mood today. Are you really that pissed off with Dad for taking Molly to play or did something happen with Doctor Patterson? You can tell me, you know. I won't freak out.'

'Kayla stop worrying. It's nothing to do with your treatment okay. Please don't get that idea.'

'What then?'

Mam takes a deep breath and tuts as if she's super deep in thought or really weirded out or something. She's not normally like this.

'We kind of kissed a few weeks back,' Mam whispers, as if it's a naughty secret.

'No way. Oh my God. Nooooo way.' My eyes widen and I'm more awake than I have been in days. 'Why didn't you tell me? And what did you do?'

'It was the day after the scare over your kidney infection, and it was a total accident of course. It's been so awkward since,' Mam says, looking mortified.

'What? How?' I jerk upright. *Oh my god my spine is on fire.* I try not to react. If Mam notices she'll morph into panic-mam mode and we'll never get to talk about this. 'How the hell can you kiss someone by accident?'

'Kayla. Language,' Mam scolds.

'Sorry,' I say. 'But, seriously, Mam, you're so bad at this. Who said it was an accident? Him or you?'

'It. Was. An. Accident, Kayla. We just kind of bumped into each other with our lips.'

I laugh. Mam sounds as helpless as some of the girls in my

year when they like a boy and just don't know what to do about it.

'Yeah, yeah. I know how that sounds,' Mam says, and I wonder if she knows her cheeks are bright red. 'But it was so awkward and...'

'And... what did you say?'

'Nothing. I just sort of left,' Mam says.

'Oh, Mam. What must he have thought?' I shake my head, super disappointed that she blew it.

Mam runs a hand through her hair and I can see her playing the kiss over in her mind. 'I doubt he cared, to be honest.'

'I'm pretty sure he did. He asks about you all the time. *How's your mam doin?*' I mimic his deep voice. '*I had one of your mam's cookies today, it was great. Is your mam coming in today* and on... and on... and on...'

Mam shakes her head and there's a new sadness in her eyes. It's not the sadness I'm used to seeing when she notices I'm in pain or when we get more bad news.

'You know he's going to think you don't like him now,' I say.

'So?' Mam shrugs, acting more like a teenager than me.

'So...' I say. 'You do like him. You're always going on about him. Nearly as much as he goes on about you. You're always saying how great he is.'

'A great doctor,' Mam says. 'But he's taken, Kayla.'

'What?' I say and my voice is starting to crackle, I hope she doesn't notice.

'He's married, Kay,' Mam says, standing up to pace the floor with her hands on her hips. 'Or, he has a girlfriend at least.'

I lick my chapped lips and I'm about to explain but Mam keeps talking.

'They're expecting a baby together,' she says.

'He's not having a baby!' I puff out.

Mam reaches for the glass of water on my bedside table and

chugs the entire thing. She slams it back down with unneces-
sary force and I'm surprised it doesn't break.

'Ugh, God. That was warm,' Mam complains.

'Welcome to my world,' I say, 'and you're always trying to
get me to drink more.'

'Right.' Mam exhales, picking up the jug. 'I'm going to get
some fresh water and see if I can find some ice too.'

'Mam wait.' My eyes are rolling closed and I hate that I'm
getting so sleepy right now.

'There's nothing more to talk about, Kayla. It was just an
embarrassing mix-up. That's all. Doctor Patterson and I both
know that. It's nothing for you to worry about.'

'Doctor Patterson?' I say. 'I thought you called him Jack.'

'No,' Mam says. 'Doctor Patterson will do just fine.'

'She's his sister,' I say, my eyes are closed now.

'Who is?'

'The woman having the baby. That woman he lives with.
She's his sister.'

'But Dad said—'

'Did Dad actually ask him? Or just assume?'

'Oh, erm, well.'

'She's his sister and do you know how I know?' I manage to
open my eyes again.

Mam straightens her head and looks at me with questioning
eyes.

'Because he told me he can't wait to be an uncle. Lucky kid
I say, Doctor Patterson is great. He'll be an awesome uncle.'

'But he lives with her, Kay. Dad says they moved in just a
few weeks ago. And it's only the two of them. I think there's
some crossed wires.'

'Yeah, your wires,' I say. 'His sister's husband died a few
months ago. She moved back from New York because Doctor
Patterson is going to help her raise the baby. He even left his

apartment nearer the hospital to move in with her so she wouldn't be alone.'

'Wow, that's some gesture.'

'Yeah,' I say. 'So the guy you pushed away is probably the nicest guy on the planet. And he's hot too.'

'Oh God.' Mam puts down the jug and flops back into the chair. The cushion puffs out under her making a whoosh sound. 'I was so rude. I've been so rude. He must think I'm a right bitch.'

'I'm sure he'll understand if you explain.'

'No.' Mam shakes her head. 'It's too messy. Too complicated. He's your doctor, Kayla.'

'And he's a great guy who super likes you.'

'No, Kay.' Mam exhales, her whole body weighed down by sadness. 'Now is not a good time. This is for the best. The only thing I care about right now is you. And you getting better. I don't have time for kisses and drama.'

'But Mam—'

'Kayla, please. Let's just concentrate on what's important. Okay?'

'Okay,' I say, so glad I have a plan. If Mam won't help herself, then I'm just going to have to do it for her.

FORTY-FIVE

KAYLA

I've really enjoyed the noise in my room all afternoon. Mam and Charlotte sat side by side in the bedside chairs. Dad sat on the end of the bed. He got up every now and then to shake his legs and I wonder if he had pins and needles or a numb bum. Aiden spent the whole time standing and Molly spent most of the time running around or asking to be taken to the toilet or down to the tuckshop to buy a lollipop. I don't even know what the conversation was about. I drifted in and out of sleep, Loving that each time I woke there was laughter and happiness in the air. It's been ages since I heard Mam laugh.

Time seems to be moving so fast with me sleeping so much. The whole afternoon flew by. Dad offered to give Aiden a lift to the train station when they were leaving and it's been very quiet and almost lonely since it's just me and Mam again.

'How you doing, kiddo?' Mam says, when I wake up after yet another nap. 'That was a long visit. You seem exhausted.'

'Yeah,' I say, honestly. 'But it was a really good day, wasn't it?'

Mam nods. 'It was nice.'

'Are you going to talk to Doctor Patterson?'

'Of course.'

'I mean about the kiss and not medical stuff.'

'I know exactly what you mean, Kayla.' Mam raises her eyebrows and I can tell she's about to launch into an excuse or a speech when her phone vibrates in her bag, distracting her. The beeping is relentless as message after message bombards her phone. I hold my breath as she reaches in, rummages around and finally drags it out.

'Oh,' she says, surprised as she stares at the screen. 'I've a tonne of messages from Aiden. I hope the train hasn't been cancelled or something. How on earth will he get home?'

I throw the covers back and swing my legs over the edge of the bed. Trying to hurry and not hurt myself in the process is really tricky, but I don't want to be here when Mam reads Aiden's messages about me stopping treatment.

'I need to pee,' I lie, looking for the only reasonable excuse I can find to leave the room so suddenly.

'Here, let me help,' Mam says, popping her phone down on the chair behind her as she stands up.

'No, no. I've got this,' I say, reaching for the single crutch next to my headboard. Mam continues to stand in front of me, blocking my path, trying to help. 'Mam.' I wince, pain shooting through my entire body as I finally stand, crutch in one hand, weird coat-stand-on-wheels drip-holder-thingy in the other. 'I really, really want to pee by myself. Really. I do.'

'Okay,' Mam says. 'But don't lock the door. Okay?'

'Yeah.' I choke back tears of agony. 'Sure.'

I hobble towards the tiny en suite, close the door behind me and flop onto the loo. I pee. Not because I need to, but since I'm here I might as well make use of the opportunity, so I don't have to go through this hell again later.

It's hard to leave the tiny bathroom knowing Mam is reading – some possibly very long – messages from Aiden. And she's been reading them while I hide in here. The longer I leave it the more time she has to stew over everything he's saying. I hope he kept to the script and didn't add in any bits that we didn't talk about. He was supposed to wait until tonight to text her. I wanted her to have at least a few hours to think everything over and then we could talk about it all in the morning. But now we're going to have to talk about it tonight. And I'm not ready. And suddenly I feel this might all be a very bad idea.

I flush and give myself a mental high five for standing unaided as I wash my hands. I grab my crutch and finally open the door and hobble back into my room.

It is painfully quiet. The only sound is the loo guzzling in water after a flush and I wish I'd closed the bathroom door behind me. Mam is still sitting in the same chair as when I left but her back is bent and her arms are folded on the edge of the bed with her head resting on top. Her shoulders are shuffling, and I realise she's crying silently.

Mam doesn't move as I brush past her. I rest my crutch in the usual spot next to the headboard and climb onto the bed. Mam lifts her head and I can't miss the mascara streaking down her cheeks as I try to get in under the sheets. Mam helps me and I note we're getting better at making it seem like much less effort than it actually is.

Mam sits back down and stares at the floor. She can't even look at me. *Oh God. Why did Aiden have to text so soon?*

'C'mere,' I say, our roles weirdly reversed as I pat my legs and Mam's head settles onto my lap. She's so careful not to touch my knee and I know she's paranoid about hurting me and won't relax fully. 'Mam, don't cry, please,' I say as I stroke her hair the way she used to stroke mine when I was a little girl. 'I've made my decision. Please try to understand.'

Mam sniffles and finally sits up. My legs are instantly cold when her head isn't in my lap and I pull the blanket over me.

Mam shakes her head while rubbing her eyes with her finger tips. 'Kayla, no,' she says. 'I can't let you do this.'

'I'm not asking for your permission, Mam.' I swallow, hating how dry my mouth feels and my lips sting where they're all dry and cracking from the hospital aircon; no amount of lip balm can sort them out. 'I'm telling you what I want.'

'You're fifteen years old, Kayla. You don't get to make this decision. I do.' Mam slaps her fingers against her chest so roughly I wonder if she hurts herself. '*I'm* the adult here. *I'm* the parent.'

Mam's words are clipped, and her voice is so angry. I didn't even know she could sound so cross. And maybe if you didn't know her as well as I do you might even believe she's furious. But, I don't believe it. Not for a second. Her scrunched-up forehead and gritted teeth can't hide her sadness. And it breaks my heart.

'If this is your way of trying to force me to talk to Doctor Patterson, Kayla. It's not cool. Not cool at all.'

'Mam, c'mon. Please.'

'Sorry. Sorry, I know you wouldn't do that,' she says. 'But Jesus, Kayla. You can't just stop treatment all together. Don't you know what that means?'

'Yes,' I say, worrying about how pale she's suddenly become. 'I do.'

'We need to talk to more doctors,' Mam says. 'Get more opinions. Go to another hospital. Maybe in the UK, or the States, if necessary. It'll be like an adventure. You'll see. We've always wanted to go to America, haven't we?'

I bum-shuffle forward on the bed, yelping when the cannula in my hand bites because I've accidently got the IV line tangled up and it's pulling. Mam jumps up and untangles the wire quickly. She's become so familiar with all the medical equipment.

'There,' she says, smiling. 'All better.'

Then she turns away from me and I know it's because her eyes are filling up with tears and she doesn't want me to see. She turns away sometimes when the doctors are talking. Or when Molly is asking about when I'm coming to Dad's for the weekend. And when she feels she's said something stupid to upset me. Like *all better*. It's never going to be all better and we both know it.

'Sorry, something in my eye,' Mam says, turning back around.

'Tears,' I say.

Mam smiles. 'When did you get so grown-up, huh? Feels like just yesterday you were sitting on the floor in Granny and Grandad's house watching cartoons and singing along to all the songs, and look at you now, towering over me. You get your height from your dad, you know.'

'Speaking of Dad,' I say. 'Do you think he'll be okay with this? With my decision.'

'Kayla, this isn't your decision, you do know that, right?'

'Mam, please. I need you to understand.'

'I know this is all scary and it hurts, but I just want what's best for you—'

'No.' I shake my head. 'You want to make me better. To keep me. But that's not going to happen, Mam. It's never going to happen. If you keep me – you keep me in this room.'

Mam looks around, sobbing and heartbroken.

'I know that's not the life you want for me. It's not a life you'd want for anyone, is it?'

'I need to talk to your dad,' Mam says, her eyes round and puffy. 'I can't do this on my own, Kayla. I can't. I can do most things alone. I've done most things alone. But not this. Definitely not this.'

FORTY-SIX

HEATHER

A week later

The kitchen is awash with muffins, cupcakes and brownies. I made extra brownies because brownies were a firm favourite with the kids on the ward, or so Kayla says, so I can only hope that the kids in her school will enjoy them just as much. I burnt the batch of cookies and had to throw them out. I haven't had to throw anything out in years. I think it's because I'm ridiculously nervous about today, for a whole variety of reasons.

I can hear Gavin, Charlotte and Molly walking around upstairs. Molly is clearly not happy to be woken at 6 a.m.

'I don't want to gooooo!' she shouts, followed by some crying.

By the sound of Gavin's gruff voice and lack of patience, he doesn't appreciate the early start either. 'You can sleep in the car, Molly. Now, *please*, will you just get dressed?'

Charlotte and I don't have to worry about being woken up before dawn because we haven't actually gone to sleep. Charlotte came downstairs around 1 a.m. and offered to help me bake. She said she couldn't sleep and she wanted to be useful.

I was nervous at first. I usually bake alone, and besides, if Charlotte's cupboards are anything to go by she doesn't stock anything that isn't either organic or vegan, or preferably both. I thought she'd be horrified to see the ingredients going in to my muffins and brownies, but she didn't seem all that bothered.

She must have been as anxious as I am because she kept checking her phone every few minutes as if she might receive wildly important messages in the middle of the night. I didn't say anything. I guess she needed the distraction.

'I'll make us some coffee,' she says, as she pulls up the kitchen blind to reveal that the sun is up and it really is morning time and today is actually happening.

'Coffee would be great. Thanks,' I say, piping some vanilla buttercream icing onto the last remaining bare muffin before dusting it with edible glitter in the school colours.

'Can I have a muffin?' Molly asks, coming into the kitchen with one shoe on and one off.

'Not for breakfast,' Charlotte says, before I have a chance to answer. 'And where is your other shoe?'

Molly shrugs, clearly unfazed as she makes her way to the table to wait for food. Charlotte pops some five-grain bread in the toaster and my tummy rumbles.

'Stick a slice on for me, Charlie,' Gavin says, appearing in the kitchen looking equally as dishevelled as Molly. 'Christ it's early, isn't it? Couldn't they have postponed the race until after lunch?' Gavin mumbles.

'It was your idea to allow Kayla to participate in Sports Day, remember?' I say, which isn't entirely true.

Gavin and I had a lengthy discussion about whether or not to allow her to take part after the school phoned me to let me know that, as Aiden said, they were holding a fundraiser in her honour. Kayla was all for it, of course. Until she realised that she wouldn't actually be able to take part in any of the games –

just watch. But she hid her disappointment admirably and insisted she was well enough to go.

Gavin and I both reached the same verdict – that it was just too much for her – but Kayla enlisted the help of Jack who seemed to concur with our excitable fifteen-year-old that it wasn't really a terrible idea. I had a million questions I wanted to ask Jack, but I found only a single desperate request tumbling out of my mouth.

'Will you come?'

Jack looked shocked. And he didn't answer at first. We're barely speaking since our awkward kiss. He almost always has a nurse or a barrage of student doctors with him when he comes by to check on Kayla now. Kayla thinks it's just coincidence but I'm pretty certain he doesn't want to be alone with me. To say I was surprised when he rang me to explain that he'd moved a few things around and he'd be happy to join us for Sports Day is an understatement. I was so relieved at first. Jack will be there to keep an eye on Kayla if she becomes overwhelmed or tired and he'll know what to do if she takes a bad turn. But it also means that Jack will be there watching me too. We can't all fit in Gavin's car, so Jack kindly offered to take Kayla and me with him. I know it's for the best – Gavin would probably drive off the motorway with panic if Kayla so much as fainted. Jack is the best person to travel with. He's also the worst and this is all so bloody intense I wish I had never agreed to any of it.

You're doing it for Kayla. It's all for Kayla, I tell myself as the smell of freshly brewed coffee wafts towards me instantly lifting my mood.

'We'll need to go soon,' Gavin says. 'We want to get ahead of the traffic. We'll drop you to the hospital, Heather, and go straight from there.'

'Thanks,' I say, hoping Charlotte is going to pass me a cup of coffee soon. I can see three full cups waiting on the countertop and I don't feel as if I can just take one, no matter how desperate I am.

'Don't we have time for breakfast?' Charlotte says, unimpressed.

'Toast to go,' Gavin says.

'I'm hungry,' Molly says. 'I want dippy eggs.'

'How about a muffin?' Gavin says.

'A chocolate-chip one?' Molly chirps, suddenly bright-eyed and awake.

'That's okay, Heather, isn't it?' Gavin asks. 'I mean, there's still enough for the kids at the school, right?'

I sweep my eyes over the countertop laden with confectionary. 'There's plenty. Actually, we could all have one now. With our coffee,' I say, dropping a hint and practically pleading with Charlotte to pass me a cup.

'I really don't think chocolate for breakfast is a good idea,' Charlotte says.

'Please, Mammy. Oh please, please. I'll be the bestest best girl today. Please. I super love Heather's muffins.'

'I don't think a few chocolate chips is going to cause any cavities, Charlie,' Gavin says, rolling his eyes. 'Go on, Molly. But just for today, eh? It's back to Mammy's yummy five-grain bread tomorrow, okay?'

Molly sticks out her tongue and I don't blame her. Yummy and grains should never be used in the same sentence. Molly hops down from her chair with a burst of energy that defies how lazy and sluggish she pretended to be just moments ago. She reaches the counter and looks up at all the treats, but she doesn't reach up to help herself.

'Would you like a chocolate-chip muffin or a chocolate brownie?' I ask.

'A chocolate-chip muffin,' Molly says, her eyes twinkling with excitement. Her happiness is quite contagious, and I find myself looking forward to my muffin too.

I reach towards the back of the countertop and pick out the muffin with the most chocolate chips and I bend over to pass it to Molly. Unexpectedly, Molly wraps her chubby little arms around my neck and says, 'Yummy. Thank you, Heather.'

Even more unexpectedly, I begin to cry as I hug her cozy little body back. 'You're very welcome, Molly,' I say. 'You're such a good little girl. Just like your big sister.'

Gavin clears his throat. 'Excuse me,' he says, leaving the room, and I know I've upset him.

Charlotte goes after him.

'You can sit aside me,' Molly says, letting me go and pointing to the table.

'Thank you, Molly,' I say, taking a muffin with considerably fewer chocolate chips for myself and, unable to hold out any longer, I take one of the cups of coffee and I follow Molly to sit at the table.

'I like Sports Day,' Molly says, mid-chew of a huge mouthful of muffin.

'Me too,' I lie, prioritising large mouthfuls of coffee over bites of cake.

My phone beeps and I pull it out of my pocket, my face lighting up when I see a message from Kayla. I open it and it's a photo of Kayla and Jack smiling excitedly with their thumbs up. Kayla is sitting in a wheelchair with Jack crouched beside her. I recognise the backdrop of the hospital canteen immediately. She's dressed in a bright-red hoodie and black tracksuit bottoms. It's the first time I've seen her in anything other than pyjamas in I can't remember how long. She looks great. Her cheeks have a hint of colour and she's wearing a new bandana I haven't seen before. It's red too and pretty. Jack's legs are out of shot but it looks as if he's in a tracksuit too. He certainly appears very different to how he usually looks. A banner streaks across the centre of the picture and the words *we're waiting* sit in the middle in bubble writing followed by a multitude of emojis.

'Take one of us. Take one of us,' Molly says, leaning close to me and pointing at my screen. 'Send Kayla our picture.'

I drape my arm over Molly's shoulder, and she snuggles close to me.

'Say cheese,' I say.

'Cheeessseee.'

I snap and – content that my phone has autocorrected my red puffy eyes – I send the picture to Kayla, with the caption: *See you soon. Can't wait.*

I've a tonne of texts on my phone. Mostly from the teachers at Kayla's school wishing both Kayla and me luck today as if we're running a marathon or moving into a new home. Not simply attending Sports Day the same, unnoticed way we do every year. Usually I turn up at the last moment after dashing out of work early, while knowing I'll have to work twice as many minutes in overtime to get my boss off my back. Last year I arrived at the school twenty minutes before the end of the day for the parents' and kids' three-legged race, which Kayla and I lost in spectacular style and spent the next week or two teasing each other about.

This year is nothing like last year. And, even worse, I fear it may be nothing like next year.

FORTY-SEVEN

KAYLA

'C'mon, Kayla! Hurry, Kayla, hurry,' people chant.

I try. I'm moving faster than I have in months and it's fabulous. I don't know who the voices belong to. It doesn't even matter; their cheering spurs me on.

'You can do it, Kayla,' they say.

My arms burn as I turn the wheels on my wheelchair as fast as I can. The wind whips against my face and I take deep breaths, loving how amazing it feels to be outside, even in the cold. I wonder why I never appreciated fresh air before. I should have.

The grass is bumpy beneath the wheels and the faster I go the more my bum bounces about in the chair. I should probably worry about toppling over or bouncing right out but I don't. Not even once.

'Go. Go. Go.' The chanting is deafeningly wonderful as the finish line comes into view.

I finish last, unsurprisingly, but it doesn't matter because I'm swarmed by a cheering crowd. Close friends, not-as-close friends and yet-to-be friends. But over their shoulder, a little further down the field, are my once-upon-a-time friends. People

I sat beside in class. I confided in these kids when I was having a rubbish day. I was on a debate team with them. Some of them are my fellow basketball teammates. They stay well away, as if I'm contagious. They're not stupid, they know I can't infect them with cancer, but getting too close could infect *them* with uncoolness and that's the worst disease of all, right?

'That was awesome,' Aiden says, wrapping his arms loosely around my neck in the way he's learned to do so he doesn't hurt me.

'What?' I scrunch my nose. 'I lost, you numpty.'

'Yeah, but you also rolled over Roisin Kelly's foot.' Aiden is laughing so hard he snorts.

'No way.' I smirk. 'Did I really?'

'You should have seen her face,' Aiden giggles. 'Best race ever, if you ask me.'

'Well done, Kay,' Dad says.

'You're very slow,' Molly adds, unimpressed. 'All the other people passed you.'

Aiden laughs louder than ever. I laugh too.

'Yeah.' I nod. 'I am.'

'Can I have a go?' Molly asks and points towards me.

'In my chair?' I say.

Molly nods. 'I bet I can go faster.'

'I bet you could too,' I say. 'But I'm a little too tired to stand up right now. But you can sit on my lap and we can go for a spin. How about that?'

'Cooolll,' Molly says.

'Kayla, I don't think that's a good idea,' Dad says. 'Your knee.' He points as if I've forgotten or could ever forget.

'I have two knees, Dad,' I say. 'She can sit on the other one.'

'Molly be careful,' Charlotte warns as Molly rushes over to me. 'Kayla, are you sure she won't be too heavy?'

'Of course you won't be too heavy, will you, Molly?' I say. 'You're only little.'

'I am not.' Molly jams her hands onto her hips in protest. 'I'm four.'

I laugh some more. 'Of course, how could I forget how grown-up you are. Now, c'mon. Hop up and let's go. Aiden will you push us?'

'Sure,' Aiden says. 'Let's go around the basketball court and Molly can throw a few hoops. See if she has the natural Doran talent.'

Dad lifts Molly onto my lap, taking ages to position her so she's to one side, avoiding my bad leg. 'Now don't wriggle or move Molly or you'll hurt Kayla.' I can tell by Dad's face that he's nervous.

Aiden starts to push the chair and we slowly begin to roll forward.

'Faster, faster,' Molly shrieks.

'That's plenty fast enough,' Dad warns. 'Take it nice and steady, Aiden. That's it.'

'Gotcha,' Aiden says, though we're barely moving. 'I'll be careful.'

I wave to Mam on the far side of the yard. She's chatting to Miss Hanlon and she's smiling and doesn't notice me at first. When I finally get her attention she suddenly charges across the grass towards us.

'Stop. Stop!' she shouts. 'What are you doing?'

'Mam. It's fine,' I say. 'Molly is just having a little spin.'

'C'mon, Molly.' Mam lifts Molly off my lap and places her down on the ground and she throws Dad a dirty look. 'What on earth were you thinking?' Mam says.

I'm not sure who she's asking.

'Gavin, really. I turn my back for two minutes.'

'No harm done, Heather,' Jack says, appearing at Mam's side. 'They were just having some fun.'

Mam sighs and suddenly seems less frantic. Jack has a real calming effect on her. It's good. And Dad looks as if he appreciates that he's not going to get his head bitten off after all.

'It's time to go inside now,' Mam says. 'It's too cold out here for you and Miss Hanlon says there'll be music and dancing in the hall soon.'

'I can't dance,' I say, becoming embarrassed that people have started to stare, obviously noticing Mam's dramatic sprint across the whole yard. *Jesus.* I wish I thought about how much I'd stand out today before I agreed to come.

I mean, it's bad enough being stuck in this chair, but my whole family being here too is a bit intense and everyone keeps staring at me as if I'm a stranger and not someone who's been in school with them for the last four years. I know I look different now. I'm pretty skinny, and even though I like this new bandana Jack gave me it's still obvious I'm trying to cover my lack of hair. I hope Jack doesn't tell anyone he's my doctor. That's a level of mortification I simply can't handle right now. It's as if I've come with a whole team of super-enthusiastic babysitters who make awkward conversation with the teachers and don't really know where to stand. I just want some space. I really thought today would be different. I thought it would be just like a regular day at school. But it's nothing like that at all.

'Kayla, I'm sorry.' Mam's smile falls. 'I didn't mean to upset you. I just mean it's warm inside and I don't want you to get sick.'

'I'm already sick,' I say.

'Kayla.' Dad says my name the way he used to when I was a little girl and I did something naughty.

I roll my eyes. I'm pretty pissed off that I'm clearly not supposed to mention the obvious. That I am sick. *Dying in fact.* I don't think a light breeze is going to change much.

'It's fine out here,' I say. And it is. Google is saying it's something mad; like it's ten degrees warmer than it usually is at this time of year. I don't even need a coat. Although Mam insisted I bring one. I'm surprised she hasn't noticed I took it off and asked Aiden to stuff it into his locker for me.

'Kayla, I'm not going to argue with you,' Mam says.

'Okay. Good. You go inside if you want, then. I'm staying out here.'

Dad's eyes narrow. 'Kayla,' he warns. 'Don't speak to your mother like that.'

'It's not cold,' I snap. 'What was the point in driving all the way down here if I can't even hang out with my friends? I might as well have stayed in bed in the hospital.'

'Kayla that's not fair to say,' Dad says. 'You know we're worried about you.'

'Why did you even let me come today if you were going to be like this?'

'Like what?' Dad asks.

'All overprotective and stuff. It's embarrassing.'

'Kay...' Dad says, crouching next to me. 'I'm sorry. You're right. Today is supposed to be fun for you and we don't want to ruin that.'

I sigh. 'It's only teachers and parents in the hall.'

'It is,' Aiden backs me up. 'My mam's in there. She's looking for you actually, Heather. She said something about muffins melting next to a radiator.'

'Look,' Jack says, 'I'll stay with Kayla if you're worried. You go on in and sort the muffin crisis.'

Mam shakes her head. 'No. Thank you, Jack. But—'

'Right,' Dad says, standing up and placing his hand on Mam's shoulder. 'Maybe we should give Kay a little space. I'm sure she'd like to spend some time with Aiden without us crowding her. And if Jack's with them it will be fine.'

Mam shakes her head again, but she doesn't bother with words this time.

'And after all your work last night you don't want your muffins destroyed now,' Dad says. 'Molly loves the three-legged race, so we'll be just over there.' Dad points nearby where some of the junior classes are partnered up and tying their ankles together with mouldy, coloured neck ties like the ones the vice principal always wears.

'Okay. Yeah. Okay,' Mam says, sounding super unsure, like she'll change her mind any second. 'Thanks, Jack.'

'Right, C'mon, Molly,' Dad says, taking Molly's hand. 'Let play a game of guess who will fall over first.'

Molly giggles with excitement as Dad, Molly and Charlotte walk away.

Mam walks away too, ridiculously slowly, twisting her head over her shoulder to say, 'Have fun. And put your coat on before you get sick.'

'Bit late for that,' someone says and there's a lot of laughing and joking.

'You got something to say there, Roisin?' Aiden snaps, marching over to where Roisin Kelly and some of her horrible friends stand in the doorway of the science building trying not to get caught smoking by the teachers. I really wished I'd noticed them there sooner. I hate that they were in earshot of our conversation. No doubt having a good laugh at my expense.

'Oh, piss off back to the cripple,' Roisin says and all her friends laugh as if she's hilarious.

Aiden sees red and charges towards her.

'Leave it, Aiden. She's not worth it,' I shout, worried he'll get in trouble if any of the teachers see him.

There's more laughing and pointing and I hope my face isn't going bright red because I feel as if my cheeks are on fire. Maybe I should have gone into the hall with Mam after all.

'Disease is a funny thing,' Jack says, suddenly standing where Aiden was two seconds ago. I didn't notice them switch places. 'You never know when or if you'll be affected.'

'I wasn't trying to slag her,' Roisin says, and her face goes as red as mine feels.

'Yes you were,' Jack says. 'But that's okay. You can't help being an asshole any more than Kayla can help being unwell. Goodbye.'

'Oh burn,' one of Roisin's friends says before they erupt in laughter.

'Is she always like that?' Jack asks coming back.

'Yup,' Aiden and I say together.

'Wow. Her parents must be proud,' Jack says. 'Some kids, eh?'

Aiden and I don't reply. There isn't really anything to say. Roisin Kelly is the type of person who puts chewing gum in your hair when you're healthy and teases you about being in a wheelchair when you're not. I guess she's the one who's really sick.

'Right.' Jack smiles, rubbing his hands together. 'Who's up for a game of basketball.'

'Really?' I smile. 'Can we?'

'Sure,' Jack says. 'I don't see why not. I mean, if you think you can make the shot from your chair, then bring it on.'

'I can.' I smile, confident and excited.

'I should warn you, I've improved a bit over the years,' Jack says.

'Yeah but you're old now,' Aiden giggles. 'And Kayla is still the captain of our team.'

Aiden's words fill my tummy with butterflies. 'They didn't replace me?'

'What?' Aiden says. 'No. Of course not, you wally. Someone stands in for you when we've a game on. But you're the captain, Kayla. Everyone knows that. And no one ever wants that to change.'

FORTY-EIGHT

CHARLOTTE

Molly is in her element as the older kids fuss over her.

'Oh, she's so cute,' a tall girl says, noticing us standing on the sideline of the three-legged race. Gavin has gone to find somewhere quiet to take a work call, so it's just me and Molly and I must admit I feel a little self-conscious because we don't really belong here.

'That's Kayla Prendergast Doran's little sister,' another much shorter girl adds.

They both seem about Kayla's age.

'Do you want to race?' they ask together, and Molly nods and smiles and takes their hand.

'Is that okay?' one of the girls asks me.

'Sure,' I say, 'I'll be right here watching.'

'What's your name?' one of the girls asks, bending to come down to Molly's level.

'I'm Molly.'

'We're Kayla's friends, by the way,' I hear them tell Molly as they walk towards the starting line and a woman I assume is a teacher hands Molly a silver dessert spoon and a potato.

Kids take their spots at the line. Some are very tall and seem very grown-up. Molly seems to get lost among them. I become quite worried that they'll knock Molly over in their enthusiasm to win. I move around to get a better view.

'Three... two... one... go!' the teacher shouts and they all take off running very slowly.

Potatoes tumble to the ground and lanky teenagers pick them up and hurry back to the starting line to begin again. Kayla's friends are on either side of Molly, shielding her, and Molly's potato is wobbling but not falling and she's pulling ahead as more overzealous racers lose their spuds and have to start over.

'Yes, Molly. That's it. Good girl. Good girl,' I shout as Molly approaches the finish line way ahead. 'Woohoo. Woohoo!' I cheer when she comes first.

Molly passes her spoon and potato back to the teacher and runs over to me with her hands above her head and a huge smile on her face. 'I won. I won. I won.'

'Yes. You did. Well done, champ.'

'Do I get a prize?'

I'm about to explain to Molly that the satisfaction of winning should be a prize enough when the two girls come running over.

'Don't forget your medal,' they say.

Molly jumps up and down on the spot with excitement. 'I do get a prize,' she says.

One of the girls slides a plastic medal from the euro shop with bright pink-and-yellow ribbon around Molly's neck.

'Thank you,' I say.

'You're Charlotte, right?' the taller of the two girls asks.

'Um, yes,' I say, wondering if Molly told them my name.

'You're Kayla's stepmam, right?'

I wince, not sure what to say. Kayla never refers to me as her stepmother and Gavin doesn't either. And I imagine Heather would rather stick pins in her eyes than use the term. But I guess as Gavin's wife that's what I am. And acknowledging that these two friendly kids see me that way fills me with joy.

'Yeah. Yes I am,' I say, owning the title, proudly.

'I'm Sarah. And this is Amy,' the taller girl says, pointing to herself first and then her friend. 'We saw your Help Fund Me page.'

'Oh,' I say, wondering if all the kids have been talking about it. Wondering if the teachers know. Suddenly I'm very aware that Heather is in the hall packed with gossiping parents and teachers.

'Did you know they were talking about it on the radio this morning?' Sarah asks.

I shake my head unsure what to think or feel.

'She lives in Dublin,' Amy says, pointing at me. 'You don't get Radio Cork up there, do you?'

'No,' I say, glad that Heather won't have heard anything.

Sarah nods. 'Ah, right, yeah that makes sense. Well, anyway, the DJs were talking about it on the breakfast show this morning. Saying how Kayla is a local girl and all. They were saying how awesome an idea it is and then loads of people were phoning in saying there were going to donate.'

'Really? People are donating?' I ask.

'Yeah. Like tonnes of people,' Sarah says, practically bouncing on the spot, the way Molly does when she is excited. 'There's a hashtag on Twitter too. #HelpKaylasCakes.'

'It's just #KaylasCakes, silly,' Amy corrects.

'Okay, whatever. It's something like that and people are really into it. I think it's so cool. You've done such an amazing thing. Kayla must be so excited.'

'And her mam must be super happy too,' Amy adds, a little more calmly than her friend. 'Like a bakery is *awesome*. And I've known Heather since I was little. She makes the best cakes. It will be so cool when she has her own shop. I'm going to go there all the time.'

'It's totally going viral,' Sarah says. 'Kayla is, like, famous.'

I pull my phone out of my pocket and log into the app. 'Oh my God. Oh my God,' I say as I see the hundreds of donations that have come in since this morning.

'See. Told ya,' Sarah says. 'And it's going up all the time.'

'This is incredible,' I say, barely able to believe my eyes. 'People are so generous. Kayla won't believe this.'

'She's on the basketball court with Aiden and that hot old guy,' Amy says. 'If you want to go tell her.'

I'm the same age as Jack. I try not to take offence that Kayla's friends think anyone in their mid-thirties is obviously ancient.

'Can we come with you to tell her?' Amy asks, beginning to become as excitable as her friend.

I really wish they hadn't asked. I'm not sure what Kayla will say when she discovers her story is all over the internet and radio, but they've been so lovely I can't ask them to leave now.

'Sure,' I smile. 'I'm sure Kayla would love to catch up with you both.'

FORTY-NINE
HEATHER

I'm in the school hall nattering to teachers I've never spoken to before and parents I barely know as I finish up taking brownies out of the large Tupperware box I borrowed from Charlotte and display them on paper plates on the tables. The school has gone to a lot of trouble. There are floral and lacy table cloths. They're horribly mismatched and a bit gaudy but they're a vast improvement on the bare desks that are doubling up as display tables. There are balloons and banners, and there is music playing. Colourful art is splashed all over the walls, along with pictures of runners, trophies and medals, scattered across the brickwork like a rainbow collage.

'There you are,' Miss Hanlon says, startling me as she appears suddenly behind me. She laughs. 'Oops. Did I give you a fright?'

I blush.

'Is Kayla here, too?' she asks, craning her neck to look all around.

'Yes, somewhere,' I say. 'Still outside, I think.'

'Oh right.' Miss Hanlon sounds surprised and my concern that Kayla playing outside is a bad idea is compounded.

'No doubt she's found her way to the basketball court if I know Kayla,' Miss Hanlon adds. 'We're hoping to get the awards ceremony started in the next few minutes so will I go out and call her?'

'The awards...' I say blankly.

'We have something very special for you both. And the hall can get pretty uncomfortably packed when all the parents and kids start coming in. It would be good to get Kayla in first, and seated so she's comfortable.'

Oh God, I think, instantly uncomfortable. I wasn't expecting any fuss. This is all a bit awkward. I hope they haven't bought some sort of a gift. Especially not if they've taken the money from the parents-association fund. I'll never hear the end of it from the bitchy yummy mummies who moan about absolutely everything and never actually help with the fundraising.

'Gosh, these look lovely,' a women says, crossing the hall to point at my brownies. 'I didn't know we were supposed to bake. I'd have made my favourite red-velvet queen cake.'

'No need, Mrs Kelly,' Miss Hanlon says. 'Heather has taken care of all our baking needs today. Thank you.'

'Well, I must say they look delicious.'

'Thank you,' I say, doubting it's a real compliment by the snotty tone of her voice.

'May I have one, please?' She picks up a brownie before waiting for an answer.

'Certainly,' Miss Hanlon says. 'The brownies are two euros each.'

'You have to buy them?'

'Well, yes.' Miss Hanlon tilts her head to one side and eyes the woman with disgust. 'That's the whole idea of a fundraiser.'

'But the kids already brought in two euros this morning for the fundraiser,' she says.

'That was two euros to wear no uniform.'

'So the children are expected to pay again for something to eat.'

'They don't have to. Just if they want to – all the cakes and treats are priced at two euros each. And like I said, Mrs Kelly, it really is all for a very good cause.'

'This school gets more expensive by the day. My God.' She places the brownie that she's held disgustingly close to her lips back on the plate and walks away.

Miss Hanlon rolls her eyes. 'I'm sorry,' she says. 'There's always one, isn't there?'

'I didn't know we'd be selling the buns,' I say, picking up the brownie the rude woman breathed all over and tossing it into the bin next to my ankles.

'Didn't you?' Miss Hanlon asks.

I make a face. 'I don't mind. I mean, actually, I think it's a great idea. It's just I didn't realise. If I'd known the school were trying to raise funds I'd have baked more.'

'What you have here is fantastic. You've so much on your plate, Heather. I don't know how you found the time to make all these. And they smell amazing. My mouth is watering.'

'Would you like one?' I ask.

Miss Hanlon shoves her hand into her pocket. 'I've no change, I'm afraid. And my wallet is in the staff room.'

'I won't tell if you don't.'

'I think my guilty face would give me away. I'll get one later when I have some money. But thank you, Heather.'

'Hey, Mam,' Kayla's voice carries through the air to tap me on the shoulder. 'I scored six baskets. Jack could only manage five and he was on his feet and jumping.'

'You played?' I say, as Jack and Kayla come into view. Kayla looks exhausted and I instantly worry but I try to hide it. Jack is flushed but smiling and Aiden has beads of perspiration dotted around his hairline and his face is redder than Kayla's hoodie. 'Good game?' I say, changing tack, trying to sound breezy.

'The best. Even though Jack used to play in college he's pretty rusty now.'

'Hey,' Jack says, trying to sound offended but his wide grin and kind eyes contradict him.

Miss Hanlon places her hand on my shoulder. 'Heather, would it be okay to get you guys to take your seats now? I've reserved the row up front for your family. I'm short a seat for your partner though but I'll get one of the students to grab another. It'll just be a moment.'

I blush and drop my eyes to the ground. I can feel Jack looking at me and I wonder what he makes of Miss Hanlon assumption that we're a couple. I don't correct her and neither does he and I wonder if that's just because it would be awkward or because we are both rather enjoying her error.

'This way, this way,' she says, ushering us towards the front row and she catches the attention of a passing senior student and asks them to fetch another chair.

'Where are Dad, Molly and Charlotte?' Kayla asks.

'Here. We're here,' Gavin says, suddenly behind us.

The hall begins to become very noisy as it fills with people taking up seats behind us. Kayla stays in her wheelchair and Jack expertly tucks it in at the end of the row so she simply looks like she's sitting beside us all. I take the seat next to Kayla and Jack sits next to me, which feels both awkward and lovely and I hope my feelings aren't written all over my face.

Gavin is next to Jack with Molly on his knee. She's stroking a very shiny plastic medal and she's showing it to everyone nearby.

Charlotte is missing and it takes me a minute to realise that she's crouched on her hunkers on the far side of Kayla's chair. They're whispering and giggling and there's lots of hand movements and excitement. I wonder what on earth they're talking about. I haven't seen Kayla look this happy in weeks. Aiden joins their conversation and two girls from Kayla's class are bending down to show Kayla something on their phones. And they're nodding emphatically as they point at their screens.

My niggling curiosity about their conversation switches into concern quite quickly as Kayla soon appears to be overwhelmed and becomes emotional. The noise in the hall is horrendous as the large crowd filing in behind us natter.

'Jack, Jack,' I whisper, tapping him gently on the arm.

'Hmm,' he says, turning to face me.

'Is Kayla okay? Do you think she's okay?'

Jack leans around me to get a better view of Kayla and the small group surrounding her. He turns back smiling. 'She looks good. Happy. Today has been good for her, hasn't it?'

'Yeah,' I say, unsure. Something is definitely going on and I hope she's as okay as she's pretending to be.

'Ladies and gentlemen, welcome to today's extra special Sports Day,' a voice carries over the speakers and a hush falls over the hall as the principal takes to the stage.

FIFTY

KAYLA

Miss Hanlon is staring at me and smiling. I haven't seen her this excited since we got new hoops and nets in the gym last year.

Mrs Maloney, the principal, is waffling into the microphone about the extension the school is building next year. 'And the planning application has just gone in to the council,' she says. Everyone claps as if it's fantastic news. I guess it is. 'If all goes to plan we hope to have a new, bigger sports hall and five new classrooms built in the next two years.'

There's more clapping as my stomach knots and I realise the new building is something I won't ever see. I'll be long gone by then. *How weird.*

Just as I'm zoning out, unable to listen to Mrs Maloney drone on anymore, I hear my name and I'm shook.

'Perhaps you could join us on stage, Kayla?' Mrs Maloney says, pointing towards me.

I shake my head. *Oh God. Oh God.* I can feel the eyes of every parent and pupil in the hall follow the tip of the principal's finger to find where I'm sitting.

'Kay-la. Kay-la. Kay-la,' chanting begins.

I shake my head again. 'No, no, no,' I say, but no one can hear me.

The other students have started stomping their feet, keeping in beat to the syllables of my name as they chant. 'Kay-la. Kay-la.'

Oh God, this is horrendous. No one warned me about having to get up on stage. My eyes widen. *Crap, Mrs Maloney isn't going to expect me to speak, is she? What would I even say?*

'Come on, Kayla. Don't be shy,' Mrs Maloney says into the microphone, so it definitely feels more like she's talking to everyone in the room and not just to me.

I'm borderline freaking out. Mam glances at me, and I notice the super-worried face on her. I bet she thinks this is a crappy idea, too. I've been on stage for awards ceremonies before. But I'm always with my teammates. It's never just me on my own. This feels so uncomfortable and forced.

Miss Hanlon disappears behind the stage curtain and within seconds she's standing beside me.

'Can you stand?' she asks.

Mam shakes her head. Answering for me. *Thank God.*

'There's no ramp,' Miss Hanlon says and I'm pretty sure she's telling Mam and not me.

'Where are the steps?' Mam asks.

Miss Hanlon points to the stage door. 'There are about four steps on the other side. They're not steep or anything.'

'Kay-la. Kay-la. Kay-la.' The chanting grows even louder. It feels as if the roof is vibrating.

I glance at Molly sitting on Dad's lap. I wonder if she'll be scared by the loud noise and I almost start laughing when I see her bouncing up and down on Dad's knees shouting her head off and loving every moment. Dad's face is hilarious because she's clearly squashing him.

'I can carry you,' Aiden says, leaning in from the seat behind me.

'Screw this,' I say, getting a fright because I didn't know that's where he disappeared to when Mrs Maloney came on stage.

'Kayla. Please mind your language,' Mam says. 'Sorry, Miss Hanlon.'

'Sorry, Miss,' I add. 'But seriously, no. How morto. Aiden cop on.'

'Well you can at least lean on me, then,' Aiden says.

'Oh, Aiden, I don't know. Steps are tricky for Kayla right now,' Mam says.

I look at Doctor Patterson. He's nodding and smiling. And even though I'm freaking out, I know I can do this. I'll regret it if I don't. The school have been so great, organising a sports day in the middle of November just for me, I probably should go up on stage to say thanks at least.

'Go on,' Doctor Patterson mouths and I smile back at him.

'Kayla, it's up to you,' Miss Hanlon adds. 'There's no pressure. If you're not comfortable...'

I listen to the noise and excitement in the hall that rings in my ears. 'No pressure,' I say, pulling a face.

'Well...' Miss Hanlon laughs.

'Right. C'mon,' I say, not sure what the hell I'm thinking as I stand up. 'Let's do this.'

Mam looks on as Aiden crouches slightly so I can drape my arm over his shoulder and Miss Hanlon supports me on the other side.

'Take it handy,' Mam warns. 'Nice and slowly, okay.'

'Okay,' I nod, putting one foot in front of the other, relieved that it doesn't hurt as much as I was expecting it to.

The steps are much more awkward than I anticipated and by the second step I'm seriously considering taking Aiden up on his offer to carry me. But I keep going – determined, and by the time we reach the stage I feel like a champion. An exhausted champion, to be fair.

'And here she is now,' Mrs Maloney says.

There's a lot of clapping and wolf whistling as Aiden, Miss Hanlon and I make our way into the centre of the stage to stand beside the principal.

Miss Hanlon lets go and grabs a chair from the side of the stage. Aiden helps me to sit down and it feels super weird to be sitting facing a tonne of people as they all sit facing me.

Aiden turns to walk away and I tug the sleeve of his jumper, just in time to catch him.

'Don't leave me,' I whisper.

'This is your moment,' he says.

'Please,' I say. 'I need you.'

'Okay.'

Aiden stands at one side of me, his face is red like he's just finished an epic basketball game. I really hope someone takes a picture so I can tease him about this on Snapchat later. Miss Hanlon stands on the other side of me, her hand gently squeezing my shoulder encouragingly every now and then.

'Ladies and gentleman, boys and girls, it is with great pleasure that I announce today's fundraiser has been an overwhelming successes. Thank you all for your kind support,' Ms Maloney says.

There's yet more clapping.

'Miss Hanlon, if you would be so kind as to pass me the envelope with the tally please?'

Miss Hanlon scurries to the side of the stage, picks up a fancy white envelope and hurries back to give it to Mrs Maloney the way they do at the Oscars. Only I've never seen a presenter at the Oscars in a tracksuit or with a whistle dangling around her neck. I try not to laugh thinking about it.

'Thank you,' Mrs Maloney says, opening the envelope super, super slowly. 'And the tally is in, we have raised a whopping two thousand euros today.'

'Wow,' I say, genuinely blown away. 'That's so cool.'

'Kayla.' Ms Maloney turns towards me, and although the microphone still picks up what she's saying she really is speaking just to me now. 'We are so incredibly proud of you. Myself, the vice principal, your teachers and all your peers think what you are doing for your mother is just wonderful. And that is why it makes me incredibly happy to say that the entire tally of today's fundraiser will be donated to the Kayla's Cakes Help Fund Me page.'

I gasp. I thought the money was for charity. I look at Mam. She's shaking her head. *Oh God. Oh God.* This is not how I wanted her to find out. I look at Charlotte. She seems panicked too. *Please stop talking, Mrs Maloney. Shh. Shh. Shh.*

There's some whispering on stage behind me and the rattle of trolley wheels. I turn my head over my shoulder to find Roisin Kelly and one of her friends behind me, sniggering. I didn't notice them come on stage.

'Thank you, girls,' Ms Maloney says. 'You can take your seats again now.'

I look at the trolley the girls have left behind. The school projector is on top. Mrs O'Hagan has moved to the back of the stage to pull down the white screen thingy that they project stuff on. I have no idea what is going on and bubbles of fear pop in my stomach. I look at Aiden, begging him to fill me in but he shrugs and I know he's totally clueless too.

'Now, if I just press this button. Um, eh, this one here.' Mrs Maloney fiddles around with the projector and within a couple of seconds it turns on and shines the school crest onto the screen. 'Ah ha, there we go,' she says, excited.

I search the stage for Miss Hanlon and when I find her she's staring back at me nodding and smiling, as if to say, 'This is awesome, right?'

This is so not awesome. I need to get off the stage and talk to Mam. I need to explain.

'Kayla, perhaps you would like to tell us a little bit about your wonderful fund in your own words.'

I shake my head and my eyes glass over as the school crest disappears off the screen and a screenshot of my Help Fund Me page appears in bright in-your-face colour. Magnified until it's bloody huge.

My name is Kayla Prendergast Doran.

I am fifteen years old and I have a stage four soft tissue cancer.

The doctors call it Ewing's sarcoma. I call it shit!

This isn't a Help Fund Me page asking you for money to help me buy expensive treatment. I've passed that point. It's also not a page asking you to feel sorry for me. I don't want a trip to Disney World. I don't want to meet my favourite celebrity – although, Zac Efron, if you see this, feel free to drop by the hospital.

What I want more than anything is to get better, but I know that won't happen. All I can do is try to make sure my mam is okay – and I need your HELP!!!

When I got sick my mam gave up her job to look after me. She makes money now baking cakes for the hospital canteen. I would really, really love if she could make money baking cakes in her own shop.

Please, please donate anything you can to help my mam set up her own bakery. I just want my mam to be okay when I'm gone.

Thank you so much,

Kayla x

I watch as the eyes of the whole school community read over my words. Charlotte, Aiden and I spent ages trying to get this wording just right. I know we put it on the internet for the whole world to see, but I always imagined the people who read it would be a world away. As if the internet was only viewed by strangers and not neighbours and friends and classmates. And definitely not by my mam. There are gasps and shocked faces as they discover how hard it's been for Mam and me this past while.

Whispering starts among the parents first and, of course, all the students join in. I even see some of the teachers, lining the walls, chatting among themselves. *Jesus. How could Mrs Maloney possibly have thought this was a good idea?*

'Kayla. Kayla.' Mrs Maloney taps me on the shoulder. She's so full of excitement. I've never seen her like this before. I don't know how to react. Mrs Maloney's enthusiasm combined with my shock makes my head spin.

'I don't have anything to say,' I manage to splutter out. The microphone picks up my voice and broadcasts it to the whole hall.

'Shh. Shh. Shh,' people encourage each other, as if I'm that guy in the kilt in *Braveheart* who makes a mad important speech to his army before he leads them into battle. I'm not a leader. I can't even manage to beat cancer.

I look at Mrs Maloney and I'm shaking.

'Okay, okay,' she says, and her excitement seems more under control and she's more like the principal I'm used to. She turns away from the microphone and bends to whisper in my ear. 'If you'd rather not speak, Kayla, I completely understand. I can imagine this is all a bit overwhelming. You're very brave.'

I sigh with relief and look to Aiden and Miss Hanlon for help getting off stage. But Miss Hanlon doesn't come to my rescue. And Aiden doesn't even make eye contact as he stands beside me like a beetroot statue. Worst of all, Mrs Maloney doesn't stop talking. She proceeds to tell the entire community about the hashtag trending on Twitter. About the DJs talking about Mam and me on the radio. About the calls from parents she's been receiving all morning asking how they can help. She makes Mam and me out to be desperate or something – begging people for money to make ends meet. I know she doesn't mean to, but I can see pity on everyone's face as they stare at me. My mind is racing. This is not how today was supposed to go.

Mrs Maloney is saying something now about how proud of me she is. And she's mentioning Aiden too. But I'm not really listening. My attention is on my mam. I watch as she sinks down in her chair, covering her face with her hands. I think she's shaking her head but it's kind of hard to tell from up here. And then she's talking to Jack. I can see she's getting angry. Or upset. Dad tries talking to her too. But she's waving her hands about now. And, *Oh my God*, she's standing up.

She stands up and stares at me and the last time I saw this much pain in her eyes was when I told her that I wanted to stop all treatment. *Oh God what have I done?* This was supposed to be a wonderful surprise. It wasn't supposed to get announced like this in front of the whole school with everyone staring at us, whispering about us, feeling sorry for us.

I read Mam's lips. 'Excuse me. Excuse me,' she says, turning towards Jack. But everyone is clapping and cheering.

I have to talk to Mam, I think. I have to get off this stage and explain that I wasn't trying to embarrass her. Or upset her. I have to tell her that I love her.

I stand up. Unaided and taking the entire weight of my own body means that pain shoots through me like thousands of small electric shocks. It hurts so much I can't see and everything goes black and the noise in the hall turns from cheers and chants to ringing and I know I won't have time to sit back onto the chair before I pass out.

FIFTY-ONE

KAYLA

A million different colours fill my head as memories explode like fireworks in my mind. I remember learning to ride my first bike. It was bright pink with a purple basket in the front for my doll. Dad bought rainbow coloured streamers that we attached to the handle bars. Mam and Dad clapped and cheered when I was finally able to keep my balance by myself.

I remember Dad's wedding. Dad was so handsome in his suit. And Charlotte had a beautiful white dress with a lace bodice and a long swishing trail. I wanted a dress just like it when I grew up and got married. I remember dancing in Dad's arms and smiling and laughing and being the happiest girl in the world.

The day Molly was born Mam cried. She said everything would be different now that Dad had another little girl and she was worried. Mam was right, everything was different. It was better. Molly is the best little sister. She is pretty and clever and she gives the biggest squeezy hugs.

I think of Ross and Rachel on a break in *Friends*. I think of how Joey doesn't share food. I think of every episode that Mam and I laughed our way through, just the two of us at home eating pizza in our pyjamas. And Mam would sometimes say that she had all her favourite things in one room. *Friends*, pizza and me.

'Kayla,' someone calls and I can feel a hand gently on my forehead. 'Can you hear me?'

I nod, but nothing happens. I try again. I'm not moving.

'Is she in pain?' I recognise Mam's voice. It's wobbly and I know she's crying, but it's definitely her.

'No.'

'I can't do this,' Mam says. 'I can't watch her go.'

'Have you spoken to Doctor Patterson today?' the voice says – it's one of the nurses, I realise. I'm back in the hospital.

'Yeah,' Mam sniffles. 'This morning. He says Kayla knows what she's asking.'

'She really doesn't even want to try a trial? It could give you a little time.'

'No,' Mam says, and I hear certainty in her voice. 'She doesn't want any more pain. She's asking me to let her go.'

'And can you?'

'No,' Mam sobs. 'How can I? How can I ever let her go? You know, Jack says this Help Fund Me thing that Kayla has set up is her way of saying goodbye. He thinks she's trying to protect me. To take care of me.'

'And you think?' the nurse asks.

'I didn't ask for this. For any of this. The media are trying to contact me. I don't even know where they got my number. They leave me voicemails, asking if I'll do radio or TV interviews. They say it will bring in even more donations.'

'Is it something you might consider?'

'No,' Mam says, sounding hurt. 'No it's not. I don't want people's money. I just want my daughter to get better. That's what I want. But no one can give me that. Can they?'

I hear a door creak open. There's footsteps. They're fading. Mam is walking away, I think. *No. Don't go. I don't want Mam to go.* I try so hard to open my eyes but they're heavy and I'm sleepy. So sleepy.

The Christmas Santa bringing me a sparkly magic wand dances across my mind as if it's a movie on Netflix. I watch as Mam tells me I'm a magic princess. And I tell Aiden I'll turn him into a frog.

I see my first day of secondary school. My jumper is embarrassingly huge on me and Mam says, 'You'll grow into it.'

There's talking at the door. It pulls me out of my lovely dreams. I hear raised voices. A man and Mam. Mam is shouting. No, crying. No, shouting. The man is Dad. He's angry too. And then it stops. All the noise stops, and I wonder if I'm still breathing. Still here.

'Kayla. Kayla, honey, it's Dad. Are you okay?'

I feel lips on my forehead. Dad kisses me. It's so nice. I want him to hug me too. But he doesn't. He doesn't know how much I want a hug.

'What are they saying?' Dad asks, all whispery and stressed.

'Not much,' Mam says.

'Jack thinks it's the growth in her chest pressing on her lungs. They did a scan this morning. I thought he'd be here by now with news.'

'And if it is? If something is pressing on her lungs...?' Dad says.

I know Dad wants to ask what will happen. Will I be able to breathe? I want him to ask. I'm scared. I wasn't prepared to be this scared.

'And... I... don't... know,' Mam cries.

I'm flying. I'm flying over school. I see the yard, and the cool kids in the back smoking and thinking the teachers don't know. I

want to shout, 'They do know. And they think you're idiots.' I
see my team. I see us winning by three baskets. I see myself
dribble past the captain on the other side to score the winning
basket.

'Did you know about this?' Mam asks.

'The Help Fund Me page?' Dad says, and I wonder if he's
looking at something. It sounds as if he's looking at something.
Like his concentration is on reading his phone, or a letter or
something. 'Oh my God, has she really raised this much?'

'Yeah,' Mam says.

'Wow.'

'Did you know. Did you know about it?'

'No,' Dad says. 'No. I didn't. How could I?'

'Charlotte was in on this,' Mam says. 'Aiden told me. Oh, he
didn't want to confess. But his mother dragged it out of him.
Did you know Mary had no idea he's been skipping school
every Tuesday to come visit Kayla?'

My mouth finally opens. *Ouch. Ouch. Ouch.* My lips sting
and I know they're all cracked and dry. *Stupid hospital air.* And
my throat is on fire. I mean actual fire. *Jesus.* But I think I can
manage words. I still can't open my eyes, that seems to be too
much effort for my stupid body right now.

'Charlotte and Aiden helped me,' I say. 'But it was my
idea.'

I sound like a one-hundred-and-ten-year-old smoker. It's
weird and kind of funny but Mam and Dad are all super serious
so I can't laugh right now.

'Oh, Kayla,' Mam says. 'Oh, you're awake. You're awake.
God you scared me.'

'Hey there, kiddo,' Dad says.

'Drink...' I croak. Okay that noise deserves at least a giggle, I
decide.

But Mam and Dad don't make a sound.

My eyes flutter open and the room is horribly bright. I close them again. I count backwards from three in my head and try again.

'There she is,' Dad says, looking at me. 'Hey you. Hey.'

'Hey,' I crackle back, blinking a lot. 'What time is it?'

'How about what day is it?' Mam says.

'Dad?' I ask, confused.

'You've been out of it for a couple of days, Kay,' Dad explains as he pours some water. 'You hit the stage like your mother hit the Barcadi Breezers after you were born. Hard.'

'Hey,' Mam says, semi-giggling, semi-offended.

It's so good to hear her laugh. Dad always makes her laugh.

'What?' Dad says, carrying a glass of water over to my bed. 'Don't you think it's time Kayla knew the truth? I snuck a couple of Barcadi Breezers into the hospital the night you were born, Kay, and your mam and I celebrated like a couple of teenage rebels.'

'Except I couldn't actually drink mine because I was breast-feeding,' Mam says as she slides her arm behind my back and helps me to sit up.

'Oh yeah,' Dad says smiling as he passes Mam the glass of water that she helps me sip. 'That's right. I drank them all, didn't I?'

Mam and Dad laugh and try so hard to keep the atmosphere light. It works, and I love that they have so much history together. But a horrible feeling grips me as I listen to them reminisce and tease each other the way old friends do.

'You'll stay friends forever, won't you?' I say, suddenly very short of air.

'Hmm, sweetie?' Mam says, and their giggling stops instantly as she gives me her full attention.

'You and Dad. You'll stay friends, won't you?' I puff out. 'Even when I'm gone?'

'Kay. C'mon,' Mam says, shaking her head.

Dad looks at me. I can see his eyes glistening. 'You're

mother and I will always be friends. Always, Kay. That's not something you have to worry about, okay?'

'It's just, you guys have stayed in touch all these years because of me.' My eyes are so heavy. 'And when I'm not here anymore...'

'Kayla please,' Mam says, the same way she does every time I start to talk about the future. A future without me. 'Let's talk about something else, okay?'

'Okay,' I say, 'you can't be cross with Aiden and Charlotte.'

'Kayla I'm not cross,' Mam says.

'Yes, you are,' I say, licking my stinging lips. 'I know you. You're all embarrassed. I'm sorry.'

'I'm not,' Mam says, and her 'I'm trying to be all cool and breezy because you're sick' voice comes out and I've learned that this voice really is her 'if you weren't sick you'd be in so much trouble right now' voice.

'I put Charlotte in a mad awkward position. I asked her for help. I told her not to tell Dad. Or anyone.'

'And Aiden?' Mam asks. 'He's been skipping school.'

'Just Tuesdays,' I say, and I have to pause to draw some breath.

'Well.' Mam takes a deep breath, almost as deep as mine. 'I think what you tried to do is very, very kind, Kayla. But you must know we can't go ahead. We can't expect people to buy us a bakery. Where would we even buy, for goodness' sake?'

Dad winks at me as Mam rambles on and on and on. And when Mam is distracted by a knock at the door, Dad whispers, 'I have an idea, Kay. I have a great idea.'

'Hi, Jack,' Mam says, as she opens the door. 'Come on in.'

'You know what, Mam?' I sigh, exhausted again but also excited to know what Dad's idea is. 'Maybe you and Doctor Patterson could talk in his office, while I get some asleep?

Doctor Patterson looks at me with a sceptical smirk, but he

nods, smiles and agrees. 'Sure. You get some rest, Kayla. I'll be back around later.'

'Thanks,' I say.

Dad gets ready to leave too, believing me.

'Dad,' I whisper gently. 'Will you stay with me for a while.'

'Sure, kiddo. I'd really love to.'

FIFTY-TWO

CHARLOTTE

December

'How do you spell unicorn?' Molly asks, sitting at the kitchen table with a pink pencil in her right hand and an even brighter pink notepad in front of her.

'U-N-I-C-O-R-N,' I reply, washing up after dinner. 'Molly that's about the tenth time I've spelt that for you today.'

'It's a hard word,' Molly says, poking her tongue between her lips and scrunching her eyes as she concentrates on writing the letters.

'Are you writing your Santa list?' I ask, trying to scrub a stubborn stain off the baking tray.

'Yes,' Molly replies, twitching with excitement. 'I'm going to show Daddy when he gets home from the hostable.'

I let the scrubbing brush fall into the sink as I turn to face my little girl. 'Sweetheart, it might be bedtime before Daddy gets home.'

'Is Daddy helping Kayla write her Santa list?' Molly asks.

'Maybe.'

'I can't wait for Christmas,' Molly chirps. 'I'm going to sit aside Kayla for dinner and I'm going to let her play with all my toys. Even my unicorn.'

Tears gather in the corners of my eyes and I look away.

'Don't be sad, Mammy.' Molly hops off her chair and walks over to wrap her little arms around my legs. 'You can play with my toys too.'

I exhale slowly and run a hand through my hair, wincing when my rubber glove lands suds into my hair.

'What are you asking Santa for, Molly?' I ask, fishing the scrubbing brush out of the sink, desperate for a distraction.

Molly hurries back to table and sitting down she takes a big, deep breath. 'Barbie with pink hair to brush. Scooter that's got shiny lights and can go fast. Fairy door so I can get new fairies.' Molly pauses for another deep breath. 'Mary Poppins dress-up dress and a unicorn teddy that's all pink and purple with multi-coloured hair.' Breathless, she nods. 'That's all.'

'Oh, Molly,' I say, taking off my rubber gloves to come and see this mammoth list for myself. 'That's quite the list, isn't it?' I read the words over her shoulder.

'I did my best writing so Santa will know I'm a good girl.'

'Your writing is lovely,' I say, proud. 'And you are a good girl. But I really think three gifts is more than enough on any Santa list, okay?'

'But... but... but...'

'Molly,' I say.

'But I gots to put on even more things.' Molly looks at me with wide, desperate eyes. 'I'm not finished.'

'Well' – I walk back to the sink, slipping my hand back into my gloves – 'you're just going to have to choose the things that matter most, Molly, and ask for those. Put the most important thing at the top.'

I watch Molly expecting some objection or perhaps some sulking, but she smiles and nods. 'Okay,' she says, tearing the list she worked so hard on out of her notepad and turning over a fresh page to start again.

'I know the thing that matters the mostest ever. I'll ask for that.'

'Good girl,' I say, wondering where I'm going to get a very specific pink-and-purple unicorn with multicoloured hair. I pick up her finished letter, which she has carefully folded. 'Okay, Molly. Put your coat on please, it's time for piano lessons. We can post this on the way, if you like.'

'But I don't want to go to peenano.' Molly drops her pencil and folds her arms. 'I want to stay at home and watch *Teen Titans Go!*'

'Molly, please,' I say, too exhausted for a tantrum. 'This is your last lesson before Christmas. You'll have a lovely long break then, okay?'

'Okay,' Molly says, closing over her notepad. 'Can we go see Kayla after peenano?'

I nod, smiling. 'Okay. But just for a little while. Remember Kayla is very tired.'

'Yay!' Molly says and scampers off to get her coat.

FIFTY-THREE

HEATHER

My phone is riddled with messages and emails. RTÉ and all the papers want to talk to me. I actually had someone from the Taoiseach's office contact me asking if I could call them back. I haven't had a chance. I don't even know what I'd say if I did. I can't deny that my heart skips a beat knowing my daughter's plight has reached the government. But, as much as I'd like to, I don't have time to entertain politicians. Every time I think Kayla is getting a hold on this thing, she slips a little. And every time I think she's slipping, she fights back. My head is spinning and the sudden attention from everyone at the hospital, nurses, doctors, the other parents, combined with a media frenzy has me completely frazzled.

'Mam,' Kayla says, waking from what seems like endless sleeping. 'Can we go home?'

'What?' I ask, rousing from the semi-sleep I fall in and out of all the time.

'Please?' Kayla breathes out.

I sit up straight. Instantly fully awake. I wonder if she's dreaming. She mumbles in her sleep a lot lately. I spend hours watching her sleep. Sometimes her lips twitch and curl into a smile and I hope she's dreaming about something wonderful. I usually ask her what she's been dreaming about when she wakes but most of the time she's too exhausted to tell me, or she can't remember.

'Home,' Kayla sighs. 'I want to go home.'

'Kayla. Sweetie. The last time you left the hospital...'

I wait for Kayla to argue back the way she always does when I shoot down her suggestions with logic but all I hear is deep breathing.

'Kayla?'

Nothing. She's asleep again.

I curl into a ball on the bedside chair. It's the same ball I've slept in for the last countless days.

Gavin drops in and out. I know he's trying to juggle work and home life and hospital time. But his visits are becoming more and more frequent and he's staying for longer each time. Sometimes Kayla is awake and is delighted to see him. Sometimes she's asleep but he's still delighted to see her. Charlotte often drops by with Molly too, though Charlotte and I don't really speak. It's painfully awkward since I know she went behind my back with all the Help Fund Me stuff. And it's also very uncomfortable since neither of us have ever acknowledged that it's been Kayla's pride and joy recently, the one thing that's given her light despite any of our grown-up reservations.

Molly on the other hand is a treat. She waltzes into the room with her hand on her hip, confident and ready to chat. She fills me in on her mean piano teacher who makes her practise and practise, and tells me about how she loves swimming and diving right down to the bottom to get the shiny beanie dolphin that her instructor throws in. I've come to enjoy Molly as a wonderful breath of innocent fresh air. Charlotte's visits are becoming more frequent. They started out once a week, then twice weekly. Now she's here almost every day when Molly finishes school and I wonder when they find time for piano and swimming, but I don't ask.

'It's nearly Christmas,' Molly says, flinging back the door of Kayla's room and charging in full of energy and excitement.

Kayla stirs from sleep at the mention of her favourite time of year, but she doesn't wake enough to open her eyes or to speak.

'Shh, Molly,' Charlotte says, placing her finger over her lips. 'What did we talk about in the car? Kayla is very sleepy. We need to be calm and quiet.'

I shake my head. 'It's okay,' I say. 'Kayla has been asleep most of the day. It would actually be great if she woke up for a little while.'

Charlotte looks at me, unsure. I know she wants to enquire about Kayla. But she doesn't say a word. I'm sure she'll ask Gavin at home later instead.

'Sorry,' Charlotte says. 'We should have called ahead.'

'No, no. It's fine,' I say, honestly. 'It's nice to have some company.'

'Santa is coming soon,' Molly reminds me, as she climbs into the chair beside me and smiles up at me with beautiful, happy eyes.

'Yes. Yes he is,' I say. 'I hope you've been a good girl.'

'I bee'd so good,' Molly says.

'That's great, Molly,' I say.

'I even goed to peenano tonight just so Mammy could be not wibbly wobbly.'

I look at Charlotte, concerned. She doesn't say anything.

'Mammy was going to cry when she was scrubbing the dishes, but I said I'd go to peenano and then she didn't need to cry.'

I look at Charlotte. Her eyes are glassy as she watches Kayla. I think about asking her what her plans are for Christmas. Gavin will no doubt want to spend some time here. Will Molly and Charlotte come with him, or would Molly prefer to stay at home with her presents? I'm plucking up the courage to ask when Molly pushes my hair behind my ear as she does often when she has a big secret to tell. Usually it's about that mean boy in school who won't let her build a colourful tower, but today she takes a deep breath and presses her gorgeous little nose even closer than usual.

'I asked Santa for a secret,' she whispers, her warm breath tickling my ear.

'A surprise,' I say, knowingly. Kayla always asked Santa for a surprise when she was Molly's age. My favourite thing on Christmas morning was waking up and seeing her little, stunned face.

'No.' Molly pulls back a little but stays in whispering distance. 'A secret.'

'Okay,' I say. 'A secret sounds very special, Molly. I hope Santa brings it.'

'He will,' Molly says, confidently. 'Santa is magic.'

'He is,' I say, nodding.

'It's okay, Heather,' Molly says pressing her lips right against my ear, and her small chubby arms tighten a fraction around my neck. 'Santa can do anything. Ben in my class said so.'

'Oh, Molly,' I exhale, wishing life were that simple.

'I can't wait for Christmas,' Molly says.

'Me too,' I lie with a heavy heart.

FIFTY-FOUR

CHARLOTTE

I drive onto our road some time before midnight. Gavin is still at the hospital with Kayla and Heather. Molly is asleep in her car seat in the back. Somehow our brief visit to the hospital turned into hours. Kayla woke up shortly after we arrived and when Gavin came back to the room, she took a couple of mouthfuls of Heather's coffee, much to Gavin's disgust.

'Seriously, Heather, you don't let her drink coffee, do you? That's so bad for her,' he said, wide-eyed.

'Really, Dad?' Kayla whispered, straining to make sound pass her lips. 'Coffee is what you're worried about. You do see the irony, right?'

Everyone laughed. Even Gavin. But there was a sad acceptance that followed our giggles. That's how most of the evening played out. Laughing and talking could only lift us for so long before the weight of sadness inevitably followed.

No one came to tell us visiting hours were over, the way they used to when we outstayed our welcome. The nurses popped in and out to perform their usual checks. We're so accustomed to them poking and prodding Kayla that conversation went on around them, or we paused to include them. There was no awkwardness and it all felt very normal, as if this is what life has become for us all now and we're so familiar that we fit in to Kayla's hospital life like pieces of old furniture that have always seemed to be there. Jack stopped by too before he headed home for the night. And I got the distinct impression he was checking up on Heather as much as Kayla, but I didn't say anything. Besides, he didn't stay very long. Heather assumed he was exhausted after a full shift, but I think he was leaving us alone to enjoy some precious family time that we so desperately needed. It was the most wonderful evening I've had in a very, very long time and I hope Molly asks if we can go to the hospital again tomorrow after swimming. Because my answer will be a resounding yes. We can go every single night. We will go every single night.

I pull into my driveway and the porch light doesn't come on as expected when I park and I guess the sensor is broken. I'll ask Gavin to fix it tomorrow when I see him for breakfast. He's staying over at the hospital tonight. He said something about watching some episodes of *Friends* with Kayla and Heather for old times' sake. I know Kayla will enjoy it.

I turn off the engine and look over my shoulder to check Molly is still sleeping. She's snoring gently, exhausted after a busy day, and I think I'll have to leave her to have a lie in tomorrow. I can drop her in to school after little break. I'm sure Ms Martin will understand.

Our little cul-de-sac is silent. The houses dotted around the horse shoe are mostly in darkness, with the odd light left on in an upstairs bathroom or the landing. I drop my head back and stare out of the sunroof above me. It's a cloudless sky and beautiful twinkling stars stare back at me. I sit for a moment, savouring the silence and enjoying the beautiful view and I don't bother to wipe away the tears that trickle down my cheeks.

I can feel my phone vibrating in my pocket. I'm not surprised. Messages have been coming in thick and fast on

Kayla's Help Fund Me page. She was replying to them all herself at first, but she's been so tired the last few days I couldn't not help when she asked me to keep replying to some.

'Please,' she said, her eyes bloodshot with tiredness but dancing with excitement. 'I really want to make sure we thank absolutely everyone who donates. No matter how big or small the donation. I want everyone to know how much we appreciate their help.'

I didn't reply at first. I couldn't find the right words.

'Aiden is helping as much as he can,' she said. 'He's staying up half the night to reply to people. But he can't have his phone in school. There's a backlog of people donating during the day who aren't getting messages back from us.'

'Okay,' I said without having to think about it. 'Of course, I'll help.'

I can only imagine how upset Heather would be if she knew I was still involved. She wanted to shut the whole page down after the fiasco at Sports Day. She was hurt and embarrassed. But Kayla had worked too hard to let Heather's pride get in the way. Besides, Jack told her in no uncertain terms that while she's entitled to refuse the donation, she couldn't shut down the page. Only the administrator could do that – and the administrator is Kayla. Well, and me, of course. But that's Kayla's and my little secret. For now, at least.

I pull my phone out of my pocket and get ready to reply to some of the messages.

'Lisa in Wisconsin wrote,' I read aloud. 'What an amazing girl you are, Kayla. Your mom must be so proud. I only wish I could give more.'

There are more messages than I can count as I scroll down. And they're coming in from all over the world. Mandy in New York says, 'I think I'll have to fly to Ireland to get me some of these buns. Kayla you are a hero.'

Anonymous in Perth simply says, 'Good work.'

I'm replying as fast as my fingers can type. I thank everyone, adding emojis and kisses. But I pause when I come to Dermot in Leitrim's message. Dermot has donated twenty euro. His donation is number 63,432 and his donation has brought us to target. I can't wait to tell Kayla. I think about texting her now so the message is there for her to see in the morning. But I stop myself. I'd much rather tell her in person. This is so exciting. Kayla will be over the moon.

My eyes scroll down on the screen. Dermot has left a message too. It reads: 'Everyone will miss you so much when you're gone, Kayla.'

I pause. My hands are shaking and my fingers won't cooperate as I try to thank Dermot for his kindness. Because I realise Dermot is right. Everyone will miss Kayla more than words can say. I've spent so long worrying about Gavin and Molly and how they will cope without Kayla I forgot to allow myself time to accept that I can't bear to lose her either. I just can't bear it.

Loud angry sobs shake and rattle my whole body and I don't bother to fight them or hold them in.

'Mammy,' Molly says, waking.

'Um-hmm.'

'Why are you crying?' she asks.

I think about wiping my eyes and I think about lying. I think about telling Molly that I have a cold. Or that the wind caught my eyes. But I don't. I simply say, 'Because I'm sad, Molly. I'm very, very sad.'

'But it's nearly Christmas,' Molly says, and I turn over my shoulder to find my little girl smiling at me with such innocence and warmth in her heart. I know she'll be okay.

'Yes, sweetheart. It nearly is.'

My phone vibrates in my hand and I glance down at the screen expecting another heartfelt message from a donating stranger. I'm surprised to find Gavin's name flashing up on screen.

'Hello,' I say, pressing the phone to my ear.

'Where are you?' Gavin whispers.

'I'm in the car.'

'Are you driving?'

'No. No, I'm home. I'm sitting in the driveway. Listen, Gavin, I have the best news to share with Kayla. Is she still awake?' I ask.

There's silence on the other end of the line.

'Gavin.'

I take my phone down from my ear and stare at the screen, wondering if the line has gone dead. But the light is on and the call is still active. I hold my phone back. I can hear heavy breathing.

'Gavin are you there?' I ask again.

'She's gone, Charlie.'

'What?'

'Kayla's gone.'

FIFTY-FIVE

HEATHER

Three days later

I stand in front of the antique, free-standing mirror in the guest bedroom in Gavin's house. A reflection I barely recognise stares back at me. I see a thin woman, with big black circles under her red puffy eyes. This woman needs to dye her roots and maybe wear some make-up. And she needs to change out of the pyjamas she's been wearing for three days straight. This woman doesn't belong in this room. She's not even sure she belongs in this world anymore.

I hate this woman. I turn away so I can't see her. I never really took the time to stop and look around the room that I've been sleeping in before now. Previously it was just somewhere to lay my head when I was too exhausted to go on. I'd fall into the bed late at night, sometimes without even bothering to turn on the light, or undress. And I would get up again the next morning and leave the room within a moment of waking in my rush to get to the hospital. But there is no more rushing. Time is standing still now.

The bedroom is decorated to be calm and soothing. There

are cream walls, cream carpet, cream curtains with a spiral pattern in duck-egg blue. There's a duck-egg-coloured satin throw on the end of the bed, too. It's all very elegant and charming – very Charlotte.

There's a gentle knock on the door.

'Come in,' I find myself saying. Even though what I really want to say is, *Go away. Please, please go away.*

The door creaks open and Gavin's head appears followed reluctantly by the rest of him. He's tall and handsome in his dark suit but his eyes are red and puffy like mine.

'They're asking if we have a photo we'd like to use in the church,' Gavin says.

'They're asking?' I echo. I know he means the funeral directors but he can't bring himself to say it.

'Aiden has some really lovely ones on his phone. All very recent. Maybe we could use one of those,' Gavin suggests.

'Yeah. Okay. Whatever,' I say.

'People are starting to arrive,' Gavin says. 'Some of your neighbours from Cork are here. They're asking for directions to the church.'

'Have they never heard of Google Maps,' I snap. 'Sorry. Sorry. I don't mean that. People are good to come. I'll be down soon.'

'Do you need any help?' Gavin looks at my favourite black pencil dress hanging on the wardrobe door. 'I can ask Charlotte to come in.'

The knot of Gavin's tie is slightly different to usual. Chunkier, less symmetrical. I can only imagine Charlotte had to tie it for him. If his hands are shaking even a fraction as badly as mine there's no way he'd have managed alone.

Gavin takes a deep breath. 'I can still feel her,' he says, 'around me, you know. It's as if she's at home in Cork with you and I'll see her at the weekend. And then suddenly reality hits me. And...'

I don't have words. I wonder if I should hug Gavin, but my feet seem cemented to the spot and even if I tried to walk over to him, I don't think I could.

'Aiden's here too. With his parents. They arrived a few minutes ago,' Gavin says, pulling himself together again, as if changing the subject somehow helps him.

'Okay,' I say, glancing at my dress hanging on the wardrobe door. I know that I have to put it on and face today but I desperately want to stay in my pyjamas and never face the world again. 'Just give me a few minutes. I'll be down in a few minutes.'

Gavin nods and slowly closes the door and I fall to the floor, my heart in a million tiny pieces.

FIFTY-SIX

HEATHER

In the churchyard people shake my hand and tell me they are sorry for my troubles. As if Kayla is a favourite handbag I've misplaced. Or an expensive watch that's been broken.

'How are you doing?' people ask.

I answer them. But I honestly have no idea what I say. Maybe I lie and tell them that I'm okay. Or maybe I open my mouth and no sound comes out at all. I really don't know.

I feel a hand on my back and someone guides me inside. Kayla's coffin is in front of the altar. It's white with shiny purple handles. I didn't choose it. Gavin must have. There are photos of Kayla framed on top. There's one of her on her last birthday. She's smiling so brightly after getting a new phone she'd been pestering me about for ages. There's another that must have been taken just days ago. She's gaunt and pale but her blue eyes still sparkle and her personality shines through. Of course, there is one of her in her basketball gear, and she has a shiny medal around her neck. I haven't seen most of these before. Aiden must have had them on his phone. I hope he'll share the rest of his photos with me. I'd love to see them all.

Gavin shuffles into the seat beside me and the church

begins to fill with people. It isn't long before it's heaving with friends and family from both Dublin and Cork. I see the school principal and a lot, if not all, of the teachers. Kayla's old teachers from primary school are here too. The students are all here in their uniform and sit to the side of the church to form the choir. They whisper among themselves as teenagers do. Some are crying. Some are simply talking and some look bored as if they'd rather be anywhere else. I doubt they realise I would most certainly rather be anywhere else too. Kayla's close friends wear their regular clothes and are dotted among the congregation. Most sit with their parents in silence with their heads low and their hearts breaking.

Kayla's favourite song begins and Gavin takes my hand and whispers, 'It's time to say goodbye.'

I close my eyes and think about the day I told Gavin he was going to be a father. I didn't know then that I was giving him the most wonderful gift in the world and that our daughter would make us so incredibly happy for fifteen amazing years.

'Hello,' a shaky voice I recognise says. I open my eyes to find a very dapper Aiden in a fine tailored suit standing next to Kayla's coffin with a piece of paper in his hand.

There's some shushing and some coughing from the huge crowd crammed into every nook and cranny of the church. And then there is silence and I know all eyes are on Aiden.

'My name is Aiden. I am... er... I was...' Aiden says, before he pauses and clears his throat. He's shaking but he's doing well to hold back tears. 'I am Aiden and Kayla *is* my best friend. She's asked me to read this letter to you all.'

Aiden shakes his head and lowers the page. This is too much for him. Too hard. His teary eyes find mine and I nod, encouraging him, letting him know without words that it's okay to stutter or cry or even fall completely apart, but he needs to read Kayla words. She trusted him. And no one else. She needs him now. She needs him one final time.

Aiden nods, and pulls himself a little straighter as he steps closer to her coffin.

'Okay,' he says. 'This is from Kayla. They are her words.' He takes a deep breath and begins.

As you know I can't be with you all today. I'm a little busy being dead. Funeral humour – sorry. Anyway, because I can't speak myself I've asked my best friend, Aiden, to read this to you all. Thank you, Aiden. Try to keep it together, man. Pretend this is English class and you're after an A for public speaking. Mrs Quinn, if you're here, I think you should give Aiden an A this year. This eulogy business is hard! I'm finding writing it tricky, I can't imagine how hard it must be to stand in front of you all now and read it.

So, here goes...

When I found out that there was nothing more the doctors could do, I began to think about my funeral. Well, actually, that's not exactly true. The first thing I did was cry and freak out. Because it just seemed so unfair that I had no control over my own life. But I slowly realised that I had control over my last goodbye. So, this might be a little long-winded or go off point, but please bear with me. It's the very last time I'll have a chance to speak to you all and I have a lot to say.

I know this is a little weird. People told me that writing your own eulogy is not what normal people do. You're right, everyone, it's not normal. But neither is dying at fifteen – yet here I am. And you know what I say? I say, fuck normal. Sorry, Father Clancy – I'm not sure if you're allowed to curse in mass. Also, sorry, Aiden if reading that part out loud has just gotten you in trouble.

I bet right now my mam is blushing because I've just mortified her with my bad language in front of all these people. But if you look over at my mam I hope you see the black dress that she's wearing – I know the one. It's her pencil dress with a silver zip up the back. She likes it because it makes her look smart for her work meetings. But she doesn't know that I like it too. But it's not the dress, I like, it's the way she feels when she's wearing it. It's her smart dress. My mam is smart – always. This dress just reminds her of that. I hope you're feeling smart today, Mam. You're the most amazing mother. You made me. Shaped me. Hugged me when I needed to feel you close. Corrected me and gave advice when I made silly mistakes, and most of all you taught me how to be loved and how to love. I'm so incredibly grateful for the gift of our relationship. Every kid should be lucky enough to have a mother like you. I love you.

Dad. Hey, you. Are you wearing your grey suit with your blue tie? I hope so. The blue brings out your eyes. The same eyes you gave to me. The same eyes that see me. Know me. Seem to understand me even when I don't understand myself. Thank you for everything. Thank you for getting drunk when you were eighteen and sleeping with Mam. Again – apologies, Father Clancy! And Aiden. Oh, don't try to play it cool, Aiden. I know you're blushing. Sorry!

I love you, Dad. And Charlotte. And Molly. Little Molly. I adore you – do you know that? Do you know that you are the best little sister in the whole wide world? No one can sing Beyoncé like you. No one can hula-hoop like you. Or wear a tutu and a tiara quite like you. And no one can own a piece of my heart like you.

I'm so sorry I won't be around as you grow up. I'm sorry that I won't get to read the rest of Fantastic Mr Fox *with you. You have to keep reading it by yourself now. I know you can. The ending is sooo good. Trust me. Mr Fox had courage when he needed it most. Be like Foxy, my beautiful little sister. Find your strength.*

Aiden. Oh, don't look at me like that. Or at my wooden box like that. 'Cos I know that's where you're eyes are wandering to. We talked about this. We knew my time was up. Get your arse out there and get yourself a girlfriend. You're a catch, just because you are my best friend and it would have been super weird to kiss you doesn't mean I didn't think about it. There I admit it. I will miss you. A lot. But I'm also expecting you to cop on and talk to Sarah in our science class to tell her you like her. Oh, and if Sarah is here... By the way, Aiden likes you. Oh, what, Aiden? I've just done you a favour, trust me. Sarah, take good care of him. He's in need of a new best friend.

At this point, I want to say something really intelligent and profound to make my English teacher proud, although profound is a pretty big word so maybe I can get some points for effort with that. But, as it turns out, words don't really matter in the end. I bet most of you have fallen asleep listening to this already. To be fair, I started writing this yesterday and I've come back after some sleep, drugs and jelly that was yellow and smelt like wee. Heads up – if you're ever in hospital and they offer you jelly, don't eat it.

So, all I really want to say is: live your best life. Live it every single day. Don't make bucket lists you won't stick to. Don't feel you need to jump out of a plane or bungee jump into a canyon. If living your best life is simply going for a walk with your dog every day – do that. If living your best life is drinking white wine that you haven't bothered to chill. Do that. Hug your family. When you're finished telling your family how much they annoy you, be sure to tell them how much you love them, too. And every morning when you wake up, take a big, deep breath and be grateful for the air in your lungs. Don't just be alive. Live. I did.

Aiden lowers the page as everyone claps and he bursts into tears and hurries down the centre aisle to slide into the seat beside his mother. Mary wraps her arms around him and cradles him close.

'Thank you, Aiden,' Father Clancy says, beginning the mass.

But I'm not listening. I run my hands over my favourite black dress – Kayla's favourite – and I make a promise to my daughter to live.

FIFTY-SEVEN

CHARLOTTE

Christmas Day

Molly bounds into our bedroom with squeals of excitement.

'Santa came. Santa came,' she says.

I open my reluctant eyes and try to shake myself awake. I have no idea what time it is but it's still dark outside. My eyes adjust to the light shining in through the open door from the landing. I roll over to find Gavin is already sitting up and I wonder if he's been asleep at all. He's been so restless the last few nights. I know Christmas is weighing heavy on him.

'Get up. Get up,' Molly commands as she climbs into bed beside me. I yelp when she puts her icicle toes on the backs of my calves.

'Okay. Okay,' Gavin says, throwing back the duvet on his side and sliding his legs over the edge of the bed and standing up.

'Come on. Come on!' Molly shouts, unimpressed that I'm not moving as quickly as Gavin. 'Ugh,' she grunts, climbing out of bed again.

I hear the pitter-patter of her little feet scurrying across the landing, followed by the slam of the spare bedroom door as it's opened with too much force and crashes into the wall.

'Heather. Heather. Heather,' Molly calls. 'It's time to get up.'

'Oh God, she's gone into Heather's room,' I say, as if Gavin can't hear what's going on.

'Yeah,' he says, pulling on a tracksuit.

I stand up and slide my feet into my waiting oversized fluffy slippers and I wrap my warm dressing gown around me. I open the wardrobe and pull out another dressing gown to give to Heather. She was so reluctant to stay with us for Christmas. I practically had to beg her. But the thoughts of her home alone in Cork today was too much to bear.

I walk across to Heather's room and stop in the doorway. 'Sorry,' I say, feeling I should apologise for the four-year-old alarm clock that has just barged uninvited into her room.

'S'okay,' Heather says. 'I wasn't really asleep anyway.'

The humongous bags under her eyes confirm it.

'She's just so excited,' I add, feeling embarrassed or awkward or something. I'm not quite sure. But Molly's excitement seems misplaced and upsetting right now.

'Did he come?' Heather asks, trying to be enthusiastic for Molly's sake. 'Did Santa come?'

'He did, he did, he did. I could hear his reindeer on the roof.' Molly spins around in a circle and jumps up and down.

'Did you now?' I say.

'Yup,' Molly says, brazen with confidence.

Molly takes Heather by the hand and tries to drag her to her feet. Heather stands and I almost gasp seeing her in her night shorts. Her legs are so tiny and thin. I hadn't realised she'd lost such a huge amount of weight since she first moved in. I pass Heather my spare dressing gown and she wraps it around herself and smiles.

Gavin appears at the door behind me wearing a Santa hat. 'C'mon. Let's go downstairs,' he says.

Molly leads Heather by the hand past us and down the stairs.

'Thank you,' I whisper to Gavin, pointing at his hat.

'Kayla asked me to make Christmas special for Molly and for Heather. And I'm trying,' he says.

'You just didn't know it would be this hard,' I add.

Gavin swallows and I can almost see the emotional bubble making its way down his throat.

Gavin and I follow Molly and Heather into the sitting room. All our stocking are hung by the fire. They're heaving with gifts. I managed to find a stocking for Heather yesterday and I've stuffed it with presents.

Molly squeals with excitement when she finds the pile of presents wrapped under the tree for her that weren't there when she was going to bed last night.

'These are from Santa,' she says as she points and jumps up and down on the spot. 'See, I told you he came.'

'Well, what are you waiting for?' Gavin asks. 'Open them.'

Molly drops onto her knees and picks up the first box. She tears into the bright green-and-red candy-cane wrapping paper.

'A scooter with light-up wheels,' she says, setting the box to one side as she reaches for the next one.

She tears the wrapping paper on the next present even faster. And looks even more disappointed when she finds a giant, fluffy unicorn inside. She casts the teddy aside. And reaches for another gift. She continues to open every present from Santa, gradually becoming more and more disheartened with each one.

'I don't understand,' I whisper to Gavin. 'It's everything she wanted.'

Molly reaches for the final present and when she opens the

paper and discovers a Barbie with long pink hair she begins to cry.

'Is this all? Is this all Santa brought?' She searches around greedily for more boxes.

'Molly, stop,' Gavin says firmly. 'Don't you like your presents?'

'There's apposed to be *more*.'

'Molly,' I say, equally as frustrated as Gavin. 'Don't you think you got enough? You haven't even looked at them.'

'No, no, no,' Molly begins to cry. 'There's apposed to be a big, special present.'

'Is this the secret you told me about?' Heather asks, and I tilt my head to one side unaware that Molly has been sharing secrets with Heather.

Molly nods as tears trickle down her rosy cheeks.

'Can you tell me what the secret is now?' Heather bends down to crouch beside Molly.

'I asked Santa to make Kayla all better 'cos he's magic. But he didn't do it. Kayla's not here. And I bee'd the best, best girl but he didn't bring Kayla back.'

'Oh, Molly,' Gavin says, crumbling.

I wrap my arms around him quickly before he falls and I watch as Molly climbs into Heather's arms and they hug and sob.

Gavin turns his head into the crook of my neck and we all take a moment to wish that Santa really was a magic man who could give Kayla back to us.

FIFTY-EIGHT

CHARLOTTE

It took a little coaxing but Molly gradually forgave Santa and began to play with her toys. She brushes Barbie's hair and cuddles her unicorn. And she laughs, like a little girl is supposed to on Christmas morning.

I make us some breakfast. I keep it light, mostly fruit and some granola. It's not easy to get Heather to eat but she eventually nibbles on a banana. Gavin doesn't eat much either. He seems to be relying on coffee to function. He plays with Molly for as long as he can keep it together before excusing himself to go upstairs.

'Mammy, Mammy, look,' Molly says, bounding into the kitchen to show me she has discovered that her unicorn talks when you press his tummy.

'I like hugs,' the soft toy says in a squeaky voice.

'That's nice, Molly,' I say, as I concentrate on preparing starters I doubt anyone wants to eat.

'He says more. Listen.' Molly presses her teddy's tummy again and again and the overzealous toy serenades us with chirpy catchphrases.

Heather sits at the kitchen table staring into a cup of coffee I made for her almost an hour ago. It must be cold and disgusting by now, but I doubt she plans on drinking it anyway.

'I love you,' the cheery teddy says. 'You are my best friend.'

'Okay, Molly,' I say, trying not to snap as the squeaky voice grates against my brain like nails on a chalkboard. 'Why don't you play with some of your other toys now?'

'But I like Mr Rainbow,' Molly says, cuddling her unicorn tightly under her chin.

'Mr Rainbow is a nice name,' I say, smiling at Molly, but my eyes are on Heather.

'Erm. I think I'm going to go for a walk,' Heather says, as she stands up slowly and shaky.

'Okay,' I say, worried that she's exhausted and dizzy and might fall while she's out. 'Maybe Gavin might like to go too,' I suggest. 'I'll go upstairs and ask him.'

'Can I go for a walk?' Molly asks. 'I like walks. And I can bring Mr Rainbow.'

'No, Molly, I don't think—'

'Walk. Walk. Walk,' Molly chants.

Heather moves into the hall. I rinse my hands quickly, washing away herbs and breadcrumbs and hope I'm not too late to catch her before she goes out the door still in her pyjamas.

'Heather, wait,' I say as she reaches for her coat hanging on the banister of the stairs. She's not listening. Her body is here but her mind is somewhere else entirely.

The doorbell rings unexpectedly and Heather jumps. As if the sudden noise has jolted her back to the here and now.

'Who could that be?' I say, thrown a little; we're not expecting visitors for Christmas.

'I don't know, Mammy,' Molly says very seriously, as if she's disappointed that she doesn't have an answer for my question.

Heather lets go of her coat, leaving it on the banister as she turns and walks back into the kitchen with her head low.

I open the door. 'Jack.'

'Hi,' Jack says, smiling.

A gush of icy December wind whips past and I shiver, blushing a little when I realise I'm facing my neighbour in fluffy slippers and an even fluffier dressing gown.

'Is Heather here?' Jack asks.

I turn my head over my shoulder to find Heather has stopped walking and has turned around to face the door.

'Yeah. Yes. She is. Do you want to come in? It's freezing.'

'That would be good. Thanks,' Jack says.

Jack steps inside and I catch the reflection of the small box he's holding behind his back in the hall mirror. It's wrapped in shiny silver paper and there's a bright-red bow on top. It's very pretty and I've no doubt it's a gift for Heather, but she hasn't touched the other presents in her stocking yet.

'Did Santa come?' Jack asks, as Molly shoves her new unicorn towards him.

'Do you like him?' Molly asks. 'He's Mr Rainbow.'

'He's very nice, Molly,' Jack says. 'You must have been such a good girl.'

'It's Christmas, Jack,' Heather says, slowly walking towards us. 'Shouldn't you be with your family.'

Gavin appears at the top of the stairs. The noise of the door-bell obviously caught his attention. The hall feels unusually crowded.

'My sister is spending the day with her husband's family,' Jack says. 'They invited me, of course, but it didn't feel right.'

'You're on your own?' Gavin says, descending the stairs rubbing his eyes and I think he's just had a nap. I'm glad. I can't remember the last time he slept.

'I don't mind,' Jack says. 'I'll stop by the hospital later. Check on some of the kids.'

'Well you must stay and have dinner with us in the mean-time,' Gavin says.

'No, really.' Jack winces. 'That's very kind, but please don't feel obliged.'

'We have more than enough,' Gavin says. 'Don't we, Charlie?'

I think of the oversized turkey that needs to go in the oven. 'It would be lovely if you could stay, Jack,' I say.

Jack smiles and I watch as his eyes find Heather's.

'It would be nice,' Heather says.

'Okay,' Jack says. 'Thank you.'

'Is that a present?' Molly says, pointing to the beautifully wrapped box behind Jack's back.

'It is,' Jack says, taking his hands and the gift out from behind his back.

'Is it for meee?' Molly asks.

'Molly,' I say, sternly. 'Don't be rude.'

'Actually it's for Heather.'

My heart sinks. I don't think Heather is in any mood for gifts, but she takes a couple of steps forward and says. 'For me?'

I step aside and make room for Jack and Heather to stand face to face.

'Yes,' Jack says. 'But it's not from me.'

There's silence. Even Molly is standing still and quiet as we watch Jack and Heather share a moment.

'It's from Kayla.'

FIFTY-NINE
HEATHER

I'm sitting on the couch, next to Jack. There's no talking but it's not weird or uncomfortable. When I appeared to be frozen to the spot after Jack passed me the box, Charlotte guided us from the hall into the sitting room. Gavin is sitting in the armchair nearby, bouncing Molly on his knee. And Charlotte is pretending to be busy tidying up wrapping paper that Molly has left strewn under the tree and all over the floor.

The fairy lights twinkle on the tree and the shiny, metallic wrapping paper in my hand picks up their pretty reflection. My hands are shaking as my fingers curl around the small neatly wrapped box. I've almost dropped it more than once. There's a tag dangling from the centre of the red bow and it simply says, *Love from, Kayla* in her beautiful swirly handwriting. I read over the three simple words countless times, tracing the letters with my finger tip.

'Open it, open it, open it,' Molly says, finally losing patience.

'Shh, Molly,' Gavin says. 'Let Heather take her time.'

Gavin's words contradict the longing in his eyes. He's as

desperate to see what's inside as much as his giddy four-year-old is. And I want to see inside, too. Very much. But every time I reach for the red bow, ready to pull it open, I stop. I'm so overly aware that this is the last gift I will ever open from Kayla. The last time I will ever read a gift tag written in her handwriting. The last time I will ever wonder what gift she has picked out for me. The last surprise.

'Would you like a moment on your own?' Charlotte asks, standing up with a mound of torn and crinkly wrapping paper in her arms.

'No,' I gasp. 'Don't leave. Please.'

Jack places his hand on my knee and lets me know that he isn't going anywhere.

I take a deep breath and tug on the ribbon, rip open the paper carefully and lift the lid on the box I find inside.

'It's a key chain,' I say, confused.

'It is,' Jack says.

I lift the rectangular silver keychain out and read the inscription on the front. 'Kayla's place,' I say.

Jack nods as if I'm supposed to understand what this means. 'There's more,' he says, pointing at the box, encouraging me to look again.

I glance into the bottom of the box at the piece of white card that says, *Call Me.* Picking out the card is difficult. My fingers are fumbling and making a complete mess of things. Finally I grip it and turn it over.

'There's a phone number,' I say.

Jack has taken his phone out of his pocket, ready and waiting. He passes it to me.

'Call the number,' he says.

I take his phone, unsure, and punch in the digits and hold it to my ear. 'It's not ringing,' I wait.

'You should get voicemail any second—'

'Hi, Mam,' Kayla's voice whispers softly into my ear. I

almost drop the phone as tears trickle down my face. Jack is smiling and nodding.

A message. She's left me a message.

'It's me, Mam. It's Kayla.' Her voice is so beautifully familiar. My heart aches.

'Happy Christmas, Mam. I hope you're doing okay. I wish I could be there with you today. But I thought this voicemail would be the next best thing. Jack helped me. He's so nice, Mam. You should get to know him better. Seriously.'

I look up at Jack and smile and he smiles back.

'Do you like your keyring?' Kayla asks, followed by some giggles. 'I bet you have no idea what it's for, do you?'

I shake my head as if she can see me. I wish she could.

'It's for the keys of your new coffee shop. Kayla's Place. I know, I know. You're not a charity case. But it's not charity if you give something back. So, how about ten per cent of all profits go to Cancer Research. Wouldn't that be great? We can help future kids get better. We can do that together, Mam, can't we?'

Fat salty tears trickle down my cheeks because it's just so typically Kayla. Always thinking of a way to help others.

'And you don't have to call it Kayla's Place, I just couldn't think of anything else. I ran out of time before all the paperwork went through, but Jack and Charlotte promised to help sort it all out. What do you say, Mam? Will you open your dream bakery and live your best life?'

I nod, unable to see though my tears.

'I love you, Mam. I love you so incredibly much. No matter where I am now. Nothing will ever change that. And whenever you're missing me, or we haven't talked in a while, just call this number and my voice will be right here with you again. Bye, Mam.'

'No. No. Come back. Kayla come back,' I cry.

Gavin is on his feet and over to me in an instant. His strong arms are around me, holding me close as I sob hard.

Charlotte takes Molly into the kitchen, making some excuse about getting dinner into the oven and I eventually peel myself away from Gavin to look at Jack.

'How long was she planning all this?' I ask.

'A while,' Jack says. 'Once she realised she wasn't going to get better her main priority became trying to take care of you.'

'But I was supposed to be taking care of *her*,' I say.

'And you did,' Jack says.

'But she's gone,' I cry, my whole body shaking. 'I'm her mother and I couldn't save her. I couldn't protect her. In the end I couldn't do anything for her.'

'You can do this for her,' Jack says. 'As Kayla would say, you can live your best life.'

'I... I...' I stare at the keyring in my hand without keys. 'I don't even know where to begin.'

'The paperwork is already in progress. After that you can learn on your feet. Kayla believed in you. I do too.'

'You can do this, Heather,' Gavin says. 'You can do it for Kay. You have to.'

EPILOGUE
HEATHER

A little over a year later

I give myself the once-over in the bathroom. I've got flour in my hair and my pretty red dress that buttons all the way down the front seemed like a good idea this morning, but it's chafing under my arms now and I'm sweating with nervous energy.

I flush the loo just as there's a knock on the door.

'Heather, are you ready?' Charlotte calls.

'Yeah. Just gimme two minutes. I'm trying to work a miracle in here.'

'C'mon. People will be arriving soon and you can't leave me out here on my own.'

'Okay. Okay,' I say. I hurry as I splash a little water onto my hair and it removes most of the flour.

I open the door and smile when I see Charlotte on the other side with her apron still on. I point and giggle.

'Gah,' she says, reaching around her back to untie it. 'I'm so nervous. Are you?'

'I'm shaking,' I say. 'Do I look okay?'

'You look amazing,' Charlotte says, sweeping her eyes over me and nodding.

'You look great too,' I add, checking her cropped black trousers and pastel-lemon blouse for any baking stains.

'I can't believe we thought six o'clock was a good time to schedule this thing. We didn't leave ourselves any time to go home and change.'

'I know. I know,' I say, making my way back into the shop. 'But it's still so exciting, isn't it?'

'It really is.' Charlotte grins as she walks behind the counter to do some last-minute checks on muffins with elaborate piped icing in the colours of Kayla's basketball team.

I glance at my watch. 'It's almost half five. What time are Gavin and Molly coming?'

'Gavin is picking her up from after-school care on his way home from work and they're coming straight here. They should be here any minute.'

I glance around Kayla's Place. Charlotte and I haven't made too many changes since we bought the premises. It's still exactly as haphazard and quirky as it used to be when Gavin and I were teenagers, frittering away afternoons here. We kept the mismatched, brightly coloured chairs, only replacing any that were worn out or broken, and we purposely chose colours that clash. We sanded down the tables and kept them all. We thought about changing the windows that don't fit in the frame properly and let the wind in during the winter. But we couldn't bear to part with them. We leave complimentary colourful scarves and blankets in the window seats instead.

Today, the whole shop is full of balloons and brightly coloured streamers ready for our first ever party. We're in business a year today and we're about to hand over our first ever cheque to Cancer Research. Someone very important from the charity and some staff from the children's hospital are coming.

When I confided in Charlotte that I had no idea what to

talk to them about, she suggested I tell them the story of how Kayla's Place came about. I still can't believe that Gavin had been bringing Kayla to this old café most Saturdays throughout her childhood. This place held as special a place in his heart as it did mine.

'Of course I love this old place,' he told me the day we opened. 'It's the place I found out I was going to be a father. It doesn't get more special than that.'

The chrome bell of the door jingles as the door swings open and Molly skips in, followed by Gavin.

'How was school?' Charlotte asks.

'Okay.' Molly shrugs casually.

She's grown up so much in a year, I think.

I never thought I'd see the day Charlotte would allow Molly to go to creche so she could go back to work. But when she told me she wanted to invest in a vegan line of confectionary I couldn't refuse. Charlotte was such a huge part of Kayla's Place coming to be, I know Kayla would be delighted to see us working side by side now.

Within an hour Kayla's Place is heaving with visitors. Regular customers mingle with the heads of the charity. Some of the nurses from the hospital have brought a beautiful bouquet of flowers and everyone is raving about how delicious the new line of vegan muffins are.

I nip behind the counter to pop another batch of brownies in the oven, worried we'll run out, and my breath hitches in my throat when I turn around and see a familiar face.

'Jack,' I say, almost dropping the tray.

'Hello, Heather,' he smiles.

I'm lost for words.

'It's great to see you.' He looks all around. 'The place looks great. Kayla would be so proud.'

'Yeah,' I say, swallowing an emotional lump. 'I hope she would.'

I set the tray down and look into his eyes. 'How have you been?' I ask. 'I haven't seen you in ages.'

Jack moved out of his sister's house a few months ago. His sister met someone and Jack wanted to give them space to be a family. And I had to stop baking for the hospital when things became super busy here. Our paths stopped crossing.

'I have something for you,' he says.

'You do?'

I'm not sure what to do. Or what to say. I haven't seen him in such a long time and he turns up out of the blue and has a gift for me. I'm blushing.

He pulls something out from his inside jacket pocket. My eyes glass over as I stare at the familiar present in his hand, its shiny silver wrapping paper tied up with a red bow. A tag dangles from the centre of the bow. I don't have to turn it over to know what it says.

'Jack,' I say, shaking my head.

'Open it,' Jack says.

My heart is beating so hard I feel as if it might beat right out of my chest. I run my fingers over the swirly handwriting on the tag. *Love from, Kayla.*

'You kept this all year?' I ask.

Jack nods. 'She asked me to. I couldn't say no.'

I nod. Understanding. I'm glad he didn't say no to whatever this is. I'm glad Kayla wanted to bring him here for whatever reason. I'm just glad he's here.

'Open it,' Jack repeats and I get the impression he's nervous.

I'm nervous too, but I do as he asks. There's no keychain inside this time. Just a piece of white paper. I turn it over.

'Ask Jack out,' I read aloud, instantly embarrassed. 'Oh God.'

'Wow, Kayla has really put you on the spot here,' Jack says, smiling.

'Did you know that's what was in here?' I ask.

Jack shakes his head. 'I honestly had no idea.'

There's such kindness in his eyes, I believe him.

'I'm sorry,' I say. 'I wouldn't have read it aloud if I'd—' I cut myself off searching for the right words. 'If I'd known this would be embarrassing.'

'I'm not embarrassed,' Jack says.

We look into each other eyes and I giggle. It's so nice to see him again.

'Well,' he says, his beautiful eyes sparkling. 'Are you going to ask? Kayla seems to think you should.'

'What?' I laugh, wondering if he's serious. 'Ask you out?'

He nods.

'Okay.' I shrug, my face no doubt reddening as I take a deep breath and say, 'Would you like to go out with me, Jack Patterson?'

'I would very much like that, Heather Prendergast.'

I smile, as subtle tears trickle down my cheeks. *Kayla knew me so well*, I think, missing her more than ever. I look down at the card and the three simple words in Kayla's handwriting that stare back at me.

'Does Kayla have any more surprises for me?' I ask, my heart aching – knowing this is her last.

'I think Kayla is trusting us to take charge of the surprises from here.'

Jack walks around to my side of the counter and when he gathers me into his arms I only pretend to be surprised. And when he presses his lips onto mine, I smile, as my amazing daughter's words play over in my mind.

I am living my best life, Kayla. I promise.

A LETTER FROM THE AUTHOR

I want to say a huge thank you for choosing to read *The Forever Gift*. If you enjoyed it, and want to keep up-to-date with all my latest releases, just sign up here. Your email address will never be shared and you can unsubscribe at any time.

www.stormpublishing.co/brooke-harris

When I sent the first, rather messy, draft of this book to my editor she replied with a profound and unexpected comment and it touched me in a way I know I'll never forget. She said, 'So, the question is: *How does it feel to be mourning someone when you need to support people whose grief is even greater than yours?*'

Well, I wasn't expecting that! Was that really what I'd written? Was Charlotte really so like me? Of course, the circumstances are entirely fictional and completely different to my real life, but I honestly think I wrote this book with that very feeling in my heart. And the truth be told, I'm still not sure I have an answer. I guess you just do!

If you liked *The Forever Gift*, and I really hope you did, I would be so grateful if you could spare the time to write a review. I'd love to hear what you think – it makes such a difference in helping new readers to discover one of my books for the first time.

I love hearing from my readers – you can get in touch on my Facebook page, through Twitter, Goodreads or my website.

All my best,

Brooke xx

www.jbharriswrites.wordpress.com

X x.com/Janelle_Brooke

📷 instagram.com/janelle.brooke.harris